DEAD MEN LIVING

DEAD MEN LIVING

Brian Freemantle

THOMAS DUNNE BOOKS
ST. MARTIN'S PRESS
NEW YORK

To Simon and Tine, with love

THOMAS DUNNE BOOKS.
An imprint of St. Martin's Press.

www.stmartins.com

Design by Nancy Resnick

Library of Congress Cataloging-in-Publication Data

Freemantle, Brian.
    Dead men living / Brian Freemantle.—1st ed.
        p. cm.
    ISBN 0-312-24379-0
    1. Muffin, Charlie (Fictitious character)—Fiction.
    2. British—Travel—Russia—Siberia—Fiction. 3. Intelligence service—Great Britain—Fiction. 4. Siberia (Russia)—Fiction.   I. Title.

PR6056.R43 D43 2000
823'.914—dc21
                                                            99-462044

First Edition: June 2000

10 9 8 7 6 5 4 3 2 1

Knowledge Itself is Power.

—"Of Heresies,"
Meditationes Sacrae,
Francis Bacon

1

The *El Niño*—Christ's Child—gets its name from always beginning in December, usually in a seven-year cycle, and reverses the equatorial winds to blow west to east across the Pacific. But there was nothing benevolent about the worldwide climatic upheaval Christ's Child caused that year.

The heavy storms that followed the wind-driven warm water washing up against the coasts of North and South America caused deserts to flood and rain-denied rain forests to wither.

Drought parched Southeast Asia and smoke from fires that engulfed Indonesia blocked out the sun and plunged the country into near-darkness for weeks. There was so little water in the lakes and rivers feeding the Panama Canal that ship size had to be restricted. Raging torrents destroyed roads and railways in Kenya and Tanzania and Uganda, and rainstorms caused more than $1 billion of damage in California. For weeks temperatures of more than one hundred degrees seared Texas. Scores of people died from heatstroke. Forest fires engulfed Florida. Canada was paralyzed by ice storms.

Siberia was also hugely affected. Tundra permanently frozen so hard that houses were built without foundations melted, in places reducing entire villages to collapsing matchwood. The thaw was particularly pronounced around Yakutsk.

It was returning home to the tiny township of Kiriyestyakh from a supply-buying trip to Yakutsk that a reindeer herder found the bodies. Had he not been on horseback—denied the more customary use of the sled the animal normally pulled—he might not have seen the upthrust, hand-clenched arm: as it was, his first impression was of a tree branch.

He was too young to have known the Great Patriotic War, although his grandfather had been killed on the eastern front and his father had lost an arm in the battle of Stalingrad. But the until now perfectly preserving ice tomb had collapsed sufficiently for him to recognize that both corpses were dressed in military uniform. Neither uniform looked like those he'd seen in any photographs of his grandfather or father. His initial impulse was to loot the bodies of whatever valuables there might be, but Siberia is the most superstitious of any Russian region and to grave-rob risked the Evil Eye. Instead he remounted his horse and hurried on to Kiriyestyakh, to report his find.

2

Although, after all he'd seen and endured and done, it would have been impossible for Charlie Muffin to believe in God, it had seemed divine intervention when he, of all operatives, got the first-time Moscow posting in the department's anxiety to justify its continued existence by becoming a quasi-British FBI after the supposed end of the Cold War.

Maybe, despite being a disbeliever, he *had* believed it was something like that, so quickly had he again come into contact with Natalia—and seen their daughter for the first time—and imagined she'd so easily forget all the hurt and all the deceit. The fact that she'd resumed their affair at all was little short of a miracle; that she was here, with Sasha, in his apartment, even more miraculous. Second thoughts—and third thoughts and fourth thoughts—were inevitable. He had, every time, convincingly allayed them, as convincingly as he'd persuaded her to move into Lesnaya Ulitza. Although, Charlie accepted, Natalia had hardly *moved* in. The belated doubt had come even before she'd unpacked.

"This is ridiculous! A mistake!"

"You're here now. Let's just give it a chance."

"We can't afford chances. Not one." She shook her head distractedly. "I can't conceive that I'm here: that I agreed to it."

Neither, in all but rare honesty, could Charlie. He'd even phrased the initial suggestion in a way that he could have dismissed it as a joke, although deep down it hadn't been. "It's not like the old days. We don't even *have* a concierge to inform on us. And you're keeping

Leninskaya on: officially that's still where you and Sasha live."

"Which will be meaningless, if we're discovered." Why didn't she tell him of the threat she thought herself to be under, despite so much of it personally involving him? Too much to think about; too much—too fast—of everything.

"I love you," declared Charlie solemnly. "Sasha is my daughter. I'm in Moscow permanently now. Officially. It doesn't make sense for us to go on living apart."

"It does if you really intend us to make some sort of life. If our being together comes out, you'll be withdrawn and I'll probably be dismissed, and then what's left?"

"London."

Natalia shook her head. "I was prepared to make that sacrifice once, remember? Risked imprisonment—worse, maybe, because I was officially in the KGB then—to get myself to London, expecting you to meet your side of the bargain. All you had to do was meet me, arrange my defection. But you backed off—abandoned me because you weren't sure. Which, in one very important way, I'm glad about now. I was so much in love with you then that I forgot I was Russian. How much *being* Russian means, which no one who isn't can ever understand. Leaving Russia—coming to London and bringing Sasha to London—is the very last thing I want to do. Which I'd ever consider doing, which has nothing whatsoever to do with how I feel about you and about us. I'll do everything I can to avoid it."

Charlie felt abruptly hollowed out and it was several moments before he replied. As he did so, he gestured around the huge room in which they were and the apartment beyond. "If you're telling me that you're not sure any longer, then I agree. This doesn't make sense. Nothing does."

"I'm telling you I've got to make up my mind whether I am or not. I thought moving in might be a way of my finding out; thought too much about what seemed my biggest problem and not enough about what others could be caused by my being here. Which was stupid."

They were talking English. Sasha, who was five, said impatiently, "What are you talking about?"

In Russian, Charlie said, "I was telling Mummy how much I love you and how pleased I am that you're here."

"Did princesses *really* live here once?" asked the child, craning her neck in awe.

"All the time. And now another one is going to. You."

"I want to see!" demanded the child.

Charlie got up almost too quickly to take the child's hand, glad of the escape from a conversation he didn't want to have. The Lesnaya apartment extended over a quarter of an entire floor of what had been, in 1915, the fifth story of one of the grandest Moscow palace-mansions of a cousin prince of the last tsar. Legends had it, as legends often do, that Tsar Nicholas had not once but several times slept there, although not in the guest rooms on Charlie's level. Rasputin, at the time caring for Nicholas's hemophiliac son, Tsarevich Alexei, *had* been on Charlie's floor, according to the same fable, but again not in any of the rooms in which Charlie lived.

Everything was echoingly enormous, following the principle that the specially chosen and therefore exalted rulers of others had to reside in surroundings built for giants. Charlie liked the leader-of-men imagery. The ceiling of the main room was high enough to have formed scaffolding for a tired moon. There was a huge Venetian mirror over an ornately carved mantelpiece, its cavorting cherubs climbing a bas relief to the faraway corniced and molded ceiling. In the main room, more a reception salon, there were three verandaed and velvet-draped windows, stretching the entire height from that ceiling to the deeply carpeted floor, and although a hodgepodge of style and period, all the furniture was of the highest and most comfortable quality, apart from some of the pieces—particularly two couches—that appeared from their pattern fade and some wear to date from the house's original occupant.

There was a separate, smaller and more convenient family room in which Charlie had installed the large-screen, transformer-operated and satellite-linked television—imported from England—and three bedrooms, two with four-poster beds around which, despite complete central heating, curtains could be drawn against a Moscow winter the El Niño appeared to have defeated. The kitchen was a burnished, chromium-gleaming contrast to the bygone age, a laboratory of microwave, ice machines, walk-in refrigerators and rotisseries. The entire edifice had been maintained and created for a relative of Leonid Brezhnev, when the most corrupt of recent Soviet leaders had ruled, taken over by subsequent Party tsars until the demise of communism, after which it had come upon the list of diplomatically offered properties through endemic bureaucratic incompetence.

Charlie had gotten it totally by chance, to support his arrival assignment cover as an entrepreneurial intermediary to infiltrate the nuclear-smuggling Russian mafia, and was reasonably confident—although not absolutely sure—that he could manipulate a matching dinosaur of Whitehall bureaucracy to go on living there by right of existing possession, even though the reason for his original occupancy had been successfully concluded.

It wasn't until the end of the tour, tightly holding her mother's hand, that Sasha said, "Where's my room?" and scuttled into the smaller one containing the curtained four-poster to which Charlie pointed. The child stood, legs apart, surveying it and gravely said, "I like it. I want to stay."

"I'm glad," said Charlie. Turning to Natalia—knowing in advance he shouldn't use the child's remark—he added, "How about Mummy?"

Natalia's answer wasn't a direct one. "I'll tell you if I decide I'm not sure anymore, about you and I."

"All right," said Charlie, unable to think of anything better.

"Does that make you think any less of me?"

"No," said Charlie, honestly. "It took me long enough, but now I'm sure."

"I want it to work, Charlie. I really do."

"So you're going to stay?"

"I might change my mind. Think I should change my mind."

They'd reverted to English. Feeling neglected again, Sasha said, "Are you going to live here, too, with Mummy and me?"

"Yes," said Charlie.

"Does that make you a daddy?"

Charlie and Natalia looked at each other. Charlie said, "Yes. Would you like that?"

"I don't know," said Sasha with childlike truthfulness.

"Let's hope everyone makes all their decisions soon," said Charlie.

The entire town council of Kiriyestyakh, led by the mayor, stood around the softening grave. The bodies were still deeply frozen, the clawed hand stiffly upright, but more earth had crumbled so that they could see the backs of both heads had been shot away.

The mayor, who had fought with the reindeer herder's father, said, "Definitely foreign. English, I think. And American. I saw uniforms like these in Berlin."

"What are we going to do with them?" asked his deputy.

The mayor had survived the long years of communism by never once making a decision. "This is in Yakutsk jurisdiction. They've got facilities there."

"They've been preserved exactly as they were the moment they were shot," the awed deputy pointed out.

"English and American," repeated the other man. "There will be a big investigation. We can get to Yakutsk in an hour."

"Do we take the bodies with us?" asked a third man.

"We don't touch them," warned the mayor. "Let others risk the Eye."

3

Yakutsk is the capital of the partially autonomous Russian republic of Yakutskaya, one of the most remote and inhospitable places on earth and provably the coldest, where temperatures plunge to minus eighty degrees centigrade. As well as being certain of the Evil Eye and the magic power of shaman witch doctor priests, the Yakut people who exist there believe unheard conversations freeze in the winter to be heard in the brief summer thaw.

In that region the summer is plagued by mosquitoes that sting so viciously that grazing reindeer and cows and horses that are not driven mad by the pain often suffocate from the attacking clog in their nostrils and mouths. Men and women have been driven insane by a concerted swarm, although the more frequent dementia is caused by the vodka intended to numb every feeling.

The freak weather of the El Niño had awakened the insects early and the melting grave was blackly thick by the time the mayor got back to it with the two official investigators. The mayor and his council were all Yakuts, less troubled by the mosquitoes than Colonel Aleksandr Kurshin and Vitali Novikov, both of whose ancestry was Russian. Kurshin, the homicide chief, at once lit supposedly repelling smoke candles that made everyone's eyes sting but did little to drive away the bugs. Novikov, the pathologist, put on a personally adapted and mesh-visored hat and gauze mask and protected his hands with rubber medical gloves. He didn't have a spare mask, but he gave his extra gloves to Kurshin, who snatched at them.

"Where's your hat and mask?" demanded Novikov, who'd made the same face protection for the other man, a boyhood friend as well as a professional colleague.

"Forgot," said Kurshin.

"That's stupid," said Novikov. Everyone drank too much in Yakutsk but Kurshin was increasingly drinking more than most and it worried Novikov. Kurshin had stunk out the mortuary vehicle on the way there. The weather and its effect worried Novikov, too. Malaria had never been a problem in such a frigid climate, but if this unnatural weather lasted, the disease could become an insect-borne epidemic. If it remained so warm for too much longer he'd warn the Health Ministry in Moscow, despite Yakutskaya's independence pretensions. He couldn't be accused of negligence if he sounded an alarm before a problem arose. It was ingrained in people whose forefathers had been exiled to permanent imprisonment, albeit without jail walls, to arrange defense before accusation.

Novikov was not, however, thinking of malaria at that precise moment. As he stared down into the grave, other thoughts—desperate, half-formed fantasies—were swirling through his mind, so distracting that he had consciously to try to push them back. He looked beyond the grave, squinting through the permanent half darkness of the Yakutskaya day over the flat, empty wasteland. He was sure he was right, but there was nothing to see, not the slightest trace. As if, in fact, a shaman had cast a spell to make everything disappear. How, he wondered, could he make it come back again?

Neither Aleksandr Andreevich Kurshin nor Vitali Maksimovich Novikov were frightened of the supernatural, although they were familiar with all the superstitions. Neither sneered at the folklore beliefs, either. Novikov, who also practiced as a general physician, knew of at least seven shamans in Yakutsk. He knew, too, that the townspeople consulted them as much as they came to him and that sometimes people whose maladies he had failed to diagnose recovered from whatever the shamans prescribed. Novikov considered himself a man of science, but didn't know of a better medicine than the power of absolute, mind-over-matter conviction. Unable to resist another fantasy, he was curious if he possessed it sufficiently himself.

Kurshin, a fat, rumpled man who had little conviction about anything apart from the anaesthesia of vodka, said, "They look like wartime uniforms." He couldn't possibly be expected to solve something that had happened such a long time ago.

"This whole area was closed then, like Yakutsk," reminded Novikov. His father, like Kurshin's, had been exiled there during the Stalin era on trumped-up charges of political conspiracy. It had left both with an inferiority complex—an apprehension of authority—that both tried hard to conceal. Too often when he was drunk Kurshin wept for no apparent reason.

"It doesn't make sense," agreed the policeman, uncomfortably.

"This is too important for us," judged Novikov, as anxious as his friend to avoid any accountability. He was a thin, nervous man whose blinking increased in proportion to his apprehension. It was very rapid at that moment. This would, he knew, attract the attention—maybe even the involvement—of faraway Moscow. Could there in some way be the salvation he almost maniacally dreamed of? Or the disaster that had overwhelmed his father?

"I know that, too. We've got to get everything right," agreed Kurshin. He'd solved each of his eight previous murders because they had all been barroom brawls or mining camp disputes where the killers had either been standing over their victims or pointed out to him when he'd gotten to the scene. He'd had to shoot dead one man crazed from vodka, not mosquito bites. The first two shots had missed. The third had only hit because the man had lunged toward him.

"I intend to," said Novikov. He checked to ensure his camera was loaded, even though he had put in the new film himself before leaving the mortuary. There weren't any proper forensic facilities in Yakutsk. The two men were expected to provide their own.

The Kiriyestyakh group, as well as the two Yakut mortuary attendants who'd come with Novikov, backed away from the grave roughly by the same distance that the medical examiner advanced toward it: a disturbed dense mass rose up toward him and before every exposure he had to shake the camera to dislodge the persistent cloud. Every print would be speckled. It couldn't be avoided. He worked his way around the entire grave, taking a picture at each sideways step.

Behind him Kurshin made a rough sketch against which to put his measurements. It was a vaguely round, banked hole, the still partially earth-covered bodies at its lowest point. Several times the measuring tape came free of the stones with which he tried to tether it, so he had to repeat the process. It would have been pointless asking any of the withdrawn group to come closer to hold it in place. Reminded, he said, "I suppose I'll have to touch the bodies as well as you to get the Eye before your people will take them out?"

"Of course," said Novikov, surprised at the question.

"I'm being stung to death. It'll be worse in there."

"You shouldn't have forgotten your hat and mask."

"It doesn't help to be told."

There was a murmur from the watching Yakuts as Novikov stepped as delicately as possible into the grave, medical bag hanging from its strap over his shoulder. Flying things engulfed him, encroaching beneath his jacket and trouser cuffs. Bites began to burn their way up his arms and legs. Kurshin was right about it being worse inside the grave, even though it was far colder than he'd expected.

Kurshin, also under attack, said, "Let's hurry."

Novikov said, "We can't afford to."

The bodies were still frozen too solidly to intrude a thermometer into any part of either body from which Novikov would have normally attempted a reading. He laid the thermometer against the outside of each grimaced face. Flies and bugs were crawling in and out of the stretched-apart mouths and their faces were swollen and bumped from stings inflicted at their moment of death, unknown years before. Novikov took close-up photographs of the obvious wounds. The backs of both heads were totally gone, exposing brain pulp. In the center of each was a trajectory hole he hoped still contained the fatal bullet. He wrote *E* for English and *A* for American in his notebook and against the *E* recorded the twist of the man's foot. It would, he guessed, be a green-bone ankle fracture, from the fall into the pit. Strangely the American's spectacles were still perfectly in place, although the left lens was shattered. Novikov himself had taken the chance and worn his contact lenses, in which he preferred to work, although he had glasses in his medical bag. Normally at this time of year it was so cold that contact lenses froze in the eye, making them impossible to wear. He was the only person in Yakutsk who bothered with what was considered a pointless ophthalmic invention. He said, "It won't be easy getting the Englishman into the van, with his arm thrust out like that."

"How would that have happened?"

"Muscle spasm when he was struck by the bullet," guessed Novikov. He tried but couldn't open the Englishman's tunic pockets. "I would have expected the clothing to have thawed by now."

"You think they were prisoners of war?"

Novikov shook his head, deciding against telling even his best friend what he thought he knew and what he was thinking. Kurshin would have laughed at him, as he'd laughed before about the things he'd tried to do for Marina and the boys. "They're too smart. Look! You can see the creases in their trousers. You want to get in here and touch the bodies, so we can get my people to move them?"

Waving his arms against a fresh insect upsurge, Kurshin stepped into the grave and tapped both corpses. Each was ice-cold and rock-hard. Looking back at the village headman, Kurshin said, "Moscow will have to be told."

"Naturally."

"Shouldn't we leave the bodies here for Ryabov to see—be photographed looking at, perhaps?" Yuri Vyacheslav Ryabov was Yakutsk's publicity-conscious, eager-to-pose militia commissioner.

"Fuck him," said Novikov.

"You don't have to rely on him like I do," complained Kurshin.

"I don't want animals eating at the bodies, even though it's still going to be some time before they thaw," said Novikov. He shouted to the two mortuary attendants, who reluctantly approached with stretchers.

Kurshin remained in the grave for the two Yakuts to see that he had touched the bodies and attracted the bad spirits, before climbing out. He was halfway toward the road, pacing out its distance from the grave, when the shout came. He turned in time to see the two attendants scrambling out; one actually fled toward the Kiriyestyakh group. Kurshin ran back himself, unable at first to hear what Novikov was yelling from the hole.

"What?" Kurshin shouted, still some distance away.

"There's a third body," said Novikov. "It was covered by the other two. It's a woman."

Taking Sasha to the state circus, all part of Charlie learning fatherhood, had been wonderful, as it always was, but they'd had to stand in line for half an hour to get into McDonald's, which was a long time for Charlie to stand comfortably. Neither Charlie nor Natalia had ordered food and now Charlie wished he'd chosen the cola instead of the coffee, which was awful. He pushed it aside. Trying to be philosophical, Charlie supposed a thirty-minute wait was practically moving at the speed of light for a Russian restaurant. And Sasha, her face greased by her cheeseburger, was enjoying it.

"I checked again," announced Natalia. "There's nothing on you apart from your appointment details." Long before Charlie's Moscow posting, Natalia had used her colonel's rank within the then-existing KGB to expunge all Charlie's records from the organization's files, as Charlie had double-checked the embassy's security archives against those in London to establish there was no file on Natalia.

Charlie looked sadly at her. "You already knew that."

"Just wanted to be sure."

"So now you are." He'd badly misjudged how difficult it was going to be. Even Sasha seemed aware of her mother's uncertainty.

Searching for a new topic, he said, "I didn't know you had a sister."

"We're not close." The letter from Irena had been among the mail she had collected from the apartment she still maintained in Leninskaya.

"What does she want?"

"Says she hasn't been able to contact me. She flies for Aeroflot and brings things from abroad for Sasha."

"What have you told her about Sasha?"

"That there was an affair that ended." She looked directly at Charlie. "I thought it had."

And maybe would have liked it to, Charlie thought. "Am I going to meet her?"

"Maybe," said Natalia, noncommittally. "I suppose I should call her or write. There's something else about us."

"What?"

"I don't expect you to ask me anything—to use my position—and I don't expect you to share anything with me."

"Neither's crossed my mind," Charlie said with a smile, trying to lighten the atmosphere. McDonald's hardly seemed the place for such a conversation, but then what—or where—was?

"That's bollocks and you know it," accused Natalia, using the word that Charlie had taught her.

"It doesn't sound the same when you say it."

"It means the same."

Charlie accepted that he'd abused Natalia's professional position badly enough in the very beginning, after he'd staged his phony defection to Moscow and deceived her when she'd been assigned to debrief him. So her distrust was justified, like everything else. Natalia had sufficient professional integrity to make up for any that he might lack. Still seemed a pity, if the facility was there. But then . . . Charlie abruptly stopped the reflection. He wouldn't cheat or treat Natalia badly, ever again. In fact, he had to do even better than that. He had to make her love him again.

4

Difficult though it was about anything involving the man, Gerald Williams did his best to remain totally objective about Charlie Muffin. And objectively he accepted he'd lost the last battle, like so many before it. But most certainly he hadn't lost the war. Nor would he. Still objective, he conceded that Charlie Muffin had succeeded in his experimental posting to Moscow by shattering a Russian nuclear-smuggling operation to the Middle East and that, for the moment, Charlie Muffin could do no wrong in the opinion of Sir Rupert Dean, the director-general. Which wasn't, by any stretch of any imagination, Williams's opinion. Charlie Muffin could—and would—break rules. The man couldn't help himself. It was Muffin's way. The way that one day—the sooner, the better—he'd make the mistake he couldn't wriggle away from, as he'd wriggled away from so many; the mistake with which he, Gerald Williams, would finally rid the service of a nuisance that should not have been allowed to exist in the first place and shouldn't be allowed to continue in these uncertain times.

There had been too many changes made too quickly in expanding the department with the hope of justifying its continued existence after the end of the Cold War. There'd actually been some personnel moves as a direct result of what the damned man had already done in Moscow. Which meant that for the moment not enough people remained in power who knew Charlie Muffin for what he truly was. But Gerald Williams knew. He knew Charlie Muffin to be an insubordinate liar and cheat with an inverted snobbery about people with better accents whose boots he shouldn't have been allowed to lick, let alone appear equal to—sometimes, even, superior.

Williams, a fat but fastidiously neat man, was sure of his strategy. Time. But with persistence. What he had to do was allow Charlie Muffin all the time—all the rope—with which to hang himself. But not let this ridiculous admiration cult grow, simply because of one initial new posting success. So there had to be constant, leveling reminders. And there was no one better qualified than he to introduce that constant balance. And he was going to be able to do that now that he was being included in these nervous discussions about the uncertainty of their organization.

Williams was happy with his reflections, quite content for the departmental conference, chaired by Sir Rupert Dean, to swirl around. For some of the time he'd only half listened, more interested in his own thoughts, gazing across the Thames to the headquarters of the MI6, or SIS, as Britain's external intelligence service preferred to call itself.

Today's meeting had been convened by the director-general to assess the effectiveness of the National Crime Squad as Britain's FBI—the role they'd fought to establish for themselves in the post–Cold War adjustments—and Williams felt the least threatened of all. The first to suffer from any retraction or functional change would be operational heads. His record as financial director and chief accountant was unblemished, although as careful as he was, Williams recognized a danger—another reason to be wary of the man—in the drunken-sailor way Charlie Muffin was being allowed to throw money around in Moscow, as if he had the key to the safe. Worriedly it occurred to Williams that the bloody man was devious enough actually to have made an impression and done just that.

"I believe they've made inroads, damaged our claim," insisted Jocelyn Hamilton. He was new to the control group, a replacement as Dean's immediate deputy. The demise of Hamilton's predecessor had come from the man's own power struggle miscalculation, but the nuclear-smuggling Moscow episode had been the trigger and Williams hoped he'd find an ally in the bull-chested, sparse-haired new deputy whose office was festooned with photographs of him as a rugby prop forward and four-time English rugby international.

"We've more than held our own," countered Dean, a disheveled man whose hair retreated from his forehead in an upright tidal wave. He'd been appointed director-general from the chair of Modern and Political History at Oxford's Balliol College and was internationally acclaimed as the foremost sociopolitical authority in Europe. There was no longer talk of his tenure being temporary, as it had been described in the beginning. Williams didn't believe the nuclear affair had anything to do with Dean's knighthood, but it had come soon afterward and some people thought there was a connection.

"It's just more duplication," persisted Hamilton. "There's already the National Criminal Intelligence Service. There's regional crime squads. There's us. What can a National Crime Squad do that we or any of the others couldn't? Or aren't already doing?"

"Focus on the criminals identified at the very top," said Jeremy Simpson, the legal adviser. Heavily he added, "And NCIS isn't operational."

Patrick Pacey, a small, dark-haired, and totally nondescript man, except for a face permanently reddened by blood pressure, said, "It makes the government's commitment against organized crime look good." He was the political officer.

"I don't think there is any cause for us yet to overreact," said Dean. He habitually spoke too quickly, his voice staccato, and seemed to make more use of his spectacles as worry beads than as an aid to reading.

"Nor to be complacent," said Hamilton.

Time carefully to venture a toe into the water, decided Williams. He said, "Certainly it would be a bad time for us to make a mistake."

Jeremy Simpson, who compensated for his alopecia baldness with a drooping bush of a mustache, sighed. "Do you know a good time to make a mistake?" He didn't like Williams and regretted his inclusion in these meetings, although acknowledging finances and costs were important in their overall future.

Williams flushed, well aware he couldn't expect any support from the odd-looking lawyer, who was buttressed against any upheaval within the department by an inherited personal fortune. "I meant that perhaps we should devote some time to anticipating potential problems."

"Like what?" demanded the political officer.

"Personnel," said Williams, shortly.

"Here we go again!" sighed Simpson, in weary anticipation. "Why *do* you have such animosity toward Charlie Muffin?"

Williams shifted uncomfortably, knowing it would be wrong for his objections to appear a personal vendetta, even though it had, for him, developed into one from how Charlie Muffin had maneuvered his attempt to impose some financial restraint into open ridicule throughout the department. Holding back from the specifics he'd intended, Williams said, "He totally disregards authority—doesn't conform. Which are attitudes I don't think we can afford in our current situation."

"You think he should be withdrawn?" asked Hamilton.

"I would not oppose the suggestion," snatched Williams, eagerly.

"Most of the cabinet Intelligence Committee would, after that most recent business," deflated Pacey.

"There's no justification any longer in his retaining the apartment he has," blurted Williams, unable to stop himself and regretting it at once.

"Now we're getting to it!" jeered the lawyer.

"It's excessive expenditure," said Williams. "My function is to control the finances of this department. I will be hard-pressed to explain the huge amount of money Moscow is costing."

"There was every justification for the apartment to distance Muffin from the embassy over the nuclear business," pointed out Dean, becoming as irritated as Simpson by the accountant's obduracy. "And you won't be called upon to explain. I will."

Enough, Williams decided; he was on record as having fulfilled his official and expected role, which was important. He said, "I felt—and still feel—that the point should be made."

"And you've made it," dismissed Simpson.

And would again, determined Williams. It was extremely important to discover everything he could about Charlie Muffin's extravagant lifestyle in Moscow. The problem was finding a way of doing it.

Vitali Novikov's mortuary, examination room and what were supposed to be his scientific testing facilities epitomized the township at the center of which it stood: crumbling and inadequate. Like the provincial government offices and militia headquarters to which it was attached, it had been built of brick and concrete, to appear impressive, before architects learned brick and concrete thawed the permafrozen ground upon which they were placed. The whole complex was now lopsided and gradually subsiding, breaking up like a sinking ship. The freak thaw had caused fresh cracks in Novikov's particular section, and down the outside wall brick dust leaked and smeared appropriately red, like blood. The space originally made for it had pulled away from the frame the only outside window in what passed as Novikov's laboratory, widening an already existing gap that needed fresh canvas packing, cardboard and binding tape to block up. Fortunately the inner autopsy room didn't have an outside wall. It had little else, either.

Novikov had only ever had one corpse at a time and was unsure how effective the two additional but rarely used freezer cabinets were. It was not an immediate problem while the bodies were still melting, but on their journey back to Yakutsk from the grave, Novikov and Kurshin had agreed, anxious to convince themselves, that Moscow would send in a team that required, ironically, that the bodies be refrozen after Novikov's initial examination. And because of the climate change he couldn't simply leave them in an outside storage shed, which he would otherwise have done in January.

There was only one examination table and there weren't replacements anywhere in town for the three bulbs that had blown in the overhead cluster, reducing his working light by half.

Novikov had both watched and conducted full autopsies at his father's side, but always the medical details of the killings had been as unarguable as the circumstances of their being inflicted. During the day and a half it still took for the bodies sufficiently to melt, he reviewed two basic guidance manuals on forensic pathology—both Communist-era unauthorized translations of American originals—and decided his best protection against professional criticism was to remove and preserve as many of the most obviously necessary body organs as possible for later Moscow analysis. Almost at once he realized that with three bodies he wouldn't have enough proper preserving containers. He supposed he'd be able to improvise with ordinary pickle jars, but he wasn't sure if he had sufficient formaldehyde. He'd have to be sparing from the start.

Novikov was not permitted to concentrate entirely upon the postmortems, which he would have liked. During the delay in being able to start them, he—together with Kurshin—was summoned before the inner governing cabinet of Yakutskaya for a meeting that was pointless, because neither could offer any evidence or theory about bodies still too frigidly rock-hard even for clothes to be stripped and examined. Equally without any practical purpose, apart from their physical presence being recorded—which it was by two photographers and a secretary—the five-man group also personally visited the mortuary to examine the ice mummies.

It was headed by Valentin Ivanovich Polyakov, the chief minister whose detestation of everything Russian stemmed from the exile and premature death of his father, banished not by Stalin but by his secret police chief Lavrenty Beria. Polyakov was the region's fiercest advocate of distancing itself from Russian domination with the end of communism. Until now Polyakov regarded as his best independence gesture persuading in 1994 the Yakutskaya cabinet now uncomfortably grouped around him to impose a local visa requirement upon any foreigner—particularly Russians—arriving at the town's airport. Although he still hadn't worked out how, Polyakov considered the finding of the three bodies—two of them Westerners—an opportunity to make another dramatic gesture of independence.

By comparison—although paradoxically by the same reasoning—there was hardly any of the outrage Kurshin had feared from Yuri Ryabov for not being alerted before the bodies had been removed from their grave. The local militia commander was well aware of their professional and technical inadequacies and saw protection in not having been involved from the very beginning. So for once local newspaper and radio headlines were secondary to an excuse—if excuse was needed—for any failure in the investigation. If there was praise, he could equally ensure he was the recipient, as the ultimate commander.

He also didn't like the way Kurshin looked from having been out there. Ryabov, a vain man constantly aware of his appearance, was as familiar with the warm-weather infestation as anyone else in the region but could rarely remember seeing anyone so badly bitten as Kurshin. The man's head and neck remained so swollen, even after two days, that he was physically unable to button his collar and his pumpkin-sized face was purpled from the insect attack.

The government visit was spoiled before it began by their entry—perhaps because of the door slamming—being the moment that the Englishman's upright arm abruptly fell perfectly by his side, as if he'd suddenly become alive. All the cabinet, apart from Polyakov, were full Yakuts, but it was Polyakov who cried out in terror, pulling back toward the door to which the rest retreated, actually huddled together as if for protection.

Recovering the quickest, Novikov said, "It's nothing: what I'm waiting to happen." He, too, was surprised by the state of Kurshin's face and was glad, now that the bodies were softening, that he'd suctioned the persistent mosquitoes, midges and gnats from the victims' mouths, noses, ears and eye-socket surrounds.

Despite Novikov's assurance, the cabinet remained tightly just inside the door. As if the medical judgment were his, Polyakov declared, "It will still be some time before we can discover anything about them. I want to know as much as possible, before contacting Moscow."

There were murmurs and shuffles of agreement from men anxious to get out of the room. Ryabov, eager to establish a working procedure, said, "It'll be their case, though. Has to be."

"We don't know what anything *has* to be, until we find out what happened, whenever it happened," disputed Polyakov. Officiously, making it a government order, he said, "We wait. I'll decide if and when Moscow is informed. And I'll do it personally."

Asshole, thought Ryabov. He said, "I've checked with wartime photographs. They're definitely English and American uniforms. Officers, too."

"What about the woman?" asked someone unseen, from the cabinet group.

"Civilian clothes," said Ryabov, unnecessarily, because the still fully clothed woman was lying on a trolley next to the momentarily unneeded freezer drawers. "But they look Russian to me. So does she. Slavic."

"This is an opportunity to bring world attention to what Stalin and the bastards who followed him did to their own people," decided Polyakov, an idea hardening in his mind. "We're going to use this for all it's worth. Embarrass Moscow. They're still pillaging our country, for what's in the ground."

"Let's hope it was Moscow who had them killed all those years ago," said Kurshin, emboldened by the vodka he'd drunk before the visit.

Novikov listened uncomfortably, unsure after all if the murders would be the chance for which he'd hoped. The more he'd thought about it, the more determined he'd become to make it so, but he couldn't achieve it if the intention was positive obstruction and embarrassment. He wanted friends, not enemies.

Novikov began the autopsies later that evening, starting with the Englishman because the body's outstretched arm had made it more convenient to put upon the examination table when they'd first arrived. Again—as he did subsequently with the American and the woman—he exhausted an entire roll of film photographing the body from every conceivable angle, reloading in readiness to record the dissection before physically touching the body. From both his father's tuition and the stolen guidance manuals, he knew it would have been professionally acceptable to cut the uniform away, but he had heard of incredible advances in forensic science—DNA, for instance, which he only vaguely understood—and used the empty threat of dismissal to force the two mortuary attendants, his only assistants, to help him lift and maneuver all three bodies to strip the clothes away intact.

Having done that, he left the naked body on the slab to go through each item of clothing, stopping painstakingly to itemize by hand each article he found. From the Englishman, in total, there was twenty British sterling, in notes and ten coins; 100 German war-script marks and $43, both currencies all in notes; a gold watch with a worn leather strap, the hands stopped at 12:43; a gold cigarette case containing six American Camel cigarettes and engraved with an inscription in Roman lettering that Novikov could not understand; a cigarette lighter, uninscribed; four keys, one designated by a twist of red cotton around its shank; a British-made Parker fountain pen, the ink inside still frozen; and a tie pin in the shape of a bayonet. The pin was still in a plain, army-issue tie, but the tie itself was snapped, close to the neck.

The clothes consisted of brown leather shoes, showing little sign of wear; army-issue cotton socks; cotton singlet vest with half-thigh-length underpants; starch-collared khaki shirt, the top four buttons undone, with two missing but already found lodged at the waist during the undressing; and a well-tailored khaki officer's uniform, around the jacket of which there was what Novikov described in his notes as a leather harness, a belt encircling the waist of the jacket, which continued to midthigh, with another leather strap looped over the man's right shoulder to be joined, front and back, to the waist belt at the left. There was brass shoulder insignia, which Novikov noted, although he was not able to identify the denoted rank. All the clothes were so perfectly preserved that Novikov thought that with cleaning—the brass buttons and leather polished—everything would have been wearable again.

The body was that of a blond-haired, well-nourished male Caucasian, approximately thirty years old. From its condition the man could have died that day. Novikov concentrated upon the obvious cause of death. At least half the cranial casing had been lost, a considerable amount driven into the brain pulp. It was easier than Novikov expected to extract the single bullet, which had entered in a downward trajectory and lodged at the Atlas vertebra at the spinal tip. The pathologist had no forensic ballistic knowledge or experience, but the bullet looked quite large and appeared reasonably intact. There were minor facial abrasions, dark with after-death lividity, and there was a lividity burn around at the rear of the neck. Apart from that there was no body wound. The wrists and ankles were bruised, predeath, indicating the man had been tightly bound.

He sawed into the sternum, continuing the chest opening to the man's pelvis, and braced the rib cage apart. Novikov extensively photographed the exposed organs before examining each intently. None looked enlarged or diseased. Finally, still working downward, he extracted and weighed the heart, aorta, both lungs, the thymus, stomach, liver, gallbladder, pancreas, spleen, both kidneys, both adrenaline glands, bladder, prostate and urethra. Having done that, he returned to the skull and removed, weighed and preserved what remained of the cerebrum and cerebellum, inserting a pencil to show the trajectory of the wound on the photographs.

Only when he finished did Novikov remember the manual guidance about stomach contents and remove enough to discover it contained a largely undigested meal: even without using his microscope, the mirror of which was tarnished, Novikov identified meat and what looked like cheese. He had actually to consult the manual to learn that stomach evidence should not be preserved in formaldehyde. He immersed everything else, carefully labeling each jar as he did so. Without a name, he used the believed nationality. Again following the manual, he took fingernail scrapings, which just looked like dirt but which he fixed onto a microscope slide.

It was at that moment he remembered he hadn't weighed the body intact, which he should have done. He weighed it anyway, adding the minimal additions of the now-removed organs. After doing that, he took height and body measurements, something else he should have done at the outset. An inevitable second, more accurate autopsy, with better equipment, would probably pick up his error.

He didn't make it on either of the other two bodies. He chose that of the believed American next. The uniform was similar to the first, without the leather harness. Again it was all army-issue, cotton socks, boxer shorts underwear and singlet. The tie was completely missing and the three top buttons of the shirt unfastened. The tunic jacket again had shoulder ranking designation, which Novikov noted.

There was a silver-cased, khaki-strapped wristwatch which Novikov took to be army-issue, stopped at 1:20, and a silver ring surmounted by a large red stone on the small finger of his left hand. The pocket of the uniform contained $75 in notes and twenty-five cents in coin and 100 war-script D-marks; five keys in a flat leather case, none with any identification; a small, ivory-handled penknife; a pocket magnifying glass with what appeared to be a matching set of tweezers; a Zippo lighter but no cigarettes or cigarette case; a silver propelling pencil; and a packet of Juicy Fruit chewing gum, with two sticks missing.

The body was again that of a well-nourished male Caucasian, age about thirty-five. The fatal wound was once more to the back of the head but more to its right than that of the first victim. Less cranial bone had been shattered. It was again comparatively easy to recover the bullet, the trajectory of which had taken it from the right to the left of the man's skull and been slightly more damaged by impact against the rear teeth to the left of the jaw. There was a lividity burn almost completely around the neck. Novikov made the same gullet-to-crotch opening, broke open the rib cage and this time used the man's own magnifying glass to examine each of the organs, none of which showed any indication of damage or disease. He patiently went through the same weighing and preserving process, once more leaving the brain until last. Again, for the photographs, he marked the trajectory with a pencil. There was undigested vegetable matter as well as meat among the stomach contents. There didn't seem to be debris beneath the man's fingernails, but Novikov made scrape slides. He continued using the supposed nationality to identify his specimen jars.

The dead woman's clothing—a dark blue three-quarter-length jacket and skirt—resembled a uniform, although there was no indication of any service or rank. There were no pockets in the jacket but two in the skirt. In that on the left side there was a single key. In the right a cellophaned pack of Camels, from which two were missing. The remainder were crushed and broken. Her watch, which had stopped at 12:05, was tin-cased, the strap imitation leather.

The woman's shoes were down at heel, the mock leather uppers scuffed. There were no stockings. Her underpants were string-tied, with half-thigh legs. She wore only a bra beneath a long-sleeved white shirt, which was marked with several days' wear at the cuffs and collar. As with the two men, some of the front shirt buttons were open—three, in her case. Around her neck, which was unmarked, a thin chain held a bare silver cross.

Although heavily blood-matted now, her hair had been black and would have been long, practically to her shoulders. Her mouth had frozen into a grimace of agony, and although that had relaxed, the features were still distorted, destroying what once would have been an attractive, even beautiful, high-cheekboned face. Her heavy-breasted body would have been exciting, too. The pelvis was marked with the striae gravidarum of childbirth as well as an appendectomy scar. The shattering wound was more to the left side of the skull and only when Novikov inserted a probe to trace the entry line and locate the bullet did he properly realize that what he'd thought to be leaked blood from the head entry was in fact congealed around an exit wound in her throat, just above the larynx. And that the bullet had not lodged in her body. As he was examining the exit wound—again with the American's magnifying glass—he isolated small black specks he couldn't immediately identify, until separately placing them under the closer and more direct arc light on his desk. They were long-dead mosquitoes and gnats. He at once returned to the two men whose postmortems he had completed, making a scalpel incision in each throat. Both windpipes contained insect debris.

The chest, stomach and pelvic opening had virtually become routine. He went almost automatically through the process of examining, extracting, weighing and preserving the organs, all of which appeared perfectly normal. Additionally, with the woman, he extracted the ovaries. They, as well as the spleen, pancreas and remains of the brain, had to go into vegetable pickle jars. Only when he was transferring the scant debris from beneath her very short and in places bitten nails did Novikov remember he had not estimated an age. It was difficult, because of the distortion he now knew to have been caused by the exiting bullet, but he guessed between thirty and thirty-five.

So intently had Novikov worked that only when he looked, virtually for the first time, toward his supposed laboratory and saw daylight through the skewed window did he become aware he had worked completely through the night. His watch showed six-thirty. Abruptly he was engulfed in a physically aching tiredness he doubted would bring any sleep, so much was there to try to understand.

He stored all three bodies, squinting at the temperature gauges outside each cabinet to ensure the refrigeration was working, shuffled across to his office and slumped into a chair that had lost most of its seat stuffing. He couldn't immediately decide whether it was good or bad. Mixed, maybe. For him, personally, more good than bad. Certainly enough to make what he hoped would be a sufficiently impressive presentation.

It took a long time for Aleksandr Kurshin to answer his telephone, and when he did his voice was still thick from vodka and it took several more minutes for the homicide detective to recognize to whom and about what he was talking.

"Who are they?" Kurshin demanded finally, his voice still slurred.

"That's the point," said Novikov. "Everything and anything that might have identified them has been taken. We don't know who they are. And there's no way we're ever going to find out."

Yakutsk is six hours ahead of Moscow time, so it was still only midday when the telephone exchanges from the far side of Siberia percolated down through the Foreign Ministry to the interior minister's secretariat and eventually to Natalia. She made only brief interjections and afterward sat without moving, even though the demand for her to attend was immediate. This could be the problem—the potential disaster—she'd prayed would never arise.

"I'm going to be late," she told Charlie, who answered the telephone on the first ring.

"What time?" He'd thought it might have been London, although telephones were normally reserved for emergencies. The sum total of his activity that day and too many before it had been to create a delta-winged paper plane that flew completely across his office, through the open door and almost reached the far wall of the outside corridor. There'd been four improvements from that morning's prototype: it all had to do with the tilt of the wings.

"I don't know. Can you pick Sasha up from the crèche?"

"Sure. Something big?"

"I'll call when I have some idea of a time," refused Natalia, ignoring the question.

"I love you," he said, but Natalia had already replaced the telephone.

When it rang again, within minutes, he snatched it up, smiling, expecting it to be Natalia again. But it wasn't.

5

Natalia was not late, but everyone else was already there. Viktor Romanovich Viskov even had his jacket off and collar unbuttoned, and she felt a fresh twitch of anxiety at the thought that the deputy interior minister trying to depose her might have already started an undermining attack in her absence. The room had gone ominously, expectantly quiet at her entry.

Only Dmitri Nikulin gave any formal greeting. Viskov, a squat, stone-faced and professional long-term survivor in the oxygen-starved near-summit of Russian government, remained expressionless. Which Natalia expected. She supposed she should also have expected only the curt, grave-faced nod from Mikhail Suslov, confronted as the man appeared to be, after only four months as deputy foreign minister, with an international situation of potentially enormous proportion.

For herself Natalia accepted that the international perception of Russia was of an out-of-legal-control country dominated by organized crime, which too much of it was, and that of anyone in the room she could be made to appear the person most closely connected to that failure and to that embarrassment.

Which didn't end that simply. There was the fact that Yakutsk was three thousand miles from Moscow, the capital of a time-warped, antagonistic, near-independent republic and that the murders appeared to have been committed decades ago.

All and every problem of which was compounded by the meeting being convened in the sixth-floor White House suite of Dmitri Borisovich Nikulin, chief of staff of the president, whose own quarters were farther along the linking corridor on the same level, a constant although unneeded reminder of the echelon at which the matter was being considered from the outset.

"We seem to have an extremely serious problem," opened Nikulin. He was a thin, gaunt man who invariably appeared to invite an opinion from the people to whom he was speaking before offering one himself.

"On the face of it," agreed Suslov, cautiously.

"We hardly know enough yet to make any sort of judgment," qualified Viskov, just as carefully. Quickly, however, he added, "What is essential today is that we ensure from the very beginning that we are properly prepared, particularly that any investigation is totally successful." He spoke looking directly at Natalia.

"The obvious first essential," encouraged Nikulin. "It's difficult from what we've received so far to judge what it is that we might be investigating."

"It will have to be officers from here," pressed Viskov, still looking at Natalia. "I think we should hear your thoughts, Natalia Nikandrova."

The invitation should have come from the presidential adviser, gauged Natalia. The cadaverous man didn't appear offended.

"We can of course do that," said Natalia. "But Yakutskaya has a great deal of autonomy. Have we been asked—invited—to take over whatever investigation is going on there?" She had to remain focused, not allow any private distractions. Why now, this soon? she thought, in familiar litany. Why ever?

Suslov was one of the new, not-yet-forty, university-educated Russian reformers impatient for changes too long promised. He nodded approvingly at the woman's political awareness. "Not in as many words. It's inferred, from the very fact of our being informed. It's a good qualification, Natalia Nikandrova."

Not the praise of someone involved in a plot before her arrival, Natalia thought, relieved. Deciding the diplomatic road the one to take, she said, "So at the moment we have no right even to go there. I don't consider we can proceed on the basis of inference."

"It's a valid point," congratulated Nikulin. "We have to ensure our participation is officially requested."

"And that cooperation is guaranteed," persisted Natalia. "It would be unfortunate if investigators from here were blamed for mistakes not of their making." She allowed her mind briefly to go sideways. An investigation seemingly involving a murdered Englishman: without question Charlie's sort of crime, according to the remit of his posting. So added to the danger of their living together was now going to be the constant conflict of interest she'd determined not to allow. She felt constricted, as if a band were physically tightening around her chest. She'd be hopelessly compromised if they were discovered; it scarcely mattered anymore whether they were occupying the same apartment or not. Her dismissal and his expulsion would be inevitable. And she'd meant what she'd said about being a true Russian with a Russian's umbilical link to her country. Abandoning it to go to live in London really would be the ultimate, unthinkable sacrifice. She supposed it came down to how much she loved Charlie. Maybe more. Maybe it was how much she truly felt she could trust him.

There wasn't actually an expression, but Viskov's features had tightened at apparently being outargued. "I'm not suggesting we go uninvited. But to believe we won't be is naive. . . ." He paused, yet again addressing Natalia more than Nikulin. "Which I find surprising for someone whose paramount function is properly considering the political implications of criminal investigations. Perhaps, for that reason, it should be her deputy—who is, after all, a trained investigator in his own right—who supervises everything on a day-to-day basis."

Colonel Petr Pavlovich Travin had been Viskov's personal choice, appointed without any reference to her, the most positive indication of an intended, almost old-time purge. Natalia said, "And I, in turn, am surprised that Viktor Romanovich, a politician, considers the political implications—surely the reason for this initial meeting—to be secondary. They are, in my opinion, no way secondary. They are the first priority. . . ." She hesitated, abruptly aware of another, so far unrealized practical difficulty, just as quickly recognizing how to overcome it at the same time as hopefully defusing Viskov's attack. "Of course, the proper Russian investigatory team is of the utmost importance. And of course my deputy shall have day-to-day responsibility."

She saw the tightness go from Viskov's face at his imagining he had won the exchange.

Nikulin appeared aware of the tension between them and said, "I think we've sufficiently covered that point. Every indication is that it's a wartime situation. Do we have any archival records of American or British presence there?"

"What archival records?" demanded Suslov, who sometimes overstressed his contempt for the Communist past. "Russia has no accurate history for the past seventy years. Not in any ministry file or, I wouldn't think, any intelligence or militia agency. Everything has been sanitized and corrected and improved, after every event, for each decision and action to be shown to be the right one."

There was momentary silence both at the cynicism and the outburst.

"But checks *are* being made in the Foreign Ministry?" persisted Nikulin.

One of Suslov's advisers came quickly forward, whispering in the deputy minister's ear. Suslov frowned, regretting the apparent prompt. "Yes."

"And also through the records of my ministry," offered Viskov, anxious to recover. "If this does escalate, it's important that everything is seen to have been done properly, in the correct order."

"Quite so." Nikulin smiled bleakly.

"Which was surely what we agreed at my suggestion a few moments ago," capped Natalia. "Which brings us to the next political consideration. What do we do about London and Washington?"

"Should we do anything, this early?" questioned Viskov, following Nikulin's lead of seeking an opinion rather than advancing one.

"Let's take the worst scenario, that an American and an English officer were murdered, together with a Russian woman," suggested Nikulin. "It would have happened too long ago for that in itself to be a difficulty for the present government, whatever the circumstances of their being in what was, during and after the war, a closed-to-outsiders Stalin gulag complex. Our concentration has got to be how we handle it now. It's essential we appear totally open, with nothing to hide. And we don't have anything to hide. . . ." The thin man hesitated, nodding in private agreement with himself. "It *is* going to be a difficult crime to solve, after such a long time. Almost

certainly impossible. There'll be mistakes. Problems. What's important is keeping us beyond all criticism for those problems. . . ." He
paused in further reflection. "It would help if they turned out to be
spies, of course."

Natalia listened intently, frowning, anxious to anticipate the point
toward which the presidential adviser was moving.

"We have an extremely backward but volatile republic, suspicious
of foreigners—with perhaps the exception of Canada, with which
they have some joint ventures—with Russia at the top of the hate
list. They're going to resent the need for us to be involved, maybe
even intentionally make it awkward for whoever we send there. . . ."
The man paused, at a moment of rare commitment. "We need insurance. And I think that insurance could very definitely be to involve London and Washington at this stage. To go as far as *inviting*
them to send investigators at the same time as we send ours. . . ."

Logically—inevitably—that would be Charlie, Natalia accepted
once more. What would Charlie's insurance be? It would have to be
her if they were to survive together, Natalia admitted. So much for
avoiding a conflict of interest. She'd still try to avoid it happening,
for as long as possible.

"At the same time?" echoed Viskov, rhetorically, wanting Nikulin
to recognize his understanding of what the man was saying.

Nikulin gave another bleak smile, unoffended at the interruption.
"Problems—difficulties—of an investigation *by* their own people into
a fifty-year-old murder of an Englishman and an American would be
their problems and difficulties, not ours, wouldn't they?"

"Absolutely!" agreed Suslov, smiling, too.

Nikulin looked directly at Natalia. "I want you to choose your
team extremely carefully. And brief them even more carefully. The
investigation will fail. It can't do otherwise. The failure must be
shown to be that of the English and Americans, not us. The agenda
for our people must be to make the foreigners provably responsible
for every error." The smile came again, at a perfectly devised
strategy. Still directly addressing Natalia, he said, "You have any
difficulty—argument—with that?"

"None whatsoever," lied Natalia.

Mikhail Suslov said, "Washington and London will have to be
officially told through my ministry. I'll do it immediately."

"This is a boring game!" protested Sasha.

"We got three planes right across the room!" said Charlie. The distance from one end of the main salon to the other was much farther than the corridor wall from his empty office desk.

"Your planes and you threw them," reminded the child. "Mine crashed."

"All your home schoolwork done?"

"Everything I had to do."

She'd made pictures of a dog and a horse and chosen their initial letters without his help. "How about a story?"

"We could watch television," Sasha suggested instead. "American cartoons. It helps me to learn the words."

Charlie and Natalia wanted Sasha to be bilingual and spent half an hour each evening talking only English. He wasn't sure of the benefit of the satellite programs and words like *POW* and *WHAM* and *BLAM*, but he didn't want to lose Sasha's enthusiasm. "Only while I get supper."

"Baked beans!" she said, in English.

They were a novelty—unavailable in Moscow—and Sasha's latest favorite, which Charlie got through the embassy commissary. He turned on the wide-screen set in the smaller room and insisted she sit properly in a chair several feet away, vaguely remembering a warning about X ray or some sort of ray that could harm children sitting too close.

"Can I have it on a tray, on my lap?"

"No."

"Please!"

"No."

"Why not?"

"It's not a proper way to eat."

"*Ley* used to let me!" said Sasha.

Ley was the closest Sasha had ever been able to get to the given name of Alexei Popov, Natalia's deputy, whom she'd planned to marry until Charlie's exposure of the man as a Mafia-linked member of the nuclear-smuggling organization manipulating her and the rank he held within the ministry. By unspoken—although in Charlie's opinion, unnecessary—agreement he and Natalia never referred between themselves to the man who had contributed to another layer of Natalia's too-miserable life. But very occasionally, like now when she wasn't getting her own way, Sasha followed her child's instinct and experimented. Charlie said, "He might have done. I'm not."

"Where is Ley?"

"Gone."

"Gone where?"

Wherever someone goes who gets shot point-blank and full in the face with a 9mm bullet, thought Charlie, remembering the final moments of the ambush in which Popov had tried to kill him. He said, "Away."

"Is he coming back?"

"No."

"Never, ever?"

"Never, ever. So you'll eat properly, at the table in the kitchen." He set her place, complete with a proper napkin, and timed the beans and toast to be ready when the cartoon program finished. He sat opposite while she ate. Beyond the child the nearly full bottle of Islay malt stood out on the drinks tray like a beacon, but Charlie ignored it, even though technically it was happy hour. There were a lot of unimagined changes in being a father.

"Shall we try to speak English?"

"If you'd like," said Charlie, pleased it was her suggestion, which was how he and Natalia always tried to make it.

"How long will Mummy be?"

She inverted the verb, but for a child of Sasha's age it was conversationally very good. "She didn't know. She's going to phone to tell us."

"Are you going to bathe me?"

Another first, by himself, accepted Charlie. "Yes."

"All right," said Sasha, gravely, as if giving permission, which Charlie supposed she was.

The downstairs buzzer sounded, making them both jump by its unexpectedness. Not Natalia, thought Charlie at once. She'd promised to phone, and in any case she had her own key. The grandiose apartment *had* been an effective part of his cover as a crooked entrepreneur and all the nuclear ringleaders had been either arrested or killed. But a lot of the minnow men, the gofers and the fetchers, would have gotten through the net and there had always been at the back of Charlie's mind the awareness that some might know this address. Might know, too, that he was the person who'd destroyed everything. But they wouldn't come at him like this: not ring the bell. Easier—better—just to wait outside, hit him when he arrived or left.

"Mummy?" asked Sasha, when the bell went again.

"I don't think so," said Charlie. He could legally carry a gun in Moscow, but didn't. He'd have liked the comfort of a weapon now, even though he wasn't very good: never able to keep his eyes open at the moment of firing. Or keep the kick from hurting his wrist, even though he adopted the correct, hand-supporting shooting crouch. He hadn't been the person to shoot Popov as Popov was preparing to shoot him.

"I'll go," said Sasha, brightly.

"No!" said Charlie, too sharply. "Stay and wipe your mouth. I'll see who it is." The downstairs door could be forced, even if he didn't operate the admission button, but it was very thick and heavy and wouldn't be easy. And there were two bolts and a crossbar as well as a chain, from the previous protection, on the apartment door which was practically as strong as that five floors below. He wasn't reassured. It had been downright fucking stupid to have let himself be trapped like this—like this with Sasha, of all things!—without any means of protection or escape. The bell sounded a third time as he reached the microphone.

"Yes?"

"I was about to give up on you." It was a woman's voice.

"Who is this?"

"Irena, Natalia's sister."

"Hello," he said to the woman who'd called immediately after Natalia, earlier. "I wasn't expecting you."

"You said it would be all right to call 'round, so I decided to at once."

Charlie pressed the release button and opened the apartment door in readiness. Sasha came to the door and, when he told her who was coming up the stairs, said, "I like Aunt Irena. She brings me presents."

Irena was in Western clothes: loafers, Levi's jeans and a designer version of a fleecy-lined pilot's jacket. She picked Sasha up, kissed her and carried her laughing into the apartment. Immediately inside, she gave Sasha a Donald Duck that climbed quacking up a cord by some mechanism triggered by it being pulled sharply downward. The child began to retreat, giggling delightedly, then stopped and said, "Thank you," and kissed the woman again. She looked to Charlie for approval. Charlie nodded.

Irena turned at last to Charlie. "So you're my sister's new partner!"

Charlie accepted that he was, as far as Irena was concerned, but didn't like the question: it inferred there'd been a lot. He didn't know, in fact, whether there had been or not. It wasn't something he and Natalia had felt the need to discuss. "Yes," he said, simply.

"And English!" said Irena, in the same language, which she spoke well. "The embassy? Or business here?"

"Something in between," avoided Charlie.

"Daddy was just going to bath me," announced Sasha. "Now you can help."

Daddy, Charlie seized at once. Until that moment she hadn't made any attempt at a name, not even a guess at *Charlie,* which they'd decided to allow if she'd tried.

Irena seized it, too. "Daddy?"

"If I can be," said Charlie. He wasn't enjoying the encounter.

"Why don't I bathe you myself—and read you a story—while Daddy gets me a drink?" suggested the woman.

Charlie decided he liked the way the title sounded. He was glad, too, that Irena had taken over bathtime duties: he was learning how to be a father at roughly the same pace as Sasha was mastering basic spoken English. "There's most things," he invited.

"Scotch. Water back."

Very American vernacular, thought Charlie, amused. He took Islay scotch as well, pouring both straight, setting out her water glass separately and putting ice in a bucket for her to add herself, to avoid it melting to dilute the drink. For someone who until that moment had been total stranger, Irena—Irena Seminova Modin, Charlie remembered, from the McDonald's conversation—seemed very adept at appearing an old friend. It probably had something to do with being a stewardess. Long-haul, he recalled: Australia as well America.

There was a lot of splashing and laughing from the bathroom. Sasha was in her nightdress, warm and fresh-smelling, when she ran in to kiss him good night. She announced, "Aunt Irena is going to tell me a story. Girls only, but you can come in to say good night later," and ran out again, giggling.

Irena emerged ten minutes later pulling her sweater down about her and said, "I got splashed."

Charlie wondered what had happened to the flying jacket. Irena was far bigger-busted than her sister and seemed proud of it, from the tightness of the sweater. He said, "What's this girls-only all about?"

Irena smiled, taking the large, enveloping chair beside the couch on which Charlie sat. "She said she wanted to have a secret, so I told her to make one up."

Charlie indicated the drink, pouring a second for himself. Irena added just one ice cube, properly sipping the water separately, and Charlie decided there was nothing wrong with a pretension if it was carried out confidently enough. Irena was doing fairly well.

"How long have you and Natalia been together?"

"A while," said Charlie, evasively.

The woman was looking around the apartment. "And isn't she the lucky one. Sasha said princesses lived here once and I believe her. You must be either very important or very rich or both."

"There's a lot of opportunities in Moscow now." Charlie decided that apart from an obvious facial resemblance Irena was different in every way from Natalia. He preferred Natalia's natural darkness to Irena's blond-highlighted hair and if he was making a direct comparison—which he was—he thought Natalia's figure was better, too. Irena verged upon the voluptuous and seemed to want to, from the tightness of the second-skin jeans as well as the sweater.

"I know someone from the American embassy trade division," Irena declared. "Saul Freeman. You know him?"

"*Of* him," said Charlie, cautiously. Saul Freeman headed the FBI's station at the U.S. embassy. It had been the Bureau's success in getting a man based in Moscow—and the dominance and Western crime links of the Russian mafia—that had been instrumental in Charlie's appointment. Freeman was a balding New York bachelor who shared with the British embassy's matchingly single MI6 resident, Richard Cartright, the apparent ambition to screw every woman in Moscow. Natalia wouldn't be happy at Irena finding them together and most certainly not at Irena knowing someone with a Bureau function from another Western embassy. "How'd you meet Saul?"

"He was on my flight, about six months ago." She grinned. "Not by choice. It was the only plane available." She looked around the apartment again. "But his place doesn't come within a million miles of this."

Cautiously Charlie said, "You seeing each other?"

Irena grimaced again, pulling down the corners of her mouth. "We went out to dinner once or twice."

"But?"

"He didn't make me laugh. And he counts."

"Counts?"

"In a notebook. Writes down what he spends, when he spends it."

"You're joking!"

"I told you, there was nothing to laugh about. I think you'd make me laugh, though. What do you think?"

"I think I know someone who'd think he was terrific making a note of his expenditure," said Charlie, refusing the flagrant invitation.

"She'd be disappointed. He makes love by number, too. Hup, one two three, hup, one two three. . . ."

Charlie laughed, because he was expected to, curious just the same. Genuine free spirit? Or something else? He shouldn't kid himself it was anything else.

"It's a man."

"Maybe that's his real interest. He tried to explore."

Time to call a halt, Charlie decided. "I'll check Sasha. Say good night."

"She's okay."

"I'll still check." Sasha was asleep, the Donald Duck string around her wrist. Charlie gently disentangled it and put it on the bedside table. Sasha snuffled but didn't wake up. When he returned to the smaller sitting room, Irena had moved from the chair to the couch upon which Charlie had earlier sat. He momentarily considered the chair but went back to his original seat, although wedging himself in the corner farthest from the woman and half turning toward her.

Irena swiveled toward him, one leg crooked onto the seat, smiling over the separating gap. "I won't bite. Not unless I'm asked."

"Good." What the hell was this all about? Careful against misinterpretation, he warned himself.

"What's Natalia told you about me?" demanded Irena.

"Very little."

"She hasn't told me anything about you, either. So why don't you?"

"Ask Natalia."

"Why so shy?"

"I don't want to bore you, like Saul seems to have done."

"I don't think you would."

He lifted the bottle. Irena nodded. Once, thought Charlie, this might even have been fun. "How do you know I don't keep an account book?"

"I'm usually good at judging men. Saul was a mistake."

So what was Irena? A prick teaser or a pubic scalp collector? One was potentially as dangerous as the other, quite apart from the embassy connection. That wasn't a danger, now that it was over. And he wasn't interested in—didn't want to answer—either of the other questions. "Maybe this is a mistake."

"What?" The smile was quite open now.

"I think you are a very exciting woman. Beautiful," said Charlie, who believed, without conceit, that he'd perfected sincere-sounding dishonesty into an art form. "At any other time I would have liked to have played these word games—every other sort of game—for a very long time. But I'm with your sister, whom I love. As I love Sasha. We're wrongly met: wrong time, wrong circumstances. Lost opportunities. . . ." Jesus! thought Charlie. There should have been violin music for that last bit. "So it's got to be just friends. Okay?"

Before Irena could answer, the telephone jarred into the room and Charlie thought, saved by the bell, and was right. He replaced the receiver and said, "Natalia's on her way home."

"No," said Irena.

"No what?" frowned Charlie, momentarily lost.

"No, it's not okay."

Fuck you, thought Charlie. At once he corrected himself. No, I won't, despite the obvious offer.

There is an elite group of men who observe with what can best be described as tolerance the comings and goings of political parties in what are described as democratic elections in the countries of the West. Invariably the word *secretary* appears somewhere in their title, which conveys totally the wrong impression of their absolute power and unparalleled influence, a misconception they foster because these are men who, if it were possible, would choose physically to be as invisible as they metaphorically are. It is they who, irrespective of briefly passing governments and electorally promised policies, ensure the stable passage of their respective countries through life's stormy seas. Each is known personally to and operates with the other in a structure without name or written rules or constitution. It is enough that they *know*, which they do instinctively, without the need to explain to one another. They discuss.

Such a man was Kenton Peters, an urbane, cultured American aristocrat of such independent means that his salary always went automatically to charity, a man who joined the American State Department during the Nixon administration, which he felt never would have ended as it did had he been in control, and who was the first person an incoming secretary of state asked to see, upon arrival at Foggy Bottom, unaware that Peters had approved his appointment before it had been offered.

Another was James Boyce, whose family was traceable to the restoration of the English monarchy, which one or other of its members had loyally served ever since. Boyce himself had entered the British Foreign Office, of which he was now permanent secretary, during the late premiership of Edward Heath. Of all this special elite, throughout Europe and North America, Kenton Peters was the one with whom James Boyce preferred to operate—*work* would have been quite the wrong word—when the occasion demanded. It was Boyce who decided the Yakutsk murders were such a demanding occasion and made contact with Peters within an hour of the Russian message arriving at the Foreign Office.

"This is something we never expected," opened Boyce. "Bit of a damned nuisance, all 'round."

"Nothing we can't handle."

"Of course not."

"How do you intend handling it, from your end?" asked the American.

"Involve every intelligence department we've got, to create the maximum confusion. And insist I have access to everything, so I know at all times what's going on and how to misguide, if necessary."

"You think we might have to stage a diversion?"

"Such as?" questioned Boyce.

"If anyone were to get too close and have to die, it could be blamed on the Russians or people in Yakutsk, couldn't it?"

"I don't think there's the remotest chance of anyone getting close, but it's certainly something we should consider."

"Your person in Moscow disposable?"

"They're all disposable."

"I could move someone in from here to do it—someone nobody knows, with no provable attachment to an agency or government," offered Peters.

"Let's make contingency plans," agreed Boyce.

"And keep in touch?"

"Absolutely."

"How?" shouted Natalia, knowing she was taking out on Charlie all the fears and frustrations of the meeting she'd just left but unable to separate them from the shock of finding Irena calmly sipping whiskey with him when she'd gotten home. And then having to sit through an hour of frigid conversation before it had been possible to get rid of the woman.

"You gave her the bloody number. And the address!" Charlie shouted back. "She rang and said she had something for Sasha and I told her to bring it around sometime. I didn't expect her to come right away."

She *had* given Irena the number, Natalia remembered. "Did you tell her you were attached to the embassy?"

"Not directly. I let her think it was something to do with joint venture trading." He wouldn't tell Natalia that Irena knew Saul Freeman.

"I'm sorry," apologized Natalia. "I'm . . ." She stopped. "I'm not being a very nice person at the moment, am I?"

"No," answered Charlie, honestly. "But you're allowed. The adjustment is bigger for you than it is for me. And obviously you've got a lot of work pressure." He waited hopefully but she didn't respond.

6

Charlie Muffin was on his first paper airplane of the day—a new prototype, with a separate tail section—when the dust-covered telephone rang and Sir Rupert Dean announced, "You'll get everything on paper, of course. But I need you to understand a lot of things that aren't written. The most important is that the future of the department—and your posting to Moscow—depends on your getting everything right."

Charlie had never wasted time over personal disappointments—apart from the death of his first wife, Edith, which would always be a personal disaster for which he'd never forgive himself—but there was a lasting surge of regret as he listened to the director-general. Sadness came close behind. And then—surprising himself—sympathy. Natalia hadn't been intentionally perverse, hadn't tried, in some way, to trick or ridicule him. Maybe she'd even thought the assignment wouldn't be given to him, although he couldn't really accept that, convenient though it would have been.

Natalia was making a mess of it. Of everything. Of their being together—living together—and by trying to keep separate their professional lives and by not being able to trust him (for which he couldn't blame her) and by trying to do everything her way, wrongly, was endangering all that they hoped to exist between them.

Which was not the immediate consideration: the immediate consideration was his need totally to concentrate and understand what he was being told.

"Every other agency is involved?" he demanded, determined against the slightest misunderstanding.

"Every other agency has been asked to search their archives: contribute whatever they can," replied Dean, equally pedantic. "The investigation is ours."

"Which you see as a test?"

"We're vulnerable: everyone snapping at our heels. We've got to answer all the questions, find out who he was and what he was doing there. We do that—*you* do that—and I'll be able to fight whatever survival battle we're confronted with."

"And if I don't?"

"Then that's what it could become: a battle for survival. At best we could become a branch of some other agency."

"What about my remaining here in Moscow?"

There was a pause from the London end. "There are arguments being put up against the posting. They'd be hard to oppose."

Gerald fucking Williams, guessed Charlie. Why did the parsimonious bugger take as a personal insult Charlie's special interpretation of an expense account? It wasn't as if it was Williams's money. Perhaps, thought Charlie, he should have considered the early challenges, too long ago now to remember, as more than the game he chose them to make it, virtually challenging the man to catch him out. Bluntly he said, "I fail to solve it, I get withdrawn? My role— my reason for being in Moscow—won't exist anymore?"

"It would certainly come up for very hard discussion."

"From what you said, these killings happened fifty years ago!" Charlie pointed out.

"I know," accepted Dean.

"And no one's acknowledging our victims belonged to their department?"

"They've only been checking for a few hours, but so far, no."

"*Supposedly* checking," qualified Charlie. "No one's going to want this coming out of the woodwork. SIS or military intelligence or Christ knows who find they're involved, they're going to bury it for another fifty years."

There was a further silence from London. "The edict from Whitehall—and Downing Street—is that there mustn't be any embarrassment, no matter how long ago it happened. Whatever *it* was."

"Which means they don't *want* it solved!" protested Charlie. "It's impossible. Ridiculous. We're being set up."

"That's why I'm calling you. I do believe we'll stand or fall by this. You've personally got every support it's possible for me to offer. I wish there were more. Better. And I know what I'm asking."

Charlie wished he did. Slipping back on to yesteryear wordage, Charlie said, "Who's my control?"

"You deal with me, direct, at all times," stipulated the director-general. "But let's stay with that. Control. Don't you even think of trying or doing anything without discussing it with me first. One mistake—one miscalculation—is all it's going to take."

This time it was Charlie who didn't speak at once. Eventually he said, "Am I expected to work with SIS and the military attaché here? Let them know everything I'm doing?"

"Not until you've talked whatever it is through with me first."

"Which is what they're being told, probably right now."

"Probably," accepted Dean again.

"You know it's hopeless before I start?"

"Close to being hopeless," allowed the older man.

"There's not a lot left to say, is there?"

"Everything we've got from the Russian Foreign Ministry is being faxed back right away. And don't forget my personal support."

There wasn't any point in further protests or arguments. "A British officer—and an American—dead for fifty years without anyone wondering what happened to them! And a woman, too! How the hell can you explain that?"

"I can't," conceded Sir Rupert Dean. "That's what you've got to do."

Natalia recognized she was the most exposed of them all: the one in the greatest danger. Although there was the outward, cosmetic appearance of personal and authoritative involvement, the presidential emissary and the deputy ministers all had their blame-ready intermediaries, after whom there was the final buffer of Natalia Nikandrova herself. It was she who provably had to select the Russian investigatory team and just as provably had to propose the precise moment to invite Washington and London to an international game of musical chairs and after that monitor from a distance of three thousand miles its progress in a time-lost republic where everyone would be trying to pull the safe seats away from everyone else at every discordant note. With one of its chair-snatching participants being

Charlie Muffin, whose feet were always too painful for any sort of musical dance.

It was a maze from which she desperately needed guidance and Charlie was the obvious person to give it. But if she did seek his guidance, this early, she'd have to tell him why Viskov distrusted her and she didn't want any reminders of Alexei Popov.

She'd grossly, stupidly overreacted the previous night to Irena being at the apartment, which had nothing at all to do with Charlie but everything to do with other fears—memories—she didn't want to share with him, either. She was going to have to share a lot of other things, though. He'd hear today. Be told by London of the Yakutsk murders and realize she could have warned him. But hadn't. Maybe, despite her aching loneliness and aching hope for her personal life at last to change, it would have been better if Charlie hadn't come back to Moscow at all.

Natalia physically shook herself, as if sloughing off her personal reflections.

She had left Charlie in bed to get to the Interior Ministry before eight, determined to preempt Viskov or Travin—or both—from imposing a squad of their choosing and their loyalty upon the investigation. She worked, wearily resigned to the fact that she would be judged from whomever she assigned and that she couldn't afford the slightest miscalculation. And to miscalculate the honesty and loyalty of the Moscow militia, in which neither existed, was the easiest possible mistake to make.

It was ironic—and she hoped to her advantage—that the investigation would be in Yakutsk and not here in Moscow, where virtually the entire militia would have been initially distracted by the automatic requirement for financial reward for doing—or not doing, depending upon the paymaster—a job they were paid supposedly to do anyway. The disadvantage was that, denied the usual bribery by both the obvious age of the crime and the inevitable hostility from the indigenous Yakutsk and the gulag descendants, finding anyone without an impossible-to-leave workload could be more difficult than solving three fifty-year-old murders themselves. For the militia homicide detective she went for comparative youth, seeking out the most recently promoted, someone, she hoped, only yet ankle-deep in the corruption swamp and, she hoped, even more, still anxious to prove his ability.

It took Natalia five interviews to reach Colonel Vadim Leonidovich Lestov. She was immediately encouraged by the thirty-year-old man's down-at-the-heel imitation leather shoes and lapel-curled dark gray suit, shiny at the seat and elbows, a clear indication that he had so far failed to establish a private tailoring allowance. He was blond, fresh-faced and when he became enthusiastic, as he did when Natalia outlined the assignment and mentioned Yakutskaya, stammered in his eagerness to get his words out.

"My grandfather is still alive: a Stalinist. He insists the Yakutskaya gulags never existed. That they were an invention of Stalin's detractors."

"There are several million people who'd argue against him if they were still alive," remarked Natalia.

"I *want* to go!"

"Then you shall," decided Natalia.

Olga Erzin was Natalia's choice for the forensic pathologist. The woman had impeccable medical qualifications, five years' experience of forensic medicine and a weight problem she appeared to be doing little to control. Natalia guessed the woman, whom she knew from personnel records to be the same age as Lestov and like the militia colonel unmarried, weighed close to two hundred pounds.

"It will be extremely uncomfortable," warned Natalia.

"It's the chance to become involved in an incredibly unique murder case."

"Which will attract attention. To you, I mean. We can't afford any errors."

"I won't make any if you don't," said the younger woman.

"I don't understand." Natalia frowned, surprised at the near impertinence.

"By choosing someone other than me," said Olga.

After so long—and with so little information from which to judge—Natalia was unsure if any worthwhile forensic evidence would remain and decided initially only to send one scientist, to become team leader if his assessment was that a full scene-of-crime contingent was justified. Natalia was able to extend her age limit choice, because scientific technicians did not have the access—nor therefore the opportunity—for contorted handshakes in dark alleys. Lev Fyodorovich Denebin was a lugubrious fifty-five years old whose pure white hair rose from his head as if in shock, which he'd never been, whatever the brutality of the crimes he'd investigated. Which, since the KGB control of Moscow had been virtually replaced by the mafia, had been a lot.

Denebin very obviously had that in mind when he said, after Natalia had outlined what she so far knew, "This could be fascinating. Very different." His voice was blurred from a lifetime's addiction to tobacco.

"And very difficult," Natalia warned once more.

"The bastards want us to admit we haven't got the facilities!" protested Valentin Polyakov.

"They're going by the book," suggested Yuri Ryabov, who'd been summoned immediately after the cabinet session that Polyakov had chaired. "Acknowledging the degree of independence we've so far achieved."

"It's important the British and Americans are coming," decided Polyakov, his decision quite positive now.

"We can't question Moscow's ultimate authority, certainly as far as foreign policy," said Ryabov.

"I don't intend to," assured Polyakov, feeling very satisfied. He was a huge, towering man, his size seemingly made greater by a never-trimmed spade beard, which, ironically for a man who despised everything Russian, was allowed to grow fully down to his chest in the Russian style of a man of deep religious orthodoxy, which he wasn't. Polyakov looked intently at his police commissioner. "But they don't have the power of life or death, like they had in the past; like they had over my father and your father and everyone else's forefathers. Here, now, I'm in charge. And here's what we're going to do. We show every consideration and help to whoever London and Washington send in. I want everyone they come into contact with to understand that. I'll actually receive them. . . ." He stopped, one idea following the other. "But we won't include the Russians. You understand what I'm saying?"

"I think so," said the militia commissioner, uncertainly.

"But don't make it too obvious, for your part," continued the chief minister. "I want you as part of whatever investigation team Moscow sends. At *all* times. It's essential publicly to appear a joint investigation, not a Moscow take over. And that's how I want our response to read: that we're inviting their *assistance.*"

Ryabov shifted, his uncertainty growing. "Why, exactly?"

"Because I'm going to ensure we're the focus of world attention," announced Polyakov, who was given to cliché in his attempt to appear statesmanlike.

"Moscow has asked for details of what was recovered from the bodies. And photographs," reminded Ryabov.

Polyakov smiled, pleased with the way he'd worked everything out. "Moscow comes to us, on our terms. They wait until they get here to see what there is."

"All right," accepted the police chief, uncomfortably.

"You realize how fortunate we are, having the media contacts we have in Canada?"

"Not really," Ryabov frowned.

"You will," promised Polyakov.

Alexei Popov's replacement as Natalia's deputy was a taciturn, sleek-mannered, sleek-featured Georgian. The deputy interior minister had outmaneuvered an unsuspecting Natalia to get Petr Pavlovich Travin appointed, making it obvious that after the Popov debacle the Interior Ministry felt it necessary to have their own watchdog as close to the top of her department as possible, which was in no way a guarantee of Travin's honesty or integrity: an enshrined legacy of communism, maybe even inherited by them from the tsars, was that poachers made the best gamekeepers.

Travin listened, wordless and expressionless, while Natalia talked and still didn't immediately speak when she'd finished and Natalia, who'd first met Charlie as his KGB debriefer when Charlie had staged a false defection, identified the familiar trick of extended silence to lure more from someone being interrogated. With that awareness came curiosity that Travin might already consider himself entitled to interrogate her. Finally the man said, "I expected to be involved from the *very* beginning: selecting the Russian team with you. I might have had some suggestions."

The burly, mustached man *did* consider himself her equal—if not more—Natalia recognized. Stressing the demand in her voice, Natalia said, "You will be in charge, from here, of overall liaison, between us and the British and Americans. We expect—in fact it's been politically decided we *want*—them to go to Yakutsk."

"What is the chain of command?" demanded Travin, virtually in open challenge.

"Mine is to Dmitri Borisovich Nikulin, the president's chief of staff. Yours is to me. It's imperative from the outset that there are no misunderstandings between us. I hope there won't be."

"So do I," said Travin, insolently.

How many times had she already said and thought those words? wondered Natalia. And how many times was she going to repeat them in the immediate future? She said, "The most important thing for you to understand is that whatever the outcome, no blame or error should attach to our people."

"I've understood that already," assured Travin.

"That's good."

It was only when Natalia was redrafting for the third time her bureaucratically necessary memorandum to Dmitri Nikulin—with copies to everyone else in the planning group—that she accepted the first version had been quite adequate and that she was stupidly delaying her return to Lesnaya and Charlie.

"I'm on my way," she said into the telephone.

"There's a lot to talk about," said Charlie.

"I know."

"It's an opportunity!" insisted Vitali Novikov.

"How? Why?" asked his wife.

"There'll be foreigners: American and English."

"What good will they be?" demanded Marina.

"I don't know, not yet. But I'll find a way."

"Vitali Maksimovich! You've tried so hard for so long. Nothing works!"

"You want Georgi and Arseni to live like we've had to live?"

"You know I don't. But there is no other way. No way out."

"My father was a clever man. A meticulous man."

"And you're clever, too, my darling. But I can't see how Americans or British can help us."

"I'll find a way," repeated the medical examiner, stubbornly. "Even if I have to cheat and lie."

Gerald Williams examined his idea from as many aspects as he could think of before telephoning his fellow finance director across the river at Vauxhall Cross. His second call was to Richard Cartright in Moscow.

"I thought I should introduce myself, now that our two departments are going to be working together," said Williams.

7

The phrase that came to Charlie's mind was *phony war*, although it didn't fit because he wasn't going to allow a war between himself and Natalia, phony or otherwise. They were moving around the apartment, overly attentive upon Sasha, overly polite toward each other, with long periods of silence, as if each were expecting the other to fire the first shot.

It was, however, Natalia who proposed the armistice. "Angry?"

"No." Charlie was on his second Islay malt of the evening, Sasha already asleep.

"What, then?"

"Disappointed."

"It had to be this way: from our Foreign Ministry to yours, in London." She shook her head to the wine he held up.

"I know that. You might just have mentioned something." Charlie was, in fact, very angry, although not at Natalia. He'd timed the telephone lecture from Sir Rupert Dean at forty minutes, immediately followed by the promised memorandum, and after that there had been the personal visit from Richard Cartright with the insistence that he was sure they were all going to work together perfectly. To which Charlie had thought bollocks and said he was just as sure.

"I've got so much to mention I doubt I'll remember it all," said Natalia, turning his expression.

Charlie looked at her curiously. "Go on."

"I'm not sure I can do it," blurted Natalia. "That we can do it: keep secret what we have to. I've almost gone mad!" And she still didn't intend to tell him everything.

"It might have helped to talk." He was glad he hadn't told her of Irena's apparently brief affair with Saul Freeman. Glad, too, that there'd been no personal contact from the woman after that one night, which she'd hinted at when he'd walked her to the street-level door.

"Perhaps. I just wanted to do it this way. Try some separation, so that we couldn't be professionally accused of anything."

Charlie smiled at her sadly. "I know I was a shit before. But I'll make you a solemn promise. I will never, ever, cheat you or use you or expose you to any risk I can possibly avoid. Or put Sasha at any risk."

Natalia stayed silent for several minutes, changing her mind and pouring her own wine. "I believe you, about us."

She didn't, Charlie decided. She *wanted* to—maybe would come to, in time—but at the moment there was too much to forget. He took Sir Rupert Dean's fax from his pocket and slid it across the table toward her. "Now it's official, I suppose we can talk about it."

She smiled, relieved it had been this easy, reading it slowly, not looking up for several minutes. "Those are all the facts there are?"

"Seems like it."

"How do you feel about working with the SIS?" she asked, anticipating the answer.

"I don't like working in groups. Cartright won't be the only person."

"It's an order, Charlie," said Natalia, at once worried.

"They won't know that, will they? They might even have their uses." He sipped his whiskey. "Read up on what I could about Yakutskaya, from the embassy library. Seems a hell of a place. There was an embassy assessment from here, in Stalin's time, just at the *suggestion* of the gulags that was marked doubtful because the descriptions weren't considered humanly possible."

"Even though Stalin's been denounced and disgraced, public records stay sanitized," said Natalia.

"I won't take a paperback and sun oil."

Natalia refused the anxious flippancy. "Be careful."

Charlie waited. When Natalia didn't continue he said, "Everyone and his dog out to screw me?"

"I won't let you be exposed to any risk I can possibly anticipate and prevent," said Natalia, matching his earlier promise.

At once, urgently, Charlie shook his head. "Don't anticipate for me! Let me anticipate for myself."

"So *you* don't trust *me!*"

"We're not talking *us!*" insisted Charlie, "We're talking gutter survival. I've been there: lived my life there. You haven't, not operationally. Leave me to watch my own back, until I ask for help. That way there's no confusion."

In his opinion she couldn't do without his help, but he could do without hers, judged Natalia. "There isn't a score to even, Charlie."

"I'm not balancing scores," persisted Charlie, unhappy at her response. "This hasn't anything to do with your not talking to me before now. . . ." He waved the London fax still lying between them. "You think the Americans got the same?"

"Positive."

"So," Charlie said patiently, although still with some urgency. "We've got fifty-year-old unreported, totally unknown murders of apparent English and American officers. We've got a hostile, probably obstructive local authority. We've got a resented Moscow intrusion. Without doubt someone involved from America. And in effect, I'm working under monitor. . . ." He paused, trying to imagine anything he'd left out. Unable to, he went on, "Each and every one of whom—with the possible exception of whoever America sends—will be trying to discredit each and everyone else. There's no way, from a distance of three thousand miles, you could or can anticipate what will be going on. Not in a way to help me. . . ." He gulped at his whiskey, needing the pause. Who the fuck was going to help him, then? It was the worst possible scenario, a bunch—a committee—of disorganized, fractious, warring people. And committees—working with them, for them, being part of them—ranked on Charlie's hate list equal to tight shoes, ice in single malt and the need constantly to justify his expenses. Maybe, even, a little higher than all three.

"I wasn't thinking of three thousand miles away," said Natalia, quietly. "I was thinking about back here, in Moscow."

Charlie drank some more whiskey, matching her seriousness. "I'd be grateful. And need it."

Maybe she needed it more than him, thought Natalia. "I'm frightened, Charlie. Nothing's working out as it should."

"It hasn't *started* yet!"

"I'm worried how it's going to finish."

Charlie responded before Natalia when Sasha cried out. He was back within minutes from the child's bedroom, after resetting her. "She had a bad dream."

"I'm having them, too," said Natalia. "And they don't go away when I'm awake."

It was Charlie's idea for he and Natalia to test their intuition one against the other by refusing any prior opinion of the Russian group with whom he would be going to Yakutskaya, not even to be told their names. It meant his going to the Interior Ministry totally unprepared, because there hadn't been the prior contact he'd half expected from the American embassy and Charlie hadn't called Saul Freeman: there was no benefit—not yet at least—and he certainly didn't intend conveying even an impression of a joint operation, despite Sir Rupert Dean's assurance that London and Washington had agreed on complete cooperation.

Charlie's initial surprise on entering Petr Travin's office was that it was Miriam Bell, the FBI chief's deputy, and not Saul Freeman himself who was already there. She had a yellow legal pad on a primly crossed leg, the skirt of her severe business suit covering her knee. The blond hair was in a tightly coiled chignon. She gave the barest response to Charlie's greeting. So, too, did the Russian pathologist and the forensic scientist at Travin's introduction, but Vadim Lestov stood, smiled and insisted in experimental English that he was delighted to meet Charlie. Seemingly reminded, Travin said there was an interpreter available if necessary. Miriam said it wasn't, ahead of Charlie.

"That, at least, might make things easier," commented Travin. "At the moment very little else does."

"I'd appreciate knowing what else there is, beyond what was sent to my State Department," said Miriam.

The Ice Maiden Meets the Ice Mummies, thought Charlie, sitting back contentedly. Except that was hardly Miriam Bell's reputation. According to Freeman, who enjoyed not only kissing but telling, she swore like the devil and was more than willing to use the body of an angel to each and every advantage. Although she did have a figure made for underwear commercials, it was in other ways he needed to know a lot more about her, decided Charlie. He wondered, idly, if Miriam had been as disappointed in Freeman's fuck-by-numbers technique as Irena.

To the side of the huge room there were two stenographers and an operator at a recording machine. International crime-fighting co-operation, like justice, had to be seen to be done, Charlie supposed. During Alexei Popov's unsuspected tenure of an office very similar to this there'd been vodka as well as tea from a traditional samovar for such encounters. But then Popov had hidden deceit behind friendliness.

"There were some belongings on the bodies but nothing that could identify them," offered Travin.

"What?" demanded Charlie, bluntly, for the benefit of the record. When it was necessary Charlie was capable of Oscar award performances.

"Personal items: we don't know what," admitted the Russian, tightly.

"They're not here?" persisted Charlie.

"No," conceded the man, tighter still.

The first publicly recorded indication of difficulties to come, judged Charlie. Making his own intentionally awkward contribution, Charlie looked between Travin and Lev Denebin and said, "So you're quite confident of the forensic facilities in Yakutsk?"

Denebin actually looked toward the note-takers before saying, "I don't think I can say that at all! I don't know . . . I mean I need to see . . . what's there. . . ."

Charlie was conscious of Travin looking very intently at him. Charlie said, "I would have thought your facilities were better here in Moscow?" Until Denebin's startled reaction, the three chosen Russians had been sitting relaxed, too obviously observers. So there'd been a separate, earlier blame-apportioning session. They should have been better rehearsed to prevent the preparation being so obvious.

Travin said, "The Yakut authorities appear to think it's better for what was recovered to remain there."

"So you did ask for it?" pounced Charlie.

"The inquiry is at a very early stage," floundered Travin, trapped. "The concentration has been upon assembling an investigation team . . . advising your respective governments. . . ."

It was sufficient, decided Charlie, allowing the pause which Miriam Bell hurriedly filled. "Have the files been checked here for any records of an American or a British officer being in that region, which I understand to have been a closed part of the old Soviet Union?"

"Yes," said Travin, grateful to escape. "Both Foreign and Interior Ministries. There is nothing officially recorded."

"What about photographs of the bodies?" said Miriam.

Travin shifted uncomfortably. "Yakutsk have said there are some, with the other material."

Colonel Lestov should have been asking questions, thought Charlie. More bad rehearsal. "What about prison records? Virtually all of Yakutskaya was a prison colony, wasn't it?"

Travin's face began to color. "It was. But the records are very inadequate. What do exist are being examined, naturally. There can be no question of British and American nationals being sentenced to this or any other region. . . ." His face began to clear, in realization of escape. "And as our advice to both your governments made clear, these officers were dressed in their military uniforms and carried some personal items, which would not have been allowed had they been prisoners. . . ." Too forcefully in his eagerness, the man finished, "So a search of records would be pointless."

"But you are still looking?" insisted Charlie. "That's what you said . . . ?"

"What I'm trying to make clear is my government's total commitment to investigate these murders."

That very definitely was rehearsed, recognized Charlie.

Just as rehearsed, Miriam said, "I've been authorized to offer every facility on behalf of my government."

Might as well go for broke with those busy little pens and recording tapes scratching away, decided Charlie. "I appreciate, as I'm sure my American colleague does, the cooperation you're offering. I, for my part, want it to be understood that I see my role as an observer—although prepared at all times to contribute in any way that I am asked—to a Russian investigation. . . ." He allowed a long pause. Come on! Come on! he thought, although not looking at Miriam.

"Yes," came in the American, as if on cue. "That's certainly how I see it, too."

Travin nodded, to disguise the heavy swallow. "I see you all acting together as a team," he tried. "We respect your ability. Don't expect you to hold back to be invited to give an opinion. This is, in fact, going to be a unique investigation."

The precise words Alexei Popov had used in this very same room about a year earlier, remembered Charlie. Popov had been a far more adept bastard than his successor. Still wrong to be too confident, too soon. Looking obviously at the note-takers, Charlie said, "I am impressed by the obvious efficiency with which this has all begun. I will, of course, make available copies of all my reports to London, for your murder dossiers. And would like copies of yours—including that of this meeting—to create my full file. . . ." He smiled sideways at Miriam. "That's the sort of arrangement to which you'd agree, wouldn't you?"

She said, "Yes. That sounds fine."

Miriam Bell offered the drink and suggested the conveniently close Intourist Hotel and Charlie accepted, although he preferred the bar of the Savoy. After they were served, she said, "You want to tell me what that was all about back there?"

"Doing my best to prevent the back of my head from being blown off, like some poor bastard's was fifty years ago." If he'd added any more water to his whiskey after the barman's adulteration, there wouldn't have been any taste at all.

"Not enough," she protested.

The bolted-door reserve wasn't the earlier suspected arrogance, Charlie decided. It was get-all-but-say-nothing.

"Things go wrong, they want scapegoats. We're it."

"What if things go right?"

"Same role."

"I thought Lestov seemed a nice enough guy."

"We'll see."

"What about you and I?"

"No reason for us to work in opposition."

"What about together?"

"Doesn't seem there'll be an alternative." He gestured for more drinks, changing his to vodka: there wasn't the need to dilute the cheaper local drink so much to get a three hundred percent markup.

"But if there was, you'd prefer it?"

"Don't want anyone else to suffer from my mistakes."

"Or suffer those of others yourself?"

"That's about it."

"I suppose it's also being honest."

He grinned at her. "You get the identity of your American first, it'll most likely lead me to my man, won't it?"

"I think I've got the rules." She sipped her drink. She'd chosen vodka from the beginning. "Surprised it's me, not Saul?"

"Yes."

"He's expecting to be called back to Washington any minute. Didn't want to be off base. So I get the big chance."

Jesus, thought Charlie: sneaky bastard didn't lie any better than Irena described the way he fucked. Emptily he said, "That's what we all need, the big chance."

"This isn't my first overseas assignment," she said, in unasked defense. "I've worked Manila. And Tokyo."

"But nothing like this before?"

"Is it too obvious?"

Charlie recognized the little-girl-lost ploy. "Not at all. You all set to go?"

"I guess."

"Pack a lot of chiffon scarves."

"What?"

"Chiffon scarves. Pack as many as you've got." The protection he'd decided upon after reading about Yakutskaya had arrived from Harrods that morning, in the embassy's diplomatic shipment. He could hardly wait for Gerald Williams to get the bill.

———

Charlie assessed his score at ten out of ten. He judged Travin to be working to a separate agenda, to which Natalia limited her agreement, but she did admit there'd been a much longer, separate briefing between her deputy and the three Russians, which was why they'd made the mistake of not asking questions. And the Yakut ruling council had refused to send any evidence in advance of the investigation team's arrival.

"Travin's furious," said Natalia, delighted with the recorded outcome of the man's encounter with Charlie. It could hardly have been better if she *had* told him the threat she believed herself to be under.

"He's not very good." It was unthinkable that he would make any comparison with Popov.

"Don't underestimate him."

"I don't underestimate anybody, not this early in a case."

"What about the woman?"

"What about her?"

"Think you'll have a problem working with her?"

That wasn't at all what Natalia meant, Charlie knew sadly. "I don't work with people, if I can help it. But there's every reason—every advantage—in cooperating here, until it proves otherwise. So I will. . . ." He was about to make a joke of her real concern but abruptly stopped himself, remembering the hurt of her past. Instead he continued, seriously, "And I seem to remember promising that I would never, ever, cheat you. And I meant cheat in every way. So no, I'm not going to try to seduce Miriam Bell. Or anyone else, for that matter. . . ."

Natalia smiled, abashed. "I'm sorry."

So was he, decided Charlie. One day, he supposed, the trust would be there. He wondered when.

Vitali Maksimovich Novikov straightened triumphantly from the attic box, gazing down at what he considered the treasure it contained. His father *had* been a meticulous man. There had to be something.

"Good to hear your voice," greeted Kenton Peters.

"And yours," said Boyce.

"Everything's in place this end. The confusion is absolute."

"That's good."

"And I've spoken to the man himself."

"How is he?"

"As overconfident as always."

"I'm glad the Yakutskaya authorities are being awkward."

So am I. Like to know a little more of their thinking, though."

"We can't have everything, James! Who's your disposable man?"

"Odd name. Muffin. An awkward bastard, according to his file. Actually caused a lot of trouble in your CIA a long time ago. Embarrassed your director as well as our director-general."

"Deserves to be punished, then."

"Quite. You briefed anyone?"

"Selected him. Haven't briefed him yet. Too early. Better send me Muffin's file. That CIA business would be 'enemy of the state' justification."

"Will do," agreed Boyce. "I think we've got everything under wraps, don't you?"

"Can't think of anything we've overlooked."

8

All of Charlie's forebodings were confirmed from the very outset. There was no trace of their confirmed reservations on Aeroflot's ten A.M. Domodedovo airport departure for Yakutsk until Charlie offered his passport with a $50 note folded inside. That still, however, didn't guarantee a seat. It was agony for him to have to run, like everyone else, but they got to the aircraft ahead of families with small children and the infirm, while there were still unoccupied seats. Vadim Leonidovich Lestov determinedly elbowed his way through to get beside Miriam Bell, and Olga Erzin and the Russian forensic scientist remained stubbornly and protectively together, which left Charlie to fight for himself, which suited him perfectly. He hoped it would be a permanently established division.

He managed a seat next to a Yakut who greeted him with a graveyard-toothed smile and a miasma of halitosis so bad Charlie was tempted to surrender his place to a loudly demanding, arm-waving woman with an apparent official boarding pass. There were, however, at least seven more identical arguments going on simultaneously throughout the aircraft, which meant it was overbooked, as Aeroflot planes always were, and that no other seat was available. Charlie was isolated as a dispensable foreigner by an androgynous stewardess, whose arrival he greeted with another $50 note, which secured his occupation and got the pass of the still-protesting woman torn up as she was escorted from the aircraft.

Immediately after takeoff the passenger directly in front abruptly and without warning fully reclined his seat, the back of which stopped just inches from Charlie's face, even though he threw himself backward. The frame of the inset meal table jammed tightly just below Charlie's knees, threatening the blood supply. The man ignored Charlie's shoulder tap and whispered plea to ease forward and told him to fuck off when he tapped harder. The Yakut obligingly made room for Charlie's legs.

Despite his advanced tooth decay Charlie's companion chewed contentedly upon an appropriately turd-shaped black and sinewy piece of pemmican he took, unwrapped, from inside an enveloping jacket. Aware of Charlie's interest, the man smiled again and generously offered Charlie a bite, wet end first. When the tepid mystery described as lunch was put before him, Charlie wasn't sure he'd made the right decision refusing the chance of even previously chewed dried meat. He offered the tray, minus the vodka and wine, to the Yakut, who eagerly accepted. The manly stewardess was just as eager to serve him more vodka when she realized he'd pay in dollars.

The visa kiosk at Yakutsk airport was shuttered. Charlie stood back to let other passengers hammer and protest against the metal grill and Miriam stayed with him. So did the three Russians, and Charlie frowned at the prospect of being the group tour guide. It was only two in the afternoon, but already it seemed to be darkening from twilight into night.

It took them more than an hour to progress into the customs hall. Their luggage was already waiting. The pathologist and forensic scientists had tried to anticipate the equipment they might need, with no way of knowing what would be locally available. Olga said at once, "I'm missing a case. Some saws, spare scalpel blades."

"You'd better report—" started Miriam, before stopping abruptly, embarrassed.

"We *are* the police," Charlie reminded, grinning at her. There was no air-conditioning within the terminal building and Charlie felt his clothes melting around him in the humidity. Already there were a lot of flies and insects.

Resigned, Olga said, "There'll be no point, will there?"

"None," said Lestov, positively. "Can you manage without?"

"I'm going to have to, aren't I?"

Yuri Ryabov, Aleksandr Kurshin and Vitali Novikov were waiting on the outside concourse. The silver-haired, urbanely mannered militia chief, who'd put on his neatly pressed and newest uniform for the occasion, looked curiously at the disheveled although obviously Western-dressed Charlie—particularly at the snowshoes-spread Hush Puppies—and said in Russians, "Who's *that?*"

Charlie said, "I'm the British investigator. Everyone able to speak Russian will make it easier to work together." Charlie wasn't offended—he never was when somebody underestimated him—but he was surprised at the stupidity. He was sure he'd caught the slight smirk of satisfaction from Kurshin. Charlie was conscious of the intense examination from the third man in the group.

Also in Russian, Miriam said, "And I'm American. Hello."

Ryabov looked more confused than embarrassed. Gesturing toward three waiting, undesignated cars, the local militia chief said, "You'll want to settle in, after such a long flight. We've booked you into the Ontario."

First stupid, now clever, thought Charlie, who'd spent the intervening days since first being alerted to the murders preparing himself far more thoroughly than by simply buying a beekeeper's hat that would be necessary in the summerlike temperatures. In the short time outside the airport terminal he'd already noted the preeminence of horse-drawn transport in his search for nonexistent taxis. And knew the Ontario Hotel, a Canadian joint venture, was a thirty-minute car ride from the Yakutsk town center: effectively they would be as imprisoned as the original Russian exiles.

It was the thin, intense man who at once introduced himself and maintained the aircraft division, hurrying forward to usher Charlie into his car, which Charlie allowed unprotesting but curious, wondering if Novikov was intended to be his personal jailer. Ryabov shepherded Miriam and Lestov into his vehicle, leaving the remaining Russians to go with the local homicide investigator. Always ready to kiss as well as look a gift horse in the mouth, Charlie said, "Is it always as dark at this?"

"In the proper summer it's lighter. Maybe for two months of the year."

The car's body shell was a Lada but the inside was cannibalized from other vehicles. It smelled of longtime dampness. Charlie said, "You lived here all your life?"

There was a quick look across the car. "Regrettably I was born here."

Charlie awarded himself ten out of ten again. Sometimes the gods, whoever and from wherever they were, truly smiled. He said, "Until a few days ago I'd never heard of Yakutsk. Or the region."

"Few people ever have. Or want to."

Charlie saw the pathologist was white-knuckled from the tightness with which he was holding the wheel. Why, wondered Charlie, had the arrival examination been so equally intense? The man was blinking rapidly and perspiration was bubbled on his upper lip. Charlie moved to speak, but before he could Novikov said, "You have come especially from London?"

The temptation to rush—to try at once to use the advantage of being alone, how he always preferred to be—was enormous, but Charlie held back. "I am permanently based in Moscow." I hope, he added mentally.

"Officially?" queried the man. Then, just as quickly, he nervously answered his own question. "Yes, of course you must be. The end of the old system, I suppose?"

"It's a very new arrangement," agreed Charlie. There were times to push against the tide and times to go with the flow.

"You are the first, under that arrangement?"

"Yes."

"You must have been special chosen? Have influence maybe?"

The man *wanted* him to be special. Why? "There were reasons," he said, seeking another guiding question to fill the emptiness of his reply.

"Are you attached to the British embassy in Moscow?"

"Yes." Where the hell was this going?

"You must know important people?"

Charlie exaggerated the shrug of apparent modesty, seeing the crack of light in the literal darkness. "I suppose I do. Things are very different in Moscow now: different in Russia." He gestured to the two cars in front. "Once our being here like this would have been unimaginable." As it was unimaginable that a British officer was here more than fifty years ago, he thought.

Novikov said, "Very little changes here. Never for the better."

It was difficult to conceive that what little Charlie could see outside the car could have been worse. The countryside was unlike anything he had seen or experienced before, ever imagined. The stretched-to-the near-horizon twilight was only broken by the stick-drawn blackness of skeletal, leaf-naked trees, a child's pencil drawing abruptly denied by the suddenly vivid, paint-box colors of rarely seen plants brought to life by the strange thaw. Most difficult of all was to believe that beneath such a barren, infertile moonscape, larger than the entire Indian subcontinent, lay the majority of the world's reserves of oil, gas, coal, gold and diamonds. Or that for so many Stalin years—and after—men, women and child slaves had little more than their bare hands, and those stick-thin tree branches for pit props, to mine it.

Charlie, with difficulty, remained silent, his foot-throbbing instinct telling him the other man had more to say. But abruptly Novikov had fallen silent, although his hands were still white-knuckled at the wheel and the perspiration still flecked his upper lip.

They entered Yakutsk along the Ploshchad Druzhby. Charlie had read, along with everything else, of the melting effect of brick and concrete houses upon permanently frozen ground but hadn't anticipated the added effect of the unprecedented thaw. One of Sasha's English-learning nursery rhyme books had a doggerel about a little crooked man who lived in a little crooked house and Charlie thought it could have been written about this place. Only the wooden buildings lifted free of the ground on stilts had any proper, houselike shape. Everything of brick or concrete was lopsided, tilting this way and that, their walls fissured, cracked and lined like old men's faces.

Novikov turned on to Prospekt Lenina, pointed to a series of buildings, all close together and said, "My professional opposition."

Outside of each were docile lines of men and women, waiting for admission.

Wrong to appear too ignorant, decided Charlie. "Shamans?"

Novikov nodded. "Healers. And a lot more besides. The local people don't understand what's happening with the weather. It should be cold now: minus twenty celcius, at least. Possibly lower. Snow a meter, two meters deep. They think it's a curse. That the spirits are offended."

"What will they do to placate them?" asked Charlie.

Novikov humped his shoulders. "There are rituals . . . offerings . . ." He caught Charlie's quick sideways look. "No," he said, smiling for the first time. "No blood sacrifices. But they're linking these killings with it. They know it would have been impossible for those bodies to have been where they were. They say spirits put them there, as a warning."

"Of what?" asked Charlie.

"That's what they're asking the shamans to tell them."

Through the topsy-turvey buildings Charlie occasionally glimpsed the Lena River, which became more visible, muddy, debris-littered and unusually fast, as they began to clear the town. He'd kept a comparison between the number of motorized to horse-drawn vehicles and decided he was right about the choice of the Ontario Hotel.

As they entered the parking lot Charlie said it wouldn't take him long to unpack and Novikov said he wasn't in any hurry.

The hotel was properly built for the normal local climate and far better than a lot of hotels in which Charlie had stayed in the Eastern Bloc during his operational days of the Cold War. There was no bribe-prompting hindrance with their reservations, all of which were on the third floor, Charlie's room directly opposite Miriam's. The shower worked and despite the promise to the waiting man downstairs Charlie used it and changed, convinced the jacket he'd been wearing retained the odorous trace of his gap-toothed aircraft companion. He took particular care to avoid snagging the mosquito net he'd had shipped in with the special hat and doused the window area with insect spray. The bath had a plug still attached to its chain, so there had been no need for the spare he'd packed, from long experience. Everything he did, however, was automatic, his mind upon the journey from the airport. Yakutsk might as well be on another planet and its inhabitants aliens, but Charlie didn't have any doubt there were messages and meanings in the curious conversation he'd had with the pathologist. They would still have to come from the man himself: someone clearly as nervous as Novikov could easily be frightened away.

It was an uneasy gathering in the bar below, an uneasiness which Charlie did not have to work too hard to maintain. Vadim Lestov remained Siamese-twin close to an accepting Miriam, while the two local police officers tried hard but seemingly unsuccessfully to ingratiate themselves with Olga Erzin and the forensic scientist. When Charlie joined them, Vitali Novikov was trying to talk to the Moscow pathologist, too. Her patronizing disinterest in the local medical examiner verged upon outright rudeness.

They ate reindeer steaks, which Charlie enjoyed, identifying from its texture the dried turd the man beside him had chewed upon during the incoming flight. The reserve was more noticeable during the meal from Olga and the forensic scientist than from Lestov, although the militia colonel kept himself to one glass of Canadian-imported wine. Miriam tried hard but failed with the other woman and Charlie concentrated determinedly upon Vitali Novikov, holding the man's total attention with talk of London and Moscow, carefully interspersed with hints of the authority that seemed important to the doctor.

It was Charlie who afterward suggested returning to the bar and its Canadian whiskey, which he considered an unexpected bonus. Everyone except Charlie, who was confident of his capacity, and Olga, who appeared uncaring, continued to limit their alcohol intake, although as the evening progressed Lestov's stammering became more pronounced.

Using Novikov's insistence that his wife was expecting him, Charlie broke the evening up, walking with the local pathologist to the lobby where the elevators were.

Charlie said, "Thank you again for being at the airport. I enjoyed our conversation."

"I did, too," said Novikov.

"I'm looking forward to starting work tomorrow. I'm going to be relying upon you a great deal. I hope we can learn to work together."

"That doesn't seem to be anyone else's idea."

"I'm only interested in my own," said Charlie. "In case you need to contact me at all, I'm in room thirty-seven."

"I'll remember that," promised Novikov.

Charlie rode bemused, silently, to the third floor but made no effort to get into bed. Within fifteen minutes he heard Miriam's quick footsteps, alone, along the outside corridor and her door open and shut. It was half an hour later when there was a second set of heavier footsteps and another quick opening and closing of the American's door.

With the six-hour time difference it was still only six in the evening in Moscow, but Charlie failed to get a connection to the embassy when he tried to dial direct. Experimentally Charlie booked the call through the hotel switchboard, where it would be logged. The connection was made immediately. Charlie smiled, not surprised.

Raymond McDowell and Richard Cartright came anxiously on to a conference call together. For the benefit of the suspected eavesdropper, Charlie exaggerated the total cooperation and assured the two men he had made the official request for the return of the body, which had amounted to the only proper conversation that evening with the militia commander.

"Do you imagine any problem with that?" asked McDowell.

"No."

"When are you meeting the council?"

"Nothing's been arranged." Which wasn't, Charlie had already decided, an oversight. He made up his mind to give the head of chancellery a gift of his special hat if McDowell had personally to come from Moscow.

"What's it like there?"

"Unusual."

"London is concerned," announced Cartright. "The finding of the bodies got leaked, it seems, through Canada, and from there, obviously, to America. There's a lot of media interest building up."

"I can imagine," said Charlie.

"I've promised a cable from here tomorrow."

"I'll try to give you something." Charlie hesitated. "If I haven't come through to you by this time tomorrow, you ring me. Telephone calls out aren't easy."

Charlie had just replaced the telephone when the knock came hesitantly at his door.

"I hope you don't mind," said the rapidly blinking Novikov.

"Not at all," said Charlie, opening the door more widely.

Richard Cartright was seeking, not providing, so it was right he crossed the river from the British embassy to the American legation on Ulitza Chaykovskovo, and when Saul Freeman said he liked Chinese food Cartright suggested they simply walk the few blocks to the Peking. It was Freeman who guided the way into the foreign currency section. Cartright deferred to the American's superior knowledge of a Chinese menu written in Russian, too.

"We heard from Charlie in Yakutsk," offered Cartright, at once. "Just arrived. Nothing's started yet."

"That's what Miriam told me. Bizarre place, apparently."

"Thought you might have gone yourself."

"What about you?" hedged Freeman.

"Would have done in the old days," agreed Cartright, as if he were volunteering something, seeing a way to follow. "MI5 in England is increasingly taking an FBI, crime-fighting role, so it had to be Charlie."

The wine—Georgian—was poured without their being asked to taste it. The surprise was that it was drinkable.

"Interesting guy," said Freeman, which was precisely the reaction Cartright wanted.

"No one at the embassy quite knows how to take him. Lot of experience, apparently. Bit unconventional." Like the second phone call from Gerald Williams was unconventional, although it was a combined operation and Cartright had checked that the two financial directors were talking to each other in London. Cartright's unease was not so much keeping an eye on a colleague as personal apprehension at that colleague being as odd and as unpredictable as he was finding Charlie Muffin to be.

"One of our guys died in that nuclear business," reminded Freeman, although without hostility.

"There were some casualties, although not physical, at our embassy, too," recalled Cartright, nervously. "You ever go out socially with him, find out what sort of guy he was?"

Freeman shook his head. "Gather he and a gal from our technical department in Washington got close on the nuclear thing, but he doesn't seem particularly social, apart from the odd drink. Got a hell of an apartment, I understand. Never been there, though."

"Neither have I." Cartright decided he was wasting his time. "Got any interesting numbers to swap?"

Freeman smiled. "Got to know a fantastic Aeroflot stewardess."

"Worth a hello call?"

"Wouldn't be telling you if she wasn't. Her name's Irena."

"It must be widely known that there was a camp nearby?" pressed Charlie.

"There were so many."

"How did you remember Gulag 98?"

"My father."

"You haven't told anyone else? Not Ryabov or Kurshin?"

"No."

"Why not?"

"I want something they can't give me."

"What makes you think I can?"

"I'm taking the biggest chance I've ever taken in my life, in praying that you might be able to. And until you do, you don't get everything. Which is how I am protecting myself."

9

In a long and often uncertain life, Charlie Muffin had met a lot of desperate men and recognized that Vitali Maksimovich Novikov was a very desperate man indeed. Without any compunction Charlie further decided it was an attitude to be taken every advantage of, certainly until the doctor stopped playing games and spelled out the deal he wanted. Everyone had to live, and to live it was first necessary to survive. It was a very good beginning.

The transport division was the same as the previous day. As they assembled in the hotel parking lot, Charlie thought it was practical for Olga Erzin to have worn trousers, but as big as she was it created an unfair comparison between the Russian pathologist and the American, whose jeans were actually tailored.

As the vehicles moved off, Novikov said, "It's getting hotter."

He'd follow the other man's pace at all times after the previous night's approach, Charlie decided, settling in Novikov's car. Which did not, of course, preclude a little prodding.

The sun was actually visible today and it was airless. The roads were permanently wet with the seepage from the deeper thawing of the road-edge tundra, and the insect swarms were much thicker and persistent. Charlie lowered the window, hoping the rush of passing air would blow them away. It didn't seem to help. Seizing the obvious opening, Charlie said, "When the weather is normal, when you have your usual spring and summer here, does it get as hot as this?"

"This would be a very hot day. Unusually so."

"At the end of your summer, after a period of warmth, how deep into the ground does the thaw reach?"

Novikov gave one of his nervous sideways glances, aware it was not a casual conversation about the weather. "About a meter, I suppose. Maybe less. Why?"

"How deep was the grave?"

Novikov drove on in silence for several moments. "Much deeper than that. At least a meter and a half. Kurshin took measurements."

"Had anything been done to disinter the bodies, before you arrived?"

"No."

"But an arm was protruding?"

"Yes."

"How much of an arm? To the wrist, the elbow, the shoulder?" asked Charlie.

"From the wrist. Not much of that."

They were among the higgledy-piggledy nursery-rhyme buildings of the town again. The lines seemed longer outside the shaman temples on Prospekt Lenina. A lot of the people there—and on the other streets—were wearing their heavy winter clothes, unbuttoned and undone, expecting the phenomena to disappear at a finger snap or a shaman's incantation.

Although it was only ten in the morning, there were already several men slumped drunkenly or sleeping against walls. One lay in the gutter. Novikov said, "Miners. They come into town once a month, to drink and fuck. There have to be houses, because normally it's too cold, but they're hardly brothels. Just shelters. There's three in the next street back, by the vodka factory. I suppose there's something significant that the factory is the biggest building in town."

Charlie thought the red, brick-dust smear down an ocher wall looked like blood several moments before Novikov identified it as their mortuary destination. Charlie made a mental note to pick up later on the mine conversation.

The transformation of Olga Erzin in the surroundings of a mortuary was almost visible. She virtually expanded into an autocratic bully, clipping her words and responses, instinctively assuming superiority. It was Olga, not Novikov, whose mortuary and laboratory it was, who led the way up the rickety stairs into the building. She stopped just inside the autopsy room, exaggerating her disdain, making no effort to help Novikov or his two tentative assistants get the three naked corpses from the storage cupboards onto examination trolleys. Already on separate tables alongside each, like produce displays at a village fete, were the proper specimen containers augmented by village fete vegetable jars holding what Charlie guessed to be every removable organ of each body. Behind each, again on separate identifying tables, were the uniforms and their contents. At once Charlie saw, dismayed, that nothing had been done to keep the uniforms or the woman's clothes in the subzero temperature at which they had survived for so long. Already mold had begun to fur the fabric, endangering possible stains or marks from the moment of death.

Charlie said to Novikov, "I'd appreciate it if you could keep it as simple—as nonmedically technical—as possible." He smiled. "I'm going to need all the help I can get and you're the only person who might be able to provide it."

"That's a hopeful expectation," sniffed the Moscow pathologist.

"Which I'm sure will be met," said Charlie, still smiling. "I'd appreciate your nontechnical input, too. That's the understanding, isn't it? Total and mutual cooperation?"

The woman looked sharply at Charlie, aware of the rebuke. She said, "I'll look forward to your input, as well."

"The sooner we start, the better, then," said Charlie, easily.

The woman made as if to respond, but then apparently changed her mind. Instead she turned back to Novikov and peremptorily said, "Talk me through your examination."

To Olga Erzin's obvious irritation, Novikov translated every medical technicality into layman's terms, identifying each organ in each container. Charlie listened patiently to the recital, waiting for the details of the actual injuries. At the same time, he tried his best to study the clothing, conscious for the first time that a space at the bottom of the individual tables was allocated to scene-of-crime photographs. They were either badly taken or badly printed—or perhaps both—but even from a distance of almost two meters Charlie thought he isolated something curious.

He concentrated totally upon Novikov when the man began to talk about the head wounds, looking around anxiously for the recovered bullets, relieved when he saw two in separate kidney bowls among the organ exhibits. Again before everyone else, he said, "All three were shot in the back of the head?"

"Yes," confirmed the local medical examiner.

"I can only see two bullets."

"The one that killed the woman exited, through the throat."

"Didn't you find it in the grave?" demanded Denebin, at once.

"No," admitted Kurshin, to the forensic scientist's sigh.

"Were there any powder burns to the skulls, to indicate the gun was held tightly against the head?" asked Miriam.

"All the skulls were shattered to varying degrees, particularly around the point of entry," said Novikov.

"What about fragments in the grave?" demanded Olga.

From the pause and looks that passed between the local pathologist and Aleksandr Kurshin, Charlie guessed no proper search had been made.

Kurshin said, "I was not able to recover any."

"Has the scene been secured?"

Ryabov looked to his homicide chief and quickly said, "You did put people there like I told you, didn't you?"

"It's intact," said Kurshin, although unconvincingly.

Charlie said, "What about shell casings in or around the grave?"
Kurshin shifted awkwardly. "I did not recover any."

To Denebin, Charlie said, "The bullets in the kidney bowls are reasonably intact. I'd say they're nine-millimeter?"

"I think so," agreed the forensic scientist. "Easy enough to establish."

Going back to Novikov, Charlie said, "Have you weighed the bullets?"

Everyone frowned at Charlie in varying degrees. Novikov said, "They're just bullets. They'll be standard weight."

"I'd like to know *precisely*," said Charlie, surprised Lestov looked confused. That's what too much sex does for you, my son, Charlie thought.

Miriam Bell actually reached out to turn over the hand of the man designated to be American. "Was there any fingernail debris?"

"Some grave dirt that I guess was forced beneath them when he pitched forward after being shot."

"The nails are manicured," said Miriam, almost to herself. "You've washed the hands. Did you take photographs before doing that?"

Instead of answering, the pathologist shuffled through the pictures on the contents table and offered her two prints.

Miriam studied them, before offering them sideways to Charlie, who at once gestured for Lestov to look ahead of him. Before he could do so, Lestov felt the dead hand Miriam had turned and said, "It's soft, not blistered. He didn't dig his own grave."

"Neither did the other two," came in Novikov quickly. "Their hands are unmarked."

Their hands would literally have been raw if they had even been made to try digging through concrete-hard ground, acknowledged Charlie. Which had been the point of his conversation in the car with the local pathologist. He was sure he knew how the grave had been created and wondered if they'd worked it out.

"The wrist bruising is very definitely linear," said Denebin, taking the hand from the other Russian. "Handcuffs, obviously."

"Were they still handcuffed?" demanded Miriam.

"No," said Kurshin.

"Why take them off?" wondered Miriam.

Charlie was sure he knew. Aloud he said, "And there were insects in the tracheae of all three?"

Novikov pointed to the microscope slides on the exhibition table. "There."

"I want to carry out a second autopsy," announced Olga Erzin. "Where can I change?"

For a moment Novikov looked nonplussed. "There's a toilet along the corridor," he managed, at last.

Sighing, the woman stomped off. At the order from Novikov the two Yakut attendants wheeled the trolley holding the corpse of the woman to the central examination table. Charlie stayed close to the uniforms, their contents and the photographs, although not at that moment making any too-obvious effort to study anything. The clothing, all heavily bloodstained around the collar, was beginning to smell as well as go moldy. Olga swept back into the room in a trousered medical tunic like a barge in full sail. Charlie waited expectantly for her to insist the room be cleared, but she didn't. Lev Denebin appeared uncertain which group to join, those at the exhibit tables or Olga and Novikov at the autopsy slab. After a moment's indecision the forensic scientist came to where Charlie stood, his back now to the second dissection of the female corpse.

Beside him Miriam said, "Bizarre!"

Charlie didn't think so at all, but he said, "Certainly a strange situation." He reached out, then stopped. He said to Kurshin, "Every hard surface has been checked for fingerprints?"

"I couldn't find anything," said the local detective, apologetically.

"I doubt there would have been, in the conditions," said Denebin.

Without any discussion they divided according to nationality, Charlie by the table holding the English uniform, Miriam to the American and Denebin and Lestov going to where the clothing of the believed Russian woman was laid out.

Charlie carefully separated the coin from the paper and war-script money, feeling the surge of satisfaction at his immediate find. In predecimalization coin there were four pennies, four half crowns and two florins. Protected as they had been in a trouser-pocket, none were affected from being buried for so long. The brightest was a half crown, dated 1944. The earliest date, 1939, was on a florin. There was another possible time frame indicator—and a very positive direction to follow—from the inscription in the case containing six Camel cigarettes: "S.N. A First. 1932. From a proud father." Caught by the thought, Charlie turned to the corpse just as the attendants were moving it, momentarily halting them while he examined each hand. The mark where a signet ring had been was very obvious on the little finger of the left.

There was no inscription on the watch case. It didn't have a date register, either, although an unspecified day of an unspecified month would have been a difficult clue. It was difficult, too, to surmise anything from the stopping time of 12:43. Experimentally he tried winding it, but the button was jammed: if it had run on after the assassination, it would only have been for less than twenty-four hours. Its significance was that it had still been on the man's wrist, Charlie decided.

He closely examined the keys, the Parker pen and the tie pin before going to the photographs before the actual clothing, wanting a sequence. The agony-rigored face was dirt-smeared but clearly recognizable, particularly in comparison against the second facial set, which, from the background, had been taken in this examination room just prior to the first postmortem. Fair-haired, not clipped militarily short, a high-cheekboned, aristocratic face badly swollen by insect bites moments before he died. And agony, too: maybe disbelieving surprise. Which didn't square with the handcuff marks. Charlie put that impression on hold, moving through the photographs, getting the confirmation of something else within the first three frames. He looked around, seeing Kurshin with the group by the Russian woman.

"Can you help me?" he asked. Everyone at the other two tables immediately looked at him.

Miriam said, "Found something?"

Too anxious, Charlie thought: so she was having difficulty. "I don't know yet."

Pointing to the photograph he held, Charlie called to Novikov, "That's how you found them in the grave? You hadn't touched them?"

"That's how they were, exactly," the man called back.

Charlie said, "They're not properly dressed, are they? Look. The fly to the Englishman's trousers is wrongly buttoned. And two jacket buttons are undone, as well as the shirt."

He was able to see the American, too. "The shirt buttons are unfastened here, too . . . ?"

"They'd been stripped of all official ID," said Novikov. "No dog tags: no military identification at all."

Charlie turned to the blood-clotted uniform, immediately seeing that there was no regiment designation on the brass buttons but that the shoulder insignia was that of a lieutenant. As casually as he was able, Charlie gently opened the jacket. Where the maker's name and customer details should have been was an empty, cotton-framed rectangle where it had been torn out: the cloth had actually been ripped, more so at the top where the initial cut, probably with a knife, was clean.

Charlie went immediately but still attempting casualness to the trousers, briefly pausing to locate the mud marks on the knees where the man had been forced to kneel to be executed, which Charlie had known anyway from the downward trajectory of the wound that Novikov had already spelled out. The tailor's duplicate label, upon which the owner's name and measurements would have been recorded, had been yanked off even more roughly than from the jacket, a scrap of the label still remaining. There was sufficient to make out what looked like a half C, which was all Charlie thought he needed. He became even more confident when he found in the record of Novikov's earlier autopsy the precise list of the dead man's measurements.

Charlie double-checked his examination to fill in the time, not wanting the others to guess what he considered quick and unexpected success. He even ventured to the adjoining table, where Miriam was still frowning over the displayed contents.

She looked up at his approach and said, "You think we're ever going to be able to make sense of this?"

"Not from what I've seen so far," lied Charlie, who was sure he could identify the dead Englishman, just as he knew that the murder had been committed certainly with the knowledge of some people within the NKVD, the wartime forerunner of the KGB, although he guessed for a reason far removed from Yakutsk.

His more startling conviction—one he knew was going to cause an upheaval of seismic proportions—was that another Englishman had in some way been involved in the killing, which totally justified his keeping to an absolute minimum what he'd so far worked out. Until he discovered much more, he'd even have to keep the English involvement from Natalia.

"Who?" queried Irena.

"Cartright. Richard Cartright. I'm a friend of Saul Freeman's. Just arrived in Moscow and trying to make some friends here."

"You at the American embassy?"

"No. The British."

Irena smiled to herself. "What have you got in mind?"

"A drink? Dinner, maybe?"

"Sounds fun."

10

The mortuary and the militia headquarters were part of the same gradually sinking administration complex: some of the corridors along which they silently followed the heavy-footed military commissioner noticeably inclined and even more steeply declined like the decks of a wallowing ship. The crepe-soled grip of the Hush Puppies helped and briefly Charlie's hammer-toed feet were at peace.

Charlie was more than content with the day so far. No one else seemed to be. Charlie was happy about that, too. The most dissatisfied was Olga Erzin and the Russian forensic scientist, the woman because she'd been unable substantially to improve on the first autopsy findings, Lev Denebin because in the woman's determination to find something the postmortems had occupied the entire day. Now it was almost six in the evening, too late to go out to the grave, which Denebin had pressed for since midday, to the visible annoyance of Yuri Ryabov, who'd refused to alter his prearranged schedule.

There was no clue to its normal use in the sag-windowed room into which Ryabov led them. It was starkly bare except for a communal table against which the precise number of chairs were already arranged, with a separate table and chair for the solemnly waiting secretary. Charlie dismissed his predictable committee claustrophobia, for once, rarely, benefiting by being part of a group. During the protracted time it had taken Olga Erzin to complete her examinations, Charlie had openly studied the clothing and the pocket contents of both Russian and American victims, maneuvering the opportunity by inviting the others to do the same with the belongings of the Englishman, confident they'd miss a lot of what was significant to him. It was important now to discover precisely what they had learned. Even more important was finding out if there was something he'd missed.

So for the moment Ryabov's tight orchestration was not to his disadvantage; in fact, it was even more to his advantage than anyone else's, Charlie hoped. He didn't have the slightest doubt that he had enough. But that wasn't sufficient. It never was. Charlie wanted it all, each and every time.

"I hope we've learned from our first day's work—made progress . . ." opened the police chief, from the very positively chosen head of the table. He looked challengingly at Lev Denebin, who sat, totally withdrawn, doodling on a pad, refusing to take any part in the meeting. Ryabov shifted his attention, going encouragingly toward the Russian pathologist. "And that work has been largely yours, I think?"

Quickly Charlie said, "I was very impressed by the detail of the original examinations, by Dr. Novikov. I'd certainly like to hear what additionally Dr. Erzin discovered."

The Russian medical examiner fixed him with the cast-in-stone look that Charlie expected and didn't care about. With what Charlie judged to be attempted—and doomed-to-failure—avoidance, the woman said, "I have to subject all the organs to appropriate scientific examination, which hasn't yet been properly done . . ."

Charlie snatched an opportunity he hadn't anticipated. "Which you will, over the coming days?"

Imagining an escape, the woman said, "It will be necessary to take everything back to Moscow for total analysis." She smiled triumphantly.

"What about your preliminary findings?" pressed Charlie, smiling not at the woman but at the tightly attentive Vitali Novikov. The woman's triumph faltered. "Comparatively straightforward," she conceded. "I believe, however, that there were burn markings to the skull fragments I extracted: that the gun was placed directly against the backs of their heads."

Which I could have told you, thought Charlie. He said, "The preservation of the bodies is remarkable, though, isn't it?" No one was opposing his taking over the meeting and Charlie was glad, needing to be the ringmaster. They probably expected him to disclose something in his apparent eagerness. Hope in vain, he thought.

"Yes?" agreed the woman, although questioningly.

"So you *were* able to secure fingerprints, despite the fact that they died so long ago?"

"Yes," said the woman, again. The reluctance was obvious.

"And you also took photographs of the faces not distorted by rigor?" Charlie had much earlier realized that the fogging of some of Novikov's earlier scene-of-crime pictures was caused by insects blocking the camera lens, not bad development. It was all going remarkably well, he decided. He could have written the script himself. In fact, he realized, at that moment that was virtually what he was doing.

"You saw me do it," said the woman, impatiently.

"So we have made progress!" declared Charlie, using the police chief's expression. "You will be able to let my American colleague and I have fingerprints *and* photographs—as they were when they died—of people we have to identify. That's wonderful."

Olga Erzin didn't immediately reply, aware not just of what she'd been trapped into conceding but that she now had no way to avoid surrendering both. Tight-lipped, she said, "Yes."

Charlie continued to smile, apparently grateful, in reality anticipating the coup de grâce. "As notes are being taken of this meeting—which I know are going to be made as available as the fingerprints and the photographs—I think it should also be made clear that the previous examination by Dr. Novikov was totally thorough and complete, wouldn't you say that, Dr. Erzin?"

"That is so," conceded the verbally straitjacketed doctor.

Charlie said, "I'd like my appreciation to be recorded as being expressed on behalf of the British government."

Novikov beamed and Charlie relaxed, satisfied. As asshole-crawling went, this had gone on long enough. He hoped he'd encouraged the local doctor beyond what the man had so far been willing to talk about.

"I think what primarily has to be established is whether, in your opinion, the male bodies are those of British and American nationals," said Kurshin.

"I'm sure they are," said Charlie.

"So am I," agreed Miriam.

"Is there sufficient to identify them?" demanded Lestov, at once.

"It's far too early to give any opinion on that," refused Charlie.

"There's more personally identifying material on the Englishman," insisted Miriam.

Not bad, acknowledged Charlie; not enough to put him under any pressure, though. He said, "We've certainly got the initials of a name, from the inscription on the cigarette case. But that just gives us one very small needle in a huge haystack. There has been an obvious attempt to remove any identification, ripping out names from the uniforms and taking all the dog tags." He waited for the challenge, although he hadn't seen anyone examine the English victim's inside trousers band.

"Why, I wonder, were any belongings left at all?" asked Ryabov.

If you genuinely do wonder, you shouldn't be chief of police, thought Charlie. Instead of spelling out the significance—that their being left proved a motive other than personal robbery, an element of premeditation, and that the killings had nothing whatsoever to do with the Yakatskaya gulags, to whose prisoners the articles would have represented a fortune—Charlie said, "Panic, perhaps. They took the obvious identification, snapped neckties and hurriedly re-dressed the bodies, anxious to get away from the scene . . ." He was conscious of Miriam Bell looking curiously at him. "What do you think?"

"That could be the reason?" replied the American, although without conviction. "What's the inscription mean in the cigarette case? What's a 'First'?"

Another good try, conceded Charlie. "A high college pass."

"So you've a direction?" she persisted.

Shit, thought Charlie. "It could be from a hundred schools: more than a hundred," he lied. "And have been gained anywhen over a period as long as twelve years, if we accept the top age estimate of thirty-five. It's a search we'll have to make, of course. But I'm not hopeful." He wasn't volunteering, but he wasn't learning, either. Which was significant enough in itself, proving how determined everyone was not to share the smallest scrap.

"Why would an American officer carry a magnifying glass and tweezers?" asked Lestov.

It was a question that Charlie couldn't yet answer, although he had a vague, half-formed thought prompted by the fact that none of the uniforms carried regiment or corps crests on their buttons. Once again it was the absence of an article rather than its presence that Charlie considered important: wearing a Sam Browne proved the man wasn't armed. Would the other officer whom Charlie was sure had been at the scene have been wearing a more practical battle dress, complete with sidearm? There were no markings on the uniform to show the American might have carried a weapon, either. Whoever they'd been and whatever they'd been doing, neither had belonged to a fighting unit. Which narrowed the possibilities.

Miriam Bell lifted and then dropped her shoulders at the Moscow detective's question. "My only thought is that it could have something to do with a hobby."

People didn't bring their hobbies to Yakutskaya then or now, thought Charlie: it was the first slip Miriam had made. Hoping to generate something—anything—Charlie said, "We need more than we've got to take this inquiry forward . . . to take it anywhere." If he suggested a comparable photographic check against graduation pictures from America's military academy at West Point she might come back at him with the British counterpart at Sandhurst, so he decided to leave it.

"In view of the media interest, there might be a response if the photographs that Dr. Erzin took today were issued?" suggested Kurshin.

There could, Charlie conceded, be satellite television somewhere in the town, but the Ontario didn't have CNN, because he'd already checked. So how, apart from monitoring Charlie's British embassy call during which Cartright had talked of the publicity leak, could Kurshin have learned of the media awareness? Charlie was glad he hadn't booked a traceable call to Natalia through the hotel switchboard. He wouldn't attempt to reach her while he was here. And needed to be more careful than he had been the previous night when he next spoke to the Moscow embassy. Charlie looked between the two doctors and said, "The Russian woman had childbirth marks. Is there any way to establish how recent to her death she'd had the baby?"

"It should be possible for a gynecologist," Novikov said at once.

"It's a test I intend to make when I get the organs back to Moscow," said Olga.

"Something else I look forward to receiving from you," reminded Charlie.

The pathologist nodded but didn't speak.

"The child could still be alive," Charlie pointed out. "Conceivably, so could the woman's partner. There could be an identification if her photograph was published in Moscow."

"I'll suggest it," agreed Lestov.

Charlie doubted that either London or Washington would issue pictures until a reason was found for the two men being where they had been, despite media pressure. But it didn't hurt to go along with the local homicide chief's suggestion.

"Now that we've agreed on the nationality of the victims, I assume there'll be no difficulty repatriating the bodies?" said Miriam.

"That's more a political decision," avoided the police commander.

"But you won't object to the release of the bodies?" pressed Charlie, hoping to infer something from the reply.

Before either local man could respond, Olga Erzin said, "I really do need to get all the organs back to Moscow. There's absolutely no reason for anything to remain here any longer."

"It has to be the decision of the Executive Council," said Ryabov.

Awkwardness for awkwardness's sake? Or something else he couldn't at that moment fully understand? Charlie's first thought would have been perverseness, but now he wasn't totally sure. There would have to have been some local official awareness all that time ago of a tweezer-carrying American and an unarmed English officer being where no other Westerner had been before. And increasingly, as he tried to fit the pieces together, Charlie was getting a nagging feeling that the reason for their presence might be buried locally far more successfully than the bodies had been. Maybe it made sense after all for him to play diplomat and meet some local leaders. He said, "Perhaps we need personally to make the request?"

"That would be best," agreed Kurshin.

The convoy arrangements definitely established, Charlie lingered for Vitali Novikov when the meeting broke.

The man said, "Thank you, for what you said. Putting it on the record like that."

"Nothing that wasn't the truth," flattered Charlie.

"You'll want some protection from insects out at the grave tomorrow," offered Novikov, trying to reciprocate.

"*Exactly* the sort of local knowledge I do need," prompted Charlie.

"Have you any arrangements for tonight?" asked the pathologist.

"None," said Charlie, at once.

"My wife would be very happy for you to join us for dinner."

"So would I be, to accept."

Charlie had completely orientated himself and knew they were driving north from the town center. Very quickly the brick houses for crooked people gave way to wooden ones on stilts, securely upright without any subsidence, although the connected streets were haphazardly disjointed, afterthoughts to link places originally erected where the whim took the builder, before roads were considered.

Novikov said, "Certain trades, professions, could get people out of the gulags. A lot of people lied, of course. When they were found out, they were shot: publicly, in front of the original camp from which they'd tried to escape, as a warning to others. Being shot was another way of escaping."

"Who was it who was exiled here?" asked Charlie, picking up the lead.

"My father."

"Was he a builder?"

"A doctor. That was even better."

"And why you became one, too?"

"Yes," confirmed Novikov, at once. "There aren't many safe professions, even now. Everything is the mines. Which is slave labor, as it's always been."

"How close are they to the town?"

The pathologist shrugged beside him in the car. "The nearest is maybe five or six kilometers."

"What about prison camps?"

"Much farther away."

"But prisoners still work the mines?"

"Until they die. Which they still do, very quickly."

Novikov's house was immaculate, the wooden lining clearly insulated against the outer wall. Novikov's family was waiting in the main room, in which a fire flickered from habit rather than need. Marina was plump and rosy-cheeked. Charlie guessed she was about forty, although her hair was completely white. The boys were fair, like their father. They were dressed in what was clearly their best and newest clothes, the woman in a thick blue wool dress, the boys in matching gray trousers and sweaters. Novikov had been sure he would accept the invitation before it was offered, Charlie acknowledged.

Everyone embarrassingly remained standing until Charlie sat, the boys waiting after that for their father's permission. Charlie estimated Georgi to be about fourteen, Arseni maybe two years younger. Novikov served vodka for himself and Charlie, a purple-colored juice for his family.

Charlie's interrogation training and techniques had been honed by his new diplomatic environment and he used it all and improvised on top of that. He coaxed the boys into talking about their schooling and their intention to be doctors like their father, and flattered that he'd guessed before being told by Marina that her father had been the qualified architect who built the house.

Charlie described where he lived in Moscow as an ordinary apartment and showed the woman the photographs of herself and Sasha that Natalia had smuggled into his suitcase. During the meal—reindeer steak again—Charlie elaborated stories of police investigations he'd read about or occasionally seen in movies and insisted against Novikov's protest that he didn't mind Arseni's question but that he'd never shot anyone dead. Both boys appeared disappointed. Charlie made a point of repeating several times that it had not really been necessary for Moscow to send a pathologist, so complete had Novikov's examination and conclusions been. "If we solve this case, it will be largely due to your father."

On their way back to the Ontario Hotel, Charlie said, "You've got a fine family."

"You were very gracious," said the doctor. "And flattering."

"Isn't it going to be largely due to you if I've any chance of finding out what this is all about?" asked Charlie, heavily, turning sideways in the car toward the man.

"Probably," returned Novikov, enigmatically.

"Your father was sentenced to Gulag 98, wasn't he?"

"Yes. But being a doctor, he was allowed to move into the town almost immediately. He was still responsible for Gulag 98, though. And two more on the other side of Yakutsk."

"Was Gulag 98 a special prison?" pressed Charlie, discarding that morning's decision to let things come at Novikov's pace.

"It was for intellectuals."

"Were the people in the grave connected with someone who might have been in the camp?"

"It's possible. But there aren't any records anymore. Officially the genocide of Yakutskaya never occurred."

The twinge in Charlie's feet told him he was missing something, maybe a key to unlock more doors. "Would you take me to surviving camps?"

"It wouldn't help."

"It would give us a chance to talk more, at least."

"I am staying with the woman tomorrow, while she carries out her tests. Maybe after you've been to the grave."

Everyone—even the two local militia officers—was waiting for him in the bar when Charlie entered the hotel. No one accepted his offered drink. Miriam said, "We kept dinner waiting."

"Decided to eat out," said Charlie. "Should have told you."

"Yes," said Ryabov. "You should."

Fuck you, thought Charlie. Being an enforced member of a committee wasn't as much of a problem as he'd feared it might be.

11

The ice grave was a crater in an earthly moonscape and the protective headgear and face masks that everyone wore, in various designs, made them look appropriately like astronauts. The insects rose in a solidly attacking mass. Charlie's beekeeper's hat was perfect but he wished he'd taken Novikov's advice about gloves.

The annoyance at his disappearance the previous night remained, so much so that Charlie suspected they would have left without him if he hadn't made a point to be first downstairs waiting, and bustled in to take Olga's place the moment Kurshin arrived. On the way to the burial spot Lestov and Kurshin had talked—the Moscow detective hoping the crime scene produced more than the autopsies appeared to have—ignoring Charlie in the back. He trailed behind, the last in line, as they straggled toward the actual spot, and no one paid any attention to him when he edged away from the huddled-together, mosquito-swatting gathering that assembled to watch Lev Denebin carry out his forensic examination. Charlie positioned himself with the scientist in his immediate line of sight and the others beyond, able to see everything and everyone.

Denebin was better protected against the insects than any of them, helmeted, gauzed, gloved and with his scene-of-crime overalls tightly held at wrists and ankles. Charlie, who admired professionalism, was at once impressed by the Russian. Before getting into the grave, Denebin exposed an entire role of film in advance of pegging its immediate surround, using the markers to secure his tape for detailed exterior measurements ahead of stretching between them a crisscross of tape to section the depression into six designated search areas.

From Novikov's earlier photographs it was obvious the ongoing thaw had deepened the grave still further from the depth at which the bodies had lain. Although he trod minimally and carefully, Denebin very quickly created an ankle-sucking sludge in places at the bottom of the depression. The forensic expert was painstakingly thorough, gently digging with a small trowel, particular always to sieve the earth back on to the place from which he'd collected it, not allowing any encroachment onto an unsearched, taped-off section.

It was only after watching the Russian probe and sift with total concentration for thirty minutes that Charlie appreciated the complete extent of his dismissal. Denebin appeared unaware and certainly uncaring of Charlie but stood always with his back to the others, for his body to obscure anything he didn't want them properly to see.

Denebin had his specimen bags in a satchel slung around his neck, returning to a separate compartment whatever he felt it necessary to collect. He retrieved a lot of what looked to Charlie like metal shards and a few pieces of blackened wood. On the third cordoned-off section Charlie was immediately aware of the man's body tightening and of Denebin more obviously putting his back to the watching group when he straightened with something small enough to hold between his thumb and forefinger. Until then he'd used one bag for several pieces of metal, but this new find got a specimen container of its own.

None of those at the grave edge appeared aware of Denebin's stiffening, all too distracted by the constant, arm-waving effort to disperse the persistent mosquitoes and midges, despite Kurshin lighting a cordon of ineffective repellent candles. Charlie's hands and arms were ablaze from bites, but he rigidly held himself against warding them off, not wanting to attract the scientist's attention.

Within minutes he was glad he'd endured the torture. At the crater's edge of the fifth section Denebin actually grunted as he stooped abruptly, troweling debris into his agitated sieve. From where Charlie stood the shell casing was obvious, and in the few seconds it took Denebin to bag it, Charlie decided it had not been from a 9mm bullet but a much smaller caliber.

It was turning out to be another good day, Charlie thought, although maybe not for the worried British military attaché, Colonel Gallaway, in faraway Moscow. Not his problem, Charlie decided. His job was to determine the circumstances and, he hoped, establish the facts, not pretty them up. Behind the forensic scientist the rest of the group waved and slapped and Charlie wondered what, apart from insect bites, they were gaining from just standing there.

Quietly, slowly, Charlie eased himself away. It *was* a moonscape, empty kilometer after empty kilometer of treeless, stunted scrubland. In a few places—other, smaller craters—the rare warmth was making mist that hung, wraithlike. A place of far too many ghosts, thought Charlie: of three in particular, but of hundreds more. But where had Gulag 98 been in which they had been kept, when they had been pitifully alive?

The killings, he supposed, would have been a day very similar to this. Not as warm but summer, the ground softening. Vehicles, although not many: a truck, perhaps. A car. Two at the most, as few witnesses as possible. It would have been during the half-light of day. The killers would have needed to see what they were doing, choose their spot, and the insects had been swarming in the daytime heat, like now, to clog the mouths and throats after the executions. There would have been panic. And fear. A lot of fear. *Don't do this! This is madness! Let's talk about it! For God's sake!* English voices— hysterical voices—in a land that had never heard English. No time to dig. Get it over with as quickly as possible. Get away. The explosions—there would have been several, from the amount of metal Denebin had collected—would have been deafening. No turning back after that. All argument, all pleas, ended by the explosions. They would have been manacled. Immobilized. Frightened people killing frightened people. But why? What could this desolate, pitiless land of ghosts have or possess to justify the ritual, cold-blooded execution of these three unknown, apparently unmourned people?

Not the land—the place—itself, Charlie decided. It would have been someone who was here, in Gulag 98. Maybe more than one. A group, like he was a reluctant part of a group now, men—maybe women, too—with a secret.

He had to examine that speculation further, justify the reasoning. He'd seen the bodies, each of them naked. Hand and ankle cuff marks, clearly visible. Shattering bullet wounds to the back of the head. But that was all. No sign whatsoever—no bruises or burns or cuts—of torture. And men prepared to kill would have been as prepared to torture if the victims had possessed a secret. So why hadn't they? Because they didn't have to, Charlie answered himself. The executioners *knew* the secret: what there was to gain. But didn't want to share what was big enough, rewarding enough, to kill for. They'd known each other, victims and killers. Would have used first names when they pleaded, calling upon friendship, acquaintanceship. Charlie was sure he had a picture, but it was misted, much more deeply obscured than the occasionally shrouded expanse across which he was looking, seeking but still not finding what he had expected to see. The foundation marks of buildings, perhaps, even those built on stilts. Certainly evidence of proper graveyards.

He turned, surprised at how far he'd wandered on feet that normally cautioned against such excess. Denebin was clambering from the grave, tidily winding up his marking tapes and retrieving the securing pegs, when Charlie got back to them. He was in time to hear the forensic scientist say, "There's very little. Too much time has elapsed from the bodies being discovered. Animals have been there, disturbing it all."

"But there are some things?" questioned Charlie. "I saw you collecting samples."

"Things I need to look at more closely," said the scientist, vaguely.

"Do we have to talk about it here!" protested the arm-flailing Miriam. She'd suffered more than anyone, with just chiffon scarves to wrap around her head and face. "I'm being eaten alive. I want to get back to the hotel, clean up."

"Of course," agreed the attentive Lestov, at once.

"I'll need until tomorrow to get any opinion of what I've got," said Denebin, awkwardly.

"We're meeting Valentin Polyakov in the morning," reminded Miriam.

"Another busy day then," said Charlie, brightly. No one acknowledged him, already hurrying back toward the waiting vehicles.

It had been Novikov's idea that they meet at the town's museum, but the man wasn't there when Kurshin dismissively dropped him off, so Charlie went inside. The museum was far more a monument to Russian persecution of Russian than Charlie had expected, whole rooms given over to photographs and paraphernalia recording the establishment of the vast penal colony. The photographs were almost uniformly of lines of dead-eyed, despair-crushed, barely human figures, the bechained walking dead, men, women and even children. It was from a variety of the pictures that Charlie believed he'd answered one question and gotten a pointer to another.

The gulags were regimented, haphazardly wire-fenced, with corner-placed watchtowers, some tilted like the subsiding buildings of today. There were lists of the minimally subsistence diets upon which the exiles and prisoners had been expected to survive, and occasional names, particularly of political figures purged during and even after the Stalin era. Charlie was intrigued several times to see a photograph of a gaunt-featured man with the same name as the chief minister with whom he had an appointment the following day.

Charlie was standing in front of an exhibition of prison camp equipment—chain-linked manacles, hand and ankle cuffs, actual posts against which prisoners were tied for execution, punishment whips and guard batons—when the tall, thin doctor found him.

"What you expected?" asked Novikov.

"Far more."

"Still want to go for a drive?"

"As much as ever."

They were driving north again, Charlie recognized. Deciding after the family encounter it was safe to try to guide the conversation, Charlie said, "What was your father's supposed crime?"

"Just being a doctor," said Novikov, simply. "Doctors were regarded as dangerous intellectuals, especially those who weren't members of the Communist Party, which my father refused to join." He snorted a laugh. "Being a doctor got him sent here and then saved him. Once he arrived, he only had to live *in* Gulag 98 for a few months. Even when he was inside, he didn't have to do any manual labor in the mines. That's why he trained me. Made me study basic forensics, later. That again was for necessity, to make myself as indispensable as possible. I can't ever return permanently to Moscow, of course. Anywhere else in Russia, for that matter."

"Why not?" Charlie frowned.

"The system," said Novikov. "People sent here were automatically stripped of their citizenship: lost their Russian nationality. So have their descendants. You need established residency in a Russian city to be allowed to leave here and you can only get that by getting away from here to establish residency. Which you can't do without an internal passport, which none of us is allowed to hold. We're imprisoned here as effectively as anyone in Stalin's day."

"So everyone who ever came here was known: recorded some-

where?" The town was falling away in the semidarkness, more moonscape stretching out in front of them.

Novikov nodded, recognizing the reason for the question. "In theory. Somewhere in Moscow, I suppose."

"What about here? Were there registers?"

"Again, in theory. Aleksandr Andreevich asked the chief minister
after the bodies were found. Polyakov said there weren't any archives,
not any longer. That they'd been destroyed when we got our limited
autonomy. And don't forget millions were sent here. Died here. It
would have needed a warehouse as big as Yakutsk itself."

After the previous day there was no love lost between this man
and Olga Erzin. No need, then, to circumvent. "Anything from today's examination?"

The pathologist shook his head. "She tried to get me to agree that
some grazes on the woman's hands and on the American's right fore-
arm were defense injuries, where they tried to fight off whoever killed
them. But I wouldn't. It doesn't fit, with the close range at which
they were shot in the back, not the front, of the head. I believe they're
scratches from pitching forward into the grave. Frozen as it was, it
would have been like hitting concrete."

Charlie thought so, too. It led perfectly to one of the questions he
believed he'd virtually resolved. "The restraint bruising, to the wrists
and ankles? It's very even, isn't it? And totally encircling, without
any interruption. Normal handcuffs wouldn't leave a band like that,
would they? There'd have been gaps."

Novikov regarded him curiously. "I suppose so," he allowed,
doubtfully. "There could have been some sideways lividity, joining
up the gaps. What's the significance?"

"In the museum photographs the wrists are completely enclosed
by a U-shaped band that goes under the wrists. The encirclement is
completed by the straight bar that slots in at the top to be ratcheted
down tightly to grip every part of the wrist."

"I still don't understand the importance."

"It would be the sort of prison equipment available at Gulag 98,
wouldn't it?"

"Yes," Novikov agreed at once. "Of course it would." Just as
quickly he said, "I understand things were found at the grave?"

"What?" demanded Charlie, questioning instead of answering.

"I don't know," said the other man. "When he came to collect the woman on their way back, Lestov said Lev Fyodorovich wanted to use what laboratory facilities I have. I had to warn them I didn't have much." He hesitated. "I thought you might know what it is he wants to examine or test."

"Denebin wouldn't say," said Charlie, moving easily on to his other query. "Have you managed to establish the weight of the bullets?"

Novikov smiled. "There's a slight variation between them. The one that killed the Englishman was ten grams, the one I recovered from the American—which was more damage—was just over nine. Does that tell you anything?"

"It might, if there was the third bullet for comparison," said Charlie. And he was sure there was. The uncertainty was whether Denebin would admit to finding it.

"There!" said Novikov, abruptly pointing through the gloom.

The gulag emerged like a mirage, at first a skeletal outline. It seemed a long time before they were able to distinguish buildings on the left of the approach road from the mine on the right. That was brightly lit, with two descent shaft derricks.

"Gold," identified Novikov. "There's three, quite close together. We won't be able to stop. As it is, my registration will be logged. There are diamond and gold mines about thirty kilometers farther on."

As they slowed, a straggled line of men emerged from the camp of single-story wooden shacks elevated from the ground. Some had their hands on the shoulders of the man in front. All walked head down, scuffling in jangling ankle manacles, crossing to the mine. They all wore uniforms padded against a cold that didn't exist. All the guards were armed. One began waving Novikov's car on urgently.

"Convicts?" queried Charlie.

Novikov nodded. "It will be the afternoon shift. The mines are worked twenty-four hours."

Charlie was concentrating on the camp. The huts were in regimented lines, five to a line. Charlie counted thirty. There were two control towers like those he'd seen in the photographs in the museum. Charlie frowned, knowing he should be aware of something but unable to decide what. Then he said, "Wire! There's no wire."

"There rarely is. Look where we are: what this place is. Where is there to run? People tried, of course. Still do. They're never chased. It isn't worth the effort. The locals find them frozen to death when the snow melts. That's why run aways are called 'snow drop.'"

The cemetery was on the far side of the camp, what appeared to be hundreds of lines of uniformed crosses. They were close enough for Charlie to see there were no names, just numbers.

"So this is what it was like?"

"No," said Novikov. "This is civilized—humane—by comparison."

Charlie had just finishing spraying the room with insecticide, after another meaningless conversation with the Moscow embassy, when Miriam's knock came at his door. Charlie thought he kept any reaction from showing when she entered the room, but he wasn't sure. His own hands and arms were swollen from bites, but the woman's face was ballooned, hamster-cheeked and bumped and very red, despite whatever cream she'd smeared upon it. There were still isolated globules she hadn't properly rubbed in.

"Meet the bride of Frankenstein." Her skin was so stretched it was difficult for her to speak. "You don't need me to tell you I'm not coming down for dinner tonight."

"No," accepted Charlie.

"You've been playing quite a game," she accused. "The consensus is you're a no-hoper."

"Everyone's entitled to an opinion."

"It's not mine," she said. "Saul filled me in before I left Moscow: it's been fascinating watching you. That's why I haven't interfered."

As fascinating as it's been watching you, reflected Charlie. "Don't read too much into it."

"I've come to warn you."

For a reason, guessed Charlie. "What?"

"Our calls to Moscow are being monitored."

There's a clever girl, thought Charlie. "Who told you?"

"Ryabov, trying to get into my pants. They know you're not getting anywhere."

It had to be getting pretty crowded inside Miriam's pants, thought Charlie: there wouldn't have been room for him even if he'd been interested. "How about you? You got anything that gives any sort of lead?"

Miriam started to shake her head but abruptly stopped, wincing at the discomfort. "Lestov says there was something in the grave: that he'll tell me when he finds out. And I'll tell you, obviously. The locals haven't got a clue. They just want to get rid of us. According to Ryabov, the Russians aren't going to be included in tomorrow's meeting and he thinks Polyakov is planning what he regards as a coup, but Ryabov doesn't know what it is."

She was wrapping up her eagerness very well, Charlie decided. For his own amusement he said, "Not sure I like being used."

"You haven't said what you've picked up," prompted the woman.

"A lot of isolated bits, nothing making any sort of sense, any picture," avoided Charlie. "I need to get back, start putting the picture of the man to work. There are a lot of checks that have got to be made with that. And I don't just want to get the body and its organs back to London, for our own pathologist. There's the uniform, too, for forensic tests."

"I thought you had more," said the woman, disbelievingly.

"Nothing crystallized yet."

"We *are* working together on this, aren't we, Charlie?" pressed Miriam. "I mean, Washington and London have agreed?"

"What I get, you'll get. Trust me."

"That's what I've got to do!" agreed the girl. "Learn to trust you."

"Perhaps things will pick up tomorrow."

Miriam said, "I'd like to think so."

When it did, neither of them was happy.

12

Charlie was totally trapped. Miriam, too. He experienced every feeling, beginning and ending with the same numbed, disbelieving fury. There was a lot of that in between, too. He was furious at being tricked—and at not anticipating it—and at not being sure what, if

anything, was salvageable—and perhaps most of all at his helplessness because Charlie Muffin hated most of all being in a situation
over which he had absolutely no control. So a lot of the anger was
directed at himself.

There'd been no warning, although maybe he should have suspected more from Commissioner Ryabov's hotel foyer announcement
that the Russians were excluded from the meeting with the Yakutsk
chief minister, wrongly assuming that to be the "something funny"
the militia commander had warned Miriam about. Charlie had withdrawn to the sidelines of the inevitable argument from the Moscow
homicide detective, uncertain whether to try to force Novikov's hand
by announcing his return to Moscow after the formal release of the
body, which was the purpose of the meeting to which he and Miriam
were going. He'd actually checked the availability of late afternoon
and evening flights.

There had been no indication, either, from their initial reception
by Valentin Ivanovich Polyakov. The full-bearded, towering chief
minister had greeted them with handshakes, samovar tea and cakes
in what had to be the only room in the government complex not in
imminent danger of collapse. He'd said he appreciated the cooperation there appeared to have been with the Yakutsk force and in return
Charlie and Miriam had promised its continuation after their return
to Moscow, from where a lot more inquiries needed to be made. And
Polyakov had agreed at once to the bodies and the possessions being
returned to Britain and America. He had, declared the Yakutsk
leader, already officially informed London and Washington and had
the necessary papers prepared and ready. Even more prepared—an
indication Charlie missed—he summoned a photographer to record
the documentation formally being handed over. Charlie was speculating again about the last evening flight when Polyakov rose unexpectedly from behind his ornately carved desk in what Charlie first
thought to be in dismissal but instead said, "Now perhaps you'd be
good enough to come with me?"

Charlie followed, imagining a courtesy meeting with the rest of
the local ruling assembly, smiling in expectation at the murmur of
people when Polyakov thrust open linking doors to a larger room.
Charlie later decided, when he saw the video, that the fatuous grin

froze on his face as rigidly—and almost as terrorized—as those of the murder victims.

The lights from the television cameras that recorded his expression made it difficult for Charlie to see the extent of the press conference. From the immediate North American–accented questions, against which Polyakov held up his hands, Charlie finally realized the surprise that Ryabov had told Miriam about was a press contingent flown in certainly from Canada and probably from the United States as well. And knew how the media leaks that Cartright had warned of had come about.

Charlie had spent his entire operational life trying always to be as amorphous as the graveside mist and until this appalling, stomach-dropping moment had succeeded. So shocked—bewildered—was he by the abrupt exposure that for perhaps the first time in that operational life Charlie's mind went completely blank, momentarily refusing to function. He was conscious of Polyakov ("the conniving, manipulative bastard!") thanking the Canadian and American media for flying in at such short notice and the inconvenience and of being introduced, with Miriam, by name (holy shit, no!) as he was herded toward a table to sit upon a raised dais behind a hedge of microphones. Yuri Vyacheslav Ryabov and Aleksandr Andreevich Kurshin were already seated, waiting. Able at last to focus, Charlie saw translation booths along the left side of the room and that a lot of the waiting journalists—close to thirty, he guessed, as well as two television teams—wore earphones.

It was at that moment, in reality only a hiatus of seconds, that Charlie began to function, to try to assess and calculate: and from whichever and whatever way he considered it, he reached the same conclusion. It was an absolute fuckup. And worsening by the second, steered inexorably toward further and greater disaster by Valentin Polyakov.

The Yakustkaya chief minister had achieved his lifetime's ambition, gaining an international audience to denounce successive Russian leaders who perpetuated what Stalin had begun by turning an entire country into a penal colony. At last, declared Polyakov, there was going to be the opportunity for the world to be made aware, after half a century, of the crimes against humanity exceeding those of the Holocaust. Six million Jews had perished in that attempted genocide. Double that number had been worked to death and put to death in the Siberian gulags. To Charlie's fidgeted discomfort, Polyakov inferred the two lieutenants ("brave, fearless agents") had been murdered because they had discovered the secrets of Yakutskaya ("a secret terrible enough to have destroyed war time alliances").

At this point Polyakov gestured to either side of him, to include Miriam and Charlie. "Now, after so long—too long—two more brave, fearless agents have come to this godforsaken country, to rediscover and expose secrets Russia even now would prefer kept hidden. Now, at last, the world will eventually be told the truth."

It *was* a disaster, Charlie recognized. An utterly unparalleled, irrevocable disaster. His cover, always the paramount consideration, was blown. Which did not create the physical, life-threatening danger it once would have, but as bad on every other level. None of which was the most important consideration. His new creed, the doctrine constantly preached, was never, under any circumstances, to become involved in a diplomatic incident. And here he was—they were—by association, by sitting beside a ranting xenophobe, denouncing Russia and by so doing causing not a diplomatic incident but an inevitable, devastating diplomatic sensation. Beyond that—worse than that— even: it was, potentially, personally devastating. This was of recall and dismissal magnitude: the collapse of the house of cards. As things were between them at the moment, he didn't think Natalia would bring Sasha to London. She'd virtually said so. And it was immaterial whether he was dismissed or resigned from the department. He'd be refused residency permission to remain in Russia.

The immediate barrage of questions, in English, were all directed at Charlie and Miriam, too many and too quick at first to isolate one from the other. Charlie didn't wait properly to hear, desperate to limit the damage. It was, he insisted, important to stress that it was neither an American nor English investigation. He and his FBI colleague were observers on a joint inquiry being conducted by a Moscow murder squad working with the local militia. To the visible face-hardening from Polyakov, earphoned for the translation from English, Charlie said the Moscow team—to which Polyakov had studiously not referred—was kept from the conference by continuing inquiries. Charlie spoke accepting that his qualifications would be overwhelmed by the carefully prepared drama of the chief minister's claims but was not, at that moment, addressing the media. He was talking to whoever later examined the transcript at whatever inquiry there would unquestionably be to decide his future.

There was an audibly shouted question—"Just what were these guys doing, all that time ago?"—directed to Miriam by name and Charlie looked along the table, unaware if she had already fully accepted their entrapment but conscious of her additional discomfort. A lot of the previous night's swelling had gone and her face wasn't as purple-red as it had been, but it was still lumped in places—one eye was half closed—and greasy from that morning's antiseptic balm. She wore absolutely no makeup. She sat apparently trying to shield her eyes from the camera lights, in reality hoping to conceal as much of her face as possible, and two still photographers crouched at the lip of the dais were repeatedly gesturing for her to lower her hands. She still had difficulty in talking, too.

As soon as she began to speak, Charlie recognized that in her anxiety to escape, Miriam Bell was panicking, offering far more than was necessary. She repeated Charlie's insistence upon jurisdiction and cooperation and babbled on that they hadn't established a reason for the killings, nor any victim identities, although they had no doubt of nationality. Her disclosure of the method of execution at once prompted a shouted interjection.

"Wasn't a bullet in the back of the head the favorite killing method of Russian intelligence in Lubyanka?"

"Yes," agreed Miriam.

"So they were killed by Russian intelligence?"

"We don't know who they were killed by," intruded Charlie, still working damage limitation. "That's what the Russian team is trying to establish. Why there is such excellent international cooperation."

He held back at a demand to know what specific leads they had, curious for his own part how Miriam would reply, but she said there weren't any.

"What's your next move?" shouted a woman from the rear of the room.

"Analyzing the autopsy and forensic evidence," Charlie came in quickly, anxious to be as vague as possible, but Polyakov added, "And the items found upon the bodies."

"Which at this moment we don't intend to make public," persisted

Charlie. Thank Christ he hadn't discussed what he considered significant. An enterprising journalist could still get a lot from the cigarette case inscription. The thought lodged in his mind. There hadn't so far been the concentrated questioning he'd feared—no one, for instance, had asked about photographs of bodies perfectly preserved—and he abruptly wondered how of and how far he could manipulate the situation into which he'd been thrust. He would be taking a hell of a risk by trying and if he got caught out it could go catastrophically wrong, but they already had a catastrophe, so there was very little more to lose.

"We have," he began, "probably one of the greatest unsolved mysteries of the Second World War. Two Allied officers. A Russian woman. And a secret that has lain buried for fifty years. . . ." He had them, Charlie decided. There was scarcely a sound in the room, the coughs muted. Charlie thought faster than he could remember in any previous back-to-the-wall situation, sifting the innocuous from anything that could give the slenderest clue to his real thinking, determined to out-exaggerate Polyakov and spread as many false leads as he could make up on the spot. He acknowledged that it had obviously been a covert mission ("What other reason for it remaining secret when it went wrong?") and invented the possibility of special German prisoners being incarcerated in special gulags ("in the remotest, most unreachable part of the world"). Hitler had Mussolini snatched from captivity after the Italian dictator's overthrow. What if, held somewhere in Yakutskaya, there had been a German, possibly several, with the knowledge of a weapon or a development—jet propulsion, of which the Peenemünde rockets had been the forerunner, nuclear fission ahead of the Americans' Los Alamos development—that would have shortened the war?

Enough, Charlie decided: stop before he became a contender for the Nobel prize for Fantasy. Time to let his still-enraptured audience work up their own embellishments. There was a fresh cacophony of demands from which he picked those most likely to mislead, ignoring those that could have been pertinent. After seeming to prevaricate, he allowed himself to concede his belief that the three victims could have been an advance reconnaissance group and that there could be other victims, in undiscovered graves. He intentionally shifted questions about surviving registers of possible German prisoners to Valentin Polyakov, enjoying the man's difficulty admitting they had either been lost or intentionally destroyed. Quickly Charlie picked up that there should be some files in British and American intelligence archives, although finding them would undoubtedly be hard and conceivably impossible if the operation was covered by a special, time-restricted security release.

Polyakov made a determined effort to stop Charlie's takeover and to bring it back to the intended anti-Russian platform by switching the questioning to the local militia, which was a mistake. Yuri Ryabov was too excited by an international spotlight, never managing to complete replies too convoluted for Kurshin to finish for him and in his desperation the homicide chief seemed to agree that the investigation was concentrated as Charlie had suggested and Polyakov hurriedly tried to conclude the conference by repeating an apparent earlier undertaking to escort everyone to the grave site. There was an immediate demand from both television teams for individual interviews with Charlie and Miriam.

Miriam followed Charlie's lead by refusing. And did so again when he insisted he would not be photographed near the grave, either.

As they hurried back into Polyakov's office, Miriam whispered in English, "We got well and truly suckered."

"We got well and truly fucked," corrected Charlie.

Charlie guessed Polyakov's anger matched his but hoped his was better controlled. He'd had time now to rationalize his mistakes, acknowledging that he'd underestimated everything and everybody, which had been foolishly arrogant. He wasn't sure how much of a recovery he'd managed, but he had to go on working at it and at the same time not lose sight of the fact that, devious, conniving bastard though he'd been, Valentin Ivanovich Polyakov was a diplomatically recognized head of a semi-autonomous republic who had to be accorded the respect due to his title. It didn't necessarily extend to the man himself, of course. Only the three of them had returned to Polyakov's suite, leaving Ryabov and Kurshin to organize the transportation to the grave. Possibly his first advantage, recognized Charlie. He'd have to make sure he isolated all the others.

For that reason Charlie waited for Polyakov to speak, but unexpectedly it was Miriam who broke the angry silence. "That was monstrous! I am going to make a full report to my embassy in Moscow. Ask that protests are made from my State Department in Washington."

Wrong, thought Charlie. There was no threat in that: Polyakov, who'd caused the offense, was the same man who'd sit in judgment upon any diplomatic complaint about it. Don't get sore, get even, remembered Charlie, calling upon another dictum. What other advantages were there? The eavesdropping was a definite advantage there: a signpost to follow, in fact. He'd told McDowell and Gallaway he was getting nowhere—probably never would—and the listening Polyakov had believed him. The bastard would never have chanced a trick like the one he'd just pulled if he'd known Charlie's bullshit was going to be spread thicker than his. The benefits were stacking up. What else? He had the official release of the body and possessions snug in his inside pocket. Important to ensure those possessions, including the uniform, weren't picked over by anyone else. There were the lists, of course, carefully prepared by Vitali Novikov. But the local medical examiner had not been able to read the English lettering of the cigarette case inscription, so the danger was minimized there.

Insufficient for a total recovery, assessed Charlie objectively. Publicly—in Moscow and London and Washington—it would still probably be regarded as an unmitigated debacle requiring his head on a pole. If he stood any chance at all of keeping it instead on his shoulders, he had to solve all the mysteries, not make up any more. But not here, at this precise moment. At this precise moment he had verbally to manacle Valentin bloody Polyakov as effectively as the victims they were trying to identify. And Charlie thought he could do it. Calmly, conversationally—no longer, in fact, furious—he said, "You should have told us: prepared us for what you were going to do back there."

"I achieved all I wanted."

Charlie discerned the faint doubt. Shaking his head, he said, "Maybe if you'd been more forthcoming we could have helped you make it better." He refused to answer Miriam's abrupt look, willing her not to say anything, make any interruption, until she understood what he was doing.

"What do you mean?" demanded Polyakov.

"I mean that both of us have been aware from the beginning that all our contacts with Moscow have been monitored," said Charlie, easily. "Which is why we've said nothing to indicate our thinking or what we've already been able to decide. But most importantly there's been no discussion, either, of what was discovered in London or Washington before we came here. Or what's been shared by Moscow."

The other man's uncertainty was obvious now. "I want to know everything about this Nazi business!"

"After what happened this morning, I don't feel at liberty to tell you," said Charlie. "As far as I'm concerned, that's something you'll have officially to approach London about."

"And Washington, as far as I am concerned," came in Miriam, once more following in Charlie's footsteps.

"Your being allowed here was on the understanding of complete cooperation," threatened Polyakov, inadequately.

"That was our understanding, too." Charlie nodded in the direction of the just-left room. "There wasn't much evidence of complete cooperation in there. And I expect London to be outraged that what were official discussions between myself and my embassy were monitored."

"Washington, too," endorsed Miriam again. "I think the whole episode was extremely unfortunate. You would probably have been able to avoid a great deal of embarrassment by first discussing the claims and accusations you made today."

Careful, thought Charlie worriedly.

Polyakov said, "I demand to know everything that's been discovered elsewhere!"

"I have to refer you to London," said Charlie. "Or my embassy in Moscow."

"You are both here with my permission: under my sufferance," further threatened the bearded chief minister. "It's I who have to authorize the release of the bodies and their effects."

Charlie thought Polyakov and Stalin would have gotten on well together. He said, "You told us earlier you'd already been in contact with London and Washington, agreeing that. We were photographed being given the official release papers."

Polyakov's face began to burn.

Sure of herself—of Charlie's script—Miriam said, "This really could get most unpleasant. My embassy has an aircraft on standby to recover our national. I think everything is out of our hands now. Any decision to hold the bodies will be taken on a diplomatic level."

The man was close to being out of his depth, Charlie guessed. His mind still on limitation, Charlie said, "I agree. I regret—and I feel sure my government will very much regret—what occurred today. At my level—the level of the investigation—I think it would be most unwise if the media for whose invitation you are responsible were allowed any more information or facilities than they already have been given. That's as far as I feel able to go, guiding you about what's known elsewhere about this case."

"I can't add to that," said the woman.

The television teams had, of course, brought satellite communication equipment and the conference was instantly syndicated by their respective stations to be seen worldwide during the course of the day.

In London Sir Rupert Dean turned to his assembled committee and said, "Charlie Muffin will need a damned good explanation for this!" For Gerald Williams it was a superhuman effort not to speak or keep the satisfaction from his face.

In Moscow, McDowell, Gallaway and Cartright looked between each other in matching incredulity. Gallaway said, "Oh, my God!"

McDowell said, "I've got to speak to the bloody man," but at once corrected himself. "No. I need to speak to London."

And in the Lesnaya apartment Sasha said, "That's Daddy. What's he talking about?"

"I don't know," said Natalia. Their situation had never stood a chance of succeeding, not from the very beginning.

"Inconceivable!" protested James Boyce.

"Definitely a need for some close control: find out what the dangers are," said Kenton Peters. "Sounded awfully like your man knew something he shouldn't."

"And your woman, too," said Boyce. "Yakutsk itself was always our greatest weakness: a problem if the bodies were discovered, not knowing ourselves precisely where the grave was. Never in a million years expected it would melt like that."

"Do you think Muffin is getting too close?"

"I've absolutely no way of knowing, not until he gets back to Moscow. I'll get a full account then," said Boyce.

"I think I should go personally," said Peters. "Best you stay clear: more to lose in some ways with your man still living. And I've got a presidential problem because the damned idiot acted without consulting me, which is unforgivable."

"You stopping by on your way?" asked Boyce.

"Think it's best if I go to Moscow first. Assess the degree of danger on the ground."

"Probably the better idea," agreed Boyce. Heavily he said, "You going alone?"

"Muffin has to be identified," reminded Peters. "It'll be the ideal opportunity."

"Try to make it on your way back," urged Boyce. "Putting the boat in the water at the weekend."

"That sounds nice."

13

It was Miriam who suggested, "What was on the bodies and the clothes?" and Charlie said, "Yes" and they went directly from the encounter with Valentin Polyakov to the mortuary. It was several minutes before either realized that with the local militia officers acting as tour guides to the visiting media, they were alone and unchaperoned.

"I *am* going to look like Frankenstein's bride on film," complained the woman.

"I'd probably pass as Frankenstein's creation as well, two dummies together."

"I'm sure Ryabov would have warned me if he'd known."

"Too late now."

Miriam said, "How much of what you told the media was kosher, how much bullshit?"

"Bullshit that fit," said Charlie.

"You think Polyakov bought the line afterwards?"

"Most of it. It helped, you picking up as you did."

She shrugged. "We're in a hell of a mess, aren't we? You see a way out?"

"Solving everything, with no embarrassments to anyone, would be a start."

"So would a cure for cancer," she said.

"You really got a plane on standby?"

"Small cargo freighter, chartered from Aeroflot. This thing's getting a lot of play back home. Secret Grave of the Unknown Soldier, that sort of thing. Good bandwagon for a president with falling poll ratings to get on board."

"Any chance of sharing?" Charlie was panting, climbing up and down tilting corridors. He wished she wouldn't walk so fast.

"That's what I keep asking you, remember?" avoided Miriam, making a point.

"What did you get out of Ryabov and Lestov?" Charlie countered.

"Nothing out of Ryabov, apart from the eavesdropping, which I'd guessed anyway. All he wanted was to get into my pants. That was Lestov's main aim, too. But he was prepared to trade, to get there. Olga didn't get anything extra from the autopsies and is pissed about it. Denebin got a lot of metal out of the grave, apparently."

"Grenades," identified Charlie, simply.

Miriam stopped, turning to look at him. "Grenades!"

"That's how the grave was made, the quickest way, throwing two or three grenades one after the other at the same place," said Charlie, grateful for the chance to rest his feet. "And they were either German or Russian. The grenades both used, during the war, had wooden handles: they could be thrown farther than the British and American pineapple type. I saw Denebin pick up quite a lot of burned wood fragments."

"You sure about grenades? You're not still bullshitting?"

Charlie began walking again. "No bullshit. Anything else?"

"You think there was?" fenced Miriam.

"Denebin picked up a shell casing. And I think the bullet that killed the woman."

"You expect them to tell us that?"

"No."

"Were you going to tell me?"

"Depends what you had to trade," replied Charlie, honestly. And she did have a convenient plane.

"That magnifying glass and the tweezers are specialized, not the sort stocked by a 7-Eleven or whatever convenience stores were called that long ago: Woolworth's I guess. Our laboratories in Washington might be able to narrow down the sort of thing they were used for. Give us a specialization."

"He was very definitely a specialist," agreed Charlie. It would be picked up by American forensic examination anyway and there wasn't anything to be gained holding it back from her. "The one unbroken lens in his spectacles was particularly thick. Your labs will be able to establish the degree of impairment, but he'd never have passed an army medical with eyesight as bad as his. He was in uniform because there was a special need for whatever he did."

"I missed that," admitted Miriam, unoffended. "What about the uniform?"

"It didn't tell me anything. Again, your forensic people might get something."

"It wasn't tailored to fit, not like your guy's," said the American. "I checked the measurements. I guess our officers didn't go in for that sort of stuff."

Charlie hadn't seen her do that. It helped having a sounding board to bounce off and the echoes were coming back loud and clear. "I don't suppose they did."

"Would there have been a name on the label ripped out from your guy's jacket?"

"Yes," said Charlie, waiting for the challenge.

Nothing came. Instead Miriam said, "Shit. Think how easy it would have made things."

"I already have," assured Charlie.

"If my guy had special talents, it follows that yours would have had, too, doesn't it?"

"I guess so," agreed Charlie, cautiously.

"So they were killed *because* of their expertise?"

"What they were here to use it for," qualified Charlie, glad they were approaching the mortuary. "You didn't say whether there was room on your plane."

"I wouldn't leave my worst enemy in a place like this longer than I had to."

They were as surprised at all three Russians being in the cramped and inadequate mortuary laboratory, with Novikov closely attentive, as the Russians appeared to be at their arrival. Charlie at once remembered Denebin's requested use of the facility and just as quickly accepted that the forensic examination, such as was possible, of the grave contents was the obvious place *for* all three to be. He and Miriam, too. The shock-haired scientist appeared to be clearing up when they walked in, a second specimen satchel in addition to the one he'd used at the scene already securely buckled.

"All over, then?" greeted Charlie. "Anything interesting?"

Denebin didn't respond. Instead Lestov said, "What happened?" The attitude was hostile.

"We were totally conned," admitted Miriam. Succinctly, missing nothing but not elaborating, either, she recounted Valentin Polyakov's stage-managed performance, frequently quoting the chief minister verbatim, which Charlie noted. He listened and watched with one hip lodged on a laboratory bench to ease his feet, intent upon the Russians. Olga's face was the most readable, instant anger, washed away just as quickly by dismayed awareness that the television coverage guaranteed Moscow seeing it. Even the normally enigmatic forensic scientist shifted beside his samples, his irritation needing movement, although his features remained unmoving. Only Lestov showed any objectivity.

"He didn't mention us: give a reason for our not being there?"

"Charlie did," said Miriam. Just as succinctly she paraphrased Charlie's responses. Before she finished, Charlie was the sole object of attention.

"Where's your evidence for all this special wartime prisoner conjecture?" Denebin demanded.

"Doesn't what you recovered from the grave support that supposition?" Charlie came back, never the poker player to miss the chance to bluff.

"No," denied the man.

Miriam was determinedly silent, recognizing the game. Vitali Novikov's eyes were everywhere, seeking guidance and not getting it. Lestov and the other pathologist were equally lost but concealed it better.

"What contradicts it?" demanded Charlie. The other man was playing well.

"What supports it?" matched Denebin.

"It was a nine-millimeter bullet, wasn't it?" tempted Charlie.

"No. It . . ." blurted Denebin, too intent, before realizing the admission.

"That certainly knocks my theory," said Charlie, in apparent defeat. "What *was* the caliber?"

"The bullet was too badly distorted for me to be certain," said the scientist. "A lot of it had splintered against a rock."

Show-your-hand time, decided Charlie. "But the casing you recovered—what was it, from that fourth section of the grave you taped off?—that wasn't damaged at all as far as I could see."

Denebin stared directly at Charlie for several moments, red-faced, throat moving. There was no sound or movement from anyone else. Even the insect buzz seemed subdued. Finally the forensic scientist said, "It was .38."

"Now, that *really* means I've misled everyone, doesn't it? But gives us a lot more to think about. What conclusion have you reached about that?"

"I haven't," said the Russian, tightly, seemingly aware for the first time of their audience.

It should all be downhill from now on, Charlie thought. "What about the shrapnel? You must have a theory about that? So much of it?"

"A bomb of some sort."

"Several small bombs? Grenades, for instance?"

"Possibly."

"That's what I thought," said Charlie. It was always essential to get a positive confirmation. It wouldn't have taken them long to realize that neither German nor Russian handguns of the Second World War fired .38 bullets, but without the significance of the torn-out trouser band label it would just be an additional mystery, most probably dismissed as having come from a captured Western weapon. And still would be because he didn't intend telling them. He turned to Novikov, offering the release papers. "Could we call the American embassy from here, get the aircraft on its way?"

"You've finished?" The pathologist frowned.

"No," said Charlie. "We've scarcely started."

Miriam emerged from Novikov's office and said, "Saul is already on his way here with the plane. All hell's broken loose."

The transportation coffins were remarkably well made, but Novikov, embarrassed, couldn't find anything better than newspaper to wrap the uniform. To keep the recovered contents safe, Charlie put them back into tightly buttoned pockets and folded the clothing in upon itself. Miriam did the same. It was all completed quickly enough for the Russians to wait and accept Novikov's offer to drive them all back to the Ontario.

The ambush—particularly the already-setup television cameras— was visible some way from the hotel.

Olga at once said, "No!"

Lestov turned to Charlie, ignoring her. "It happened just as you told us?"

"Exactly how Miriam said," assured Charlie.

"Then yes!" insisted the homicide detective.

They were briefly engulfed as they got out of the car, and Charlie swallowed against laughing. There clearly hadn't been sufficient graveside protection and everyone was gargoyle-faced from bites and stings, some more bubbled and bumped than Miriam had been at her worst. One very badly swollen TV reporter was making a point of his appearance in a live introduction: Charlie heard "hell on earth" and decided the country-proud Valentin Ivanovich Polyakov was going to be a very pissed off chief minister and that the bastard deserved it.

It got worse the moment Lestov began talking, but the melee helped cover Lestov's initial stammering, which quickly went. He was glad, said the militia colonel, that the Russian participation had been made clear at the earlier meeting. He could not understand why they had been excluded from that meeting. He could only assume a misunderstanding, which was unfortunate, or intentional obstruction, which would be curious and which he understood even less. He expected Moscow to ask the Yakutsk authorities for an explanation, Russian help having been very specifically asked for because of local investigative limitations. It was fortunate the working relationship with the two Western investigators had, by comparison, been so good. It was only when Lestov suggested that the Yakutsk militia commissioner might be able to explain the problem that Charlie became aware of Ryabov and Kurshin at the edge of the press pack. The attention and the cameras immediately switched to the word-blocked local police chief.

Vitali Novikov hadn't moved from beside his car. Neither had Charlie. The pathologist said, "You're going back immediately?"

Charlie said, "Yes."

"I wanted more time!"

"There isn't any."

The pathologist swallowed, not immediately finding the words. Then, in a rush, he said, "Get us out: me and Marina and the boys. Please!"

"What have you got?"

"Get us out first."

"Do you know the whole story?"

"Most of it."

"You don't, do you?" challenged Charlie.

"More than anyone else. I told you about the camp."

Quickly Charlie passed the man his official card with his direct embassy number. "I will do everything I can." It would surely be easy: Natalia worked in the very ministry necessary to grant permission.

"Get us out and I'll give you everything."

"You'd have to."

There were two waiting demands from Raymond McDowell for his calls to be immediately returned when Charlie finally entered the hotel, warding off, as he walked, repeated demands for individual interviews and photo opportunities. His telephone was ringing as he entered his room.

McDowell said, "This is terrible!"

"No it's not," contradicted Charlie. Polyakov wouldn't have canceled the monitor.

"London wants a full explanation at once."

For the benefit of the listening public, Charlie said, "I'm sure they do. I think there should be an official note to the government here, asking for one."

There was momentary silence. "What are you talking about?"

"Our calls are tapped!"

The silence this time was longer. "What's happening?" asked McDowell, less stridently.

"I'm coming back tonight, on an American charter. With the body and what was found on it."

"What shall I tell London?"

"That I'll speak to them tomorrow. And to go on watching television."

It took another $50 note to persuade the hotel receptionist to summon a taxi, which seemed to be collapsing as dramatically as most of the buildings they passed on their way to the airport. The two coffins were already there. The Aeroflot charter wasn't. Its arrival was promised within thirty minutes.

Both Charlie and Miriam chose to remain in the luggage shed with the bodies rather than go into the hard-chaired, tobacco-fugged departure lounge. They didn't find a lot to say. They were both alert to the entry into the shed of any vehicle or uniformed official, other than those handling the luggage of schedule flight passengers. Charlie thought his newspaper-wrapped uniform was better-packaged and -tied than a lot of the items that went by on the arthritic conveyor belt. Miriam hadn't surrendered hers since bundling it up in the mortuary, either.

The charter was an hour late. Saul Freeman flurried officiously into the shed, immediately set off balance by Charlie's presence beside a second coffin.

At once the FBI chief said, "There's no agreement about this! We've got enough—"

"Saul!" stopped the woman. "Shut the fuck up. We're getting out together. No discussion. Okay?"

Freeman looked hesitantly between Miriam and Charlie. "You've got to understand—" he tried, but again she cut him off.

"Saul! You're not listening! Let's get the coffins on the plane and the plane off the ground, while we're still able. I'm sure you've got a great speech prepared and I can't wait to hear it later. But *later*!"

There were some luggage handlers, none Asian-featured superstitious Yakuts, hovering and Charlie waved more $10 notes like flags at a parade. At once the coffins were loaded onto trolleys. Automatically Miriam and Charlie walked beside that for which they were responsible, each with a protective hand resting on the lid. There was only a very small passenger area beyond the hold, but neither Charlie nor Miriam looked for it until after the coffins were not just roped securely into their carrying space but the loading bay ramp was raised. Both finally sagged with the click of its lock.

"I want to know what went on—*is* going on!" demanded Freeman, when they finally pushed aside the curtain separating the cargo bay and slumped into canvas bucket seats.

"It's a very long story that can wait," said Miriam. "Charlie and I have a lot to talk about ourselves first, before we can make any sense of anything. So please, let's wait until we can get our heads straight."

"We've got people flying in from Washington, for Christ's sake!" said Freeman, awed.

"Good," said Miriam. "You brought anything to drink?"

"A little Jack Daniel's," admitted the Bureau chief, blinking.

Miriam held out her hand, unspeaking. From the briefcase beside his seat Freeman produced a bottle three-quarters full and when she remained with her hand outstretched followed with polystyrene cups.

Miriam drank deeply and, looking out of the window at the moment of takeoff, said, "It's like being in one of those great escape movies." She lifted her cup in a toast. "We made it!"

"I wasn't sure we would," admitted Charlie.

"For God's sake, will someone tell me what's going on?" implored Freeman.

"We got set up," conceded Miriam, simply. "But out of ten I'd score our recovery at six."

"That's about right," agreed Charlie.

"And we got our Unknown Soldier back. Both of them." Miriam

stretched out, pushing herself as far back in the stiff canvas as she could. "Now I'm pretty exhausted."

"You're happy for this to be your thing, is that right?" demanded Freeman, hopefully.

"I guess that's it," sighed Miriam.

"Your choice," said the man. "It's your ass."

"I just made it," said Miriam. "And the ass is intact."

They all settled as best they could, trying to sleep, but Charlie was always subconsciously aware of being aboard a droning aircraft and gave up after about an hour. As he thrust himself up in his seat he became aware of Miriam sitting up, too. Freeman snored on.

They didn't speak for a long time, their refilled cups in their laps. Finally Miriam said, "You know what I think?"

"What?"

"I think if some gal had something you needed badly enough to know and if to screw her was the way to get it, you'd screw her."

Charlie said, "There a point to this conversation?"

"Don't want you sitting in judgment on me, like you've got the moral high ground, Okay?"

"Okay," said Charlie. There was a lot he liked about Miriam Bell.

"I thought he did something dull . . . something to do with trade!" said Irena. "Now I learn he's . . ." she waved her hands across the dinner table, seeking a metaphor. Remembering a Russian-dubbed English series that had just ended on Moscow television, she finished, "A Sherlock Holmes!"

Probably not for much longer, thought Cartright, glad he was on the absolute edge of the hurricane that was sweeping through the embassy. He was still recovering from the revelation that Charlie was living with Irena's sister. "It's kind of an unusual job."

"How'd he get an apartment like they have? It's in what used to be a palace. Incredible!"

"So I understand."

"Does everyone at the embassy live like that?"

"He's not properly attached to the embassy," said Cartright, knowing from the military attaché that deniability was already being considered. "I guess you'd say he was freelance."

"Obviously a very successful one!" Cartright was much better looking than the American and she hoped he would be better in bed, too. He obviously wasn't so mean. The restaurant was just off the Arbat, called the Here and Now, and was the social spot of the moment at which to be seen, which she considered promising. So was the imported champagne he'd automatically ordered. She was glad she'd worn the Donna Karan she'd bought in New York. He couldn't keep his eyes off her cleavage.

"Hasn't Natalia told you all about him?" questioned Cartright, trying to get the conversation on track.

"We're not particularly close," dismissed Irena. She was sure the five-man group at the bar were mafia. One smiled at her. She smiled back.

"See a friend?"

"I thought I had. It wasn't."

"Natalia probably considers herself very lucky, able to live in an apartment like that. Accommodation isn't easy in Moscow, is it?"

"She had a pretty impressive place before." Irena didn't return the mafia man's smile this time.

"If it's as grand as you say, they probably do a lot of entertaining?"

"I wouldn't know. Like I said, we're not close." The quail was wonderful and from the attention she was attracting Irena was sure the dark-haired girl who'd just come in was the star of the gangster series getting the top TV ratings. Irena was enjoying herself. The tuxedoed band began playing Glen Miller's "In the Mood." "A girl could get jealous at someone being more interested in her sister than in her," Irena protested, pushing her plate and her chair away at the same time. "Come on! Let's dance. And stop talking about Natalia and Charlie."

Enough, decided Cartright. There was absolutely no hurry, she had the most spectacular tits and there was Saul Freeman's recommendation.

During the evening the man she was sure was mafia intercepted Irena on her way to the washroom and asked her if she needed rescuing. She said no but added that she appreciated the gallantry and when he said anytime she gave him her telephone number.

Cartright started to get out of his car when they got to her apartment, in the Moscow suburbs on the way conveniently to Sheremet'yevo airport, but she stopped him, lying that she had to be up very early the following morning for a flight.

"Perhaps next time," she said. Maybe she'd found herself someone with money, like Natalia. Discovering what he was like in bed could wait.

14

They had remained in conference practically the entire day, broken only by Sir Rupert Dean's summons to Downing Street. Patrick Pacey, the department's political officer, went with him. The director-general had also several times spoken to the Moscow embassy by telephone—to the ambassador as well as to the head of chancellery—and when he'd finally managed a connection to the Ontario Hotel in Yakutsk it had been eight P.M. local time there and he'd been told that Charlie had checked out.

Throughout the day the attitudes toward Charlie Muffin ebbed and flowed. Initially, after his Nazi-secret declaration, the criticism and accusations had been virtually unanimous, determinedly led by an inwardly very satisfied Gerald Williams, totally supported by the deputy director-general. A lot of the condemnation became muted—or stopped altogether—after the second TV transmission of the hotel parking lot interview with Colonel Vadim Lestov.

Dean said, "We don't know enough to reach any conclusion or judgment."

"And whose fault is that?" demanded the finance director. "Muffin was repeatedly told—*ordered*—to maintain the closest contact and report back everything we needed to know and at all costs avoid any reference to possible intelligence and difficult diplomatic situations. He's done the total and complete opposite, as he always does. And as I have consistently warned that he would. To relay a message telling us to watch television was arrogant impertinence."

"Made sense, though, to see and hear what the Moscow detective said, didn't it?" sighed Jeremy Simpson, the legal adviser. "Muffin also told the Moscow embassy his phone was tapped. Seems a good enough reason for saying nothing."

"He said a lot *on* television," pointed out Jocelyn Hamilton.

"Which remains the problem," agreed Patrick Pacey, knowing the political thinking from having attended the cabinet Intelligence and Security Committee meeting at Downing Street with the director-general. "The last thing the government wants is reminders of Germany's wartime past, now that we're European partners. Or having one of our people sitting beside the Yakutsk leader like that, publicly associated with an anti-Russian attack."

"Made worse by drawing attention to the sort of place Yakutskaya was," persisted Gerald Williams. "I can't imagine Russia wants that raked over. From whichever way we look at it, Muffin has put us—this department—in an appalling situation."

"One, in fact, that we've already agreed we had to do everything to avoid, with our whole future so uncertain," endorsed Hamilton. "There might be an explanation of sorts, but I'll need a lot to convince me it was justified."

"That's a gross exaggeration," argued the bald, mustached lawyer. "Quite obviously there were a lot of local problems we don't yet know anything about. The Moscow detective went out of his way to *say* how good the relationship was. Which was exactly what Muffin was told to establish."

"I think the enormous publicity is unfortunate," said Pacey, echoing another concern from the earlier Downing Street crisis meeting. "There'd been no public announcement of our being officially allowed to have a man in Moscow. The inference that Russia needs Western help to fight its crime isn't something we wanted to become too obvious."

"Which it didn't. And hasn't," insisted Dean, forcefully. "It's entirely acceptable that someone from the UK—whose department was never identified—should have been in Yakutsk looking into the murder of a British officer, whenever the killing occurred. It was never stated that Charlie was based in Moscow or that he had any intelligence agency background. You inferred it was said, because you *know.*"

Pacey flushed, caught out. "No," he remembered. "It wasn't, was it?"

Williams felt a further fray in what he'd been so sure was the noose from which Charlie was at last going to dangle. He said, "With anyone else, it would not be necessary for us to be having this discussion: having to defend ourselves, cap in hand, in Downing Street! If this department becomes subsidiary to all those willing and eager to take over our traditional role, it will be dated back to this episode." The finance director looked to the required records taker. "None of us will be here in a year's time for us to be reminded of the warning I've just given."

"If, on the other hand, we were all here—and I called for a transcript of what you've said all day—you'd be shown to be an absolute fool, wouldn't you Gerald?" said Simpson. He stroked the drooping mustache. "And I will. There! You've got a whole year to work out an explanation for being so wrong."

"I don't want this to become personal," warned Sir Rupert Dean.

"Unfortunately—and usually unfairly—it's always been personal between Charlie Muffin and Gerald," said Simpson.

"Every complaint and every warning about this man has been justified by what's happened," insisted Williams. "It's no pleasure for me to have been proven right."

"You haven't been," said Simpson. "Not yet."

"When's our first chance to speak to him properly?" asked Hamilton.

"Tomorrow morning," said Dean.

"Every conceivable thing that could have gone wrong has gone wrong," insisted Gerald Williams, desperate for the last convincing word.

At that moment Natalia was entering the Russian analysis meeting thinking exactly the same thing. She also suspected her personal survival could be at risk. She hoped she hadn't miscalculated as she believed her opposition had. It wouldn't take her long to find out.

"Outrageous!" declared Dmitri Nikulin. "Internationally we have been made to look ridiculous by a tinpot quasi republic still living in the Stone Age. How? Tell me how!"

The head of the presidential secretariat talked directly to Natalia, who in turn looked to Petr Travin beside her. She said, "My deputy has had all the operational dealings today. Unfortunately, there hasn't apparently been time for him to advise me."

Travin had three times claimed he was too occupied talking direct to Yakutsk to give her an account of what was happening, an open challenge to her authority. She knew the man wouldn't have attempted that without the backing of the deputy interior minister, Viktor Viskov, who sat opposite, fixed-faced, studiously avoiding the man he'd personally appointed to be her deputy and his spy. If this was their chosen moment for a coup, they'd mistimed it.

This afternoon's meeting had initially been scheduled for the following day, which would possibly have given them the opportunity to complete whatever they were manipulating. But Nikulin's unexpected decision to bring it forward gave her the most influential audience in front of which to fight, turning Travin's evasion back upon the man by insisting—in memoranda to the president's chief of staff—that Travin attend to explain his lack of contact. And bringing the meeting so abruptly and unexpectedly forward hinted the intervention of the president himself, which she guessed to be the main reason for Viskov's discomfort. From his implacable silence she decided presidential pressure was also the inference drawn by the deputy foreign minister, Mikhail Suslov, the fifth person in Nikulin's office.

Nikulin frowned between Natalia and her deputy and then said to Travin, "What's going on here?"

"It's been very difficult . . . bad communications," stumbled Travin, losing his usual smooth-mannered control. "From what I understand, there was no warning, no agreement, to meet the press. The Westerners imagined they were only going to see the chief minister, possibly the Executive Council. We were specifically excluded."

Charlie had looked trapped, Natalia remembered. Why hadn't he called? She would have been so much better prepared if they'd talked. It was like trying to walk blindfolded in the dark, but she was sure there was some high ground she could gain if war had been openly declared. She said, "Colonel Lestov was my choice and I think he's proved to be a good one. He made the whole episode, which I accept we still have properly to have explained, appear the mistake—the stupidity—of the Yakutsk authorities. . . ." She looked directly at

Travin again. "He talked on television of our demanding an explanation. What did he say to you about that?"

"We didn't go into that," said her deputy, uneasily. "At the moment there's some difficulty about the release of the body they believe to be that of a Russian woman. The Americans and the English are on their way back with their nationals."

Natalia avoided any surprised reaction to the news of Charlie's return. "Our pathologist has conducted her own autopsy, hasn't she?" she persisted, not allowing Travin any relief.

"As far as I understand it, yes," said the man.

"Don't you know?" demanded Nikulin, exasperated.

"Yes," blurted Travin.

"What about everything else? Is there anything more for them to do there?" demanded Natalia.

"I don't . . . I thought they should wait, to bring the body back. To avoid it appearing that they weren't in control. The media are still there. You've seen the headlines in our own press. I gather it's much more in the West."

"I don't think they should wait at all!' said Natalia, looking more fully around the chief of staff's office. "Let's use the media and the Yakutsk stupidity. Recall our people, having completed their investigation, and let them announce their regret at the body being held and prevented from a civilized burial. Match it with a statement from here, formally asking why that proper burial is being prevented of someone obviously the victim of a terrible crime. Yakutsk will be caught, whichever way they respond. If they return the body, they'll be complying with our demand. If they don't, a proper burial there will also be what we demanded. . . ." She looked at the deputy interior minister. "Don't you agree that publicly we would appear to be in control either way?"

"I suppose so. Perhaps," conceded Viskov, reluctantly.

"It sounds good to me," said Mikhail Suslov.

"I can't see a problem with it, either," said Nikulin. "In fact, I think it's something we should do. . . ." Pointedly addressing her, the presidential aide said. "And I think it is something that you should do personally, Natalia Nikandrova. Brief Colonel Lestov and prepare our announcement from here."

Travin was white-faced, staring accusingly at Viskov, who still refused to answer the look.

Carefully trying to judge a safe contribution to the discussion, the deputy foreign minister said, "What do we know about this Englishman's story of wartime mysteries?"

Travin shifted, the attention back upon him. "Colonel Lestov was only with him and the American woman for about two hours before they flew out. It was the woman who gave them a résumé of what he'd said but not any explanation—any facts—to support it."

"So we *are* dependent upon cooperation?" said Nikulin.

As I have been from the beginning, acknowledged Natalia, finally. Charlie would tell her all she needed to know, to answer all the questions, but most importantly to defend herself—themselves—from any internal attack, within the ministry. Refusing to give up on Travin, she said, "You brought them officially together, as a group. Will there be sufficient cooperation?"

Imagining an escape, Travin said, "I don't believe there's been a lot of exchange so far. I found the Englishman belligerent: obstructive. The impression in Yakutsk has been that he's ineffective."

Charlie's favorite chameleon color, Natalia recognized. "Let's hope you're wrong."

"What do we know about him?" asked Nikulin, abruptly.

Natalia felt the first jump of concern. Quickly she said, "He was posted here by agreement, about a year after the official assignment of FBI representation, to cooperate on organized crime—"

"And was largely responsible for the breaking up of a nuclear smuggling incident involving Natalia Nikandrova's previous deputy," came in Viskov, accusingly.

"And other government officials," fought back Natalia.

"He's here by our permission, like the FBI?" queried Nikulin.

"Yes," agreed Viskov.

"Then I don't see that we have a problem," said the presidential adviser, going to the deputy foreign minister. "If there isn't a full exchange, we tell his government to withdraw him."

How much more impossible was it all going to get? Natalia wondered.

The man traveling on the State Department plane with Kenton Peters lay Charlie Muffin's file aside and said, "Ornery son-of-a-bitch." There was a strong Texan accent.

"Who did the Agency a lot of harm in the past," reminded Peters.

"You want it to be an accident? Or obvious?" The operational name on the passport was Henry Packer. It was his own idea of a joke to describe himself as a pipeline specialist on his visa.

"I haven't decided yet. At the moment you're just getting sight of the rabbit."

"Whatever you say."

"Does it matter one way or the other?"

"No," said Packer. "Just want to provide maximum satisfaction. I aim to please as well as aim straight.

That was another joke, but Peters didn't smile.

15

It was what Muscovites call a Napoleon Day, the dawn sun burning from a cloudless sky to set fire to Moscow's near-deserted streets as they really had been torched to drive out the briefly occupying French emperor. Charlie hoped it wasn't an omen. The Americans had transportation—a van large enough for both coffins—at Domodedovo airport and Charlie continued to impose, actually being driven first and direct to the river-bordering Morisa Toreza. He parted from Miriam Bell in the British embassy forecourt with promises to talk later in the day.

"Make sure you do," insisted the woman. Saul Freeman barely waved.

The embassy watchman complained he hadn't been warned about the arrival of a corpse and wasn't sure about storage because he hadn't had to deal with a dead body since his posting. The man couldn't find a cart and he and Charlie needed several stops staggering with the coffin between them to the canteen's walk-in refrigerator in the basement. The watchman said the chef wouldn't like it and Charlie agreed he probably wouldn't and promised to take the blame.

"You've got a rotten job," remarked the man.

Charlie said he knew. The night duty officer at the embassy switchboard was dozing when Charlie walked in, snuffling awake at Charlie's greeting. It only took Charlie minutes to discover what he wanted in the London telephone directory and he smiled at something proving easy for a change.

Everything in his hutchlike officer was filmed with dust. The paper plane prototype he'd been working on lay forgotten under the desk: the cleaners had obviously forgotten the room altogether. There were three demands for immediate contact from Sir Rupert Dean on his voice mail, the last at ten the previous night. Charlie put messages on theirs for McDowell, the military attaché and Cartright, telling them he was back.

So clear was everything in his mind that it only took Charlie an hour to write what he intended telling London at that stage, which wasn't everything. There was, for example, no mention whatsoever of Vitali Maksimovich Novikov, only of Gulag 98. It was still only six-thirty when he made his way familiarly to the cipher room for his findings to be encoded, satisfied that because of the time difference it would reach London to coincide with Sir Rupert Dean's arrival for his normal day.

Charlie guessed he had about half an hour. Natalia answered on the first ring. "Good to hear your voice."

"My telephone was tapped."

Natalia smiled bleakly to herself. "I guessed there was a reason."

"How's Sasha?"

"Missing you."

"How about you?"

"Don't ask a silly question."

"Can I speak to her?"

"She's still asleep. She wondered what you were doing on television."

"A lot of people did. And still do. You all right?" He thought she sounded subdued.

"There's another problem, to go with all the others."

"Serious?"

"Could be. Depends how I handle it."

"Connected with this?"

"People seeing an advantage in it."

"Who's ahead at the moment?"

"I think I am."

"We'll keep it that way."

Natalia smiled again, warmed by the confidence. "I saw both television transmissions. It looked chaotic."

"Something like that."

"How'd it work out?"

"Pretty good, I think. We'll talk about it."

"We need to," she said, pointedly.

The final good-bye to separating integrity, he guessed: it would be a giant leap forward. "I can keep you ahead, believe me." I hope, he thought.

"What about Yakutsk itself?"

"Unbelievable."

"How was the American girl?"

"Clever."

"She looked a mess on TV."

Charlie frowned at the obviousness. "That's why I didn't sleep with her."

"You get the chance?"

"Natalia!"

"I was joking."

Charlie wasn't sure she had been, but either way that was an improvement, too. Past pressure or whatever had arisen now? "So was I."

"When will you be home?"

"It's going to be a busy day. Do you want to talk on the telephone?" It was a coded question.

"Maybe not."

So she wasn't sure if the Lesnaya telephone was clean. But it was his apartment: if their telephone was tapped, their being together had already been discovered. Natalia wasn't thinking clearly. "We could lunch?"

"Maybe walk, like we used to a long time ago."

She *was* worried, Charlie realized. During his phony defection, when their relationship would have meant automatic imprisonment or, for her, even worse, they'd risked trysts in the botanical gardens on Botanicheskiy Sad. "Noon," he suggested.

"It *is* good to have you back." Her relief was obvious.

"For me, too." The second line on his console began flickering urgently. "I've got to go."

"At last!" greeted the director-general, when Charlie pressed the button.

"No one's going to like the idea of another English officer being a killer," criticized Dean at once. The man had the calm, encouraging voice of the university professor he'd once been, inviting debate.

"The inside of a uniform jacket would have been the obvious place to look for names, the tailor's or the owner's," set out Charlie, patiently. "The inside of a trouser band wouldn't be, to anyone but another Englishman who would *know* British military tailors duplicate like that. Only officers get their uniforms tailored. Only another officer would have known."

"Tenuous," challenged the other man.

"The Russian military Makarov fires bullets slightly larger than those of the nine-millimeter German Walther from which it's copied," said Charlie. "They weigh ten grams, the weight and size of the two recovered from the male bodies. The bullet that killed the woman was .38 caliber. The British army Mark IV Webley fires .38."

"By 1944—the marker date on the coin in our man's pocket—every army was fighting with every other nation's weapons!"

"I think a British caliber bullet is significant and I think it's worth checking, against the tailoring" persisted Charlie. "And we *can* check. We've got sufficient label material for a positive identification. And it shouldn't be particularly difficult."

"Take me through it," demanded the director-general.

"There are only five military tailors in London: I checked the London directory as soon as I got back here this morning. And only one of those five has a name with an initial letter to match a scrap of the label left inside the trouser waistband. It's so small it looks like a *C*, but it's not. I think it's *G*—Gieves and Hawkes, at 1 Savile Row, London. From the inscription in the cigarette case we've got the initials of the customer's name, S. N. And his specific measurements, to help the trace. . . ."

"It all sounds remarkably simple," agreed Dean.

"The cigarette case inscription helps a lot, apart from the initials," suggested Charlie. "You'll know far better than me, but I don't believe there were more than a handful of universities in England in 1932, when we know he graduated. We know, too, that he got a First, which should narrow the search down. And we also know— for whatever reason—there was only a father. No mother."

Charlie heard the rustle of turning pages from the other end. Dean said, "The marks of a missing signet ring? No wallet? No military identification? Why take away the obvious identification but still leave enough from which we can possibly get a name anyway?"

"I don't have an answer to that," admitted Charlie. "Maybe they thought they had it all: did the obvious, as you say, but didn't look for other things. They were killed in what passes for summer there: the medical examiner found insects in all three bodies. Yet they had to use grenades to get them buried as deeply as they did. Perhaps they never thought there'd be a thaw this severe. There hasn't been, for more than fifty years."

"You're sure there would have had to be official Russian knowledge of their being in Yakutsk?"

"Totally," said Charlie, at once. "That was a closed penal colony—not even known about in the West during the war."

"So how did a British and American officer come officially to be there? And then get murdered?"

"Another question on a long list I don't have the answer to," said Charlie, in further admission. "Something else I think we should bear in mind is our man's uniform. Buttons on officers' uniforms usually carry their regiment's insignia, don't they . . . ?"

"I believe so," agreed the director-general.

"The buttons on this lieutenant's uniform don't," reminded Charlie.

"You suggesting a secret intelligence unit?"

"I'm not ruling it out."

"A British officer, possibly intelligence-linked, in a part of the Soviet Union where he had no right to be—and therefore no permission to be—killed for being there," mused Sir Rupert Dean, reflectively. "Working, somehow, in some way, with an American of matching rank. Somewhere there has to be a record."

"Of the operation, perhaps," accepted Charlie. "What would it say about their disappearance?"

"Stalin was too paranoid ever to have allowed British and American intelligence into a place like Yakustkaya," insisted the sociopolitical professor. "Whoever got them to Yakutsk did it without Kremlin knowledge or agreement."

"So they just had to disappear, without explanation?"

"It was wartime," said Dean, reminding in return. "Hundreds—thousands—disappeared without explanation. Stalin was our ally. Neither Britain nor America could have *admitted* spying on him, although of course we did."

"That's all a long time ago," said Charlie.

"But not to be dismissed until we know what they were doing there," persisted the director-general. "It *is* a long time ago. All the history has been written: tidied up, as history always is. Two possible intelligence officers, together as they were, *where* they were, *is* phenomenal. If the secrets of what Stalin had created in Yakutskaya had leaked out—after the war had turned in our favor—it could have been enough to break the West's alliance with Russia. And had the West split with Stalin, there wouldn't have been the division of Europe at Yalta and Potsdam. Imagine that. No Soviet Union, no forty years of communist stranglehold on Eastern Europe, no Cold War, no God knows what else. . . ." He snorted a laugh, unamused. "You could have been inches from the truth, not fantasizing, when you talked of wartime mysteries!"

Charlie Muffin, who prided himself as an Olympic-class mental sprinter against his physical difficulty to reach a shuffling trot, recognized that his academic controller was practically out of sight ahead of him. Struggling to keep up—an unpleasant experience—Charlie said, "Can we speculate that much, this early?"

"We can imagine a possible scenario," insisted the other man. "Gulag 98 is the obvious key."

"I understand no records exist in Yakutsk."

"Mosow's the most likely," suggested Dean. "Trial and deportation documents, even."

"I would think so."

"How much of what you've told me—written in your report—do the American and the Russians have or know?" demanded the director-general.

"The local autopsy reports, detailing all the body marks, were shared," recounted Charlie. "So were the lists of belongings found on each body, but there was a mistake I didn't correct. The inscription in the cigarette case is copperplate, all swirls and curlicues. The initials were copied down wrongly: the sweeping old English *F*— representing an *S*—was taken really to be *F* so it's inaccurate. The Russian forensic scientist has full and undistorted photographs of all three faces, which we should get copies of. We can get our own from our own body. The two nine-millimeter bullets are common knowledge. And the .38 and the shrapnel from the grenades that made the grave. I'm sure neither have the waistband label. . . ." He hesitated. "That's all, I think. They would have seen the marks where the ring was missing on our lieutenant, as I saw that things had been snatched or ripped from the other two bodies."

"You haven't mentioned Gulag 98."

"I'm going to need the Russians to trace records," said Charlie. "I don't think the Americans have it."

"We're supposed to be in tandem with Washington," reminded Dean.

"Tell Washington that."

"You think they're holding back?"

"I think for a situation involving so many people, agencies and government departments there's an echoing lack of reciprocal information."

"The same has occurred to me," said Dean.

"Until we start getting a little back, it might be an idea to keep our hand covered."

"You didn't *offer* anything: interpret the fact they weren't armed, anything like that?"

"No," assured Charlie.

"You got a lot, Charlie—concluded a lot," praised Dean. "And you're right. We should be able to find a name, this end. But until we do—and get an idea of what our dead man was doing—I agree we should keep a tight lid on things."

How difficult might it be following that instruction and resolving

Natalia's new, as yet unknown problem? Everything had to be adjustable, as long as it was in his favor. He said, "The people at the embassy here will want an explanation."

Sir Rupert Dean was silent for several moments. "And we've got to maintain a working relationship there," he agreed. There was another silence. "Keep it all general, without positively lying. Particularly test out Gallaway. When this first broke, I expected it to be a military investigation, but the Defense Ministry ran a mile, not wanting to dirty their hands. Maybe they know something they're not telling us."

"*Will* they tell us, ever?" questioned Charlie, more to gauge the other man's thinking than for the answer. He was pleased at the director-general's acceptance of what had, until now, only been a suspicion.

"Not if they don't want to. Or can't," said Dean, simply. "It's not just identifiable responsibility everyone's running from. The publicity is hysterical. Questions are being asked in the House. Daily demands for a statement from the prime minister. It's all getting out of hand."

"I'll have whoever's job it is get the body and belongings back today," promised Charlie.

There was another silence. Then Dean said, "I might bring you back: continue here what you've started there. Be ready, if I do."

That would leave Natalia—and Sasha—alone. Which he couldn't do, not immediately—not until he'd sorted out whatever it was that was worrying her. Quickly Charlie said, "Shouldn't I first see what the Americans and Russians are prepared to share? There seems to be some anxiety in the American embassy about people flying in from Washington."

"This has waited more than fifty years. I'm not counting in days," said Dean.

He was, thought Charlie, if there was any danger to his Moscow appointment. Or to Natalia. And apart from the voice mail impatience and the director-general's initial greeting, there hadn't been any rebuke. Praise, even. Probingly he said, "I'm sorry I wasn't able to say more from Yakutsk. If it caused any problems."

"Nothing serious," dismissed the director-general. "Certainly nothing that needs to be discussed after this conversation."

"I got the impression of a lot of angst in London."

"Your only concern is my support. And you have it."

Charlie celebrated the moment of satisfaction by picking up the airplane with the separate tail section and on impulse tried a test flight at the moment Colonel John Gallaway flustered into the room. The plane crashed at the military attaché's feet. The immaculate, cologne-smelling man frowned at the bristle-chinned, crumpled Charlie and said, "What in God's name is going on?"

"Just seeing if it would fly as well as my ideas," said Charlie.

"It didn't," said Gallaway.

They gathered in Gallaway's office because that was where the six surviving wartime photographs had been assembled. Charlie carried with him the lieutenant's uniform, which he decided smelled only slightly worse than he did, and everything it had contained. While McDowell, Gallaway, and Cartright prodded and poked among it all, Charlie took the pictures to the window, where the sun's early promise had been fulfilled with a brilliantly bright day. The glare made him feel gravel-eyed, from tiredness.

The photographs were grainy and sepia-faded from age. Among the recommendations he'd already sent to London—carefully retrieved from the cipher room, with everything else, on his way to Gallaway's suite—was that a Foreign Office and Defense Ministry archive search be made there for wartime pictures and Charlie decided to ship Gallaway's trove back with the body of the dead man, despite there being no one in the prints even vaguely resembling the long-dead man in the basement refrigerator.

He didn't hurry providing a greatly edited account of Yakutsk to the other three men. He omitted completely his belief of there being a second British officer involved.

"So!" he finished, looking at the military attaché. "That's my story. What's yours, from the Ministry of Defense files about an intelligence operation?"

"Absolutely nothing!" declared Gallaway, glibly. "There wasn't one."

Charlie let the silence settle, until the others began to stir uncomfortably, not understanding. "Okay," sighed Charlie. "The body of an English officer, wearing an English officer's uniform, is in a grenade-created grave in a part of Siberia no one fifty years ago could get to. The Defense Ministry, which inherited the War Office, has no record of any lieutenant being there. Or here. . . ." Charlie paused, feeling another snatch of tiredness. "You tell me, John . . . you don't mind me calling you John, do you? I'd like you to call me Charlie." Unable to anticipate what was coming, Gallaway shook his head. "Thank you, John," Charlie resumed. "So you tell me, John, what our man was doing there unless he was on a covert operation? And then you try to convince me—with the amount of publicity that this is getting—that your ministry hasn't gone through every bus ticket and postage stamp receipt of its archives of fifty years ago to find out why a British army lieutenant was where he was. But before you do all that—John—you tell me what your brief is from London right now. 'Cause if you don't, I'm not going to share with you any more than I'm going to share with anyone else. And the loser—John—will be you. You think about it. . . ." Charlie looked sideways to Cartright. "And I'd like you to take that on board, too, Richard. Strikes me I'm doing all the work, being stung to buggery possibly in more ways than were obvious in Yakutsk, and getting very little back in return."

"I shall most definitely report everything about this conversation to London!" said Gallaway. His face was puce but not totally: there were isolated white blotches, making him lizard-skinned.

"I obviously will, too," said Cartright. "I've done everything I could think of to help. You can read my cable traffic if you like."

"I want all of you to do that," encouraged Charlie but ignoring the offer. "Just as I want you all to know I'm not making any accusations against you personally. It's not the way those bastards on the top floor operate. When you complain to London about me, you also tell them that I've got a lot more they'd like to know but I've got to get a lot more in exchange."

Gallaway was gulping for words when his telephone rang. He answered without greeting and just as wordlessly handed it to the head of chancellery. Raymond McDowell's face contorted into disbelief. "The body's in the canteen refrigerator! None of the staff will go in to get the food for breakfast!"

"I'm sorry," apologized Charlie. "I haven't got 'round to telling you."

Gerald Williams was right, thought Cartright. This man was practically beyond belief.

Natalia listened intently as Colonel Vadim Lestov recited back to her the statement she'd just dictated to him, knowing even the intonation was important, correcting the detective twice.

"We're going to issue something similar from here," she said, finally. She'd spent an hour that morning suggesting the phrasing with the deputy foreign minister, Mikhail Suslov, and a further hour waiting for any correction from their presidential adviser at the White House. Dmitri Nikulin hadn't called. There was only forty-five minutes before her meeting with Charlie.

"I'm very sorry," apologized Lestov. "Nothing has gone as it should have, as it was intended."

"You're not being held responsible."

"Why, then, is it you I'm being briefed by, not Colonel Travin?"

"This is political as well as being operational," said Natalia, cautiously. Politically survivable for whom? she wondered.

16

Belying the appearance of a man who always looked as if he'd crawled out from under an ancient hedge, Charlie Muffin was fastidiously clean: the way he dressed was camouflage for him to be overlooked, hopefully not even seen. Necessarily going back to Lesnaya to shower, shave and change—and even then make a telephone call—delayed him, but Charlie wouldn't anyway have arrived at the gardens ahead of Natalia.

She had never been operational, walking dark streets and even darker alleys; couldn't instinctively recognize the difference between shadows and shade, which after so long was second nature to Charlie. Not yet knowing her latest concern, he had to protect her, ensure she was alone. It had been Natalia who'd remembered their old rendezvous, so she'd remember the rules: expect him to check from somewhere unseen and know that if he didn't approach after half an hour he wouldn't make the meeting, not believing it safe.

She had to be wrong, overreacting, he told himself as he emerged from the Botanicheskiy Sad metro, cloaked by the crowd. This sort of thing had been necessary in the old, paranoid past, but one of the few real changes in Russia—Moscow, particularly—had been the ending of the KGB's spy-upon-spy internal control. In addition to which officially Natalia was no longer attached to an intelligence organization since her liaison transfer to the Interior Ministry.

His going through the charade of a clandestine meeting, behaving in the ways of that old, obsessive past, was important, though, for what it told him. Natalia *was* becoming paranoid: overpressured and overstrained trying to live as they were. As they had no alternative but to live. Charlie tried unsuccessfully to recall the Shakespeare quotation about a tangled web he'd had to learn at school, unable to remember if it was the same play that had the phrase about protesteth too much that had occurred to him that morning, confronting the supposedly outraged diplomats and offended intelligence officer. School had been a long time ago, like so much else seemed to be.

But not tradecraft.

Sure of the geography, Charlie eased into the park by the side gate, the one that gave him immediate cover from the arch-roofed hothouse and the branch-skirted gymnosperms. He saw Natalia at once. She was sitting on what he'd taught her to be their marker seat, from which he could isolate the people around her, seeking out the seemingly engrossed newspaper reader on adjoining benches or entwined lovers whose eyes never closed in ecstasy or pet owners whose dogs couldn't pee anymore.

Dutifully Natalia got up after a few minutes, striding forcefully off toward the rear gate, as if leaving: a never-fail trigger to startle a watcher into movement. Two newspaper readers read on. A third continued dozing. The solitary dog walker went on in the opposite direction. It was too early for lovers. Natalia sat as abruptly as she'd risen, on the seat closest to the first hothouse, not more than five meters from where Charlie stood beneath the tree canopy. The gardens remained tranquil, apart from the entry of a noisy school party of giggling girls who *were* giggling schoolgirls. Charlie still gave it another five minutes, smiling toward Natalia as he eventually approached.

He said, "That was nostalgic."

"I didn't need the memories."

"You'd better tell me about it."

Natalia did, at last, in short, tight sentences, finally holding back nothing, looking away from him most of the time.

Charlie didn't speak for several moments after she'd finished. "It was ridiculous, stupid, not to have told me from the beginning."

"I know. Now. I didn't guess how you'd react at there being an overhang from the Popov affair."

"There was an official inquiry. You were completely exonerated."

"Viktor Ivanovich was a member of the tribunal," she reminded Charlie, in turn. "He obviously didn't accept the finding."

"There couldn't be any other reason?"

"Not that I can think of. And I've thought about it a very great deal."

Charlie raised his hands, warding off apology before he spoke. "You couldn't have misunderstood?"

"Not after yesterday."

"Which you seem to have won?"

"This time. I need to go on winning."

"More than that, even. If they're trying to destroy you, you've got to destroy them."

"I'm so tired of playing games: our games, their game, anyone's game!"

"We're not playing games anymore," insisted Charlie. "We're going to fight."

"With what? I was lucky yesterday—the timing was in my favor—but it was a fluke. If I don't stay ahead on this every step of the way, I'll be replaced."

Charlie lapsed into silence again, immersed in thought. He wouldn't say it—couldn't say it—because the resolve had been obvious for a very long time and they'd shaken it to death like two dogs holding on to a single bone, but if Natalia *were* forced to leave the ministry—to become simply but all-importantly his proper legal wife, Sasha's mother—all their personal working difficulties would be ended, at a finger snap. But Natalia needed her job, as much as he needed his. Until now—uncertain, unsure now—both their personal lives had been a litany of one disaster imploding upon another. They were only confident about their professional ability and success, clinging to it as a blind man tightly holds his stick to get through each day without colliding with unseen obstacles. He said, "If they want a war, we'll take it to them."

Natalia said, "I've talked to Lestov. He thinks you had a lot you hadn't shared. According to the American woman, you're a sneaky son-of-a-bitch. Her words." That was an exaggeration, but Natalia had no difficulty with it.

So, thought an unoffended Charlie, was Miriam Bell. "You knew that without being told."

"Have you got something I can fight with?" demanded Natalia, gazing steadily at him.

Decision time, Charlie recognized: shit or get off the pot. Loyalty to the department? Or loyalty to Natalia? The department had cheated him and been disastrously cheated in return; and they'd cheat him again, if it became expedient to do so. Natalia had never cheated him—tried to even any score—despite the times and the ways he'd failed her. Nor, he thought, would she ever. And was the job as important to him as he'd tried to make out, with his elaborate blind man's analogy? Charlie was surprised he even needed to pose himself the question.

He stood, breathing in deeply, offering his hand to bring her up with him, and began slowly wandering the path toward the hothouses. And as they walked, Charlie told Natalia all he knew or thought he knew: even, toward the end, his director-general's now-ignored insistence that he offer as little as possible to gain as much as he could, until a reason was established for the English lieutenant being in Yakutsk.

"Miriam Bell's right. You are a sneaky son-of-a-bitch."

"Do you still have sufficient authority to try to find the records of Gulag 98?" demanded Charlie.

"It would have been Beria's time. The NKVD," Natalia recalled, talking as much to herself as to Charlie. "It's said that for more than a layered mile beneath the Lubyanka there's a virtual city beneath a city stretching as far as Red Square and the Kremlin and Ploshchad

Sverdlova, under the Bolshoi: Stalin had his own railway system, to move around it. One entire level is occupied by archives, hundreds of millions of them. Yakutskaya *was* one of the biggest secrets, so records might have been destroyed, as they were in Yakutsk itself. But we won't know that until we look."

"Don't be specific," warned Charlie. "A general inquiry about camps is an obvious extension of the inquiry: something you'd be expected to do. Isolating a specific camp at the very beginning wouldn't be, unless the information came from your own people."

"Charlie!" she protested, pained.

"If we're not going to take chances, we're not going to take chances," he said, offering Charlie Muffin logic. "Channel everything through you. You'll know what you're looking for. Dump the rest on Travin. Drown him. Nikulin is your secret weapon—so secret that he doesn't know it."

"You're going to have to spell this out for me step by step!" protested Natalia.

"You'll understand every little skirmish," promised Charlie.

"Recognize something?" she demanded, stopping abruptly where they were.

Charlie gazed around the huge glassed building with its giant, roof-sized fern leaves, realizing for the first time they'd actually gone into one of the houses. "No," he conceded.

"It's the same one you walked me to when you admitted your defection was phony and that you'd lied," identified Natalia. "It was right here you told me you were going to abandon me and go back to London."

The recollection—and the remorse—was immediate. Charlie said, "I came back. And this time I'm not abandoning you."

"No," accepted Natalia. "It's a good feeling."

Going personally to the American embassy, leaving the protection of his own territory for the uncertainty of theirs, was as conscious a psychological act as dressing to be despised and therefore underrated, despite Miriam Bell's suspicion. Charlie didn't expect an identity for the murdered American to be freely offered if it had already been found, but he'd sense the nuance if there had been progress. There were other considerations, too. The FBI quarters at Ulitza Chaykovskovo were far more extensive and certainly more luxurious than his badger's hole in which more than three people at any one time risked suffocation, and the American embassy mess extended happy hour to two and on occasions three. There was no drink price concession at all at the British bar. Charlie suspected Gerald Williams.

It had been Miriam's number he'd called from the Lesnaya apartment before leaving to meet Natalia, and the Americans were waiting for him, easily accommodated in Saul Freeman's office. It was little more than a passing impression that Miriam had showered and washed her hair and tried makeup on a face showing scarcely any sign of the Yakutsk ravages. His immediate concentration was upon two men already in the room, against a far wall almost as if they were not part of the intended gather. Charlie looked curiously, invitingly, to Freeman, who instead of introductions said, "Coupla guys from State. Just sitting in."

The elder, white-haired man was clear-skinned and tight-bodied and beak-nosed, which, combined with the length at which he wore his hair, gave him a patrician appearance. It was the second man who held Charlie's attention. He was slightly built and unobtrusively dressed in muted gray and sat completely unmoving. What registered most was washed-out blue eyes that never blinked. In Charlie's experience men with no name who didn't blink either wore six-guns in Western movies or ear protectors on practice ranges, where he'd never been able to stop blinking. And this man didn't look at all like an actor.

Determinedly Charlie said, "Hi. Charlie Muffin."

The two men nodded back but didn't speak.

Freeman said, "Must be good to get back?"

"Great," said Charlie. And waited.

"Good of you to come," said Freeman.

"We're all working together, aren't we?" Charlie spoke looking at the two silent strangers, able to see Miriam at the same time. She was subdued, unsmiling.

"Like to think so," agreed the FBI chief.

"So would I," said Charlie.

"Everything escalated while you were away. It's been a media circus. The president's responded with an executive order demanding answers. Plans an Arlington burial."

"Very impressive."

Freeman shifted, seemingly uncomfortable. "Thought it might be useful to talk through everything we've got."

Who thought? wondered Charlie. "I'd like to hear that, too." He took from his pocket a much-edited and sometimes altered version of the account he'd earlier sent to London. "That's all I've got together at the moment."

Freeman's forced bonhomie faltered at being outmaneuvered. His eyes flickered to the men against the wall.

Miriam said, "I'm afraid I haven't worked as fast as you. All we've done is talk it through in very general terms."

Charlie estimated it had been a full five minutes since the blue-eyed man had blinked. He wondered if he could make him now. He said, "Okay, so let's talk. It was clearly a combined intelligence mission. Records of American military intelligence, G2, are stored at Adelphi, Maryland. With the urgency and authority of an executive order, you'll have accessed them by now, so I'd appreciate knowing the result of that. It's too soon, obviously, to have got your own photographs of your body, but you're quite clearly geared up to run graduation checks at West Point. What sort of time frame are you running on that? You have a Rapid Physiognomy Comparison facility at Bureau headquarters, don't you? It shouldn't take long, if you use that. I'd be interested in your theories about the missing articles, against what was left on the bodies. We've quite a lot to talk about, in fact, haven't we?"

The stranger didn't blink but Freeman did, looking even more obviously at the Washington visitors. He said, "You've covered quite a lot of ground there."

"I thought that's what we had to do," said Charlie. "What's come out of Adelphi?"

"Nothing so far," said Freeman.

"But you're checking there, so you've already decided it *was* intelligence," accepted Charlie, smiling at the unintentional admission. "That's something, I suppose. Means you're already wondering, as I am, how two officers could disappear like they obviously did, for so long. So you'll be organizing a records search of your CIA forerunner, the Office of Strategic Services . . . ?" He gestured to his specially prepared report, lying unread and untouched on Freeman's desk. "You'll see we're carrying out those sort of inquiries in London. I'd appreciate your letting me have your results as soon as possible, as you'll see I've promised to let you have ours . . . ?"

"Yes, of course," said Freeman.

"What's the State Department guidance about possible embarrassment?' he asked, directly addressing the two unspeaking men.

"That's the big question," tried Freeman. "What was our guy—your guy, too—doing there in the first place?"

Which wasn't even an attempt to answer the question, Charlie acknowledged. An executive order from the president himself was certainly important enough for someone to have traveled all the way from Washington. But it was a very long way to come to sit and say nothing—practically like a performance in a B-movie. Unless they *did* know and their participation was turning into a damage-limitation exercise better planned than his at Yakutsk.

As if aware of the reflection, Freeman said, "That Nazi business really was a hell of a bluff."

"Thanks."

"It was that, wasn't it? A bluff, I mean, like you told Miriam it was."

"Absolutely." Or were they groping more than he believed? If they were, he'd already achieved all there was to achieve, misdirecting sufficiently and disclosing nothing he shouldn't have disclosed.

"You really can't take it—anything—any further?"

"Everything I've got is there," said Charlie.

"I'll get something to you," promised Miriam.

"With whatever there might be from Washington," added Freeman.

"That's about it, then," accepted Charlie. There wouldn't be the expected happy hour invitation today.

"We'll keep in touch," insisted Freeman.

Freeman had to accompany Charlie to be officially signed past embassy security. As they walked, Charlie said, "You want to tell me about that?"

Freeman said, "I'm sorry. They made the rules."

"Which were?"

"That's how they wanted it done."

"What are their names?"

"I can't tell you, Charlie."

"And you expect me to cooperate!"

"How do you think I feel?"

"I don't know, Saul. How do you feel?"

"Like a prime cunt."

"That's about right," said Charlie. "I'm sorry for you."

"I'm sorry for myself." The man straightened as he walked, as if trying physically to cast off the episode. Actually smiling, which he hadn't done so far, he said, "Dick Cartright tells me a girl I introduced him to is related to the one you're with. Isn't that a fantastic coincidence?"

"Fantastic," agreed Charlie, without a pause. Sometimes gossip and an inferior man's need to boast was a wonderful thing.

"I've never known arrogance like it!" protested Kenton Peters, who hadn't from anyone who knew who he was. The appalled indignation echoed over the line from the embassy's secure communications bunker.

"That's appalling," sympathized James Boyce. "But you've no doubt there is something he's keeping back, not telling London?"

"None."

"It can't be about there being a second officer. I've seen what he sent today. It's there."

"Our people haven't. So he hasn't shared it."

"So you could be right that he's got the connection. Is it time to eliminate him?"

There was silence from Moscow. Then Peters said, "I'll leave everything in place. We'll take him anytime, when it suits us. Maximum effect."

"I'm not happy," complained Boyce.

"Neither am I."

"Damned nuisance."

"Yes."

17

Natalia recognized that with the open support—at the moment, at least—of Dmitri Borisovitch Nikulin and the now totally shared guidance of Charlie Muffin, she potentially held a very sharp two-edged sword. The importance was properly using it against the attacks of the deputy interior minister and his acolyte, not falling upon it herself. Which made Charlie, whom she could easily believe a reincarnation of Machiavelli, the more important: the one from whom she had to learn.

It was certainly Charlie's survival plan for her that, although incomplete, sounded feasibly straightforward when he sketched it out in the botanical gardens but less certain when she was alone, as she was now, back in her echoing ministry office, knowing that Petr Travin, two doors along their shared corridor, and Viktor Viskov, on the floor above, were plotting her overthrow with equal determination.

Lead, Charlie had insisted: that was the way for her to remain ahead, from the front, not by following from behind. And she'd substantially increased her lead, she knew. The Moscow homicide detective had performed far better than she'd expected at his departure press conference from Yakutsk—Natalia made a note to congratulate the man—and her unattributed statement accusing the Yakutskaya authorities of inexplicable obstruction had chimed perfectly with it. The overseas digest of the foreign press frenzy—circulated to Viskov as well as to her—from the Foreign Ministry showed it quoted favorably by every major print and network television outlet in America, Canada and England, as well as being widely reported throughout Europe.

Leading from the front did, of course, expose her back to be stabbed. The cynicism actually surprised Natalia. More Charlie's mind-set than hers. Maybe the way she had to think—*try* to think—if she could in the future. No question of trying, she told herself at

once. There was Sasha, always Sasha. Natalia had been too long alone
ever, completely, to lose her most deeply rooted fear of all, of being
alone again.

Which wasn't a consideration of the moment, she decided, rising
positively from her desk. The consideration of the moment was continuing to follow Charlie's script ("mountains can be made from bureaucratic bullshit"), which she'd already initiated by a telephone call
to the Lubyanka. Now that had to be followed immediately by the
personal visit, because everything had to be in sequence. She made
a point of announcing to her secretariat that she was going out but
not saying where—happy for the gossip if not the positively offered
information to permeate along the corridor—and used the metro instead of an official car and driver, by which and through whom she
could have been quickly traced.

She got off at the Bolshoi station, preferring to walk the rest of
the way, seeing as she crossed the final square that the briefly removed glowering statue of Felix Dzerzhinsky, the founder of the
Soviet intelligence service, had been replaced in front of its yellow-
washed headquarters building while so many other, less despised reminders of communism had been removed.

Fyodor Lyulin, the chief archivist to whom she had already spoken, was obediently waiting. He was a bespectacled, anxious-to-please
and unexpectedly young man apprehensive at personally being sought
out by someone of Natalia's rank and authority, which immediately
registered with her as an advantage, alien though it was for her to
bully. Something else she perhaps had to learn.

Lyulin believed there were records of Yakutskaya, nervously
pointing out that it was all too long ago for him to have had anything
personally to do with them and certainly for which he had no responsibility, apart from their being somewhere in the intelligence
service archives. He did not know if they were complete—indeed,
even where they might be kept—but he would, of course, search at
once.

The man twitched more than blinked at Natalia's demand for details of gulags for the ten years between 1935 and 1945. "I've no way
of estimating at the moment, of course, but that could conceivably
run into tens—hundreds—of thousands. They might not be indexed.
In any chronological order. Material often isn't, from that period."

Better than she could have hoped, thought Natalia. "I want whatever exists—all of it. Don't worry about indexing or chronology. As they're found I want them shipped immediately to me at the ministry."

"Just located and sent to you?" pedantically qualified the relaxing archivist, seeing an insuperable job becoming comparatively easy.

"That's all," agreed Natalia. "Until I tell you to stop."

"Going through so much could be a monumental task for anyone, for a team of people," cautioned the relieved man.

"I am organizing that. It's a survey that has to be made."

"The instruction will be confirmed in writing?" requested Lyulin, protectively.

"Of course. But I want the search begun at once. It has the highest priority, from the White House itself."

"I'll put every available person on it," undertook Lyulin.

"But supervise it yourself. Nothing must be overlooked. And each camp must be identified in a summary of each shipment, understood?"

"Completely," assured the man.

There was a benefit Natalia hadn't anticipated when she got back to the ministry later that afternoon. Dmitri Nikulin's congratulatory memorandum for the effectiveness of the previous day's Yakutsk statement was marked as having been copied to the deputy interior minister, which forced a matching note from Viskov within thirty minutes. By which time Natalia was dictating memos of her own.

To the president's chief of staff she wrote that the reason for the murdered Westerners being in Yakutsk could well lie in the slave colonies that existed in the vicinity at the time of their deaths and that she intended as comprehensive a check as possible of all surviving records at Lubyanka, particularly for any Western prisoners. Her deputy, Petr Travin, would be in personal charge of the search, authorized to employ as many extra staff as necessary for it to be completed as soon as possible.

Her instruction to Travin was for a daily summary, as well as a detailed assessment of the total number of camps that had existed around Yakutsk and for any that had a specific purpose other than simply housing prisoners or exiles. She dictated the authorization that the Lubyanka archivist had asked for and duplicated everything to everyone—including Viskov—satisfied that she had effectively buried Petr Travin beneath Charlie's bullshit mountain that hopefully really would become her deputy's career grave if Camp 98—the records of which she'd sift first—had held someone of linking significance to the dead officers.

Natalia felt better—safer—at the end of the day than she had at its beginning, especially when another memorandum was delivered just as she was leaving.

It had been a good evening. They'd eaten Scotch beef from the embassy commissary and gone through in detail all that Natalia had done that afternoon to overwhelm Petr Pavlovich Travin. Charlie insisted Nikulin's memo as she'd been leaving the ministry, praising her for making the gulag check, prevented either her deputy or Viktor Viskov from maneuvering an escape. "You're not just ahead, you're out of sight."

"What happens if it's Petr Pavlovich who comes up with something from one of the *other* camps?" questioned Natalia, still needing to be convinced.

"It was still your idea," Charlie pointed out. "So it's still your success, whichever way it goes."

They went to bed early, Charlie having been awake for almost forty-eight hours, but he wasn't too tired to make love and it was perfect, as it always was. Afterward they lay side by side, their bodies touching, and Natalia said, "Yakutsk was the first time we've been apart—your not being in Mosow—for over a year."

"I know."

"I didn't like it."

"Neither did I."

"I hope it doesn't happen again too often."

"Me, too." He hadn't told her about Sir Rupert Dean's talk of his being recalled to London and decided not to. Or of the unspeaking men at the American embassy, one trained not to blink. He said, "You hear from Irena while I was away?"

He wasn't sure, but Charlie thought he felt Natalia stiffen, imperceptibly, beside him in the darkness. She said, "No. Why?"

"No particular reason. You've never told me much about her." There was definitely a stiffness.

"There's nothing much to tell."

"Why didn't you see her, for such a long time?"

"What is it, Charlie?"

"Just curious." This hadn't been the right moment, he realized. Or had it?

"She make a pass at you?" demanded Natalia.

"No," lied Charlie.

There was a long silence. Then Natalia said, "Konstantin left me for Irena."

Konstantin had been Natalia's first husband, Charlie remembered. It had been so long since they'd talked about the man that Charlie had forgotten the name. He said, "What happened?"

He felt Natalia shrug. "He was a lecher, like I've told you. But he'd never left me before. She always wanted anything I had, from when we were children."

"How long did it last?"

"Until I divorced him so he could marry her. She didn't want him then." She was quiet for several moments. "I'm sorry I've been so stupid. About us, I mean."

"No real harm done."

"There could have been. I can't think how awful that would have been."

"It's over," assured Charlie. Irena knowing someone at the British embassy was something else he wouldn't tell Natalia. Their holding-back roles had been reversed, he realized.

"I'm glad you called," said Miriam. She really wasn't sure who was the better lover, Cartright or Lestov. Which wasn't the most important comparison. Cartright's usefulness, apart from in bed, was what she could get from his involvement in the case.

"It's good to have you back." said Cartright. "It must have been appalling."

"Known better."

"How did you get on with Charlie?"

Miriam was surprised Cartright had managed to hold out through dinner and the before-and-after drinks. "Fine. He sure as hell knows how to operate."

"How's that?"

"We wouldn't have gotten on that plane if he hadn't known how to flash dollars around."

"He seems adept as making money work," prompted Cartright.

"But I gave him a ride back, so I guess we're even. What happened while I was away?"

"Nothing of any consequence. London doesn't seem to be able to find any trace of our man. Or why he should have been there. How about you?"

"Lots of questions. No answers."

"You think Charlie's being straight with you?"

"Don't you?"

"No. This is a joint operation. Anything I get from London I'm quite prepared to share with you. We do have rather a special relationship, don't we?"

"Very special," agreed Miriam, happy in every way with her night's work.

18

The first shipment from the Lubyanka archives—yellowing, crumbling folders and box files, mostly handwritten and detailing five camps, none Gulag 98—was waiting for Natalia when she arrived at the ministry the following morning.

So, too, were all the replies from Petr Pavlovich Travin to her previous day's flurry of messages, although none from the deputy foreign minister.

Travin's overall response—to complain of insufficient staff and inadequate funds temporarily to employ the extra people necessary for such a mammoth task—was precisely what Charlie had predicted, but Natalia felt a flicker of uncertainty at the next step. Just as quickly she realized there was no going back.

She ordered Travin to withdraw clerk and office staff from every militia district station in Moscow and volunteered three of her own secretariat, suggesting that Travin and Viskov match the transfer from their staff. She proposed that Travin organize a shift system extending until midnight—around the clock, if it became necessary—and in a separate although copied-to-everyone note asked the deputy interior minister to allocate emergency funding for the extra hours' payment. She reminded her deputy there was a planned meeting that afternoon with the returning Colonel Lestov and suggested they finalize the operation then. Her last message, over which she hesitated longer than any other in the batch she enclosed to him, invited Dmitri Nikulin's suggestion upon anything she might have overlooked.

The speed of the deputy interior minister's return brought the stomach-dropping realization of how carefully Viskov and Travin had set their imagined trap—even to corresponding through Nikulin—and how close she was to the final confrontation. She wished Charlie would be with her when it came.

It was to the presidential office that Viktor Viskov's memorandum was sent, marked copied to her as a matter of courtesy, and Natalia accepted at once that Viskov's denunciation was intended to be all the more effective by its careful understatement. She was referred to throughout by her cumbersome official title: Interior ministry director of militia and internal security liaison. Nowhere was there a direct condemnation. But to crush her as completely as possible by gaining an overwhelming support as well as an audience, duplicates of the memorandum had also gone to the Finance and Foreign Ministries.

Viskov wrote that although the Lubyanka search ordered by the liaison director had already begun, it had not been possible for staff there accurately even to estimate the documentation involved. It was certainly well in excess of a hundred thousand, possibly treble that number. None of it was indexed, properly annotated or in any dated order; the history of some camps occupied half a dozen dossiers, others as many as twenty. Virtually the entire archival staff of the intelligence headquarters had been assigned to the recovery, but it would be at least a month, possibly longer, before it would all be finally transferred to the ministry. Even then there was no guarantee everything would be included. The archivist—Natalia assumed it would have been Fyodor Lyulin—had warned the material would eventually occupy several thousand square meters of space. The archivist had been given no indication or guidance by the liaison director concerning what was being hunted but thought it could take as long as six months, depending on the number of people allocated, for everything to be read—longer if the search was for a specific individual. The lists of names ran into the millions.

Viskov estimated thirty clerks could be withdrawn from district militia posts to supplement a possible further twenty within the ministry, as suggested by the liaison director. Their working a shift system—even around the clock, as also suggested by the liaison director—for anything up to six months would cost three times the total yearly clerk and secretarial budget of the entire ministry. It would also, of course, mean none of the normal work of those involved could be done, which would require a further period of overtime working, logically a further six months, which would bring the budgetary overspending to four times the salary allocation. A further but very practical problem was that in the ministry building there was insufficient storage space for the files, the first of which had already arrived.

Such a commitment—in terms of cost, manpower, time and space—was unprecedented in the history of the Moscow militia, the intelligence agencies or the Interior Ministry. Nothing Viskov had so far been told by the liaison director supported such an undertaking; indeed, he was still waiting to learn precisely *what* was being sought. While in no way criticising the liaison director—nor, even less, questioning its immediate endorsement by the president's office—Viskov urged serious reconsideration until they were convinced of the need and importance of an operation that quite clearly had not been properly thought through.

The deputy interior minister proposed that the already arranged meeting with Colonel Vadim Leonidovich Lestov be expanded to the whole committee for the liaison director personally to justify her actions. Until then, and their confirmation by the full committee, he had suspended the archival transfer.

Natalia read and reread the denunciation, knowing she could not afford to miss a single accusation. It was far more detailed than Charlie had predicted and for some time she felt hollowed—fleetingly, even, angry at Charlie—before gradually forcing the acceptance that Viskov and Travin had fallen into Charlie's trap, not she into theirs. And that it looked as if this really was the last battle in a sniping war of attrition. She was frightened, which she supposed people were before knowingly going into battle. She hoped the very particular rules of engagement devised by herself at Charlie's direction proved sufficient. They seemed to be, so far, but there was a long way to go.

Her only real concession would be to admit a total inspection was impractical, and that wasn't planned as an admission. Everything after that was to lure Viskov on, turning the man's blind determination back upon himself. And he had been blinded. Or rather unable to see properly, over the bullshit mountain. Possibly the politician's greatest weakness—despite his attempted insistence to the contrary—was having no alternative but to link Dmitri Nikulin in the attack, because of Nikulin's endorsement of Natalia. More than a weakness, she corrected: it was a very definite tactical error.

Natalia used her private line to dial Charlie's direct embassy number, anxious for his reassurance, wincing when she finally got his voice mail. She didn't leave a message.

She was sitting contemplatively at her desk when the announcement came from Nikulin's office that the afternoon's meeting was being extended, as requested by the deputy interior minister. Natalia was sure she had sufficient evidence to confront those trying to destroy her, but following Charlie's dictum, she wished she had more. It wasn't until Lestov's arrival that she considered she had it. Still a long way to go, but the route was better lit.

At Miriam Bell's entrance at least twenty male heads turned at the same time, as if attached to the same wire. Charlie sat facing the door of the Metropole Hotel's Minsk Restaurant and didn't have to make the effort but thought he might have, just for the fun of it, if he'd had to. Charlie wasn't sure if the smile was all for him or had to be shared with her awareness of the effect she knew she was having throughout the room.

He said, "You ever get into any trouble you couldn't handle?"

"I hope I don't with you." She wore a shimmering green silk trouser suit over a white silk blouse and he didn't think there was a bra. Her hair was bobbed much shorter than in Yakutsk and all the swelling had gone from her face.

"I don't mix business with pleasure."

"I still believe what I said on the plane, that you would if it was necessary, and I could be sad you don't think it's necessary now," she said, nodding acceptance to the vodka he offered from the carafe already on the table. "But that wasn't what I meant, which I think you knew. So we really do need to have this lunch, don't we?"

As they touched glasses, Charlie said, "Who the *fuck* were the Men of Stone?"

Miriam shook her head in matching incredulity. "The old guy's name was Peters. Don't know his first name. Never got one at all for the second one. Peters only dealt with the ambassador, who decreed every wish was our—and anybody else's—command. I guess State Department, God and presidential executive order is a pretty powerful combination."

"The younger one wasn't State," insisted Charlie, positively. "I've met people like him before: recognize them as a type."

"Peter's bodyguard," identified Miriam. "Saul says State was taking seriously all the kidnapping and killing that happens here in Moscow."

Bodyguards got in the way of trouble or caused it, decided Charlie: they didn't sit in on what might—but hadn't been—sensitive debriefings. "Peters really that important?"

"You wouldn't believe how the ambassador and head of chancellery and Freeman were shitting themselves. Practically a hygiene problem."

"Why the act?"

"The way he is, apparently. Although I don't know how Saul knows."

Miriam's responses were too ingenuous to be prepared, but his warning feet were throbbing to the beat of drums. "Where are they now?"

"Gone."

"Quite an experience." Was it over? he wondered.

"Haven't we got other things to talk about?" demanded Miriam.

"Could be," encouraged Charlie.

"We're working against each other, Charlie! Which doesn't make any sense. You made it very clear in Yakutsk you don't like company. I didn't set out to do any deals, either. It's going to be my tit in the wringer if this goes wrong. *How*ever it goes wrong."

Charlie poured more vodka for both of them and said, "Let's

order, after a speech like that." When they had—Miriam with hurried disinterest—he said, "Wrong like failing to solve it or wrong like Peters would judge to be wrong?"

Her smile this time was ruefully admiring, at Charlie's perception. "We got a knee-jerk president, with ratings in free fall. Without talking to anyone except his own reflection in the mirror, to get the wet eyes right, he declares an unknown, wrong-place lieutenant to be a national hero whose death will be avenged. And then has to be told the reason for his very own Superman being where he was could be a monumental, fucked-up embarrassment, even after all these years. And that he's tied the rock around his own neck and could be dragged down by it faster than he was already dropping."

Charlie exhausted the vodka with the arrival of their caviar and ordered another carafe. "So if the reason for your guy being in Yakutsk doesn't qualify for the Arlington Cemetery burial, it'll be interred with him to remain the great unsolved mystery?"

"It *is* going to be Arlington," confirmed Miriam.

"Did Peters stop in England on his way here?" asked Charlie. It looked as if London and Washington were thinking with a single mind, London with perhaps more reason, if he was right about a second Briton being involved. He'd never liked being part of diplomatic house-tidying: the dirt always had a habit of bulging the carpet under which it was swept.

"According to Saul, he wanted to get as much as he could here first," said Miriam. "He's doing it on his way back."

"Seems like it's all being settled at a much higher level than us."

Miriam shook her head. "According to Saul, who's busy digging himself out from under, Peters didn't like your meeting. Doesn't think you told the whole truth and nothing but the truth. And sometimes—too many times—what gets fixed at the top fucks up on its way down because no one has the full game plan. Won't want to play it, even. Especially someone who doesn't like working in tandem in the first place."

"This approach your idea or Peters, via Saul?"

"Mine." She waited for her trout to be served. Not looking at him—squirting lemon onto her fish—she said, "You think that scrap left in the trouser band label is enough to identify your guy?"

Charlie laughed outright. "Why didn't you call me a sneaky bastard?"

"I just have. I wanted to choose my time to trade."

"What've you got?"

"A photograph. Or rather a piece of a photograph, like it's been cut in half because he didn't want the other piece. He's in uniform, in front of a building that could be a bank or a college: it's very big. He's with a girl. She's maybe thirty. Blond. There's nothing written on it to say who she is or where it was taken."

"You make a copy before it went to Washington?"

"I back up everything," negotiated Miriam. "I have your word about the trouser label?"

"My word," promised Charlie.

Miriam took the copy from her purse and slid it across the table to him, with the supposed duplicate of her Yakutsk report to Washington. Charlie pocketed the envelope but studied the picture for several moments before putting that away.

"You think there's enough of the background for your people to identify?"

"They hope so."

"I watched you pretty carefully when you went through the clothes," said Charlie, curiously.

"Like I watched you," reminded Miriam. She put her hand to her waist. "There was a small pocket, just here. For tickets or small change, I guess. The picture must have been important to him. It was all by itself in a little plastic wallet."

"Anything else?"

"You were right about the spectacles, which you can see he's wearing in the photograph. According to our laboratory guys in Washington, he suffered severe astigmatism: particularly bad unequal cornea curvature. Whatever he did or knew, he was in uniform for a very special reason."

"What about the tweezers and the magnifying glass?"

"Tweezers are medical. There's no maker's mark, which is a bastard, but our forensic guys think the magnifying glass was custom-made by optical specialists."

They both finished eating at the same time and for several moments looked steadily at each other across the table.

Miriam said, "You want to call it a draw?"

Charlie didn't want to admit but had to. "Okay."

"We got a deal?"

"That won't be enough, will it?"

"How so?"

"What about Lestov and the Russians? And Yakutsk, for that matter. It was Polyakov who made the finding of the bodies public in the first place, through Canada."

"And got badly burned doing it," said Miriam. "For Russia to be a problem, it'll have to be something forensic. Lestov got nothing from the woman's body that we didn't see."

"You sure?"

"I'm sure." She smiled.

"He could have been lying."

"He wasn't."

And if he had been it wouldn't matter, acknowledged Charlie. Because Natalia would tell him. He was edging toward his favorite position, right in the middle of the spider's web, with everything coming in his direction. Richard Cartright's interest in Natalia's sister still had the irritation of an untrapped fly, though.

Throughout the lunch, to which Henry Packer had followed Miriam undetected from the embassy, the man had sat at the bar watching them, drinking mineral water. And had seen the woman pass an envelope and what looked like a piece of a photograph to the man he had to kill. Which was all he had to do, Packer reminded himself. It wasn't his business what they were exchanging. They were supposed to be cooperating, according to the meeting he'd sat in on. Peters was an asshole, imagining there could be any problems from that shambling hayrick, whatever the man's file said. There was only one professional between himself and Charlie Muffin, and Packer knew he was it. He hoped he wouldn't have to wait long to prove it.

Colonel Vadim Leonidovich Lestov hid his apprehension well and had it not been for her earlier training and debriefing expertise it might have taken Natalia longer to recognize it. But he'd arrived nervously fifteen minutes early—giving Natalia the advantage she hadn't expected—and phrased everything he initially said defensively. It took several minutes for the stutter to subside. Natalia used every psychological trick she could remember to calm the man, intent upon getting whatever she could for what was to follow. And when it came—knowing that Charlie didn't have it but realizing at once how it could be used—she felt a warm spread of satisfaction. At once she realized that it would destroy what Charlie was trying to achieve, but that was inevitable now. At least she would be able to tell him.

"You're sure?" she insisted.

"Absolutely," said the man. "Both uniforms were still at the mortuary when Lev Fyodorovich carried out his preliminary forensic examination in what passed there as a laboratory. I counted, specifically. They were both complete."

"That's very important." Charlie had talked about wandering away from the grave before the forensic search had finished, looking for traces of Gulag 98. He'd be annoyed with himself; more than annoyed. He was always furious at personal mistakes.

"It was a forensic discovery. I don't consider I did as well as was expected," apologized the fresh-faced man. He was wearing the same shined-by-use suit of their first meeting.

Natalia said, "You did brilliantly. Far better than could have been expected, under the circumstances. You recovered completely from what was intended as a huge embarrassment. . . ." She hesitated, caught by an idea. "In fact, this afternoon's meeting has been expanded, for what you did to be properly recognized." Could it be that she was becoming as devious as Charlie?

When Natalia told him who the additional officials would be, Lestov said doubtfully, "There must be other, more important reasons."

"The worldwide publicity has escalated everything," Natalia pointed out, easily. "And there's been some misunderstandings. Nothing, though, to do with you."

"Because of what happened, there wasn't any chance for me to discuss anything with the American or the Englishman, apart from his saying he'd made up what he said at the press conference—"

"Did you believe him?" broke in Natalia, recognizing again how perfectly what she'd just learned fit everything else. There was, she thought, such a thing as coincidence. Or was it luck?

"I do believe he had no warning of the media: the American was adamant neither of them knew. It was very quick-witted of him."

Which Charlie was, among so many other things, Natalia thought. And which she had to be in the coming hours. She said, "I've got my own ideas about that, particularly after what you've just told me."

"I wish I understood more," admitted Lestov.

"I'm beginning to," said Natalia.

It continued far better than Natalia could have hoped. Everyone except her deputy was already waiting when she led the homicide detective into the Interior Ministry conference room and she was halfway through the introductions before Petr Travin flustered in. He got halfway through, "Security told me . . ." before seeing Lestov.

"The colonel arrived early," picked up Natalia. "It gave me the opportunity personally to congratulate him, as I am sure the rest of you would like to do."

She was pleased by the confusion. Petr Travin looked to the deputy interior minister for guidance and Mikhail Suslov, from the Foreign Ministry, deferred to Dmitri Nikulin. The president's representative told Lestov, "You came out well from what could have been a very embarrassing situation for us. So yes, congratulations are in order."

"Which is why I am proposing an official commendation," said Natalia, looking at Viskov. "You'd support that, wouldn't you, Deputy Minister?"

Viskov was totally wrong-footed. "I thought . . . yes, I suppose. Of course."

First blood, Natalia decided, conscious of Nikulin's frown. "Is there something else, Deputy Minister?"

"A lot, I would have thought," Viskov came back, eagerly.

"Indeed," agreed Natalia, anxious to orchestrate as much as possible. "But surely we need logically to keep to the original agenda and hear first what Colonel Lestov has to tell us?" She felt confidently relaxed, although properly so: sure of her strengths—of being stronger, in fact, than she'd imagined—but not complacent. Viskov and his puppet might not have played their full hand yet, although she believed they had.

"That was the original intention of the meeting," reminded Nikulin.

This afternoon's success or failure depended, ultimately, on the presidential aide: his were the attitudes and nuances she had most accurately to gauge, above all others. She already knew those of her immediate superior and her intended replacement. Everyone else were unsuspecting spectators.

"Of course," agreed Viskov, at once.

Uncertain, assessed Natalia at once: good. She said, "Perhaps, Colonel, you'd go through again what we've already discussed?" aware of Travin's face tightening at having missed out on the preliminary account.

Calmed by that rehearsal and buoyed by an official commendation, Lestov spoke virtually without stammering, the hesitations appearing to be more pauses to move from one episode to another than an impediment. It was only when the man had been speaking for several minutes that Natalia remembered everyone but herself was hearing the Yakutsk story in full for the first time and that what she was listening to amounted to the final preparation for her own performance. Her concentration was absolute upon her two attackers, alert for anything and everything. Their absorption, in turn, was entirely upon the homicide officer, ignoring her. If they were that attentive, anxious for something more, maybe they *had* shown their full hand.

Everything depended upon how she played hers. The slightest miscalculation, intruding too soon, before the detective finished, risked confusion, which could deflect her counterattack. But if she waited until Lestov completely finished, the danger was Viskov or Travin realizing the significance of the homicide detective's revelation and possibly outmaneuvering her before she outmaneuvered them. Or was there that danger? She *had* heard it—or almost all of it—before. Been able to analyze it—even listened to Charlie analyze it, talked it through with him step by step as she'd demanded he do. No one would be able to respond as quickly as she was tensed to. Certainly not Viskov or Travin, whose determination to topple her she was increasingly coming to think—although still not complacently—exceeded their conspiring ability. The right moment—the most effective, destructive moment—would be at the very end. Which again she could anticipate.

Natalia pounced the moment it came. "Everything we've heard totally justifies the commendation we've already agreed," she declared. "And from what we've heard, it also justifies the Lubyanka inquiry. . . ."She looked directly at the deputy interior minister. "I'm personally sorry you don't seem to have agreed to its need . . . ?" She stopped, invitingly. Come on, she thought. Jump into the gaping hole.

Once more there was confusion throughout the room. Nikulin said, "I think we all might benefit from a detailed explanation."

The president's official was cautious, Natalia gauged: ready to change sides. "I am afraid there was a regrettable misunderstanding— one that's easily resolved—between myself and the archival staff at the Lubyanka," said Natalia. "And I take full responsibility for that. But I did not ask for the *entire* records of Yakutskaya. That would—"

"Your memorandum—" Travin tried to stop.

"Does not ask for that," stopped Natalia, in turn. "Read it, more thoroughly than you appear to have done so far . . ."

There was concerted movement as everyone except Lestov went to their dossiers. The homicide colonel looked curiously at her. Natalia smiled back. Her stomach was churning.

"There can be no other conclusion—especially with your suggestions on how a necessary staff can be assembled and the work routines established—than that you intended every record to be withdrawn," insisted Viskov, triumphantly.

"My first instruction to my deputy, yesterday, asks for—and I quote—'a daily summary, as well as a detailed assessment, of the total number of camps that existed *around Yakutsk*.' And even more specifically for any that might have held particular prisoners. . . ."

"That's true," said Nikulin. "That's what it quite clearly says!"

The man was taking his escape with her, decided Natalia, relieved. If this was indeed a battle, then Nikulin was her reinforcement. More than that. Nikulin was the man who had to award the victory laurel. Natalia hesitated. She might be acquiring Charlie's deviousness, but she wasn't sure she could manage his final them-or-me killer instinct. Yes, she could, Natalia decided at once. There was Sasha—always Sasha.

Color began to suffuse Viskov's face. "The memorandum is contradictory."

"I don't consider it is," refused Natalia, directly addressing the presidential chief of staff. "At worst the request to the archives is too general. It could have been resolved by a simple telephone call to me, from either the deputy minister or my deputy. My deputy could, in fact, have simply walked along our linking corridor. Neither chose to talk to me. Instead, from the correspondence that has been exchanged today, it would appear there has been a positive attempt to undermine my authority. And by suspending what I had already initiated, an investigation that has the president's personal interest has been seriously delayed, possibly even jeopardized."

Natalia stopped, pleased with her concluding reference to the president, which had only come to her as she talked and identified her unquestionably with Dmitri Nikulin. Committed, she accepted. In the middle of the battlefield, openly wielding her two-edged sword, with no retreat. There was a strange comparison between the two men she was confronting, Viskov's face bulged and purple, outraged veins pumping in his forehead, Travin ashen in his awareness that he was indeed caught up in a war zone.

"I'm not at all sure what this dispute is all about or how it involves me or my department," complained Mikhail Suslov, easing himself as far away as he could from the firing.

Wonderful! thought Natalia. "You are one of the *most* involved," she told the deputy foreign minister. "There was always the need to look for foreign prisoners in the Yakutsk camps, which is why I suggested it. And why, by proposing the staffing I did, it could be completed as quickly as possible, certainly not over a period of six months, as has been ridiculously claimed. You've just heard from Colonel Lestov that our forensic examination of the grave uncovered a Western uniform button. . . ."

Natalia's pause was intentional, concentrating their attention. "You also heard from Colonel Lestov that the buttons on the uniforms of both the dead English and American lieutenants were complete . . ."

It was the newly confident Lestov who finished for her.

"Which can only mean that there was another Westerner present during the murders . . . perhaps someone in or on his way to a nearby camp. . . ." The man hesitated. "Or actually involved with the murders."

The detective's statement shocked the room into total silence. Natalia sat happy for it to continue, for the awareness fully to settle, only breaking it when she saw Nikulin move to speak. To Viskov, she demanded. "Now do you still oppose the *limited* Lubyanka search?"

"It wasn't properly explained," protested Viskov. He was flustered now, sweating, a lost man.

Almost there, thought Natalia. "I wasn't asked for an explanation . . . it seemed more important to denigrate the proposal, and me along with it. Which is astonishing, considering the Englishman's press conference remark about the obviousness of a connection with the area itself. . . ."

Natalia paused once more, hoping for a questioning interruption, although she was prepared to bulldoze on. But the question did come, from Nikulin. "You think he—maybe the American as well—knows there was a second Westerner there at the time?"

"I haven't been told yet by my deputy what has come from either the English or the Americans," said Natalia, looking demandingly at Travin. She knew Charlie was withholding even an edited account until after this connived challenge. What they hadn't anticipated was that it would come so soon. And now, Natalia thought, Charlie's eventual offering couldn't be as edited as he'd intended.

"There has not yet been any exchange," said Travin, trapped.

"When did you ask for something?" pressed Natalia. "You'll have logged your request, of course?"

"I was waiting for the return of Colonel Lestov," tried Travin, desperately.

There was another long silence, which again Natalia ended. Soft-voiced in apparent disbelief, she said, "They've been back for two days!"

Travin looked fervently for help from Viskov. The deputy minister ignored him. Travin said, "I have been too busy following your other instructions."

"But you *haven't!*" rejected Natalia, louder now in outrage. "*I* initiated Lubyanka. Nothing arrived until today . . ." She feigned the sudden awareness of Suslov and the homicide detective before looking to Nikulin. "I don't consider this is the time or place to continue this conversation. But I do think it should be continued . . ."

"I totally agree," said Nikulin.

———

Charlie was sitting with Sasha on his lap, watching her permitted thirty minutes of English language cartoon, when Natalia got back to Lesnaya.

"Well?" he asked.

"I won," declared Natalia. "But they know a second officer was there at the murder."

"Oh, shit!" said Charlie, unthinking.

Sasha said, "What's 'shit' mean?"

"Maybe I could have done better," conceded Novikov. "I hadn't expected everything to end like that, so quickly. I wasn't properly prepared."

"He seemed a good man," allowed Marina. "Did he promise to help?"

"He told me to call," said the doctor, fingering the pasteboard on the table between them.

"When will you?"

"Soon. When this business with the woman's body is settled. Polyakov realizes he's been outsmarted. Still might try something."

"Do you think the Englishman believed you had more?"

"I'll hint what it is when we talk."

"He's definitely working to an agenda of his own," complained Peters. His hair was too long for sea trips, blowing disordered around his face. Hurriedly he pulled on a sailing cap.

"It hardly matters," Boyce pointed out, at the helm. "Whatever he keeps back from your woman, you get from me. Just as you get whatever our other departments contribute. We can't be caught out."

"Only by the Russians."

"They're not likely to do anything, are they?"

"They're an uncertainty, and I don't like uncertainties."

"Their reaction would be intriguing, if we used Muffin as a diversion."

"That's increasingly what I'm thinking."

"It would have to be an obvious assassination, of course."

"Of course."

"Your man ready?"

"Whenever I blow the whistle."

"Let's give it a day or two; there's no urgency. But then make a sensation out of it."

"Fine."

"How was Moscow?"

"Appalling!" said Peters. "Dirty, uncomfortable and the ambassador served the most disgusting food I've ever eaten. Which I didn't, hardly."

"It was good of you to go," said Boyce, repeating the earlier gratitude.

"Necessary, particularly in view of events," said Peters. "Have you ever seen Muffin personally?"

"Of course not!" said Boyce, surprised at the question.

"Peculiar man. Looks like a bum. Won't be any loss at all to your service."

19

Charlie let Natalia feed and bathe the still-demanding Sasha ("If it's a silly word, why did you say it?"), needing the escape more than the time. He still used the time, though. It was necessary to rethink. Reevaluate. It had been stupid leaving the grave when he did—downright bloody stupid. Not a disaster—easily recoverable, in fact—but that wasn't the point. The point was getting everything—getting it *all*—the first time, and he hadn't, which was more arrogance, hurt pride, than professional objectivity. So what was professionally objective? London's secrecy intention—perhaps Washington's, too—was now at Moscow's mercy. A *major* reassessment. But more a diplomatic consideration than his, at operational ground level. What was there at his level? Vadim Lestov hadn't told all to Miriam. So much for pubic power. Which wasn't an irrelevant reflection. Told him something about the Russian detective. Had to keep it in mind. What else? Get it all, this time. Which he could. And would. So that wasn't the point, either. The primary consideration—the *sole* consideration—was whether Natalia had been as successful as she obviously believed herself to have been. Everything else, for the moment, was secondary.

She accepted the wine he had waiting when she emerged from the bedroom corridor and said, "I told Sasha you'd be along in a minute to say good night."

That, like so much else, was becoming a ritual he enjoyed. "Of course."

"I had to tell her what shit meant. She still thought it was silly."

"I'm sorry," apologized Charlie.

"Is what Denebin found a major problem?"

Charlie poured himself a second malt and said, "Not even one we're going to think about yet. First priorities first. You."

Natalia smiled, knowing the preference might have been difficult, the triumph rehearsed during the homeward drive. He listened leaning forward from his encompassing chair, looking into the glass cupped between both hands but not drinking. The silence unsettled Natalia, who'd expected—wanted—as much excitement, as much enthusiasm, as she felt.

Charlie didn't immediately speak, even when Natalia had obviously finished. Natalia waited, becoming more unsettled. Finally Charlie said, "The adjournment was limited to just you, Viskov and Travin? And Nikulin?"

Natalia nodded. "Lestov was called back at the end, when Nikulin announced he was to take over operational control."

"But he wasn't officially appointed by title as your deputy?" pressed Charlie.

"Nikulin talked about there having to be changes, but there was nothing official, no. Letting them sweat, I suppose."

"Which of them do you think Nikulin was talking about?" demanded Charlie.

Natalia allowed another pause. "Travin, primarily. Reducing his responsibility to the Lubyanka documentation was total humiliation. For him *and* Viskov, after the way they dismissed it and tried to use it."

Charlie had hoped for more: a dismissal, even. "Are there any arrangements for you to see Nikulin again? By yourself?"

Natalia shook her head once more.

"Ask for a meeting," urged Charlie. "It might have been too much to hope that by itself it would have been enough to get Viskov moved, as well as Travin. But you've definitely got to get rid of Travin. Totally. He and Viskov *have* been humiliated, as well as caught out. They're a threat as long as they're still together in the same building, able to plot. Maybe more so than before, after what happened today. They're fighting for their very existence now."

The final vestiges of Natalia's excitement seeped away. Charlie's killer instinct, she remembered. "So I haven't won?"

"Not yet." Seeing her need, Charlie said, "But you will. That's what we decided, didn't we?"

"How?" she asked, despondently unsure.

"Using what we've got," he said, inadequately. "Now tell me about the button from the Western uniform."

"It's not like those on the uniforms the dead men were wearing—not the same metal. And it's definitely not from a Russian uniform."

"Were there any special markings on it?" asked Charlie, urgently. There was another possibility that actually fit the way the English lieutenants had been dressed. There were two uniforms, dress and battle dress.

"I haven't seen it yet. I will, of course."

"I need a photograph," insisted Charlie. He fell silent. Then he said, "I made a bad mistake—a stupid mistake—leaving the grave too early. Don't like fucking up like that."

"You'd decided there *was* someone else," reminded Natalia, trying to help.

He had, acknowledged Charlie—from the .38 bullet as well as another person's military knowledge of the waistband label. Charlie said, "It was a possibility that had to be considered. This is *proof*." He straightened positively, dismissing the self-recrimination, at the same time topping up both their glasses. The immediate future was more important than the immediate past. Natalia's survival was still *the* priority. "What was decided to do about a second English officer?"

Natalia made an uncertain gesture. "I used it as an accusation, as part of the argument: turned it against Travin that he hadn't approached you or the American to get your findings. Your idea, remember?"

"What about disclosing it? I challenged Denebin in Yakutsk about everything else I saw him recover."

"They know you went off before Denebin found the buttons—that you don't know. That the American doesn't know, either."

"So?"

"It comes down to what you—and she—officially offer," said Natalia. "Maybe not even then. It's a hell of an advantage for us: the worst imaginable, as far as you're concerned—" She hurriedly stopped. "The worst imaginable for Britain. I didn't mean you personally."

Was there a differentiation? wondered Charlie. There shouldn't be, logically. But logic had very little to do with getting out from under when the toilet was flushed, and Charlie had a longtime aversion to getting covered in little brown bits. His *was* the name on everything: even on television, the identified person at the bottom of the toilet bowl. Charlie said, "But I *know*! And by knowing I can avoid a mistake." He paused. "Any *more* mistakes," he added, refusing himself an escape.

"I hope," said Natalia, at once wishing that she hadn't.

Charlie didn't pick up on the remark. He said, "Lestov, with whom I always had to liaise anyway, is effectively your deputy?"

"He was the obvious choice," Natalia pointed out. "Suddenly to have introduced anyone else as an operational controller—apart from his need to be totally rebriefed—would have shown our internal problem. Lestov getting the job can be explained, even if there's a need to explain, as a promotion. Which he rightly deserved."

"And which he must get, by title," insisted Charlie. He hadn't done enough to reassure her, he decided. He really wasn't used to worrying about people and protecting people other than himself. It meant a further delay in talking to Natalia about Novikov, too: her involvement in that was the last thing that could be risked with Viskov and Travin still in place and working against her.

"Which you still haven't told me how we're going to achieve?" prompted Natalia.

"You *are* still going to get the camp archives before Travin?"

"I insisted upon it," confirmed Natalia. "Said I wanted personally to be sure that a search neither Travin nor Viskov judged important was carried out properly."

"Excellent," exaggerated Charlie. It would have heaped further humiliation, increasing their determination to hit back.

"I'm waiting!" protested Natalia.

"I already think Colonel Vadim Leonidovich Lestov is a good policeman," said Charlie. "We're going to make him better. . . ." He paused again, remembering Miriam's lunchtime phrase. "Superman, in fact. And when the great discovery comes from Gulag 98, Petr Pavlovich Travin is going to miss it."

"What if there isn't anything *to* discover about Camp 98?" argued Natalia, raising at last one of her nagging doubts. "We don't even know that the records of every camp have survived."

The reason to get Novikov and whatever the man had to Moscow as soon as possible, thought Charlie. "We do know there was a Gulag 98 for special prisoners?"

"Yes?" agreed Natalia, doubtfully.

"None of whom, after fifty-four years, will still be alive today?"

"I wouldn't have thought so," Natalia further agreed.

"All we need is a name. I can invent an importance supposedly from an English source," said Charlie, simply.

"What if there *isn't* a surviving file?" pressed Natalia, relentlessly.

"The three bodies were where a special camp once existed, weren't they?" coaxed Charlie. "The information from England—from me— will still be that it was vital to trace a prisoner there. The failure to locate the file will be Travin's, won't it?"

Natalia shook her head. "Sometimes you lose me, Charlie."

"That's something I'm never going to do," he said, using her remark.

She started, at the strident sound of the street-level bell. So did Charlie. Shit! he thought. "I forgot to tell you," he apologized. "I invited Irena to supper."

"Why, Charlie?" demanded Natalia, seriously.

"I'm not sure yet. I'll tell you if I find out," he answered, obscurely. "Maybe it's nothing."

"You're not making sense."

"Trust me."

Natalia wished Charlie wouldn't keep asking her to do that.

———

Irena's last flight had been to Japan, where there is a theme park dedicated to the cartoon character, and Sasha's present was a Thomas the Tank T-shirt, complete with a smiling-faced railway engine printed on the front. Sasha, who was still waiting for Charlie, insisted upon putting it on and announced she was going to sleep in it.

"No," refused Charlie. "You can wear it tomorrow."

"Shit!" Sasha challenged, in English.

Irena sniggered, turning away.

Charlie said, "I told you that was a silly word. I don't want you saying it again."

"Why did *you*, then?"

"To see whether you would be silly and repeat it," said Charlie, desperately. "Or whether you were a big girl. So now we know: you're silly, like the word. And you can't sleep in the T-shirt."

"I want Mummy!"

"Take it off and go to sleep."

Sasha sat in bed with her arms tightly folded, not moving, glaring although not directly at him. Her lips were tightly together, too. Irena said, "I don't think I want to talk to silly girls. I'll come back later."

Sasha's bottom lip didn't stay tight. Charlie was hot, sweating, a never-lost man completely lost. It was unthinkable—literally—to slap her. Charlie said, "I'm waiting."

Sasha said, "I want Mummy."

Charlie didn't turn at Natalia's arrival. Natalia said, "What has Daddy told you to do?"

"He's not my daddy!" said the child.

"He is and you do what he tells you," said Natalia. "Take the shirt off."

Sasha started to pull it over her head and to cry at the same time, pointedly offering it to Natalia, who didn't reach for it. Charlie held out his hand and after a moment's hesitation Sasha gave it to him. Natalia kissed Sasha and left Charlie in the room with her.

Charlie said, "Do I get a kiss?"

"No," said Sasha, her voice muffled in the pillow, her body rigid.

"This isn't much fun, is it?"

There was no reply.

Charlie leaned forward, kissing Sasha's turned away head. He said,

"I am your daddy and I love you very much." It was a whisper, but he still heard her say, "shit," before he got to the door.

The two sisters were waiting for him in the smaller lounge, Irena already with the whiskey Natalia had poured for her.

Irena said, "What was that all about?"

"Growing up," said Charlie. "Sasha and I together." He still felt hot, disoriented by something he hadn't known how to handle or control and wished hadn't happened. How difficult was the rest of the evening going to be?

"It's a learning curve, I guess," suggested Irena.

"Maybe I've got more to learn than Sasha," conceded Charlie.

"I certainly have," simpered Irena. "Learning the man my sister's involved with is an international detective was a hell of a surprise!" She was wearing one of her second skin outfits, a black catsuit that didn't show panty or bra ridges because she wasn't wearing either. "I thought you looked terrific on television."

"I didn't," said Natalia. She was serious, subdued.

"What sort of policeman *are* you?" persisted the younger woman.

"A clerk," dismissed Charlie, his script ready in outline at least. He should have prepared Natalia; prepared himself better. Another stupid mistake. Too late now. "I just exchange information between London and here."

Irena made a sweeping gesture around the apartment. "Clerks don't live in palaces."

"There are ways," He smiled. Would this eventually qualify as another learning curve? He hoped so.

Irena regarded him curiously. "Like what?"

"Always useful, having access to foreign currency."

Now Irena smiled, although uncertainly. Natalia was looking at him in bewilderment, mouth slightly open. Irena said, "You don't, do you?"

"You should know how to turn dollars around: the best use of any foreign currency in the financial mess this country's in."

He refilled Irena's empty glass. Natalia shook her head irritably against any more. He left his drink as it was.

With forced indignation, Irena said, "I don't deal in foreign currency!"

"I don't believe you," challenged Charlie, expansively. "You'd be a fool not to, with the chances you've got. We've got it made, people like you and me."

Irena looked at her sister. "Is he telling the truth?"

"I don't know what he does or what he's saying," Natalia, said with a shrug, angrily soft-voiced.

"Aren't you worried?" It was still a question addressed to Natalia.

"If it's on a scale to support this place, I suppose I should be." Natalia was looking intently at Charlie, seeking a lead.

Irena went back to Charlie. "You could be arrested!"

"You show me a Moscow policeman you can't bribe," demanded Charlie. "Most of them would sell their mothers for fifty dollars. And I'm on the inside, as a liaison officer. Who's going to go up against me?"

Irena shook her head in bemusement. "You *are* serious, aren't you?"

"You shocked?"

"No, of course I'm not shocked! And you're right, I have sold a few dollars, here and there."

"Of course you have," said Charlie. "It's the system: the way the world goes 'round. The Arbat's best, I've found. A lot of conmen, hunting tourists." He looked at Natalia. "What about that prime Scotch steak I brought home?"

Natalia hesitated before moving off into the kitchen. Irena waited until her sister had gone before saying, "I knew you and I had a lot in common."

"And I told you I was in love with Natalia," he said, hoping she could hear from the kitchen. So far, so good, but this wasn't the way he wanted the conversation to go. But he'd play this different sort of word game if he had to.

"You don't seem to be worrying very much about her, doing what you've just told me. What about her position?"

Charlie felt the icy fingers run up his back, all the heat of his previous discomfort gone. Why the hell hadn't he talked to Natalia first? "I don't understand."

"Couldn't she get into trouble if there was a problem you couldn't bribe your way out of?" suggested the woman.

"Of course not," said Charlie, with seeming carelessness, flourishing the bottle between the two of them. "I told you: there's never going to be a problem. So the question doesn't arise."

"There's still another unanswered question from last time." Irena smiled.

"You got your answer then."

"Where's the danger in a little adventure?"

"In setting out on it." He was glad to see Natalia emerge from the kitchen: time for him to manipulate the guidance he hadn't given her.

Natalia said, "Ready when you are."

Charlie said, "Irena's worried you'll be fired if someone blows the whistle on what I'm doing."

Natalia's pause, retrieving her wineglass, was far too imperceptible for Irena to notice, although Charlie readily saw it. "I don't see how it could affect me, even if it did happen."

It was enough and Charlie felt a sweep of relief. "That's what I told her."

"You work for the government, don't you? You did when . . ." The woman stumbled to a halt, briefly flustered.

"Pensions!" jeered Natalia. "I'd get a medal for finding money where there hasn't been any to give out for months!"

Charlie couldn't believe that until that moment he'd never known Moscow and London used pensions for the same cover! So many learning curves. He said, "See? Nothing can happen to us."

"I'm fed up with this conversation," stopped Natalia. "Let's eat."

A completely sober Charlie continued playing the genially tipsy host but dropped the bombast, refusing to talk any further about imaginary illegal currency transactions or what his supposed job entailed, switching the conversation instead on to Irena. She responded with air stewardess anecdotes, some genuinely amusing, leading easily into Charlie's demand about Irena's love life, to Natalia's stiff-faced concentration on her food and to Irena's insistence that she wasn't involved with anyone in particular. "Still looking for someone who lives in a palace."

Charlie walked Irena to the street-level door, which she ignored when he opened it.

"I don't give up when I've set my mind to something."

"You're going to have to this time."

"We'll see. Do I get kissed good night?"

"No."

Natalia hadn't moved from the table by the time Charlie returned. Looking steadily at him, she said, "Well!"

"She's got a situation with Richard Cartright," said Charlie. "You would have thought she'd have mentioned it, wouldn't you?"

"I would have expected you to mention to me what the fuck you were doing."

"Another silly word," he tried, hopefully.

"Stop it, Charlie!" she refused. "Not telling me was stupid—ridiculous!"

"I didn't want to rehearse you: make it look too obvious. But I should have said something, I know. Irena arrived before I expected her."

"She's not a nice person, Charlie." She hesitated, looking directly at him. "She's bound to talk to Cartright about us, isn't she?"

"So what?" said Charlie, forcing the glibness.

"What if he tells London?"

"Why on earth should he? And what would there be to tell? That I'm living with someone who works for the Russian pension authority?"

"I thought this had been a good day," said Natalia. "Now I don't, not any longer."

"I didn't do very well with Sasha, did I?"

"It was a point in the relationship waiting to happen."

"I hope it doesn't again."

"So do I," said Natalia, although not referring to Sasha and Charlie. She'd call Irena, she decided: call her and warn the bitch that there wasn't going to be a repetition of what had happened with Konstantin. Which wasn't Natalia doubting Charlie. It was her awareness of her sister's determination.

"There's something important I want you to do," said Charlie.

Natalia listened, her face furrowed into a deep frown. "You want me to check if he officially saw anyone at our Foreign Ministry?"

"No. Just use the name Peters to trace that of the other man. The visa should give us a hotel, shouldn't it?"

"Miriam said he'd gone."

"I just want to make sure he has."

"What could he be here for?"

"I don't know," lied Charlie.

When he arrived at Morisa Toreza at eight the following morning, there were already two demands from Sir Rupert Dean on Charlie's voice mail.

The director-general said, "The name of your man is Simon Norrington. He was the elder son, thirty-one when he died, of Sir William Norrington. The younger brother, Matthew, automatically inherited the title upon the death of his father. And is still alive—"

"What was—" tried Charlie, but Dean talked over him.

"According to the family, Simon Norrington graduated with a Double First in fine art from Oxford University in 1932. He was attached to the War Office from 1940 as liaison with de Gaulle's Free French forces. He was seconded in 1943 to 140 Provost Company, a specialized unit officially part of the military police, with the rank of lieutenant, to provide the necessary authority for what he had to do—"

"Which was?" tried Charlie again.

"*Listen!*" insisted Dean. "The family believes Simon Norrington died in April 1945 and is buried in a Commonwealth military cemetery in Berlin."

20

Charlie sighed at the familiarity of a mountain of questions and a molehill of answer, not knowing the base camp of either. He hoped they wouldn't be too difficult to locate. "But the body at Yakutsk *was* Simon Norrington?"

"Definitely," said the director-general. "Sir Matthew personally identified it at the mortuary, not from after-death photographs. Gave us wartime pictures of his brother in his uniform to satisfy ourselves."

"So who's in the Berlin grave?"

"We've no idea," said Dean. "We want to exhume it, of course.

We've got to get a court order, but the War Graves Commission says Sir Matthew is still legally the recorded next of kin and wants his legally granted authority prior to a court application. And the lawyers are arguing about applying for that in camera, which we've got to do to prevent any news leak. The media pressure is bad enough as it is. God knows what it would be like if this became public."

"What was Simon Norrington's job after the War Office?"

"Tracing Nazi looted art," announced Dean.

Mystery upon mystery, or the very slightest clarification? One step at a time, thought Charlie. "Needing a lieutenant's rank, for the necessary authority?"

"Seems that way. One forty Provost Company was composed mostly of civilian police, with an occasional secondment of Foreign Office people. The police had the investigatory expertise, Norrington was the art expert."

"How extensive is his War Office record?"

"There isn't one."

"What?"

"All this comes from the family."

"This is bollocks."

"I don't like the word, but I agree the sentiment."

"What I don't like is that we seem to be all on our own."

"Neither do I."

Gulag 98 housed special prisoners, remembered Charlie. Artists and art historians would qualify as intellectuals. It was at least a fit, of sorts. It most definitely took that particular archive beyond guessed-at importance. Initially more so, perhaps, for Natalia than for himself. "Does the family have any idea what Norrington was supposed to be doing in Berlin? What he did anywhere, in fact, after 1943?"

"No," said Dean. "It seems Norrington was fanatical about art recovery—was determined to restore everything he could to its rightful owners. But the family can't offer much more than that. We've got a mystery twice as big as the one we already had, with even less chance of solving it."

There wasn't the frustration there should have been, Charlie determined. The secrecy intention, he guessed. "Have you met the American from Washington? Name's Peters."

"Kenton Peters," filled out Dean. "I'm supposed to be seeing him either today or tomorrow, depending on developments. I gather from the Foreign Office you weren't helpful."

"I didn't think I was supposed to be," said Charlie, pleased with the character assessment. "What about the other one?"

"What other one?"

"There was someone else with Peters in Moscow. I didn't get a name."

"I don't know anything about another man. And I'm glad you didn't offer too much.

"The decision's already been taken that their man is a hero, whatever he was doing or had done," said Charlie. "They won't want anything to spoil the story."

"I know what they want," said the other man, testily.

Charlie didn't like the idea of manipulating Sir Rupert Dean, the first of a very long line of directors-general not to look upon him as if he'd crawled out of a primeval swamp. But it was for both their eventual benefits, although perhaps more for his than the director-general's. Because Charlie was getting a very distinct impression that he was personally being very badly jerked around: His feet ached, which was always a sign. And a very important Charlie Muffin rule was always to be the manipulator, not the manipulated. As far as the director-general was concerned, it was more persuading the man to be receptive to alternative reasoning. "Seems pretty close to our thinking?" Not ours, yours, mentally adjusted Charlie, who hated prearranged plans or decisions that all too often in the past had rebounded dangerously close to his crotch. And this case had every hallmark of being the biggest ball-breaker ever.

"Which is why I'm being included in the Foreign Office discussions," said Dean. "Coordinated intention."

Everyone who might conceivably know something saying nothing about anything, one of those anonymous Whitehall gatherings playing verbal pass-the-parcel, guessed Charlie. He very definitely didn't want—nor intend—to be the parcel. "So our position hasn't changed?"

"At the moment our position is confused, not just by a gap of fifty years," qualified Dean. "Sir Matthew has agreed not to make any public announcement. But naturally he wants to bury his brother properly: there's a family vault. The Norringtons are a prominent dynasty: Sir Matthew got to be a permanent secretary to the Treasury in the sixties and early seventies. Left early for the city. On a Bank of England committee for a while before being seconded to the IMF in Washington. Came back to directorships of quite a few major companies. Stately home in Hampshire. Married three times with a penchant for actresses, which makes him a favorite with the media. He also gets a lot of coverage for opposing Britain's entry into the European Monetary Union. The press will have a field day if it all gets out. And they're already crucifying us."

"How likely do you think it is that as well as being useful for his art knowledge Simon Norrington might have worked for military intelligence? Or SOE? Or MI6 . . . ?"

"I've already made the list, Charlie. And the inquiries."

"And then there's the Ministry of Defense, who took over the War Office. None of which are acknowledging anything but all of which seem hugely interested in what we're doing."

"I know," repeated Dean.

"There's something you don't yet know, from here," said Charlie, preparing the director-general for the disclosure he couldn't, at the moment, openly make because he wasn't supposed to know it. "I'm pretty sure the Russians believe like I do that there was another Westerner at the murder."

"Not based solely on a bullet caliber?" rejected Dean.

"There could be something else I didn't see. Don't know about."

"What makes you think that?" demanded Dean.

"Their man, Lestov, is back from Yakutsk. We've already spoken on the telephone," lied Charlie, easily. "He said he expected the breakthrough to come from England . . ."

"There has to be a reason for his saying that," cut in Dean.

Charlie's pause had been intentional, inviting the interruption. "Of course there has. That's why I suspect there's something I don't know about. And won't unless I offer something in exchange."

"I've just told you there's more reason than ever to keep everything under wraps."

Charlie was disappointed, although Sir Rupert had sounded halfhearted about it. If you don't first succeed, try, try again, Charlie told himself. "Are the Americans going to be told who our victim was?"

"I'll listen to what they have to say first."

A sudden awareness of what Berlin could mean swept over Charlie, so encompassing that for a few moments he couldn't totally absorb it. When he did, he decided at once it made as much logic—more, perhaps—as anything else so far. But it was completely unsubstantiated—nothing more than the wildest speculation—and most definitely nothing he could suggest to the already distracted director-general. From whom he still needed to extract far more than he had so far. He couldn't afford to be sidetracked from the primary consideration of self-protection, which from now on always had to go beyond self to include Natalia and Sasha. Quickly Charlie went on, "Miriam Bell saw the waistband label, expects an identification from it. And their victim carried a photograph I didn't see her find, either. Apparently it was taken with a girl against a background it might be possible to identify." A big building, Charlie remembered—as likely to be a museum or an art gallery as a college. *Whatever he did or knew, he was in uniform for a very special reason.* Miriam's words. There was the vague outline of a hidden picture beginning to form, thought Charlie, enjoying the pun. Still wrong to be sidetracked, although he was impatient now to think solely about his sudden theory.

"She seems to have been remarkably forthcoming?" queried Dean. "What did you tell her?"

Charlie frowned. "I'm trying to give some idea of what the Americans have—so you'll know how honest they're being when you meet. You already know I didn't give anything back."

"Point taken," apologized Dean.

Getting there, Charlie thought, hopefully. "If Sir Matthew Norrington is a media figure, there's the danger of this leaking. *You* reminded *me* about the media. And I'm sure the Russians have something I don't."

"Charlie!" stopped the director-general. "I hear what you're saying. Understand it, too."

"There'll be no way to trace a leak!" protested Charlie.

"Don't let it be traced to you, from anything you might say to the Americans or the Russians," insisted Dean. "Not a millimeter too far, Charlie. One slip, and to preserve this department I'll push you the rest of the way. That clear?"

"Very," accepted Charlie. He shouldn't, he supposed, be offended at the bluntness. Indeed, he supposed he should appreciate it. At least this director-general was honest enough to tell him he was the first and prepared sacrifice. Others hadn't. And he had the leeway he wanted.

"You have anything else to talk to me about?" asked Dean.

"Are there any details of *how* the Berlin body was identified as that of Simon Norrington?" pressed Charlie. It was a safe enough question, without giving any hint of how his mind was working.

"Not yet."

"Have we asked for it?"

"We've asked for everything."

Determined to leave the other man's perception as he wanted it, Charlie said, "The body itself—particularly a recognizable face—would have suffered serious injury. So it could only have been from personal belongings. Which would have been returned to the family. Could we ask Sir Matthew what they were?"

"Maybe you should ask him yourself," suggested the other man.

"What?" asked Charlie, sharply.

"I'm restricting the number of people who know *all* of what's going on," disclosed the other man. "You're one of the few—certainly the only fully operational officer. I want you to handle it all from now on: here, Germany, America, wherever. Understood?"

"Yes, sir," accepted Charlie, keeping the reluctance from his voice. Very much the trussed and offered sacrifice, he thought. He couldn't—wouldn't—leave Natalia alone in Moscow at this stage of her ministry conflict. Nor—equally to protect her, to continue his life with her and Sasha—could he afford to let anyone else get ahead of him and risk his very future in Russia. Time to start using Charlie Muffin rules, which allowed eye-gouging and crotch-crunching. Allowed every dirty trick ever invented, in fact, providing he inflicted the damage first.

The temptation to be sidetracked, now by the thought of following the investigation outside Russia, was greater than ever, but Charlie forced the concentration totally upon the idea that had so abruptly occurred to him.

And the more Charlie thought—putting up and then knocking down the counterarguments—the more he became convinced that what had been taken from the Yakutsk bodies had not been stolen to *prevent* identification.

It had been to *provide* it, on the wrong bodies.

Which created practically a mountain range of new questions, this time without even the suggestion of a molehill. Where were the answers to start building one?

If he was right, then there had to be one, possibly two bodies in Berlin cemeteries carrying the identification of the other two Yakutsk victims: they'd died together, so their substitutes would have at least to be buried close to each other, to account for their deaths. From which it followed that the Yakutsk murders were not panicked, spur-of-the-moment killings, but the complete reverse: assassinations so carefully planned they amounted to a very positive and until now successful conspiracy. Neither had it been quick expediency to make a grave almost two meters deep by using grenades. Whoever had done that were local, with local knowledge that the tundra never melted to a depth of two meters. Which it hadn't, for more than fifty years, until the onset of El Niño.

The logic continued that the local killers had never expected—and certainly never intended—the three victims to be found. If they'd anticipated that possibility, *every* identification would have been removed, possibly even the uniforms.

The key *had* to be Gulag 98, Charlie determined. To open the door to what? Norrington's function was to trace art looted by the Nazis, about which he was fanatical. Were the special tweezers and magnifying glass that the sight-impaired American carried sufficient to suggest he was an art specialist, too? They were, for the moment, as far as Charlie was concerned. What about the woman: a specialist or an official escort? An unanswerable question for the time being, along with so many others.

Charlie stretched back in his chair, unconsciously fashioning another delta-winged paper plane. From what—or where—would come the proof, an indication that his supposition was at least worth considering? The most obvious would be finding bodies buried in Berlin in the names of the still-unknown American and Russian. A cul-de-sac, Charlie recognized. If either identity was uncovered—and shared after that—it would be from Washington or Moscow, not from any source available to him. Or was there a source? Norrington most definitely should *not* have been in Yakutsk. But for the man supposed to have been Norrington to be buried in Berlin surely proved the man *should,* officially, have been in the German capital. So in early 1945 there would have been a proper, filed in triplicate (or however many copies army bureaucracy required) order stating why he was there but hopefully—and at the moment more importantly—*who* he might have been with. If Norrington had been able covertly to go at least three thousand miles, possibly more, from where he was supposed to be, someone *in* Berlin had approved and known about it. The American was German-based, too, Charlie accepted, remembering the war-script D-marks among the dead man's belongings.

Awareness piling upon awareness, Charlie recognized where he had to look not just for the American identity—maybe even the Russian woman's, too—but for the second British officer who'd been at the Yakutsk murder. But would anything still be in Berlin? He hoped he had an advantage in the amount of time he'd spent and worked in the city over the Cold War years when, sometimes, he'd started out with less than he had now.

Charlie stirred, positively, with things to do, becoming fully aware of the absentmindedly constructed airplane. He launched it as he stood. It spun immediately into an arc and fell flat on its back. Charlie hoped it wasn't an augury.

The archives of the British embassy in Moscow are part of its basement, which have been tanked with two insulation-separated brick walls to prevent the incipient dampness of the Moskva river from mildewing the documents stored there ahead of their eventual transfer to London. In addition, humidifiers are kept constantly running. The artificial light, the only source, is harsh. Despite the brightness, the curator, a diminutive, quickly moving man with spectacles pushed up into disordered hair, blinked a lot, like a furtive animal accustomed to living permanently underground.

The man, whom Charlie had not met before, pedantically insisted upon telephoning personnel to check Charlie's authorization, appearing disappointed when it was confirmed. He recovered the moment Charlie asked for any records of a Lieutenant Simon Norrington having been at the embassy in early 1945.

"Don't have to look," said the man, cheerfully. "Already have, for Colonel Gallaway. We don't have anything."

"When?" asked Charlie.

"Yesterday," said the archivist. "Told Mr. McDowell and Mr. Cartright this morning, when they inquired. This man Norrington must have done something pretty unusual?"

"He did," said Charlie. "He died where he shouldn't have and ended up in the wrong grave."

Cartright was standing in the corridor outside Charlie's office when Charlie returned because there wasn't enough room with McDowell and Gallaway already inside. Both men were staring down at the paper plane.

Charlie said, "Pilot error."

That day they used McDowell's office, which was larger than the military attaché's. The head of chancellery accorded Charlie the padded leather chair, ordered coffee and dolefully said, "Seems like we're all getting involved in this affair."

"I thought we already were," said Charlie, studying each of them in turn over the rim of his coffee cup. McDowell was an apprehensive, first-tour diplomat frightened of any mistake, up to and including breaking wind at the ambassador's cocktail party. Foreign Office instructions would be holy writ, never to be queried and certainly never modified by any personal initiative. Charlie had already judged Gallaway a military dinosaur mistakenly laid to rest in Moscow, which the Defense Ministry was now probably regretting but which could very definitely be to his advantage. The only uncertainty was Cartright, about whom he knew practically nothing but about whom he was most personally curious because of whatever was happening with Irena. Professionally Charlie was sure he could suck up the younger man and blow him out in bubbles and wondered if he'd have to. As he was sure he could the other two. To begin with, the use of each would be to relay back to their individual departments whatever he wanted circulated to mislead and confuse. And to make them responsible for everything and anything he considered personally or professionally dangerous. The day was beginning to pick up very well indeed. With luck it could even get better.

"I don't want to repeat myself," encouraged Charlie, easily. "So it'll help if I know what, between you, you've already got from London."

The other three men looked among themselves. McDowell said, "I was simply asked what the embassy here had on an army officer named Simon Norrington."

The other two nodded in agreement.

"Without any reason?" questioned Charlie.

"Just that he was the man in the grave," said Cartright.

"But that he's supposed to be buried in Berlin," added Gallaway.

Wrong! decided Charlie, in belated realization. Cartright was MI6, which was responsible to the Foreign Office. So why the duplication to the head of chancellery? McDowell was a professional diplomat. And professional diplomats were *always* separated from each and every sort of intelligence field activity to avoid embarrassment. The molehill was taking shape. Returning to an earlier, possibly more immediately relevant thought, Charlie said to the military attaché, "Now we've got a name, your people should be able to find Norrington's service record easily enough?"

"I'm not sure that they can," said Gallaway. "It was a long time ago."

How far could he take this? wondered Charlie. As far as possible, he decided. "They going to let you have it, if it's found? It could be useful." For me more than any of you, he thought.

"Why?" demanded Gallaway, a soldier checking the barricades.

"The Russians are more convinced than me that there was another British officer there when Norrington was killed." Within twenty-four hours that would become established as a positive fact within every necessary Whitehall department, its source lost in the retelling.

"Oh, my God!" said Gallaway.

"That's appalling," said McDowell.

Still not sufficient reason for McDowell and Cartright to double up, Charlie decided. Concentrating upon the attaché he said, "You're in the hot seat, John. I'll do all I can to help, obviously. But I do need *everything* you might get from your end. And let me warn you, John. Whitehall never makes a mistake: it's always down to us poor bastards on the ground. We've got to look after ourselves, every time. . . ." He looked to Cartright. "Wouldn't you say that?"

"Absolutely," said the intelligence officer, at once.

Extending his hands, palms up, to include all three men, Charlie said, "For each of us to look after the other, you'll have to pass on all the guidance you get from London so I'm not caught out with the Russians. Everyone prepared to go along with that?"

"I certainly am," said Gallaway, eagerly.

"Me, too," accepted McDowell.

Cartwright said, "It's strictly between us and these four walls, right?"

What had he done to please God so much this day? thought Charlie. "That's most important. None of you must show me to be your source. I won't tell you anything that I'm not a hundred percent sure about."

"Thank you," said Cartright.

You won't if I decide you're trying to find out things about Natalia and I that don't concern you, thought Charlie.

Charlie went as far as to suggest a records check on the wartime prison camps at Yakutsk, which Vadim Lestov agreed was worth considering instead of disclosing it was already under way, and Charlie openly wondered how a Western-caliber bullet had come to be in the Yakutsk grave, to Lestov's shrugged insistence he had no idea. Charlie spent most of the time urging Lestov to release the photograph of the dead Russian woman, which he'd discussed at length with Natalia as a possible way of confirming Lestov's appointment as her deputy: even if it achieved nothing, the publicity was guaranteed to convey the impression that the Russian was making a positive contribution.

Charlie also provided his written impression of the Yakutsk inquiry with only the waistband label omitted. Miriam only left out her discovery of the photograph and the fact that the dead American's eyesight would have normally failed him for military service. In apparent exchange, the Russian handed over copies of the second autopsy report, virtually identical to that of the first, and announced that a photograph of the so-long-dead woman was being issued to Moscow television and newspapers in the hope of an identification.

They hadn't before met in the deputy director's suite, on the same floor as Natalia's, whose closed door Charlie had seen on arrival. Only slightly smaller than Viskov's, the room was ornately baroque and at least five times the size of Charlie's. The homicide colonel hadn't yet adjusted to such surroundings, actually on more than one occasion gazing around as if surprised to find himself there, which Charlie supposed he was. When Charlie asked directly about Petr Pavlovich Travin, the Russian detective said the man was otherwise engaged, which Charlie acknowledged to be an absolutely honest reply.

Miriam again suggested a drink as they left the ministry building and this time Charlie insisted upon the Savoy. He still hadn't resolved the uncertainty of how much to tell the American of what had nagged him throughout the meeting. Simon Norrington's identity would be known by at least three different officials from three separate Whitehall departments at the Foreign Office meeting with Kenton Peters, he reminded himself. And Miriam was his only possible Moscow source for the dead American's name. Those who gave received, he told himself.

Miriam said, "You think Travin's working on something good?"

"Could be," said Charlie.

"Jesus!"

"Maybe you'll have to try your very personal way to find out from Lestov?"

"Already in hand," said the woman, quite seriously and unembarrassed. "You were far more open with him than I expected you to be."

"Not really," said Charlie, finally deciding.

Miriam was gesturing for the second round. She turned sharply back to Charlie. "What?"

"Heard from Washington on the picture?"

Miriam shook her head, but didn't speak.

"It'll have been taken outside an art gallery or museum," he said.

"Go on."

Charlie did, telling her about Simon Norrington, leaving out only the reference to Berlin.

Miriam finished her second drink before speaking and by then any astonishment had gone. Solemnly, slowly, she said, "You think we're ever going to understand it all?"

"I don't know," admitted Charlie.

"I'll tell you what I do know," said Miriam, positively. "Something as complicated as this, there'll be a lot of people very anxious that we don't."

Which is why I've thrown the stone into your pool, to see how far the ripples spread, thought Charlie. Had Natalia's visa check not shown that Kenton Peters's companion, whose name was given as Henry Packer, was still in Moscow, staying at the National Hotel, Charlie conceded he might just have missed the man's too-hurried, attention-attracting move from the table of the hotel's pavement café, although he preferred to think he'd have still gotten it. As it was, he didn't hurry helping Miriam into her car and then strolling along Ohotnyj Rjad to the metro.

Over almost too long experience Charlie knew just how much of a surveillance nightmare the lofty, pillared and marbled halls of the Moscow underground could be, but today they were to his advantage. Within seconds of pulling himself behind one of the pillars, Charlie saw the open-eyed Packer fluster down the steps, looking wildly around, and chance getting on the train already at the platform, which would, in fact, take him in the opposite direction in which Charlie would normally have gone. Charlie went back up the stairs and into the Savoy bar again, with things to think about.

"He *told* you that he speculated in currency?" demanded Cartright, in the darkness.

"Boasted about it," said Irena. He'd been very good, the best for a long time. The apartment was a disappointment, though, compared to Lesnaya.

"What about Natalia?"

"Something to do with pensions," dismissed the woman. She hesitated. "You're not going to tell anyone about Charlie, are you? Not to get him into trouble, I mean."

"Not something I want to get involved in," avoided Cartright, which was an honest answer. He'd taken a big enough risk, agreeing in the first place to help Gerald Williams without fully understanding a reason. Now he was dependent upon Charlie's guidance and wasn't sure he could risk that, either. It was a mess.

Irena was sure Cartright would. Which would teach the blabber-

mouthed Charlie—and Natalia, with her warning telephone calls—
not to treat her like shit. The most appropriate word, she decided,
smiling at the memory of the episode with Sasha.

Charlie and Natalia were still up in their apartment on the far side
of Moscow. Natalia said, "You will have to go everywhere else, won't
you? Leave us?"

"Not until I can't any longer avoid it," promised Charlie. "Dean
said today's meeting ended as confused as it began, no one telling
anyone else what their part of the story was."

"What are you going to do, Charlie?"

"What I've always done. Look after myself."

"Look after yourself?" challenged Natalia.

"Us," corrected Charlie. A man with staring blue eyes came immediately to mind. The most worrying thing about Henry Packer
was the ineptness of the surveillance. To someone of Charlie's professionalism it was further proof that it was not the man's real job.
Charlie no longer had any doubt what that was.

"If it all does go wrong—and you're dumped because of it—it'll
all be over for us here, won't it?"

"But it wouldn't be the end of the World," qualified Charlie.

"No," agreed Natalia. "It would just seem like it."

"It's only been days!" protested Charlie, urgently. The telephone had
been ringing as he'd entered his office that morning. Afternoon in
Yakutsk, he calculated.

"I have something about Gulag 98," said Novikov.

"I could arrange for you to come to Moscow by yourself." Even
that would be a risk, Charlie accepted.

"Only with Marina and the boys. And with the residency per-
mits."

"I'm doing everything I can," said Charlie.

"Make it soon."

"As soon as I can."

21

The release of the Russian victim's photograph caused a continuing series of sensations far greater than Charlie had anticipated, although it made perfect something else he had in mind. He hadn't really expected an identification, either, which was the ultimate phenomenon.

The predictable excitement, from the existing press hysteria, was the publication itself. Despite the written and verbal insistences that all three bodies had been preserved in their ice grave, the first visual proof of just how perfect that preservation had been caused shock not just in Moscow but throughout the West. The *New York Times'* caption—"as if she died just hours, not half a century, ago"—was echoed in hundreds of newspapers and on television throughout the world.

It also brought about an unremitting media clamor for photographs of the British and American lieutenants as well as for Charlie and Miriam Bell publicly to be again made available for interviews. The FBI's inept reason for refusing—that photographic publication or a press conference could possibly interfere with ongoing inquiries—brought an even greater clamor to know what those inquiries were and within twenty-four hours newspapers in America and Europe were speculating with ironic accuracy at a cover-up.

Encouraged by the American president's already declared insistence that the American was a hero to be given a hero's burial, the free-reined theorizing spiraled into total fantasy, up to and including—disregarding both the history of the time and the fact that Yakutsk is three thousand miles from Moscow—that it had been a mission to assassinate Stalin to end communism, prevent the division of Europe and stop the Cold War before it began. Germany and France—and Charlie—preferred the suggestion that it had been a joint operation to rescue Princess Anastasia from imprisonment in one of the Yakutskaya gulags after escaping the Ekaterinburg slaughter of the Imperial Russian family in April 1918. Claimed former gulag inmates recounted stories of a beautiful woman with black hair to her waist, living in moonscaped isolation in her own crenellated, barbed-wire-enclosed dacha guarded by watch towers and an elite Cossack troop.

Brighton Beach, on New Jersey's Atlantic coast, is a ghetto of Russian émigrés, although demographically the majority are Ukrainian by birth or ancestry. They also represent the broad spectrum of Russian mafia in the United States. It was from the Beach—the waterfront avenue itself—that the first claim came from a man insisting the victim was his mother's sister, with whom they'd lost contact after leaving her the custodian of priceless heirlooms, including a selection of icons for which he now sought reward or compensation from the Russian government. The virtually immediate FBI location of a three-page rap sheet for fraud, criminal deception and larceny didn't prevent a day of headlines in the nearby New York newspapers.

There were three similar deception attempts in Moscow, two of which drew heavily upon the Anastasia invention, the third stretching it with the assertion that the victim was the secret daughter of Rasputin. Each demanded money, always in dollars, for their stories and family photographs, all of which were faded and blurred and none anything like the dead woman even before scientific examination.

Charlie made his own very personal contribution to the media frenzy on the third day, deciding it might be physically dangerous to delay any longer, although he hadn't again picked up Henry Packer despite walking far more than he normally did and always going through a series of cut-out-detours to get back to Lesnaya, pointless though that belated caution might be.

On the morning of that third day he got to his office early, wanting Packer still to be at the National Hotel. The series of quickly dialed and even more quickly disconnected telephone calls only took thirty minutes and Packer was actually breakfasting in the hotel dining room when the anonymously alerted Moscow-based international press corps descended, en masse.

Such was Packer's reaction and the momentum of the Yakutsk mystery so self-perpetuating that the entire—and continuing—confrontation ran on television almost in its entirety during the course of the day and what was cut was easily filled in from the blazoned newspaper headlines and Charlie's various conversations with Miriam and Natalia.

The dining room corner into which Packer had protectively placed himself became instead a trap from which he couldn't escape through the solid pack of journalists and cameras, and most of the television footage actually showed him wide eyed, like an animal in a snare.

Charlie's calls had identified Packer as an American State Department official on a secret mission to Moscow personally to explain to the Russian president the mystery of Yakutsk. Packer visibly cowered under the welter of questions, at first doing nothing but shake his head. When he did speak—in a surprisingly high-pitched New England voice—he appeared to confirm the suggestion. In his panic he babbled about speaking with Washington, too late remembering his pipeline engineer cover, which fell apart when he said he couldn't remember the Russian company he'd come to Moscow to see. When his panic worsened, he tried to force his way through the wall of people confronting him and when they wouldn't move lashed out, physically trying to fight his way through. At first that was panicked, but when he was shoved in return he openly tried to catch one thrusting reporter with an upward blow to the chin with the heel of his hand, which, if it had connected—which it didn't, because of the madhouse scene—would have snapped the man's neck. He chopped and jabbed several more times, very professionally, but again because of the jostling just one cameraman was hurt, a rib broken, because the knuckled punch again missed the fatal heart spot.

At least six reporters and cameramen went down with Packer when he fell, struggling, and he was gouging his way out of the melee when the militia arrived. At the police station, according to newspapers and later confirmed by Miriam, Packer first claimed diplomatic immunity, which immediately involved the embassy, and then claimed he was the victim of assault. Miriam told Charlie it took less than an hour for the State Department in Washington to disclaim any knowledge of the man and insist he in no way qualified for any immunity. It was midafternoon, according to Natalia, before Vadim Lestov got to Militia Post 23 to question Packer about Yakutsk. Fully recovered, the man insisted he knew nothing whatsoever about the television and newspaper stories running by then, nor why they should have imagined he did. Just as doggedly he maintained he'd come speculatively to Moscow as a pipeline engineer but had not yet been able to make contact with any oil exploration companies. He now demanded to leave the country immediately.

The colonel in charge of Militia Post 23 consulted with the Foreign Ministry after a junior counselor from the American embassy talked of an irritating diplomatic incident and Packer's visa was revoked. Packer's luggage being collected from the National Hotel by a second counselor, who also paid the man's bill, would have been clue enough for the waiting press pack, even without the telephone calls from Militia Post 23 police on the media payroll. Packer arrived at Sheremet'yevo airport in an embassy car to another press ambush, which provided more footage of Packer fleeing across the concourse, knocking two people over as he ran.

It was when Charlie was assuring Miriam that evening he had no idea how the press had discovered Packer's presence—reminding her she'd told him the man had returned with Kenton Peters—that he learned of Washington's disavowal: "The goddamned embassy's in an uproar: the ambassador didn't know what to do." Charlie guessed it had been a badly conceived, independent CIA operation, which was the explanation he later put to Natalia. When he put the suggestion to Sir Rupert Dean, the director-general said, "You really think so?"

"You saw the way he fought on television."

"And he definitely had you under surveillance?"

"Definitely," insisted Charlie. "I think it should be officially logged."

"So do I. And it will be. And I'll ask Washington for an explanation, through the Foreign Office. It'll all be denials and claims of misunderstanding, of course." There was a pause. "You think you've removed the danger?"

"The publicity will have frightened Peters." I hope, thought Charlie.

"Wonder how the Moscow press got on to him?"

"No idea," said Charlie.

The confirmed recognition of the woman in the Yakutsk grave came on the fourth day after the publication of her photograph and literally relegated the Henry Packer fiasco to a one-day wonder. The identification came from a man who walked into the offices of the English-language *Moscow News,* which with admirable journalistic initiative obtained what they believed to be everything it was conceivably possible to get from Fyodor Ivanovich Belous before contacting either their local militia station or the Interior Ministry. And in addition to what Belous had to tell, which upon analysis was quite meager, the well-documented background ensured a story that within a further twenty-four hours brought the announcement of movie intentions from a leading Hollywood studio. One of the photographs Belous produced of his mother, Raisa, even appeared to show her in the same white shirt, dark jacket and skirt she had been wearing when her body had been found.

Belous's story was of never having known either his father or mother. His entire knowledge of them had come from his now-dead maternal grandparents, who had brought him up in Moscow, where he had lived his entire life, mostly as a clerk in the central division office of the Communist Party and latterly as a bookkeeper at the Moskva Hotel.

His father, Ivan, had died in 1943, just days before the end of the Germans' nine-hundred-day siege of Leningrad. His mother had fled, unaware of being pregnant, one week before the siege began in September 1943. She had worked in the curators' department at Tsarskoe Selo, the "Tsar's Village" of five spectacular palaces established on the outskirts of St. Petersburg by its founder, Peter the Great. Raisa Belous's particular responsibility had been the palace of Catherine the Great. It had been her job to organize the rescue convoy to Moscow of as much of the Catherine palace treasure as she could, in advance of the Nazi army and its Einsatzstab Reichsleiter Rosenberg für die Besetzten Gebiete, named after Alfred Rosenberg, who in 1940 had been personally appointed by Hitler to confiscate, loot or steal every work of art from Nazi-occupied territory for the world's most complete museum Hitler planned for his Linz birthplace.

It was a matter of historical record that the Catherine Palace had housed one of the world's greatest but now lost art treasures, the Amber Room presented to Peter the Great in 1711 by the Prussian warrior-king, Friedrich Wilhelm. And that Hitler had personally ordered that the twenty-one honey-yellow amber panels, four gold-framed with jeweled landscapes picked out in Florentine mosaic, the others carved in flower and fruit motif, should be restored to their original splendor in East Prussia's Königsberg Castle in what he intended to be his personal study.

According to Belous's grandparents, his mother's greatest regret had been her failure to strip the three-hundred-year-old amber from the Catherine Palace walls to prevent it from falling into the hands of the Nazi E.R.R. looters. As it was, for what she had saved, Raisa Belous was made a Hero of the Soviet Union by Stalin. It was to let as many people know—not just in Moscow but in the West—that his mother had been such a heroine that he had approached an English-language publication.

As well as the photograph of his mother dressed in what she had been found in the Yakutsk grave, Belous produced four others, one of her standing in the middle of the Amber Room showing it in the dazzling glory that earned it a nineteenth century British ambassador's description as the eighth wonder of the world. There was also the official notification of his mother's death, which he now didn't understand and wanted explained.

It was recorded as having occurred in Berlin in early April 1945. Raisa Belous had died, according to the notice, in an antipersonnel mine explosion.

"Which will have caused severe facial injuries," predicted Charlie, during one of the twice-daily telephone conversations he maintained with London.

"I think you should come out of Moscow: pick up things here," said Sir Rupert Dean.

"I want to speak to Belous myself," avoided Charlie. "And there's Gulag 98."

The inmate register of which, building up the impression of a momentum, landed on Natalia's desk the following day.

It was one of a batch of ten, all former camps in the immediate vicinity of Yakutsk itself, and was one of the few to have been divided between male and female prisoners. The batch brought to fifty-three the number through which Petr Pavlovich Travin was supervising the search—already extended since the emergence of Fyodor Belous—

for anyone whose history hinted German, English or American connections or art or antique links.

The Gulag 98 records were among the largest and certainly the most complete so far delivered, the main dossier running to three hundred pages, annexed to which were the personal files of what, from the dates, appeared to be the last inmates sentenced before the camp's 1953 destruction. Only the names remained, in faded sepia-brown ink, of the original thirty artists, writers and teachers who with little more than their frostbitten hands had built the original camp in 1932. Five were registered as having died during the construction. Against the names of all—and the majority who had followed in the subsequent nineteen and a half years—were listed unspecified crimes against the state. Fifteen years appeared to be the minimum sentence, thirty the maximum. Hard labor, within the dozens of mines, was mandatory. Without exception, permanent exile followed every jail sentence.

Charlie and Natalia had exhaustively researched the discovery. The year of the coins found on Norrington and the April 1945 dates for the Berlin burial provided a year-long time frame for Natalia to work within. From that period she gleaned the names of fifty-five men and thirty-seven women whose records—spanning a range of art, art history and academic professorship—suggested people or occupations that might have been sufficient to lure the three murder victims to Yakutsk. Among the men were fifteen whose names and details identified them as German. There were no personal records for any of those fifteen, nor any reason for their imprisonment. Each was simply described as being of "special category." Twelve were marked as having died before the closure of the camp. The location to which the other three had been transferred was not given.

Following the step-by-step preparation she had gone through with Charlie, Natalia delayed sending the Gulag 98 dossier to the man who was still her official deputy, needing to copy what she considered relevant sections. With the rest she sent a note, duplicated to everyone involved, reminding him the concentration upon anyone with fine art or antique expertise was now even more important in view of Raisa Belous's history. Because it was also a connected part of the necessary further undermining of Viktor Romanovich Viskov and Petr Pavlovich Travin, she ambiguously worded her agreement to

Lestov sharing with the British and American investigators that afternoon's interview with Fyodor Belous as if it were the homicide colonel's idea rather than hers, curious if Charlie would again be proved right.

He was.

To Viskov's anticipated, within-the-hour objection, copied to the same circulation list to which she had also sent hers, was attached the minutes of their very first coordinating meeting, at which Dmitri Nikulin had specifically forbidden such cooperation. Viskov's memo demanded an explanation for her disregarding the instruction of the presidential aide.

Natalia's rebuttal was even quicker than Viskov's to her: she'd had it already prepared, complete with her marked version of the same initial meeting. Dmitri Borisovich Nikulin had also specifically ordered that everything should be done to discover the undisclosed progress of the two Western investigators, which they might be able to estimate by carefully monitoring a shared interview with someone whose story was already public knowledge. Unable to prevent the bubble of uncertainty, Natalia wrote that she regarded the intervention of the deputy interior minister even more counterproductive than his brief cancellation of the gulag search. As the authority of Dmitri Borisovich had been invoked in both their exchanges, she was, of course, prepared to defer to his judgment, but unless she heard from the president's chief of staff she intended the shared encounter with Belous to go ahead as planned.

No intervention came from Nikulin.

Charlie's invitation to the Interior Ministry, personally telephoned by Lestov, was the prearranged signal that Natalia had won another battle. It would not be difficult for him seemingly to let something slip, apparently to show Lestov to be making all the right moves. Charlie wondered if out of it all he'd be able to extract a little in return. He expected to, because he hadn't wasted the intervening, personally unproductive days. He'd read quite a lot about specific war history.

Charlie Muffin was a diligent reader of body language, too, and believed there was initially a lot to be learned in the first few nearwordless moments of the encounter with Vadim Lestov. Charlie's immediate impression was of the Russian colonel himself. Charlie knew from Natalia there had been further recognition from Dmitri Nikulin for Lestov achieving an identification by releasing Raisa Belous's photograph. The change in Lestov was practically visible, as if he had grown in stature, filling out, becoming taller. There was nothing left of the earlier, close-to-overwhelmed reserve in the official surroundings of the ministry. Instead there was a smiled greeting, without any stammer, and tea—although no vodka—and the easy acceptance of Charlie's congratulation at the quick discovery of Raisa Belous, without any acknowledgment that the picture-release idea had been Charlie's. The Russian even wore a newer suit that didn't shine with wear at the elbows.

Fyodor Ivanovich Belous's did. The striped jacket had once been part of a long-ago-divided suit and the gray trousers were bagged and shapeless. But here again there was no awkwardness and, re-membering the *Moscow News* details of the man's Communist Party past, Charlie guessed the confidence lingered from Belous once having been part—albeit a very small cog—of the ruling machine. The handshake was firm, the eye contact direct through rimless spec-tacles. When Lestov complained, mildly, at Belous telling his story first to a media outlet, Belous at once said he'd explained his reason for doing that in the article and Charlie further guessed the man's imperiousness would have exceeded his position in a mourned regime Belous would clearly have welcomed back. Charlie also suspected Belous's going to a newspaper had as much to do with a personal protest against the supposed and resented new order as it did with establishing his unknown mother's reputation.

There was a stenographer at a side table and Lestov carefully took the man through what, at the first telling, was virtually a repetition of his newspaper account. Belous also produced the originals of his now-much-copied souvenir photographs, along with Raisa Belous's award citation.

"That's all I can tell you," concluded the man.

"Let's see," said Lestov.

The homicide colonel's questioning was thorough although uni-maginative and Charlie decided the man would make an excellent support deputy for Natalia; the lateral thinking might come with time and encouragement. Belous was discomfited conceding that his mother's personal belongings had been disposed of after her death—refusing to use the word *sold* when Lestov talked of jewelry and the hero medal itself—and insisted he didn't know what his grandparents might have done with any letters or documents apart from the medal certificate. Certainly nothing had survived. Belous couldn't remember any discussion, ever, about his maternal grandparents and had always assumed they'd died before he was born.

"Where did your father's parents tell you she was buried?" demanded Lestov.

"They didn't. I mean, they didn't know. They said there'd just been a notification that she'd been killed."

"Where?" persisted the Russian detective.

"I don't know that, either. They never said."

Charlie deferred to Miriam when Lestov invited them to join the questioning, as always wanting the benefit of everyone else's input before making his own. And was disappointed, even wondering if Miriam was using the same ploy to hold back for his contribution before making hers.

Charlie took his time, actually repeating some of Lestov's questions hopefully to lessen the slightest edge of resistance he detected in Belous's response to the American.

"Your grandparents were extremely proud of your mother?" he asked, edging toward his own agenda.

"Rightfully so," said Belous. He had wispy, receding hair and the pallor of a permanent indoor worker.

"Indeed," agreed Charlie, wondering at the defensiveness. "But they were your *father's* parents?"

Belous frowned. So did Lestov. Questioningly Belous said, "Yes?"

"Weren't they proud of a son who died in one of the most heroic episodes of the Great Patriotic War?"

"Of course they were!" replied Belous, indignantly.

"None of your photographs show him with your mother."

"The newspaper appeal was for information about her, not him."

"So you do have photographs of them together?"

"Not now."

"What happened to them?"

"I don't know. My grandparents showed me some, when they were telling me about my parents. I don't know what happened to them after my grandparents died."

"What were they photographs of?" demanded Miriam.

"Their wedding."

"When was that?"

"June 1941."

"How many were there?" Charlie bustled in. He didn't believe parents would dispose of photographs of their son but keep those of their daughter-in-law.

"Four, I think."

"Doing what?"

The man shrugged. "They were wearing the same clothes in each, so I guess they were all taken at the same time. There was one I remember showing them relaxing; nothing in the background. It was dated June 1940. The other two showed the Catherine Palace behind them, so it had to be Tsarskoe Selo, where they worked."

"*They* worked?" seized Charlie. "You hadn't told us that. What did your father do?"

Belous flushed. "He was the senior restorer at the palace. That's how they met, when my mother joined the curator's staff." The man shifted uncomfortably.

Charlie's feet gave a psychosomatic twinge, a usual body and mind indicator that he was going in the right direction, even if he didn't know what the destination might be. Lestov and Miriam sat unmoving, waiting, as if they expected to learn something, too. Cautiously Charlie said, "I think we might have gone too quickly over what you told the *Moscow News*. And us, earlier. I'd like to make sure I've got everything right. Your mother and father worked together at Tsarskoe Selo until the German invasion in 1941. Your mother escaped, rescuing a substantial amount of the Catherine Palace treasures, and your father stayed behind and died just before the siege lifted, in 1943 . . . ?"

"No," said Belous, shifting again. "The paper got that wrong; made it a better story, I suppose. My father was drafted into the army long before the invasion. He left St. Petersburg—or Leningrad, as it then was—almost immediately after he and my mother married.

According to my grandparents, they *got* married because he was being moved."

"So where did your father die?" came in Miriam, again.

"They were never quite sure. My mother never showed them the official notice. They thought it was somewhere near the Polish border, Lvov in the Ukraine or on the other side, near Lublin."

"You told us your grandparents virtually brought you up by themselves, after your mother came to Moscow?" probed Charlie, hoping Miriam wouldn't interrupt again too quickly.

"I believe so. I can't remember my mother."

"Not ever having been with you?"

"No."

"What age would you have been when they told you about her and your father?"

"I'm not sure. Seven, eight, nine—something around that age."

"Is that when you saw the photographs of your mother and father together?"

"That would have been the first time, I suppose, yes."

Charlie was intrigued at the man's apparent selective memory. This was turning out to be a far different encounter than he'd imagined. "They were proud of her? Talked about her a lot?"

"Yes." Belous relaxed slightly.

"When they told you about her for the first time, did they tell you she was away a lot?" Charlie was aware of the other man relaxing further. So what had made him tense?

"She had an important job, they said."

"Doing what?" demanded Lestov.

"They never told me."

"You don't have any photographs of your mother in any sort of uniform?" Belous was lying, Charlie knew. To have told her bereaved son what his mother had done would have been the first thing proud grandparents would have done.

"No."

"What about your father? Any photographs of him in his army uniform?"

Belous hesitated. "It looked like a uniform in the pictures in Tsarskoe Selo. I'm not sure."

He was, Charlie decided. "Weren't you ever told what army group or unit he was in?"

Beious shrugged. "He was killed at a battlefront. He must have been a soldier, mustn't he?"

No, thought Charlie, who from his previous days' study and the emerging attitude of Fyodor Belous believed he had a good idea of the wartime employment of both the man's parents. The outside bits of the jigsaw were beginning to fit, but the center of the picture remained blank. He was curious if Miriam and Lestov thought the same. "You were seventeen when your grandparents died, within a month of each other?" said Charlie, picking up on what had been established in Lestov's earlier questioning.

"Yes," said the man.

"And you lived all that time in an apartment at Ulitza Kirova?"

"Yes."

"They're impressive apartments. Big," said Charlie, who'd specifically gone there on his way to the ministry. "Your grandfather must have been an influential man: a Party worker like yourself, perhaps?"

Belous stared back warily, unspeaking for several moments. "It was allocated to my mother as a reward for what she did in Leningrad. They were allowed to keep it, after she died and was honored. Why is this important?"

"We're trying to discover how and why your mother was murdered," reminded Charlie. "Everything's important. Tell us about things you remember in the apartment. Were there pictures, prints, on the walls. Ornaments around the place?"

"I don't understand that question!" protested the man.

"Your mother worked in the palace of Catherine the Great: enjoyed things of rare beauty," said Charlie, whose reading had extended to studying the illustrated masterpiece catalogue. "I would have expected her to try to decorate such a special apartment with things of special beauty."

"You are suggesting my mother stole things!"

"Not at all," lied Charlie. "Anything from the Catherine Palace would have been too well known, too well documented, for anyone to have kept them in Russia. Your mother would not have been honored as she was if there had been the slightest doubt about her honesty."

Belous regarded him doubtfully. "There were some pictures, I suppose. A few ornaments. Nothing I remember particularly."

Back to the selective memory, Charlie recognized. "Do you still have any of them?"

"No," said the man, too quickly.

"They were sold?" demanded Charlie, directly.

"I don't know."

"If they weren't sold, you'd still have them, wouldn't you?"

"I don't remember. They just weren't there, after my grandfather died."

"Not even the medal, about which they were particularly proud?"

"No."

Charlie leaned forward, picking up the citation, caught by a sudden thought, hoping but not expecting to find what he did. "Your mother got to Moscow with everything she saved from the palace in late 1941?"

"Yes," said the son, swallowing.

"And was made a hero of the Soviet Union for doing it."

"That's what the citation says."

"No, it doesn't," corrected Charlie. "It's for 'Special Services to the Soviet Union.' And is dated December 1944. That would have been almost four years after she saved what she did from the palace, wouldn't it?"

"If those are the dates," conceded the man. "Things take a long time to get done in a bureaucracy. Particularly in wartime."

There would have been treasures, Charlie knew. Maybe from the Catherine Palace or from what—and where—Raisa did for the remainder of the war, after 1941: maybe even small works of other people's and other countries' art. How much and how many would have been hoarded by Raisa Belous and gradually disposed of by this man over the years, for a few rubles—kopeks, maybe? Even a prized medal, which Charlie now doubted she'd gotten for what she'd done at Leningrad but for a far greater contribution afterward.

Belous was looking fixedly at him, apprehensively. The man hadn't gone to an English-language newspaper to honor his mother.

He would have demanded to be paid. Probably had been. And by some of the foreign correspondents he'd spoken to, as well. There wasn't anything to be gained, challenging the man. Charlie recognized he'd gotten all he wanted. It had, in fact, been a far more productive afternoon than he'd expected. He hoped Lestov had, as well. It was as much for the Russian's benefit—and ultimately Natalia's—as it was for him. His curiosity about Miriam could wait. Charlie said, "Thank you. It's been very helpful."

Belous blinked, surprised. "You think you can find who killed my mother from what I've told you?"

Belous would have been prompted by the *Moscow News*. Charlie guessed; maybe by some of the Western correspondents, too. "Not by itself. But it's added a lot to what we already know."

"What was she doing at Yakutsk, with the officers?"

"That's one of the things we don't yet know," said Charlie. But I'm getting closer by the day, he thought.

Natalia was for once already at Lesnaya when Charlie got home. Sasha was bathed and settled in bed and his Islay and glass were set out in readiness.

Natalia said, "We've got Gulag 98. As well as a lot of other obvious possibilities."

Charlie sipped his whiskey, knowing she hadn't finished, enjoying her excitement.

"Guess who was sent there, as well as the fifteen Germans?" she demanded.

"Who?" asked Charlie, dutifully.

"Larisa Yaklovich Krotkov. Who was on the curators' staff at Tsarskoe Selo. The complete staff list still exists. I ran a comparison with the names at Gulag 98. And there she was!"

Charlie stopped drinking. "What was she jailed for?"

"Assisting the enemy."

"Any details?" Coincidence, or another piece of the jigsaw?

"Not so far."

"We can use it," insisted Charlie. "*You* can use it."

"How?"

"You've sent the Gulag 98 file on to Travin?"

She nodded. "In this afternoon's consignment. But how can Lestov be shown to discover it when he's not examining the camp material?"

Until this moment it had been a problem Charlie hadn't known how to overcome, but now he did. "Did Lestov pick up on the interview with Fyodor Belous?"

"You made it clear enough. He's having Belous's place raided tonight, to see if there's anything the man hasn't already sold. And Raisa was Trophy Brigade. So was her husband, from the very beginning."

"One thing at a time," said Charlie. "Have Lestov do what you've already done, run a check on all the curator staff at Tsarskoe Selo, which he could logically do after today's interview. It'll throw up Larisa Krotkov's imprisonment. And where she served it."

"Yes," agreed Natalia, distantly. "That'll do it, won't it?"

"It's them or you," urged Charlie, knowing her difficulty. "Them or us."

"I know."

"Arrange a personal meeting with Nikulin, include Lestov, for him to get the credit," advised Charlie. "But you make the direct accusation, against Viskov and Travin."

"I know that, too," said Natalia. "And I'm as frightened as hell."

There wasn't the hiss-voiced fury of Kenton Peters's first telephone calls, a loss of control Boyce had never before known. Now the anger was in the frustrated determination to find out how Henry Packer had been exposed.

"Only you and I knew he *was* still in Moscow. And neither of us made the calls," said Boyce. It was Cartright who'd discovered the anonymous contacts. "And there wasn't any way Charlie Muffin could avoid recognizing him, after the amount of television coverage."

"Still damned impudent of Dean to put what he did in the exchanges."

"It would have been wrong for me to intervene."

"I quite understand," said Peters. "I don't know or understand how, but the information must have come from a Russian source."

"From which it follows that Moscow has more than we suspected or guessed about Raisa Belous and Yakutsk," suggested Boyce.

"I'll not give up," insisted Peters. "I'll go on until I do find out."

"We both will. But shouldn't we move on a little?"

"I don't like Norrington being identified," said Kenton Peters, taking the suggestion.

"I'm not letting it be made public," assured Boyce.

"I'm surprised the Russians allowed the photograph to be published, to let Raisa Belous be identified," continued Peters. "I've always said they're the uncertainty, didn't I? This and Packer confirm it."

"You didn't know your president was going to make his hero announcement until it was too late," gently reminded Boyce.

"What the president did will never occur again," said Peters. "He knows just how annoyed I am about that. I've told him enough to understand what the effect could be. He's terrified."

"I was merely pointing out that oversights can happen. And we can hardly remind Moscow, can we? We're not supposed to know."

Unable to move his mind for long from what came close to being the first embarrassment of his career, Kenton Peters said, "The Agency lost a good man in Packer. He's useless now that he's been so publicly identified."

Boyce said, "We'll have to put on hold any move against Muffin for the time being. Nothing too close."

"I've asked for someone else to be selected," disclosed Peters. "Muffin's an uncertainty and you know I don't like uncertainties."

22

Again it was the absence of anything positive or worthwhile that confirmed for Charlie a suspicion he didn't need proved any further. It wasn't even the fault—or obstruction—of the other three with whom he'd yet again gathered in the military attaché's office. They were as much puppets as he was intended—chosen—to be. The difference was they didn't know how their strings were being pulled. Charlie did and was thoroughly pissed off at the realization. With his feet, dancing was a dirty word anyway; it was equally forbidden when he was the puppet.

"My people can't trace anything on a Lieutenant Simon Norrington, either by name or by the army serial number his family gave," apologized Gallaway. "Nor any cross-reference to a Raisa Belous. Whatever existed must have been destroyed."

"What about an art squad?" persisted Charlie, as a test, already knowing that one existed.

"I only filed that request yesterday," said the attaché. "I'm still waiting."

"So am I," said Cartright. "So far I haven't even had an acknowledgment. As far as I know, SIS didn't have an interest."

From that morning's conversation with London, Charlie knew Sir Rupert Dean was also still waiting for a reply to his inquiry, made even earlier. The director-general hadn't argued with Charlie's open accusation that they were being played with by every other interested government ministry and department. Instead he'd told Charlie he wanted him back in London by the end of the week.

"It's put a lot of extra pressure on me," complained Raymond McDowell. "The biggest continuing diplomatic dispute between Germany and Russia is stolen or disputed wartime art, even after all these years. I've averaged four cables a day from London since Raisa Belous was identified. So's the ambassador."

"I thought everyone was supposed to be fighting a war after 1939," said Gallaway.

The limited military attaché probably did, accepted Charlie. He decided to excuse himself as soon as possible from this aimless discussion. He wanted to be at the end of a telephone if Natalia called. There was even more to talk about after Dean's week's-end ultimatum.

McDowell said, "The Nazi treasure looting was more efficiently organized than the Final Solution. There was even a connection, of sorts. Hitler considered the people of Eastern Europe subhuman. He didn't intend just to eradicate the Jewish race. Eastern Europeans were to go, too; become a vast slave resource while the Germans expanded eastwards to take over their countries. Anything of any cultural, artistic or historical significance was seized by Alfred Rosenberg's E.R.R. organization: entire museums, libraries. And not just by them. Goering, whose favorite was nudes, had Hitler's permission to take whatever he wanted from occupied countries for an art gallery that was to be as big as Hitler's, in Linz. Hitler had the plan and model of it with him when he committed suicide in the Berlin bunker; the speciality was to have been heroic Aryan portraits and sculptures. Himmler, Bormann, and von Ribbentrop each had their art squads; von Ribbentrop took every Renaissance painting he could lay his hands on in Italy. He had his own art-scavenging battalion, with three companies from it working exclusively for him in Russia alone. . . ."

Charlie began to concentrate, looking at the lecturing head of chancellery with sudden interest. It obviously all came from London and the detail was surprising. Maybe even more surprising was that the Foreign Office clearly considered it necessary to provide such an intense briefing. Calling upon his own specific, self-imposed modern history lesson, hopefully to encourage the diplomat further, Charlie said, "And the Soviet Union had the sort of Trophy Brigades that Ivan and Raisa Belous belonged to, with every front line regiment. The Soviet Trophy Brigades virtually trawled the countries—Germany particularly—when the war turned against Hitler. The almost obscene irony is that the Nazis made it easy for them: they'd stolen and got a lot of it conveniently together, for the Russians simply to pick up. Germany has officially listed something like three hundred thousand heritage treasures Russia refuses to give back. Moscow claims they're war reparation."

Gallaway snorted a laugh. "How can anyone argue the legality of that?"

"London did. And Washington," deflated McDowell. "America's OSS formed a special Art Loss Looting Investigation Unit. President Truman personally signed the order to ship two hundred European paintings to America, to go on touring exhibition. The intention was to hold on to them until Germany made its financial reparation. The paintings were only returned after American and European academics and art historians pointed out that America could be accused of the same cultural rape as the Nazis . . ."

Not all take and no give, thought Charlie; not a wasted morning, either! He hadn't known of the existence of an American unit. But the FBI would. From which it logically followed that Miriam Bell would, too. It had been almost forty-eight hours since Raisa Belous had been named and her art connection established. Time enough to have had the photograph Miriam had recovered from the body—and more recent ones of the corpse itself—checked through OSS archives. It might, even, account for the woman's seemingly casual questioning of Fyodor Belous the previous afternoon and why, for the first time, she hadn't wanted to talk things through after leaving the Russian ministry. If she already knew who her victim was—what he had been doing, even—all she would have needed to do was sit and listen during the meeting with Belous to ensure nothing emerged to endanger Washington's cover-up. In fact, thought Charlie, warming to his speculation, it all made perfect sense of that intended cover-up and what he'd guessed to be the runaround to which he was being subjected. Still encouraging, he said to McDowell, "You're remarkably well informed."

"So are you," challenged the man.

"Homework, here, after the *Moscow News* account," said Charlie, more or less honestly. "I didn't learn all you appear to have."

"I asked for as much guidance as possible," admitted McDowell.

"The Foreign Office suddenly seems to have a lot of information available," suggested Charlie.

McDowell made an uncertain gesture. "It's a sensitive area, particularly after all that business with Switzerland and Holocaust gold and bank accounts of Jewish concentration camp victims."

"That's spreading the net a bit wide, isn't it?" questioned Cartright. "I can hardly imagine there was art treasure or looted Nazi gold in the prison colonies of Yakutsk!"

Charlie suddenly realized from the previous night's conversation with Natalia what could have been there and was irritated for not thinking of it sooner. Natalia had even shown the way! Maybe, at last, there were a few pieces becoming clearer for the center of the jigsaw. There was actually an immediate direction—and reason—for his taking up the investigation away from Moscow as soon as possible, although not immediately to London. He'd already considered Berlin the place to go: where, hopefully, something no matter how small might have been overlooked.

He said, "It occurred to any of you we're being jerked around in one bloody great cover-up?"

"Ours is not to reason why," irritatingly clichéd Gallaway. "We've got to obey orders."

Charlie said, "I'd like to think that if I got shot in the back of the head, somebody, somewhere, someday, would try to find out why. Orders or no orders."

Just the sort of cocky bloody-mindedness Gerald Williams had warned him to look out for, Cartright recognized. And by which his career could be badly affected—ruined—involved as he now was in this damned affair. And then there was that currency speculation business that the gorgeous and willing Irena had told him about. Definitely things he needed to talk about with Williams. Maybe even with his own department, too. Gallaway was right. If there was a cover-up there was a good reason, and it wasn't their business here—certainly not Charlie Muffin's—to question it.

The only sound in the White House suite of Dmitri Borisovich Nikulin was the faintest rustle as the president's chief of staff turned the pages of what Natalia had placed before him thirty minutes earlier. Now she sat unmoving, outwardly in complete control, inwardly in turmoil. She knew—had known for months—that this moment was inevitable. But it had seemed so much easier—foolproof—talking it through with Charlie at Lesnaya than it did now, making the accusation to one of the most influential members of the Russian government about a deputy minister in that same government. The fact that the accusation was true—only this last, hopefully decisive device connived—wasn't a reassurance. Nikulin had only moved Travin sideways. What if the presidential aide was a friend of Viktor Romanovich Viskov? Or Viskov had a protector even more influential and powerful than Nikulin?

Beside her, Colonel Vadim Lestov sat similarly statued, no longer awed or ill-at-ease in such baroque surroundings, although Natalia had no doubt he was as inwardly agitated by the sudden awareness of what she had directly involved him in.

Lestov had easily and professionally followed Natalia's lead, not needing anything more than the initial prompt to make the same intriguing discovery about the Yakutsk jailing of a former Catherine Palace curator employee. But only Natalia's insistence that there were other, previous circumstances of which he was unaware stopped the man from positively arguing her determined conclusion. It had been an impromptu gesture to show Lestov her memorandum recommending his official appointment as her deputy. She hoped ambition— and of being in Nikulin's presence, only a few meters from the president himself—would prevent the man from voicing any further doubt.

The chief of staff looked up at last, pushing the folder slightly away from him.

"You've no doubt it has been deliberately withheld?" demanded the harsh-featured, emotionless man.

"None whatsoever," said Natalia, pleased with the strength of her own voice.

"There is no proof."

"Of course not," she accepted, at once. "I'm asking you to judge it with what you know to have happened since this began. It's been a campaign of positive, personal obstruction. A permanent vendetta against me. The inquiry itself—the need to protect this government, which was your specific instruction—has been totally and consistently disregarded." Natalia gestured sideways. "Everything positive we have suggested has been opposed, to erode my authority; the camp search, which from Colonel Lestov's discovery *is* proved to have been essential, needed your order to be reintroduced, after its arbitrary cancellation. . . ." She hesitated, at a prepared accusation. "I actually wonder to which government or country the deputy minister and Petr Pavlovich, who still holds the title of my deputy, are giving their true allegiance."

"That's an astonishing allegation!" protested Nikulin, genuinely shocked.

"And one I do not make lightly," said Natalia. She felt numb, striving to keep control. "I do not believe it's possible to continue this investigation—to achieve everything it's necessary to achieve— under these conditions. Which is why I am making this a formal, official complaint."

Nikulin stared down at the closed folder on his desk for several moments before coming up to Lestov. "Do you feel yourself to have been positively obstructed?"

Natalia felt a fresh jump of apprehension.

"I do not know all the circumstances that have been referred to . . ." the homicide detective began to hedge.

"Have you had any contact from Petr Pavlovich about Gulag 98?" broke in Natalia.

"No," said Lestov.

The presidential aide said, "What contact *has* there been between yourself and Petr Pavlovich?"

"We speak daily," confirmed Lestov.

"Who calls whom?" seized Natalia, knowing the answer.

"I call him."

"He has never initiated an approach?" queried Nikulin.

"Not since the rearrangement of responsibility."

Without explanation Nikulin picked up the telephone, dialing the number himself. It wasn't until he began to speak that Natalia realized he'd called the deputy interior minister. Natalia's emotions switchbacked. Momentarily her mind blanked, refusing any thought. Then she heard how Nikulin was speaking and gauged that he was favoring her against the man. Nikulin said nothing about her or her accusation, instead asking about the progress of the investigation and particularly the assembly and search of camp records. And from Nikulin's next question accepted that, in his determination still to denigrate the idea, Viktor Viskov must have continued to belittle its purpose.

"It's being carried out, though?" Nikulin was saying. Viskov must have assured him that it was because the chief of staff next said, "Completely up to date? That's good."

Nikulin redialed immediately. The conversation with Petr Pavlovich Travin was virtually a repetition of that with the deputy minister, except for Nikulin demanding a second time to be assured that there was no backlog in the prison file examination.

Nikulin replaced the telephone for the second time and Natalia waited, hopefully. With creaking formality the man said, "I'm sure you're very busy, as I am. Thank you for bringing the matter to my attention."

Natalia's numbness wasn't as bad, but it was still there.

Gerald Williams had always been sure he'd win. It had been his strategy that had been wrong. Which he'd recognized and adjusted. He'd never imagined that in front of embassy witnesses the arrogant bastard would openly infer his intention to question or disobey a definite instruction. Or, better still, boast of currency speculation, a virtual admission of the blatant robbery he was so determined to expose. He'd found the Achilles' heel in Charlie Muffin's ridiculous shoes, the weakness with which, finally, he'd bring the man down.

The ideal, mused Williams—the absolute, orgasmic ultimate— would be for the man to be arrested in the act by the Russian authorities.

Williams sat transfixed at his office desk at which he had just concluded his telephone conversation with Richard Cartright, consumed by the idea.

It was a very different and exciting strategy indeed. And such a perfect one. So excited was he by it that on his way home he abandoned his usual train to stop at a Westminster wine bar to buy himself a small glass of sparkling wine, savoring it as if it had been an 1890 Roederer Cristal.

By coincidence there were two other real champagne celebrations that night, both separate and both in Moscow.

"I had lunch with him," said Boyce.

"And?"

"He complained about the wine, which was Lafite. God, he's insufferable!"

"I wasn't asking about the wine."

"He said we were worrying too much."

Peters sighed. "You know what I'd like to do?"

"Yes," said Boyce. "And I'd like to help you do it."

"Maybe we should and stop thinking of Muffin," reflected Peters.

23

"You won!" said Charlie.

"*We* won," said Natalia.

Charlie waved dismissively, curious at how subdued she was. His news rather than hers, he supposed. "More than won," he said, topping her qualification. "Travin exiled to the Chertanovo militia station, not even the colonel-in-charge, so far removed it might as well be to Yakutsk itself rather than a Moscow suburb! And Viskov dismissed! You're safe!"

"Viskov is still a member of the Duma: in parliament."

"Where he'll stay, powerless. It's you who's got the ear of Nikulin. And more. It would have been the president who sacked Viskov."

Natalia smiled faintly. "It's going to take time adjusting to it." Yet again, she thought. She finally sipped the champagne Charlie had insisted on opening when she'd told him of Nikulin's late afternoon announcement. Charlie had allowed Sasha a thimble measure before she'd been put to bed demanding to know if she'd get a party for being clever like her mother, which had been Charlie's explanation for the celebration. He'd said maybe. Natalia's smile quickly faded now. "How long will you be away?"

"No longer than absolutely necessary," Charlie promised. He was as satisfied with his afternoon as he was with Natalia's. The director-general's announcement of the exhumation of the supposed grave of Simon Norrington had given Charlie a valid reason for going to Berlin, which after a lot more embassy library reading he'd decided was more important, initially, than anywhere else.

"I don't like doing business this way," Dean had protested.

"It's the way everyone else is doing theirs. It was you who warned me at the beginning that this could destroy the department—might even be intended for that purpose."

"Certainly things haven't been done properly, but I can't believe that!"

"I can."

"You don't want anyone to know where you're going?" qualified Dean.

"Not even within our own department."

"I'll overlook the impertinence of that, but only just."

"I wouldn't ask if I didn't consider it necessary."

"The military attaché is going to be the official representative, maybe with others from the embassy."

"I'll fix everything myself from here. Which will make it my personal responsibility."

"If you get it wrong, it'll be mine as well."

So obvious was Natalia's continued uncertainty about surviving her own internal war that Charlie decided against telling her his suspicion of being a chosen victim in another. Neither would he ever admit to her his impatience to pursue the investigation outside Russia. From her reaction already to his going, he knew she could never have been convinced his eagerness was entirely professional, a determination to at last become the hunter, not the hunted, which didn't quite fit but was good enough in his own mind. Perhaps a better analogy would be getting off a stage upon which everyone else had been watching his blindfolded performance without taking part themselves.

"I shall miss you," Natalia said. "So will Sasha."

"You don't need me to tell you the same."

"I do," Natalia said, urgently.

"My life's perfect here. And this is where my life is, from now on. With you and Sasha."

"Don't put it in danger, then," Natalia urged.

"How?" Charlie frowned.

"Go with the system, darling, not against it. Even if you do find out everything, go along with the cover-up if that's what's demanded. The three of us are more important than anything else."

"I will," said Charlie. The problem was having to take every conceivable risk to find out the truth. Only then would he have any protection from unblinking men like Henry Packer.

Miriam handed the champagne to Lestov, lifting her own glass in a toast. "Congratulations."

The Russian said, "I still can't believe it." There seemed, in fact, a lot of personal benefits he still had problems believing, the most pleasant of all being in Miriam Bell's apartment, drinking Miriam Bell's wine and knowing that eventually that night he would share Miriam Bell's always welcoming bed. He hoped, too, to share other things, which meant he would not even be neglecting his professional duties.

Miriam was having her difficulty understanding the dismissals that had accompanied Lestov's promotion, but needed to because of the obvious connection with the investigation. "It happened, just like that?" she questioned, snapping her fingers.

"There was a previous episode I was only partially involved in and don't know enough about: something to do with the deputy minister opposing the prison camp search."

"And didn't that turn out to be a good idea!" flattered Miriam. She grinned. "I'll show you later just how grateful I am getting the outcome of that." She picked her glass up to take to the kitchen. "Come and talk to me while I cook." Her persistence wouldn't seem so blatant there, preparing dinner.

Lestov followed dutifully, happy for Miriam to consider herself the leader. He leaned casually against the food bar dividing the kitchen in two, watching her and anticipating the prospect of that familiar body under the concealingly loose caftan. If only he fully understood that morning's White House meeting, he'd be a very happy and contented man. "I'm not sure I shouldn't tell Charlie. He seems to have been pretty open with us . . . you, at least, which amounts to the same thing."

"Only as much as it suits him," objected Miriam.

And you, thought Lestov, curious how much there was she hadn't told him. "You think there are things he's kept back?"

"I'm sure of it." She'd expected something from the OSS archives by now. She hoped the bastards in Washington weren't working the well-known need-to-know shell game to sideline her. She still didn't fully understand the business with Henry Packer. Charlie insisted he didn't understand it, either, although there was the suggestion of a separate CIA operation, which the Agency people at the embassy denied, which of course they would if it had or if it hadn't been.

"He might offer something back." Was she sleeping with Charlie Muffin, as well?

"Let's wait, see what you get from following up the Larisa Krotkov lead," suggested Miriam. "Always best to negotiate from a position of strength."

Miriam lived outside the embassy compound and from the kitchen of the apartment there was, paradoxically, a superb nighttime view of Moscow's Catherine Palace. Nodding through the window, Lestov said, "I had that checked, hoping someone there might have known Raisa Belous or Larisa Krotkov." He shook his head. "No one did, although some of the stuff rescued from St. Petersburg was stored there until the end of the war."

"And there was definitely nothing in Fyodor Belous's apartment when you went there?" pressed Miriam.

"Not that we found. I think he would have been expecting us, hidden things away. I might wait awhile and jump him again."

Lestov topped up her glass, leaning immediately forward to kiss her, and Miriam kissed him back, enjoying it, like she enjoyed the man himself. As well as being sure Charlie was still keeping something to himself—despite chest-clutching denials—she was equally sure she was ahead of everyone, largely as a result of sharing her favorite hobby with this militia colonel. Who was better than a lot in the past with whom it had been necessary to sleep in the call of duty and Miriam Jane Bell's personal advancement. Vadim Lestov hadn't so far failed to make the chimes ring in bed and was more interesting than most on the embassy fuck circuit, including Richard Cartright, who hadn't offered anything worthwhile outside the sheets, either. "What, objectively, are the chances of finding Larisa Krotkov's trial records?"

Lestov shrugged, with his back to her. "Doubtful."

"You honestly think there might be something in them to account for Raisa being in Yakutsk?" questioned Miriam, going back to a suggestion Lestov had offered when he'd told her of the Gulag 98 discovery.

"Anything else would be too much of a coincidence, wouldn't it?" He was disappointed that the totally logical speculation hadn't encouraged a more forthcoming response from her: it was always questions, never answers.

"So where do the two lieutenants come in?" Miriam hadn't given Lestov the Englishman's name. Or told him of the OSS possibility. She served the steak and handed Lestov the Napa Valley chardonnay to open.

"If I knew that, it would be the end of the mystery," exaggerated Lestov. He really had hoped to get more—or the hint of more—from her. He hesitated a little longer from making the commitment that had occurred to him on the way to Miriam's apartment. He hadn't wanted to disclose the German names, but he'd exhausted all possible Russian sources. But the FBI would have access to more. So the sacrifice was necessary. He said, "Fifteen Germans were sent to Gulag 98 in April 1945."

She looked fixedly at him across the table. "You got the names?"

"For yours and my information only."

"Absolutely," agreed Miriam, at once. All this and a good fuck, too.

"Vitali Maksimovich Novikov," identified Charlie. "He's got a wife and two boys." Natalia had relaxed during dinner, laughing more readily and genuinely than Charlie could remember for a long time. The last few weeks had been a greater strain upon her than he'd fully realized.

"The Yakutsk doctor?" she remembered, at once.

"He claims to have more. The exchange is to get him and his family out."

"You promised him?"

"I said I'd do what I could. Without him I wouldn't have known about Gulag 98, which we used to destroy Viskov and Travin. It was one of the camps Novikov's father looked after. Was originally sentenced to. I've got to know what it is he's got."

"We both have," she agreed.

Charlie's telephone call to Vitali Novikov was the last of several he made from his embassy office the next morning before leaving for the airport. Miriam Bell was not among them.

Novikov said, "I was beginning to think I wouldn't hear from you again."

"Just make the application. It's being supported through the embassy," lied Charlie. "Don't mention that, of course."

"How can I thank you?"

"You know," reminded Charlie.

24

Charlie gazed through the window as the plane banked for landing, feeling the usual surge of nostalgia for a city in which he'd worked so often that Berlin had once seemed more like home than London. He couldn't pick out the odd memorial scraps of the Wall, but didn't anyway need markers for where, like a bloated aorta along which so much real blood had run, it had gone through the heart of the city. He didn't see the Commonwealth war cemetery, either. He didn't bother trying to locate from the air the other building he was anxious to get to, knowing very well where it was.

What embarrassment—what need—could there be after all these years for not one but two countries to be so determined to cover it up, as America and England appeared to be? Something both had combined upon, clearly. Big, then. Mammoth, even. All securely hidden for fifty-four years, never ever intended to be revealed, as the bodies had never been intended to be discovered. A shared secret of one agency? Or several, each in some way involved in some small part? Would the telephone calls he'd made and the ambiguous conversations he'd initiated in the last few days, spreading the inquiry too wide, he hoped, for anyone to see a direction, be sufficient? Or would whoever the puppet masters were have been too clever, getting there ahead of him—years ahead of him? He was pinning a lot of hope on bureaucracy getting in its own way, which in his experience it nearly always did. And on the fact that he'd worked in Berlin so often and knew so well just how many institutions had been created there in the immediate post and Cold War years. He hoped most of all that his memory and knowledge were better than any Whitehall or Washington chair-bound keeper of secrets. And Kenton Peters had another secret now, not one to keep but to discover. Charlie's whereabouts. Persuading Sir Rupert Dean not to disclose his movements was as personally self-protective as it was to guard the department. More so. The American mistake—Peters's arrogance—had been letting him know what Henry Packer looked like, not knowing how well tuned Charlie's antenna was. It was going to be much harder to recognize Packer's replacement if one was sent.

Charlie had made his reservation at the Bristol Kempinski, the hotel in which he always stayed, without asking the current prices, not thinking until he was checking in of the distress it would cause Gerald Williams to authorize these expenses as well as maintaining the rent on the Lesnaya apartment. Letting the thought drift, Charlie acknowledged it had been several weeks since any expenditure inquisition from the zealously attentive financial controller. He'd almost been disappointed that the cost of his beekeeper's hat hadn't been queried. Perhaps, mulled Charlie, the man had given up. Then again, perhaps he hadn't.

Natalia had insisted on packing for him, everything laid out in his case in meticulous comparison to his customary haphazard effort, and when he lifted out the spare jacket Charlie knew why. There were two notes, with another framed photograph of Natalia and Sasha. Natalia's note said simply, *Hurry Home*. Sasha's was much longer, the laboriously printed English attempt interspersed with cyrillic letters, each line dipping dramatically at its end, literally falling away. It said, *I love you and miss you and I am sorry about that silly word.* Charlie liked best that it was addressed to Daddy.

He was at the room bureau, writing an immediate reply on a hotel postcard, when the telephone jarred, startling him by its nearness. With a befitting, machine-gun delivery, the voice said, "Jackson here. Thought we should meet, as you suggested. Downstairs when you're ready."

Lieutenant Colonel Rupert Jackson's age—at least half that of Gallaway, Charlie guessed—marked him at once as the complete antithesis of the ineffectual Moscow attaché, a fast-track career professional for whom the promotional escalator would never rise fast enough. He came up from the barstool like a spring, the flick of fair hair that would give him problems on parade days falling over his left eye. He managed to push it back and shake hands at the same time. The handshake was firm but not arm wrestling. Orange juice, Charlie noted, automatically ordering Islay malt, knowing the hotel stocked it, which was another reason for staying there.

"A table's probably better," Charlie suggested, moving away from the bar at which there were only two other people anyway, and they at its far end.

"Of course, sir."

"You want me to call you lieutenant colonel?"

The man frowned, confused. "No."

"Then it's Charlie."

The frown became a grin. "Not sure what the form is with you chaps. . . ." He looked down at himself. "Thought mufti was best." The trouser crease of Jackson's muted checked suit would have been dangerous to the touch and the man risked severing an artery moving his head too quickly against the stiff collar. The burnished brogues reflected sufficient light to send SOS signals.

"Fine," said Charlie, aware for the first time that Natalia must have pressed his trousers, too. It still amounted to a before-and-after comparison. "Sorry to barge in like this at the last moment."

"Glad to have you aboard. Saw the television from Siberia. Can't have been much fun."

There'd been a reference from the attaché to seeing him on television when they'd spoken from Moscow. Charlie hoped that had been sufficient official identification, without the man feeling it necessary to check with the Defense Ministry in London. If he had—and there'd been objections—Jackson would hardly have kept the suggested meeting or been so amenable. Charlie said, "It was pretty rough."

"Any idea yet what happened to the poor bastards?"

Open sesame! thought Charlie. "Not a complete picture. What guidance have you got from London?"

"None," said the other man, apologetically. "Just told to attend, as official military observer."

Bugger it, thought Charlie. "What's the setup?"

"Haven't arranged anything. Waited for you. Got a car outside. Thought you might like to look around."

"What about the exhumation?"

"There's a security blackout on it, of course. Ministry insistence. Fortunately the Commonwealth cemetery at Charlottenburg is under military jurisdiction. Makes it easy. The section we want has already been sealed off. The grave itself has been screened. The workmen haven't been told whose grave it is they're opening. Apart from them, there'll just be us, the embassy padre, a medical examiner and someone from the Berlin coroner's office. There might be someone from the War Graves Commission; they're not sure yet what to do about the grave marker, now they know it's not Simon Norrington. . . ." He paused. "You know what you're looking for?"

"Not yet," said Charlie. Hopefully he added, "Anything else London had you do? Don't want any confusion between the briefings."

"Little risk of that," assured Jackson, still apologetic. He'd been told the Gieves and Hawkes customer archive had provided the address of the family seat in Hampshire and Sir Matthew Norrington had produced the War Office's 1945 notification of his brother's death and burial in Berlin; having visited it, Sir Matthew had even known the plot number. He had, it seemed, considered it fitting his brother remain in a soldier's grave rather than be reinterred in the family vault in England.

"Located the grave myself from the plot number," said Jackson. "Usual inscription: rank, name, unit, date of death."

"Everything based on what the family supplied?" queried Charlie, disappointed. "What about from the ministry itself?"

"Family told the ministry, the ministry told me," said the attaché.

"Nothing more than that?"

"Afraid not."

"Was the Provost Company properly established here when Norrington was supposed to have died?" asked Charlie.

"I doubt it, that early. From what I gather no one knew where anybody was in Berlin in April 1945: whole regiments split up, platoons and squadrons fighting on their own. And the Russians were here first, of course."

"What about wartime archives here?"

"Military police headquarters are at Rheindahlen. You might try there."

"What about records of stolen art?"

"There's an art recovery center at the university here. Others at the universities of Bremen and Dresden, too." He stopped, thinking. "The grave of the American wouldn't be here in Berlin. There aren't any military cemeteries here."

Charlie felt a sink of further disappointment. "Where are the American dead buried?"

"There are a lot of cemeteries throughout Europe. I wouldn't even like to guess. Do you have a name?"

"No."

"A unit?"

"No," lied Charlie, not wanting any destroying or concealing visits ahead of his own.

"But you do have a photograph of the American body found in Yakutsk? Know what he looks like?"

"Yes," said Charlie.

"That's something, perhaps."

"But not enough," said Charlie, deciding upon the need for another lie. "Anyway, it's Norrington I'm interested in, not the American."

Charlie was surprised, momentarily bewildered, at his feeling of déjà vu upon entering the military cemetery, until the comparison came to him between the regimented pattern of so many headstones and crosses and the stunted, number-only wooden markers by the Yakutsk gold mine.

The control office was in the middle of the cemetery, the grave areas radiating out like spokes in a wheel. There were manicured trees bordering the paths. Initially he and Jackson ignored the building, going instead to the grave, Jackson confidently leading the way. Some of the trees would anyway have partially concealed it, but screens more than two meters high completely encircled it. The cross naming Simon Norrington was still in place, but there had been some digging at its base to lift it. About a third of a meter of topsoil had already been dug out. At least, thought Charlie, there weren't any man-eating mosquitoes.

Jackson said, "What was the Yakutsk grave like?"

"A bomb crater. They used grenades."

"Whoever this was had a proper burial."

"But was probably killed to order."

Jackson regarded him quizzically. "You sure about that?"

"No," admitted Charlie. "I'm still not sure about anything."

The duty registration clerk in the control office was a rigidly coiffed, rigid-faced woman who just as tightly demanded the military attaché's identification, despite their having met earlier when she had been informed of the exhumation, and who regarded Charlie with disdain and his Moscow embassy accreditation with suspicion. She insisted on telephoning some unidentified official in another cemetery office before accepting Charlie's right to examine records, and stood at each man's shoulder to ensure they fully completed the perforated, hole-punched entry slips with their names and details of their official identity documents.

Considering the outside appearance of hundreds of graves, the archive vaults were surprisingly small, two linked rooms about fifty meters long and half as wide, totally bare except for central tables and row upon row of filing cabinets against every available wall space. On both tables, In Memoriam books were set out in symmetry matching that of the grave markers, in alphabetical order to replace the current page-a-day book displayed in its glass case in the entrance to the British lodge house.

Charlie supposed there was an index system linking name and burial place, but they didn't need to consult it, already knowing the plot number, which enabled the clerk to lead them at once to a cabinet halfway along the first room. She insisted upon retrieving and finding the Norrington entry herself, not trusting them to handle the paper-aged ledger, and laid it open on the central table, clearly unhappy at disturbing the neat arrangement of the waiting commemorative books.

She said, "The paper's fragile. I'd appreciate your not touching it."

The entries were listed in numerical order, by plot allocation. Norrington's—Plot 442—was a third of the way down a right-hand page, the details occupying just one line, each fact fit into a designated box. There was his army officer's six-digit serial number—*987491*—rank, full name—Simon St. John Norrington—unit and finally a date, *29-4-45*. Under the box headed CAUSE was *KIA*. The number three was written in a final, far-right-hand column. There were various numbers against other names above and below in that column.

Charlie said, "KIA? Killed in action?"

"Yes," sighed the clerk, confirming the obvious.

"What's the three refer to?"

"Visitors asking to examine the register. The man's entry has been read three times since his interment."

"London told me Sir Matthew said he'd been here," reminded Jackson.

Charlie's feet twinged, a physical response to the feeling of expectation that had been all too rare on this operation. Gesturing back toward the outer office, he said, "Is it regulations that everyone who wants to see the registration has to complete an entry slip?"

"Of course," said the woman, impatiently. "There is a responsibility to the dead as well as to the living."

"Which I'm sure you fulfill admirably," flattered Charlie. "What happens to the slips?"

The clerk frowned at him, making vague movements toward the still-open drawer. "Each is quite properly transferred to the cabinet log. As it should be, of course."

"I'd like to see the log. And the slips," said Charlie.

"I'm not sure I can permit that," said the woman.

"And I'm sure you can," said Jackson, at once. "You need authority, make another phone call."

The clerk hesitated, face burning, before taking a separate, thicker book from the bottom of the cabinet. Again she carefully turned the crackling pages, appearing to find her place but then turning one sheet back and forth several times. She finally looked up, frowning more genuinely this time. "I don't understand that."

"No slips?" anticipated Charlie.

"You knew?" she challenged.

"Guessed," said Charlie.

"This is against all regulations! I'll have to report it!"

"Yes," agreed Charlie. "You should. No one can get access without accredited authority, can they?"

"No! You saw the procedure."

"What about another nationality?"

"I don't understand the question," she protested.

"Immediately after the war, when Berlin was occupied by the Four Powers? And later, when it was divided?" coaxed Charlie. "Could, say, an American or a Russian have examined the entry? Needed to complete a slip like we did?"

The woman digested the question. "I suppose so," she said, although doubtfully. "I've been here fifteen years and it's never happened while I've been on duty. This is very irregular. There'll be an inquiry! It won't stop here!"

"It probably will," predicted Charlie.

As they got back into Jackson's car, the attaché said, "Bureaucratic cock-ups happen every day."

"But this isn't one of them," said Charlie, who was hoping fervently for others.

"What, then?"

"A second, much deeper burial that this time won't be affected by freak weather."

"The bastard!" exclaimed Miriam. "No reason at all!"

"Just that he'd been recalled immediately, he didn't know why or for how long. And that he'd either call from London or be in touch as soon as he got back." The Savoy barman ignored Lestov's ruble-waving effort to attract attention, concentrating upon the dollar-tipping Americans at the other end of the bar.

"That's bullshit! Of course he knows why!"

"I already worked that out," said Lestov, pained.

In her fury Miriam missed the sarcasm. It had to be something very dramatic indeed for Charlie to have been called back like this. So she wasn't ahead of everyone after all. The opposite. Way behind. But why hadn't the son-of-a-bitch called? Making a point, obviously. Bastard! And why was Washington closing her out, insisting they couldn't locate the relevant OSS files? Or trace any of the German names she'd asked to be identified, which she didn't think Lestov had believed when she'd told him? Who the fuck's side were they on? She grew angrier at her impotence. Petulantly she said, "So much for share and share alike! All right by me. I'll play his rules from now on. Cut him out."

Well aware by now of Miriam's stop-at-nothing ambition, Lestov was not surprised at her peevishness but thought she sounded vaguely ridiculous. "Don't you think we should wait to see if we can afford to?"

The Russian was right, Miriam accepted. "Let's take a rain check on tonight, darling. I need to get back to the embassy and tell Washington straightaway." She couldn't think of a way to avoid admitting Charlie had gone off without telling her and knew she was going to appear pretty damned stupid.

Lestov wasn't surprised at that announcement, either. His own possible benefit already worked out, he said, "One thing this should prove to us is the importance of you and I exchanging absolutely everything: no holding back, whatever we might be officially told to do."

"I thought that was our understanding already," said Miriam. She probably would have to do so if she stood any chance of catching up and saving her ass.

"It's certainly mine," said Lestov. He wasn't particularly upset at Miriam canceling the evening. On his way to the hotel he'd become excited by an idea he had no intention whatsoever of discussing with her, as well as an oversight that needed correcting. Now he could go back to the ministry and start working at once. The barman finally condescended to move toward them. It gave Lestov a lot of satisfaction to walk away before the man reached them. He didn't leave a tip for the previous drinks, either.

At the Lesnaya apartment Sasha handed the telephone back for Natalia to finish the conversation with Charlie and afterward said, "He is going to stay my daddy, isn't he? He is coming back?"

"Yes," said Natalia. "He's going to stay your daddy forever."

"Good," said the child, positively. "I don't want anybody else."

"Neither do I," said Natalia.

"The Foreign Office has been told by the State Department Charlie Muffin is here in England," protested Patrick Pacey, the political officer. "According to the Ministry of Defense he's turned up in Berlin. Both want explanations why they weren't informed!"

"Charlie must have detoured," said Dean, easily. "And have a reason. And we're not required to advise departments either in advance or after initiating an inquiry in an investigation that we're officially in charge of. The Ministry of Defense and Washington can go to hell."

"He should have advised us," said Hamilton. "He just can't go wandering off."

"I warned you," said Gerald Williams. "Warned everyone. The man does what he likes and we'll all suffer because of it."

Charlie had been right about the reaction from the rest of Whitehall, thought Dean, reflectively. And why was it so important to America?

"Berlin *is* quite safe," insisted Boyce. "We tidied it up when it all began."

"Where, exactly, is the damned man? England or Germany?"

"Dean thinks he's moving somewhere between the two."

"Thinks! Why doesn't he *know*? I don't like this man doing what he likes, when he likes. We're not properly in control," objected Peters. "I've got a replacement for Packer. I don't think we should wait any longer."

"It wouldn't look right, so soon. Don't forget what Dean put on record. He's too independent: he'd make a fuss. I'm still seeing everything that's coming in. Muffin's still way off course. We'll let him continue going around in circles. It's actually causing more confusion than we'd hoped to create."

"I'm going to close down my end," decided Peters. "I think you should do the same."

"Not yet, Kenton," said the other man, who disliked the American's need always to be in complete charge. "We'll let my end run on for the moment."

25

It rained, very softly, a drenching mist. The ground had become soaked before they tried to extend the surrounding plastic for some overhead protection. There wasn't enough sheeting. All it had done was narrow the gap through which the water came, adding to the morass in which they stood. The mud of the partially redug grave came up to the diggers' ankles and the surrounding grass was quickly churned into mire beneath the shuffling feet of the rest of them. Jackson's inappropriately bright red and white golf umbrella kept their heads and shoulders dry, but Charlie could feel the dampness seeping in through his spread-apart shoes. The need to wear them into comfortable collapse was always a problem in the wet.

There had been formal introductions at the cemetery lodge but no conversation afterward. The German officials hunched under their own umbrellas. The plump medical examiner, whose name Charlie had caught as Wagner, kept looking accusingly at Charlie, as if their dawn misery was his personal fault. The embassy padre, now occupied in head-bent prayer, had earlier looked equally upset at Jackson's umbrella. The priest himself didn't have any covering. His hair and nose dripped. It was more crowded than originally intended inside the dank enclosure because of Charlie's visit the previous day.

Charlie and Jackson had gone directly from the cemetery to the embassy and failed to find any official approach to account for the three recorded but untraceable visits, which, inexplicably in Charlie's opinion, had caused the head of chancellery to send a second secretary today. His attendance had, in turn, ensured that of the previous day's registration clerk, no longer patronizingly hostile but instead anxious for them to know she had gone through the entire ledger to ensure the slips hadn't been wrongly indexed, which they hadn't been, and a nervous official from the War Graves Commission, who'd assured Charlie there was nothing in their local Berlin directories, either, but that a full search was being carried out in London. Charlie acknowledged that the official motions had to be gone through and didn't tell them they were wasting their time. He also didn't tell Jackson.

The diggers were even more deeply immersed when they located the coffin, which they did at first by feel, and sunk even farther, up to their elbows, groping into the quagmire to slip lifting canvas beneath the casket.

There was a muffled, shoulder-shrugging conversation between the German officials before Wagner said to Charlie, "What are you looking for?"

Charlie shrugged back. "Whatever's there."

"Anything of forensic importance could be destroyed, attempting a preliminary examination in these conditions."

"Don't let's try, then," said Charlie, who'd already decided that, as he'd also decided that, remote though the possibility would have been, anything outside the coffin, at the bottom of the grave, would have been lost, too.

The embassy padre invited them all to pray as the slime-coated coffin came into view with a slurped, sucking sound, and Charlie dutifully bent his head with everyone else, wondering idly where God had been when Simon Norrington's head had been blown off in Siberia, or, indeed, throughout the entire Second World War. Perhaps He'd been busy.

Instead of edging back against the sweating plastic to make room for the box, Charlie led the way out. The ambulance attendants, who'd so far remained dry inside their vehicle, emerged reluctantly to accept the body. Jackson promised the medical examiner he knew the way to the mortuary and the registration clerk and the War Graves officially repeated that they'd go on looking for the missing dockets and Charlie said he appreciated their continuing efforts. The cemetery official exchanged signed documents with the medical examiner.

Their wetness inside the BMW caused the windows to steam when Jackson put the heater on full. Charlie knew it wouldn't be sufficient to dry his feet. He was lucky, he supposed, not to suffer from rheumatism.

Jackson said, "You think you'll learn anything from whatever's inside the coffin?"

"Just confirmation of what I already suspect, if indeed there is a body."

The car swerved slightly at the attaché's snatched sideways look. "You think it might be *empty?*"

"I wouldn't be speechless if it were."

But it wasn't.

The skeleton, largely in its expected shape, was still inside the now-opened coffin being extensively photographed when Charlie and Jackson were shown into the glassed observation annex raised above the forensic pathology examination room. Because of the elevation

Charlie could see almost everything inside the box. What remained of the hairless skull was on its left side, horizontal to the shoulder area, which also appeared disarranged. There were isolated wisps of a thin, gauzelike cloth that Charlie presumed to be the shroud.

The medical examiner was standing back for the photographs and saw them enter. He was gowned, despite there being no risk of outside contamination of a corpse so long dead. Only when the German's voice echoed into the viewing chamber ("There's communication between us; there are permanent microphones on the ledge in front of you") did Charlie see the pathologist was wearing a headset and voicepiece.

"Anything specific you want to establish?" Wagner added.

"Extent of the injuries that killed him," set out Charlie, his list mentally prepared. "Every possible body measurement. And height. Your opinion, if you can reach it, about his possible body weight. It looks from where I am as if all the hair has gone, but if there are traces I'd like to know the color. Any orthodontistry which might help. Any indication from the bones of injury prior to his death: broken leg or arms, something like that. Anything, obviously, that might be in the coffin that you wouldn't expect. Particularly personal objects. And anything else you can think of and I haven't."

Jackson sniggered at Charlie's final remark. Wagner didn't. After a pause the German said, "I will talk as I examine."

The pathologist worked alone, lifting what sometimes appeared bone only a few millimeters in either length or diameter, virtually dismembering and reassembling the entire skeleton. Everything was measured and weighed in the transfer, every piece identified by its proper medical name, its size and weight itemized. What Charlie regarded as of major significance registered very early in the examination, but he did not interrupt until the pathologist finished the reconstruction.

"Severe physiogmatic trauma?" echoed Charlie.

"That's what I said."

"Would the face have been destroyed beyond recognition?"

"Without any doubt. There's no trace of either cheekbone or the left jawbone, including the eye socket surround. Any teeth that remained have been shattered beyond any orthodontic comparison. There's no nasal formation whatsoever. In my opinion he got hit directly in the face: death would have been instantaneous."

"You also used the word *severe* to describe the hand injuries?" said Charlie.

"You can see for yourself, from where you are," said Wagner.

"From where I am it looks as if both hands were totally smashed."

"They have been," agreed the doctor. "There is no right thumb or index finger."

"What about the tips of fingers?"

Wagner had been looking toward the panoramic window separating them. Briefly he turned to bend over the examination table before coming back to them. "No finger—nor the left thumb—extends its full length to the final joint. Perhaps he put his hands in front of his face at the last minute, to shield himself from whatever hit him."

It was a further two hours before the examination was complete. It was established that the unknown dead man had been one and three-quarter meters tall and from chest and body structure reasonably thickset. The dead man had suffered no bone damage injury prior to his death. There was no surviving hair, nor any unexpected personal objects in the coffin.

It was still only midday when they emerged from the mortuary. The rain had changed, driven down in solid walls by a wind that hadn't been blowing earlier. Charlie didn't think the graveside plastic would have survived if it had been. His feet got soaked again on his way to the car.

"Well?" queried Jackson, once they were inside.

"Sometimes it's not what you find but what you don't," said Charlie.

Natalia was thinking the same, in Moscow.

She looked up from the yellowed sheets that Lestov had set out in front of her. "It could simply have failed to be recorded."

The homicide colonel, bristle-chinned and light-headed from a totally sleepless night at his desk, shook his head. "It was my first chance fully to examine the records of Gulag 98, after getting them back from Travin. We all missed something important. They're *perfect.* No omissions, no gaps. It was a very special camp indeed, at least while it existed."

"So?" demanded Natalia.

"Look at the plot numbering," urged the man. "It's consecutive, a name recorded against every plot in a cemetery that no longer exists. There isn't an entry for Larisa Krotkov. She was sentenced to life imprisonment, but there's no record of her dying there. Or being buried there."

What possible connection could there be with the disappearance of the visitors' slips in Berlin? Natalia wondered, remembering the previous night's telephone conversation with Charlie. "Gulag 98 was closed very soon after Stalin's death. Inmates were either released or transferred."

"She wouldn't have been released, for conspiring with the enemy. . . ." He gestured to the mound of papers in front of Natalia. "Two hundred people were transferred. *Every* name is there. Larisa Krotkov's isn't."

"What have you done about it?"

"Asked St. Petersburg for trial depositions. There aren't any, for her. There are for five others, all men, accused of the same crime directly after the siege was lifted. The sentence was mandatory: execution."

Natalia had spread the papers across her desk for comparison. Slowly she began stacking them, one on top of the other. "Conclusion?"

"Larisa Krotkov wasn't *sentenced* to Gulag 98. She was *sent* there, a supposed prisoner, for a reason. And the only possible reason is something connected with Tsarskoe Selo. Which links her with Raisa Belous."

It was wildly speculative, thought Natalia. But then so was everything else. "It could only have been with the knowledge—the positive direction—of the NKVD."

"A search would need your authority," Lestov pointed out.

Always looking backward, thought Natalia. "We've got a name and a date. It shouldn't be too difficult to locate, if anything exists. She could even still be alive!"

"All we need to understand it all is someone living, not dead," agreed Lestov.

"I'm station chief!" yelled Saul Freeman.

"And I'm the person you were happy to assign to this because you were too fucking frightened of all the political implications to get involved yourself!" Miriam shouted back. She was red-faced, sweating, needing to support herself as she leaned across his desk to confront him, which was what she'd been waiting to do when he'd entered the office that day. Her overnight cable to Washington and its response lay between them.

"I don't remember you putting up much of a fight."

"I'm putting one up now. It's totally political, isn't it?" She put a flat hand close to her chin. "Right up to here? And I'm the fall guy if anything goes wrong—so fucking anxious to get there, fight for everything, that I didn't see the curve. You bastard!"

Freeman picked up the cables. Miriam's read, *Demand immediate OSS identification of American victim, which understand British already have. Further understand London about to go public.*

Freeman said, "You should have cleared this with me."

"If I'd known what the fuck was going on, I would have. And that's what I'm going to tell each and every inquiry when I get back to Washington, as ordered."

Freeman made a warding off movement toward Miriam. "Ignoring all the rules, first cabling, then calling Kenton Peters direct at the State Department instead of going through headquarters, was unforgivable! You know that! What else did you expect?"

"What I expected—but sure as hell didn't get-—was to be properly treated as a special agent of the Federal Bureau of Investigation. And told the true reason for monitoring an investigation by Britain and Russia which I was not intended in any way to contribute to. And obstructed as much as possible so that I couldn't."

"What did Peters tell you?" sighed Freeman.

"That I didn't have to bother. That Russia would never find out and if they did, would admit nothing. And that whatever Charlie Muffin and his department came up with would stay as buried as it had been for the last fifty years and that they were fall guys, too. And then he realized what he'd said—including me as a fall guy— and said he hadn't meant it the way it had sounded and that I was to forget that, too."

Freeman indicated Miriam's just-replaced telephone. "And then you called him a son-of-a-bitch and to kiss your ass."

"And enjoyed doing it: he qualifies."

"He might. It was still the worst career move you ever made."

"You going to tell me what it's really about—not some shit about saving the current president?"

"I don't *know*! Peters said it would embarrass the president now, although it was a long time ago. That it was all I needed to know— that anyone needed to know."

"You feel good about this, about screwing me like this?"

Freeman lifted and let drop Miriam's cable. "You sent it. I wouldn't have let you."

"Conscience clear, right?"

"Conscience clear. Say hello to Washington for me."

"You can kiss my ass, too!"

"I did, remember?"

"All I remember is that you were a lousy fuck. At the time it was just a physical judgment. Not now." The bastard would shit himself if he knew what she had, but she wanted a bigger reaction than the one she'd get from Saul Freeman.

Directly after the war and the control division of Berlin between the four Allied powers, America created the most comprehensive archive of the taking of the city and its postwar history right up to the bringing down of the Wall in 1991. It was called simply the Document Center and after 1991 America made a gift of it to Germany. There were more than a million photographs included in the material.

The hair of the archivist who greeted Charlie appeared to have receded in equal proportion to his beard, as if it had simply slipped from the top to the bottom of his face. His English was faultless but sibilant. He said, "We've had researchers come for a month work for more than a year, there's so much here."

"I've got quite a narrow time frame," said Charlie. "And a positive direction."

"That should certainly help," agreed the man.

"I hope it will," said Charlie. It would be good not having to work in the rain, although not for more than a year.

"We understand each other?" demanded Kenton Peters, who had come personally to Pennsylvania Avenue rather than have the FBI director come to him at Foggy Bottom, which was unprecedented.

"Yes sir," said the director.

"It's totally unforgivable."

"I agree."

"And you understand about the investigation?"

"Yes."

"I want this to be the last I hear about it from this Bureau."

"It will be," assured the other man.

26

There was still too much fury-fueled adrenaline for Miriam Bell to feel tired, although she would have liked to shower, but the car was waiting at Dulles, as she'd been told it would be, so the strip-down in the aircraft toilet would have to do. She hadn't slept at all during the flight, using the time, and was glad. She was thinking very differently now, much surer of herself, than she had been during the initial confrontation with Saul Freeman. Wished, indeed, she could turn the clock back for a rerun: she'd thought of a lot of better answers after it was too late. To rebuff Saul-the-Shithead, that was: there was still the confrontation to which she was going, where the in-flight rehearsal—and what she'd brought with her from Moscow—could hopefully be put to better and more effective use. At least she'd been thinking more clearly—leaving things as they should have been left—when she'd spoken to Lestov.

Washington seemed oddly colder than Moscow, although there was a pale sun, but there was a lot more color from the trees on the Parkway and once they crossed the Potomac by the Key Bridge everything appeared much cleaner and people on the sidewalk seemed to move with much more purpose. When she said so to the driver, he remarked that Moscow must be a god-awful place to live. Miriam said it had its moments.

There was an escort waiting for her at the reception desk of the FBI headquarters, which was completely unnecessary because she probably knew the building as well as he did, but she guessed it was part of the disapproval she was supposed to be aware of from the beginning. Which she was, but she was not intimidated by it. There was, in fact, still a lot of anger, but well controlled now. She was ready and believed herself prepared to fight back.

Nathaniel Brindsley, the Bureau deputy director in charge of overseas personnel, was a balding fat man whose cheeks puffed when he breathed because of emphysema. He'd transferred to the Bureau after ten years with the CIA, which permanently tagged him an outsider despite his working twice that long at Pennsylvania Avenue. Considering his official title and position, it was also considered unusual that Brindsley had never served outside Washington, not even in a local FBI office within America. Brindsley so snugly fit his chair that Miriam thought the man would have brought it up with him, like a permanent appendage, if he'd politely risen at her entry. But he didn't. Instead, as she sat in the chair he indicated with an impatient head jerk, he said, "As foul-ups go, you're scoring ten. And rising."

"You—and whoever's pulling the strings—are way ahead. With ten as crisis meltdown, you're at twenty." With some irony Miriam estimated she'd been roughly over Yakutsk, crossing Siberia, before she'd properly acknowledged she was flying into a put-up-or-shut-up survival situation, with no second chance. And decided to put up.

"You're forgetting our respective positions and authority here!"

Committed now, Miriam determined, "Question for question. You've forgotten how you were staking me out in the sun: leaving me to sweat with a totally inadequate briefing!"

"You were briefed to the extent you needed to be."

"Bullshit, Nat! Which you know it is! We got a long-ago secret to keep that way, I need to know what it is. Need to know what I have to hide, if one of the others—too many of the others—come up with it. You sent me blindfolded and naked into the ring, with a target on my fanny. Which makes you a bastard."

"You swear at me, it's insubornation. I swear at you, it's sexual harassment."

"You try and drop me because I offended some sphincter-stricken cocksucker who considered I was a disposal item, then you—and he—are looking at a lot more than a complaint of sexual harassment." Hardly any of this was part of the rehearsed script. She might not have anything more to lose, but this wasn't put *up*. It was personal put *down*, a suicide jump.

Brindsley was initially speechless. When he did speak, he said, "You have any idea just how far out of line you are?"

"You tell me—tell me honestly for the first time."

"You've broken every protocol in the book. And then some. Kenton Peters *is* the State Department; doesn't matter who the secretary is or who's in the White House. And *you* told *him* to kiss your ass. Used those very words!"

"And you know what he told me! He told me I was a fall guy. Used those very words!"

The sigh puffed Brindsley's cheeks more fully than usual. "He doesn't remember saying that."

"He knows official telephone conversations to and from the Moscow office are recorded, as a matter of routine?"

The only sound in the room for several moments was the rasping of the deputy director's heavy breathing.

"I'm going to forget you said that—along with its implications. And remind you whose property any tape is, recorded on FBI material on FBI premises."

Miriam took the tiny cassette from her handbag and tossed it onto the man's desk. "Just thought you'd like to hear the conversation for yourself." •

The speed with which the man grabbed the recording was surprising for someone of his size, his hand snatching out to enclose it like a lizard's tongue plucking an insect in midflight. "This the only copy?"

"With two messages. One that's on it, one that isn't."

"I don't think I want to hear the second."

"You do," insisted Miriam. "And so does Peters and anyone else who thinks they've got the lid on whatever it is that has to be locked away forever. There's too many people—too many chances for the smallest fuckup"—she nodded in the direction of the desk drawer into which Brindsley was putting the tape—"like an ill-considered remark being recorded—for anyone to believe they can control things from a distance of eight or ten thousand miles. This way, the way Peters wants to work and how you've been telling me to work, there's going to be something that someone doesn't know they're saying or doing and all the demons are going to come out of Pandora's box and land right in your laps!"

"Peters is sure he's emptied the box."

"How can he be?" demanded Miriam, careless of the exasperation. "It's his job to be."

"You going to tell me what it's really all about?"

"I don't *know*!" protested the man. "That's how tight it's being kept. I pass everything you send to the director, the director liaises with Peters, Peters tells the director how to respond, I tell you. And I don't like it any more than you do, but I'm five years from pension, so I don't tell Peters to kiss my ass."

"He want me fired?"

"Yes."

Miriam felt the stir of apprehension, a hollowness. "You going to?"

"You got a good argument against it?"

"Peters sure he's got the British under control?"

"Totally. Seems they've got as much to hide as we have."

"But he can't have the Russians . . ." She extended a cupped hand, closing her fingers. "But I have. Colonel Vadim Leonidovich Lestov, right here in the palm of my hand. You can't afford to put anyone else on the case, not at this stage. It would be even greater madness than the way it's being run at the moment."

Brindsley's smile was of resignation. "That's what I told the director, even without knowing about Lestov."

"What did he say?"

"That we didn't have a choice but that your future with the Bureau, after this, hangs on the thinnest thread you ever saw. And that you had to be brought all the way from Moscow to be told that in person, so you'd believe it. So tell me you believe it."

"I believe it." She was going to survive!

"And don't you ever again foul-mouth me like you have today."

"I'm sorry. And I won't." It wasn't Nathaniel Brindsley who was the cocksucker; it was Kenton Peters.

"Another thing you won't ever do again is communicate outside this Bureau to anyone about anything."

"I won't," promised Miriam. "But Nat, I need more than I'm getting, for all the reasons we're talking about. It *is* OSS and their art-looting investigation unit, isn't it?"

"That seemed to ring the alarm bell," agreed Brindsley. "And because the OSS became the CIA after the war, that's where the records are. Or were. And why Peters is sure everything's either gone or locked away forever."

"Who was Henry Packer?"

"Agency," said Brindsley. "And *was* is the word. He's out. Any idea how he was blown?"

Miriam shook her head. "None."

"Could it have been the Brit, Muffin?"

"I don't see how. As far as I was aware, Packer was Peters's body-guard. What was he really supposed to do?"

"Your guess is as good as mine."

Miriam felt a sudden coldness. "You're kidding!"

"I didn't say anything. Don't know anything."

"It's got to be a hell of a thing they want to stay covered up."

"You still need me to tell you that?"

"Does Peters know who the guy is in the Yakutsk grave?"

"I guess so. I don't."

"And what he was doing in Yakutsk?"

Brindsley shrugged. "I don't *know*!"

Miriam extended her hands again, a gesture of helplessness this time. "What the hell am I supposed to do?"

"Exactly what you have been doing. Passing back everything. Giving away nothing."

"Monitoring, not investigating? I could have been told that in the beginning."

"Now you have been. What about the Englishman?"

"Maybe you should tell Peters he was withdrawn to London the day before me. Left without telling me . . ." She made a vague gesture again toward the drawer containing the tape cassette. "I don't understand how Peters's remark about the British being fall guys squares with your telling me they've got as much to hide as us and are cooperating."

"Neither do I," admitted the man, miserably. "Like I said, I don't enjoy working like this any more than you do."

She was safe, Miriam abruptly realized. She might have gotten the thin-thread lecture, but after today she couldn't be blamed for the failure of an investigation that had been intended to fail from the very beginning. As the awareness settled, she said, "How's this going to be marked on my file?"

"I'm not sure that it is going to be marked," said the department chief. He hesitated. "*Is* there another copy of the tape?"

"No," lied Miriam. Altogether, she decided, everything had turned out very satisfactorily indeed. It would still be nice to have Peters kiss her ass; something, in fact, to look forward to with the tape she'd copied. It would be good to have more. To get which she needed to go on poking around, despite what she had been officially ordered to do. Do a Charlie Muffin, in fact. There was no way she could try to access the old OSS files without the Bureau finding out, but there were the Nazi prisoners at Yakutsk and New York was only an hour away from Washington on the shuttle.

Before her transfer to the overseas division, Miriam Bell had been attached to the FBI's New York office and had twice found the records of the World Jewish Congress on Madison Avenue a mine of information about Nazi Germany and the Holocaust during war crime inquiries.

She was directed to the desk of a man whose nameplate said E. Ray Lewis. He was a small, balding, bearded man whose vaguely distracted ambience of an academic changed at once to obvious daydreams at her approach. Miriam was glad she'd worn the sweater that accentuated her cleavage. He promised to do whatever he could to help her when she showed him her Bureau shield and Miriam knew how he would have liked her to help him.

His fantasies went abruptly the moment she produced her list. He said, "I know without checking who most of them are. The others would be the same. You know what happened to them!"

"I think so. Can you tell me what they did?"

"Immediately," said Lewis. And he did.

The afternoon sessions had become routine, an examination and often reexamination of everything from the previous twenty-four hours unless there was something Lestov considered more urgent, which he did the recall of Miriam Bell so soon after Charlie Muffin's departure.

"You think there's a connection?" demanded Natalia, who knew well enough from Charlie's Berlin calls there wasn't. Would Charlie have come up with anything by the time they next spoke?

"It's too much of a coincidence," insisted Lestov.

"What did she say?"

"That she'd been summoned to a reevaluation conference in Washington."

"How good has her cooperation been, until now?"

"She wants more than she gives. I'd guess we're holding back in equal measure."

"What do you think about this?"

"The most obvious is that they've identified their victim. Maybe even know why he was there," suggested the man.

Knowing from Charlie of the soft, late-night knocks on Miriam Bell's Yakutsk hotel room door, Natalia said, "Who's cooperated the most, out of the two of them?"

"Nothing in it," judged Lestov, at once.

"So a reevaluation conference is a lie?"

"Inevitably," accepted Lestov.

"What do we do?" Natalia invited.

"London and Washington have got to think we've got more than we have."

"Yes," agreed Natalia, doubtfully.

"Has there been any response about Larisa Krotkov?"

"Nothing."

"Why don't we use it?" questioned Lestov.

"Use what, how?" Natalia frowned.

"Issue a statement, without naming Larisa Krotkov, of a further mysterious connection with Tsarskoe Selo: generate the sort of publicity we did with the photograph of Raisa Belous. Maybe hint it has something to do with a second woman. It'll bring them back, force them into an exchange."

"Yes," agreed Natalia, needing only to know what the Americans had. "It would, wouldn't it?"

In Berlin Charlie eased back in the tiny cubicle that had been made available to him at the former American Document Center, gazing down tired-eyed but briefly euphoric at the photograph included in the comparatively small amount of material devoted to the American OSS period in the city, prior to the CIA. So small, in fact, that it probably shouldn't have been there at all. And more probably still was unknown to the CIA, which grew from the Office of Strategic Services, or any other Washington department, certainly none overseen by the ubiquitous Kenton Peters.

Incredibly it was the instant recognition of the girl, not of the heavily bespectacled man, that had first registered with Charlie from the copied scrap Miriam found. But this print was intact, not cut as it had been to fit into the dead American's pocket in the Yakutsk grave. There were a further seven men and two other girls smiling out at the camera. Charlie's second instant identification was of a dress-uniformed Simon Norrington, without having to read the captioned name. He didn't need the caption, either, to pick out Raisa Belous as one of the other two girls.

There was none of the previous day's frigidness from the cemetery registration clerk when Charlie shuffled into her office two hours later. She said at once, nervously, "I'm sorry. We still haven't sorted it out."

"I'm sure you're trying," soothed Charlie. "I was wondering if you could do me a slightly unofficial favor."

"Maybe," the woman said, doubtfully.

"You've got contacts with your American counterparts in their Battle Monuments Department?"

"Yes."

"Do they have their Second World War dead on computer?"

"Yes," she said again.

"To save me time, could you give them a call to see where Lieutenant George Timpson is buried?"

"Could it help with our problem over the three missing visits?" she asked, anxiously.

"It very well could," said Charlie, smoothly. "I like to know about visits to Timpson's grave, too."

The clerk only had to hold for the time it took the American official to check his Arlington, Virginia, register alphabetically. Lieutenant George Timpson had been killed, according to the file, on the same day as Simon Norrington and was supposedly buried in Plot 42 in the American cemetery at Margraten, in the Netherlands. Into the telephone the woman said, "No. We don't understand it here, either. Of course I'll let you know."

She put the telephone down and said to Charlie, "They don't have any supporting dockets for the five visits to Timpson's grave, either. This is incredible."

"Something like that," agreed Charlie.

She nodded to the telephone. "You won't tell anyone I did that, will you?"

"I won't if you won't."

When Charlie got back to the Kempinski, Lieutenant Colonel Rupert Jackson was in the foyer and Charlie decided he'd already learned more from the man's presence than the military attaché was going to discover from waiting so patiently.

Charlie parted from the military attaché after an hour and two malts, insisting he was flying directly back to Moscow, and used the public telephones in the lobby to avoid the switchboard. Natalia answered at once, expectantly, hearing Charlie through to the end before bringing him up to date.

"I agree with Lestov," said Charlie. "Two people at the same time from Tsarskoe Selo can't be a coincidence. What's her name?"

Charlie's hesitation at being told lasted so long that Natalia thought they'd been disconnected, calling his name. Charlie said, "Larisa Krotkov is the woman next to Timpson in the photograph I've got in front of me right now."

Now it was Natalia's turn to remain silent for several moments. "What about the statement Lestov suggested?"

"Make it!" said Charlie. "It's true, isn't it? But have Lestov get back to Tsarskoe Selo, for anything they might have about her."

"He's already doing that. This make anything clearer to you?"

"Not yet. What about Novikov and his family?" Could the lead come from whatever the doctor knew?

"Shouldn't take any time at all. I've approved his application."

"Sufficient for me to go to London, though?" He was still unsure whether it would be necessary to go to America, so he decided against mentioning it.

He was glad he had when Natalia said, "But not for any longer than necessary, remember?"

The director-general was just as quick personally answering his direct line and, like Natalia, let Charlie talk without interruption.

"That's preposterous."

"It fits."

"Prove it."

"Allow me to."

27

Sir Rupert Dean's Hampstead house adjoined the heath and had an expansive garden of its own, adding to the intended country impression. As he walked up the long, low hedge-lined path, Charlie saw a woman wearing a shapeless gardening hat and gloves among a jungle of large-leafed greenery in a conservatory attached to the right of the house. It was she who answered the door, a trowel still in her hand. The hair beneath the hat was gray and a face that had never known makeup was unlined and tranquil. She smiled as if he were an old friend.

"He's expecting you," she said, when Charlie identified himself. Appearing aware of the trowel, she said, "Repotting xerophytes. They're not as hardy as everyone thinks they are, you know; you need to be careful."

"I wouldn't know. I don't have a garden," said Charlie, following her into the house. He wondered if she'd have any use for the now-redundant beekeeper's hat.

The room to which she directed Charlie was a true bibliophile's library. Every available space was shelved from floor to ceiling, but there was no obvious order to their packed-together, one-on-top-of-the-other contents, books of every size hodgepodged unevenly together, waiting to be read or reread, not assembled for wall decoration. Others overflowed onto the floor, forming tiny battlements. Dean sat beneath a bright reading lamp in front of a dead fireplace, its emptiness unsurprisingly filled with a profusion of still more greenery. The book was bastard-sized, the cover print original German.

The disheveled former university professor nodded Charlie toward a chair on the opposite side of the fireplace. On a table alongside was a cloth-covered plate. Dean said, "You won't have eaten. Jane made sandwiches."

"That's very kind," said Charlie. They were cheese and pickle.

"Her idea, not mine," said the director-general. "It's scotch, isn't it?"

Charlie saw that was what Dean was drinking. "Thank you."

"I won't say 'Cheers,' " refused Dean. "I'm not sure we've got anything to be cheerful about."

"Probably not," said Charlie.

"I don't want a full summation," ordered the older man. "That can wait until tomorrow. I want an explanation for what you told me on the telephone."

"The department has been set up: all of us," repeated Charlie. "We've never been expected to solve or discover anything—"

"We were told from the outset there would be a cover-up, if it turned out to be embarrassing," stopped Dean.

"They *know* what the embarrassment is!" insisted Charlie. "Have from the beginning: not from the finding of the bodies but long before then. And it has *been* covered up, for God knows how long. The Yakutsk grave was an inconvenience, something never expected to happen. There has had to be the *appearance* of an investigation, particularly because of all the publicity. But not the sort we thought there was. What we've been doing—I've been doing—is proving whether or not the cover-up is going to hold—"

The director-general raised his hand. "Stop! Who are 'they'?"

"I don't know," admitted Charlie. "A government department, ministry, but I don't know which one."

"Our own people?"

"That's what I believe. As I believe the moment we find something taking us where we're not supposed to go, they'll clean it up before we get there."

"America?"

"*Has* to be involved, too," picked up Charlie. "Again, I don't know how. Or again, which department or agency."

"You basing this entirely on some missing cemetery records?"

Charlie offered the Berlin group photograph he'd been allowed to copy at the Document Center. "You'll recognize the man on the left as the American found in Yakutsk. His name was George Timpson. His phony grave is in a Dutch cemetery. I don't know why the Netherlands; I was told there aren't any American war cemeteries in Berlin. Timpson is supposed to have died the same day as Norrington. All evidence of five visits to Timpson's grave has disappeared, just like those to Norrington."

"There could be a far more reasonable explanation a lot different— *totally* different—from what you're drawing. Don't forget the number of departments and ministries who've got a hand in this."

"I'm not forgetting that for a moment!" said Charlie, urgently. "I'm asking *why*. Okay, a lot of other departments have a legitimate interest. But we've been given the investigation. So why's it stayed as diverse as it has? You've shared everything we've discovered, right?"

"Right," agreed Dean, thoughtfully. "Those are my instructions."

"What's been reciprocated from here, let alone America?" demanded Charlie. "The only echo we've got, as far as I understand, is that all the records and files have either been destroyed or can't be found. . . ." He paused, gulping his drink. "If we hadn't had that scrap of label that took us to Gieves and Hawkes we wouldn't have got Norrington's name. And if we hadn't done that—and got the family through it—we'd be no further forward than the day we began. Because the *only* information about Norrington has come from his family: we haven't been offered a single thing from another single supposedly interested or involved department here in England. Or from America. According to the military attaché in Berlin, the Ministry of Defense is in uproar because I went to the exhumation: they're sending in their own investigators. With so many people— *countries!*—already in on the act, there's not a chance in hell of getting close enough to understand anything—the perfect way to create the perfect confusion."

Dean leaned forward, adding to Charlie's glass. "It's an argument," he conceded, reluctantly. "The sort of argument that builds unsupported conspiracy theories into accepted fact."

"I thought the journalists in that hotel dining room were lucky not to be more badly hurt—killed, even—by Henry Packer, didn't you?"

Dean sighed, nodding. "You're asking me to trust you over my own operational group: knowingly—consciously—to deceive them!"

"Patrick Pacey is the political officer," listed Charlie. "His function is to liaise politically with the very departments—and the Intelligence Committee itself—who aren't reciprocating to us. Jeremy Simpson would have to consider everything legally. Your deputy *is* your deputy, subservient to you. Gerald Williams is only concerned with finance: wouldn't normally be part of the group. . . ." Charlie paused. "All I'm asking for is time—time to work without knowing someone's going to be ahead of me every step of the way . . ." Charlie paused, to make his point. "If I'd wanted to deceive them—and you—I could have. *You* ordered *me* back, to investigate anywhere I felt it necessary. I'm telling you *why* I think it's necessary."

"How do you intend using this time you're asking for?"

"I've got names, from Berlin. And others, Germans, from the Gulag. I want to establish the connection I'm sure exists. And I want to speak to Norrington's family. And I want to do it without people knowing in advance that I'm going to: without meeting Packer's successor."

When the director-general didn't speak, Charlie said, "All I'm asking to be allowed to do is work by the same rules as everyone else. And not have to put forward my interpretation that we're being blocked by our own people."

"I'm not sure anyone else would have given you as much time to argue that interpretation as I already have," said the director-general.

Charlie said, "There's a second interpretation I believe you should consider."

"What?" demanded Dean.

"Our department—now *your* department—wasn't in any way a

part of whatever happened, before or after, when these murders were committed."

Once more Dean did not respond.

"So after fifty years, with an undecided remit and an even more undecided future, we were the obvious choice when the bodies were found, weren't we?" continued Charlie. "A test for us, desperate to prove ourselves. A test for others—whoever *they* are—anxious to know if the concealment thus far is good enough to withstand an investigation: remain a mystery forever. But not *that* anxious. They've got the final say before it becomes final. If we get too close, they can misdirect or close it all down, citing without explanation the embarrassment they've already insisted to be the primary concern. But to keep everything properly hidden, no one is going to be able to know what the embarrassment is, are they? So there's an easy answer: we're made to be seen to fail. Which makes us even more vulnerable to everyone snapping at our heels."

"That's pretty convoluted logic," protested Dean.

"But it is logic, for the environment we live in," insisted Charlie. "Not even in national archives closed for the next fifty or a hundred years will there be an admission of a secret that's literally been buried for the last fifty. It'll be our inability properly to fulfill the investigatory role we're trying to establish, against all the other competing agencies. How about a second—or even third—agenda? If we don't get beyond all the obstruction of our own people—quite apart from that of America or Russia—to find out *everything,* there's every reason to disband us. We're set to be the losers, any which way."

There was a further long silence, this time for the incredulous director-general to find the words. He eventually said, "You have any more conspiracy theories? Or is this the last?"

"That's it," said Charlie. "Our only protection is to find out everything. Only by knowing it all can we defend ourselves." But more importantly defend myself and Natalia and Sasha, although not in that order or priority.

"I'm compromised, aren't I? By having agreed to meet you like this?"

"No," said Charlie. "This meeting never took place."

"Would you swear to that, under oath, if this evening was ever discovered and put before a tribunal inquiry?"

"Yes," said Charlie, at once. "If it's morally—and philosophically—right for a wartime general knowingly to sacrifice the lives of eight hundred men to save those of eight thousand, isn't it morally—and philosophically—right to tell a small lie to establish a more important truth?"

"No!" refused the other man, just as quickly. "Your morality and your philosophy don't work. Any more than your logic."

"They do if I discover that truth," insisted Charlie. "That's what's going to keep us in existence." And me in Moscow, he thought.

"What happens if you fail to discover it?"

"I won't." Because I can't, Charlie mentally added.

"You haven't eaten your sandwiches," said the older man.

"They're very good," Charlie said politely, beginning at last.

"The pickle's homemade," said Dean. "Jane does her own. She likes growing things."

"I can't get anything like this in Moscow."

"Perhaps she could find you a pot, before you leave."

"That would be very kind."

"Don't ever imagine that this evening has established any special, back-channel situation between us, will you?"

"No, sir."

"Good. Never take my inexperience for softheartedness."

After more than a week of being starved of any apparent progress, the Moscow announcement of a further although unspecified development caused the renewed media uproar that Vadim Lestov had predicted.

"Having finally returned to give us an explanation, you can't explain it!" attacked Gerald Williams, eagerly and at once. He'd definitely made his mind up: anything he could do to show up the man's inability would all contribute to what he intended at the end.

Cunt, thought Charlie. The seating arrangements put him at the bottom of the table, with the control group pincering him from either side, which Charlie supposed would be the composition of the sort of tribunal Sir Rupert Dean had talked about the previous night. To which he'd said he'd have no difficulty lying under oath, Charlie remembered. Doing just that without an oath, he said, "Not about today's announcement, no. But as it *has* been announced, I'll obviously be told, won't I?"

"Will you?" demanded Williams.

For the most fleeting of moments Charlie allowed himself to imagine the effect upon the overweight man if he'd said just how sure he now was of being told and by whom. He contented himself—only just—by saying, "Trust me."

The financial director's face mottled at the awareness of being mocked, but before he could speak Jocelyn Hamilton said, "We've heard through the Foreign Office that the FBI has been on from the American embassy in Moscow, wanting to speak to you."

"She's been on to Cartright, too," hurried in Williams, determined that nothing should be left out.

"So it could be a breakthrough," finished the deputy director-general. "If it's that important, perhaps this is a mistimed visit?"

"I ordered the recall," reminded Dean.

"It will be easy enough for me to return Miriam Bell's call from here, later," said Charlie. It wasn't Miriam Bell's style to chase like this. So she was panicking. So, too, were the Foreign Office and MI6. Everyone running around like chickens with their heads cut off. But who was wielding the ax?

"Considering your apparent belief that another English officer was involved, you seem remarkably relaxed," suggested Hamilton.

"That, above all else, is what we need to discuss," said Patrick Pacey, the political officer.

"Perhaps we'd get a more comprehensive picture if we let Charlie talk without so much interruption," proposed the director-general.

"A comprehensive picture would be very welcomed, if it's at all possible," said Williams, overstressing the condescension.

Fuck you, like you want so badly to fuck me, thought Charlie. While he sat, waiting, he decided that although he scarcely needed any preparation, the previous night's never-happened encounter with the director-general had been more than a useful rehearsal, sifting in his mind the gold nuggets to keep back from the obscuring silt. Reminded by the same conversation, Charlie decided that so many organizations, agencies and people *were* involved that there was absolutely no risk of his inadvertently even hinting at his very special source. Abruptly, disconcertingly, Charlie was seized by the thought that he'd missed something, failed to realize or recognize something that he should have. The men at the table began to shift impatiently—Jeremy Simpson very obviously looking questioningly at the political officer—and Charlie tried to push the unsettling impression aside but only partially succeeded. He had to force the intended ridicule. "I thought I'd wait to make sure the finance director had finished."

Gerald Williams's face flooded red. Before the man could speak, Dean said tightly, "I think we're all waiting," and Charlie acknowledged he'd gone too far. He still thought, Fuck it.

Then he thought bullshit baffles brains and set out his encapsulation in what appeared great detail, beginning chronologically, from the reindeer herder's discovery of the bodies. He went through the first and second autopsies, itemizing what had—and had not—been found in the grave and on the bodies. He gave a lot of time to the entrapping press conference—conscious of Gerald Williams's smirk at the admission of being tricked—to illustrate the animosity between Yakutskaya and Russia. He talked of Gulag 98 being a special prison, although keeping back his first nugget, the names of the fifteen German prisoners who had been there in 1945. Neither did he say anything about his full discovery from the Document Center in Berlin. And he didn't disclose the name of the dead American as George Timpson. With their art-connected background the presence of Raisa Belous and Simon Norrington had in some way to be linked to looted Nazi art treasure, a suggestion Charlie offered with the reminder that Raisa had belonged to the specially formed Russian Trophy Brigade that matched and at times exceeded the Nazis in Moscow's indiscriminate art rape of Europe. The injuries to the skeleton in the Berlin grave proved, Charlie insisted, that the man had been killed to provide the identity for Simon Norrington, from dog tags and personal items stripped at Yakutsk and put on the Berlin body: the face of the victim had been destroyed beyond recognition, all teeth smashed and no finger ends—and therefore no possible fingerprints—left.

"Killed to order?" demanded Jeremy Simpson, the prescient lawyer. "Are you suggesting Norrington was killed to order? A far-reaching, carefully calculated conspiracy?"

"It fits," asserted Charlie, unworried by the obvious disbelief from everyone in the room, even shared maybe by Sir Rupert himself. What concerned Charlie more was the still persistent, intrusive feeling of having overlooked something!

"Stuff and nonsense!" sneered Williams, who never swore. Addressing the lawyer, Williams said, "Is there anything we've been told this morning that you'd be prepared to argue in a court and expect to be taken seriously?"

"I'd like better proof," conceded Simpson, uncomfortable at being Charlie's critic instead of his defender. Pedantically he said, "Your main premise that there was another Englishman at the murder scene is the apparent finding in the grave of a button from a British officer's battle-dress uniform, as well as a torn-out label and British-caliber bullet? But we don't definitely know about the button; that's based on a remark the Yakutsk pathologist *thinks* he overheard the Russian forensic scientist make when the man was using his laboratory facilities?"

"Yes," said Charlie, accepting it to be his weakest evasion but with no way of telling them how he knew the button to exist.

"What on earth does a Yakutsk medical examiner know about an English officer's battle dress or its fastenings?" demanded Hamilton.

"Absolutely nothing!" snatched Charlie. "Which is why he couldn't have misheard or imagined the remark! Moscow knew it was an apparent British officer before sending their forensic expert. Who would, obviously, have been chosen for knowledge beyond his particular discipline. He *would* have known what a British uniform—and its buttons—looked like!" On second thought, maybe it wasn't as weak as it had initially sounded. The rehearsal really had been useful.

"I think the suggestion is absurd," rejected Williams. "Does the report of the Berlin pathologist state that the body in Norrington's grave was murdered?" This really was going far better than he could have hoped, Williams thought. The man was being made to look ridiculous.

"No," admitted Charlie. "That would be impossible, after so long."

"So it's purely your interpretation!" sneered Williams.

"The body was chosen to be that of Simon Norrington—had the

man's identity planted on it," Charlie pointed out. If Gerald Williams hadn't existed, he would have had to be invented; the man's unthinking determination to oppose and argue with everything was taking all their minds from any awkward questions. Most importantly Charlie was able so far to avoid volunteering anything new.

"You think it could have been the Russians who tampered with the visitors' records at the cemetery?" asked Patrick Pacey.

It could, even, have been possible, Charlie accepted, but he had to be careful with the reply. "The Russians took Berlin—totally controlled it, initially—and were responsible, I suppose, for the burials during those early days. But the Four Powers were in control when the Allied cemetery was created." If there'd been colored ribbons and a stake tall enough, he could have led everyone a merry dance around the maypole. He was aware of the director-general regarding him quizzically.

"I don't consider there's anything to support the idea of another British officer being involved in this," insisted the political officer, siding with Williams. "I expected a lot more from this meeting."

"So did I," said Hamilton.

"In fact," said Williams, recognizing his support, "I think you should go back to Moscow as soon as possible, pick up whatever crumbs drop from the table of others and leave us to reach far more sensible and acceptable conclusions than you're offering."

Charlie gazed unspeaking at the fat man for several seconds, aware at last what had been nagging him, the feeling at once relief more than apprehension. Quietly, almost humbly, he said, "There are some more inquiries I want to make here first."

"Which I've approved," came in the director-general quickly, ahead of any opposing argument. "There's certainly the need to speak again to Sir Matthew Norrington."

"Isn't the more immediate urgency finding out what the FBI in Moscow wants, as well as what this latest Russian declaration is all about?" demanded Hamilton.

Charlie was almost sad at the adjournment, so well did he consider the encounter to have been going, but it gave him time fully to consider Gerald Williams's slip. The assertion to Sir Rupert Dean the previous night that Williams's participation was entirely financial was unarguable. How, then, could Williams have known that Miriam

Bell had been in contact with Richard Cartright unless he, in turn, had been in direct touch with the SIS officer in Moscow? Cartright's communication route was through his own, separate department. Which in turn, according to regulations, should have advised the director-general—as the Foreign Office had told the political officer—not the finance director. So Gerald Williams was talking, unofficially, to Richard Cartright. Who in Moscow had formed some relationship with Natalia's sister. What silly men, Charlie thought. What silly, silly men.

The connection, from a side office off the director-general's suite, was immediate. Miriam said, "You don't write, you don't phone, you don't send flowers . . . ?"

Forced cool, judged Charlie. "You called?"

"You didn't, before you left."

"It was a rush."

"You still in London?"

Keep the pot bubbling, decided Charlie. "People aren't happy." Maintaining the pretense, he said, "Particularly when I'm here and Moscow's issuing enigmatic statements."

"It's something to do with Tsarskoe Selo is all I know. I don't know how it fits. If it fits at all, although I suppose it's got to, somehow. Lestov wants to know when you're getting back."

Charlie frowned, not just at the immediately volunteered information—which he knew from Natalia to be accurate—but more at the tone of Miriam's voice. "What's the matter?"

"Problems with Washington. I could do with your being back here: talk through some stuff. When *are* you getting back?"

"A few things to sort out here first. You want to talk now?"

"Later. But not too much later. And you watch your back, you hear?"

"You think I need to?" asked Charlie, seriously.

"Yeah, I think you need to. Maybe we both do."

"You think this new Tsarskoe Selo stuff is important?" Charlie pushed on.

"Lestov says it'll take a few days to sort out."

There was his excuse for not immediately returning, Charlie recognized. Still more, possibly. "You called the embassy twice?"

"Thought we had a deal. Wondered what happened to it."

Ignoring her implied question, he said, "You spoke to Cartright?"

"My call got redirected. Anything wrong?"

"Not at all," assured Charlie, who hadn't initiated such an arrangement. "Obvious person to backstop."

"There really are things to talk about when you get back." Now that she was working to her own, different agenda there was no reason why she shouldn't tell Charlie of the conversation with Kenton Peters, although she wouldn't throw it away. She wouldn't offer too quickly what she'd gotten from the World Jewish Congress, either. She had a lot of things to trade: to buy insurance with.

By the time Charlie got back to the conference room, the coffee was cold. They didn't bother to reassemble for the result of his phone call.

"It seems very much like the blind leading the blind," said Williams.

But who'll be seeing more clearly by the time it's all over? wondered Charlie.

Richard Cartright wasn't happy with the way things had evolved. It was, for all intents and purposes, a combined operation that initially and on the face of it had made quite acceptable his talking as he had with Gerald Williams. But he wasn't sure any longer. From the sheer restriction of anything and everything he was begrudgingly being allowed to know by his own department—against their constant and unremitting demands for any scrap from him—it had become increasingly obvious this was a very important assignment indeed for someone on his first tour of duty and that it was anything but the combined operation he'd first imagined it to be.

And now he was trapped. On the one hand he'd already cooperated too much with someone from another department suddenly to seek authorization for doing so from his own controllers, which too late he now realized he should have done from the start. On the other, and by the same measure, he didn't see how he could abruptly refuse, not knowing how much power or influence Gerald Williams possessed.

"You're not saying a lot," complained Irena. The man she believed to be mafia was in the restaurant again and if the evening didn't pick up soon, she was considering changing partners.

"Sorry. Things on my mind. Seen Natalia lately?"

Irena shrugged. "We had a row."

"So you didn't know Charlie was back in London?"

"Permanently?"

"Just a discussion recall, as far as I know."

"Probably banking his profits," suggested Irena. "Not a bank I'd trust in this city."

Cartright regretted most of all telling Williams of Charlie Muffin boasting of currency speculation. "I can't think you're right about that."

"You imagine he could afford that apartment any other way?"

It was difficult, acknowledged Cartright, although if Charlie Muffin was doing something as bloody silly as that, it did justify his cooperation with the man's finance controller. It was a total mess and he desperately wanted to be out of it.

28

After driving parallel to it for what seemed forever, Charlie decided that the redbricked perimeter of Sir Matthew Norrington's Kingsclere estate must have been modeled on the Great Wall of China although probably went on for much longer. The gate he finally located opened noiselessly to his identifying himself at the security voice box and closed just as quickly behind him. The wall was lined inside by trees and there were more meticulously cultivated on either side of the paved drive that ribboned away ahead of him. He could not see the house. Through the trees to his left there was a herd of disinterested, unafraid deer. He thought there were some white ones but wasn't sure. To his right, sheep grazed. Far beyond them, too far away to distinguish man from machine, a figure rode a disappearing tractor over the brow of a hill tufted with more trees. Would this have been the scene of perfect, safe tranquillity that Simon Norrington thought about kneeling in front of a grenade-made grave on the outskirts of Yakutsk, waiting for a pistol shot?

Not suspecting its length, Charlie had not timed how long it took to circumnavigate the outer wall. It was a full five minutes before the house came into view, a huge square pile—Georgian, Charlie guessed—with creeper-clad walls and a flagpole on the central turret for the proudly flying red cross on white pennant, the whole thing a monument to the permanence of the English landed class.

Sir Matthew Norrington waited by one of three parked Range Rovers, white-haired, tweed-suited and brogued. The spectacles were horn-rimmed. As he got out of the rented car, Charlie decided it was impossible to decide between his or the other man's whose suit was the more comfortably shapeless.

Norrington said at once, "Glad to see you. I want to understand what this is all about." The voice was firm, like the handshake.

"I don't fully understand myself, but I'll do my best," promised Charlie.

"But you are definitely in charge of the investigation? That's what Sir Rupert said on the phone." There was an impatience in the question.

"Yes," said Charlie. I wish, he thought.

The house into which the elderly man led him was as comfortably lived in as the suit and Charlie decided that perhaps it wasn't a monument to anything after all. The cavernous flagstoned entrance hall was lined with oil paintings, which continued along a paneled corridor. Aware of Charlie's interest, Norrington said, "The Holbein and the Reynolds are ancestral, but a lot of the more modern collection was Simon's choice. It's thought to be quite remarkable."

The door at which Norrington stopped was halfway along the hall, from the far end of which—or maybe from another room—there was the sound of people. A dog barked, very briefly. The library into which Norrington took Charlie was more neatly arranged than Sir Rupert Dean's but at the same time more obviously occupied. There were more framed oils, men in ermine and robes, bejeweled women and velvet-dressed children with ringlets and spaniel pets, but there was an obvious working desk dominating the window looking out over the rolling grounds. Charlie was immediately aware of a lot of photographs on its top and even more, practically overcrowding, on side tables at either end of the huge, inglenooked fireplace. He recognized a lot of Simon Norrington, two in the uniform the man had been wearing in the Yakutsk ice tomb. Another had him in gradua-tion gown with a man Charlie assumed to be his father, who'd looked remarkably similar to Sir Matthew Norrington now. There was a photograph of a teenage Matthew smiling up toward Simon in visible bigger brother admiration. The chairs, also by the fireplace, were leather, which creaked when they sat.

Norrington said, "Tell me what this is all about." It was the voice of a man accustomed to being obeyed.

Charlie left out all his supposition and suspicions and anything about a second English officer, so it only took minutes.

"I'd expected more," the dissatisfied baronet said, at once, with a frown.

"I wish there were more," apologized Charlie, meaning it.

"They were planned killings? Of my brother and the man in his grave in Berlin?"

"Undoubtedly."

"Why him?"

"I don't yet know how or why, but I believe art is the most obvious factor: something to do with its looting. But not that by itself. There's a lot more."

"Simon despised the Nazis, Rosenberg's lot, for what they did to art. And the Russians' Trophy Brigades. Judged one as bad as the other. He knew it would be impossible to reassemble the European art heritage, no matter how hard he and others like him tried." The man stopped, pointedly. "You imagine you'll ever find out who killed him?"

Charlie hesitated. "Who committed the actual murders, probably not, not after fifty years. They would have been functionaries." Which was true, he realized. It had been a Russian bullet that killed Simon Norrington.

"What about the people who ordered it?"

"That's who I'm trying to find. If I do, we'll know why."

Norrington stirred in his chair, which creaked again. "What are your chances?"

A lie wouldn't help and Charlie didn't want to slip sideways into his theories and guesses, either. "I'd like them to be better. I'd ap-preciate a lot of your time."

Norrington shrugged. "As much as you need." He got up. "I drink gin."

"Whiskey."

The old man returned from a separate side table with their drinks, settled noisily and said, "So?"

"You were, what, sixteen when it happened?" Charlie spoke looking at the young Matthew gazing up at his elder brother.

"Just seventeen, at the war's end. Felt cheated. Was an officer cadet at Eton, all ready to go. Wanted to go even more when Simon was killed; thought it had been in action then, of course. Imagined I'd find the actual person who did it." The man snorted humorlessly. "Some irony about that now, isn't there?"

"Let's hope not," said Charlie. "You can remember everything about the time? Not simply the death but immediately before? And afterwards?"

"All of it."

Everything from the family, recalled Charlie, remembering the Berlin conversation with the military attaché. Charlie indicated the photographs of Simon Norrington on the table closest to him and said, "He was—is—obviously deeply mourned?"

"My father was devastated. We all were, naturally. But my father took it dreadfully. The war was over, for God's sake!"

Charlie thought it was too much to hope, but he hoped, just the same. "*How* did you learn?"

The older man frowned. "Letter. Official notification. June third."

That was encouraging, thought Charlie. "There were some personal belongings returned?"

"Arrived much later, from his unit: cigarette lighter—it matched a case my father gave Simon when he graduated—his wallet. Family ring. There was a personal letter of regret, too, of course. From his commanding officer."

"And then there was the notification of the burial?" coaxed Charlie.

There was another snorted, empty laugh. "Of the wrong man."

"But you visited the grave?"

"Once, with my father. He was annoyed that we hadn't been asked about the body: that it had been already buried. We've got our own chapel and vault here, in the grounds. But there was a dedication service in Berlin and afterwards we decided to leave Simon . . . we thought it was Simon . . . where he was."

"How many times did you go?"

"Just the once with my father, for the service. It was an official affair, for a lot of families with relatives there."

Charlie was immediately alert to the qualification. "Was there any sort of registration at the official ceremony?"

"Not then."

"But?"

"I went again, by myself, on the first supposed anniversary. My father was ill by then, couldn't travel. There was some form-filling nonsense that time."

Charlie realized he'd drifted away from the directions in which he'd been heading but decided to finish this now. "How many other times did you go: need to fill in the visitor's form?"

"That was the only occasion," said Norrington. "Father had a commemorative plaque put into the chapel. We could mourn well enough here."

Which almost brought him back on track, Charlie recognized. "Who else from the family, apart from you, visited the grave you thought was Simon's?"

"No one." The man frowned. "Why do you ask?"

"I'm trying to build up as complete a picture as I can," Charlie avoided, not wanting to enter still-unexplored territory. Quickly he said, "You mourned here?"

"Yes."

Charlie indicated the picture-crowded tables and desk again. "You kept a lot of photographs?"

"Yes?" There was a defensive sharpness in the questioning reply.

"What about other things? Did you keep the notification of Simon's death—the personal things that were returned?"

"I told you my father was devastated. In the first two or three years it was almost a shrine. It worried me."

Sometimes it worked to hope against hope, Charlie decided. "Do you still have it all?"

"Yes. Father kept everything. So I did, too."

Don't rush, Charlie warned himself. It still might be another blind alley; this was going far better than he'd expected and there still might be more Norrington could help with. And there were the names from Berlin. "Later, when we've talked some more, could I see it all?"

Norrington hesitated. "Could it help you find the people you're looking for?"

"It's my best chance so far," replied Charlie, honestly.

"Some of the letters are personal."

"Letters!"

"I told you, Father kept a lot of stuff. Letters that Simon wrote when he got posted abroad. And before."

Now it was Charlie who hesitated, and when he spoke he did so slowly, not wanting to lose the chance. "Sir Matthew, I have what could be leads to whoever murdered your brother. But I don't know how to follow them. How, in fact, to take this investigation very much further. What you have, of your brother's, might show me."

"Then you must see it all," agreed Norrington, at once. "Now?"

"Let's talk a little more," said Charlie. There had to be something in what was promised: by the sheer law of averages and the way his luck was running, there had to be *something* that took him forward! Which made waiting a minute—a second!—close to impossibly difficult, but he kept to the determination not to hurry. Get it all, he reminded himself: an inch at a time, a step at a time.

"What else can I tell you?" questioned the baronet. He got up to go to the drinks tray.

Charlie shook his head against the gestured invitation. "It was big jump, wasn't it, from Free French liaison at the War Office to a special art-looting unit?"

Norrington frowned on his way back to his chair. "You don't know anything at all about Simon, do you?"

He didn't and it made this encounter too long overdue, Charlie conceded, although refusing completely to blame his personal situation in Moscow. There had been reason enough to remain there as long as he had. "The Ministry of Defense can't find any records about your brother."

Norrington's smile was slow, an expression of belated understanding. "He didn't tell me that."

It came close to Charlie's breath being taken away by a deluge of fittingly iced water. "Who didn't tell you what, sir?"

Norrington got up again, went to his desk and took the small rectangle of pasteboard from a top drawer. "Burbage, Lionel Burbage. Defense Ministry. Said there was a *confusion* about the records, which was why he wanted what I had."

The iced-water feeling stayed with Charlie. "Did he take them?"

"Asked to, but I wouldn't let him, like I'm not going to let you. Allowed him to read them, as you can. That's all."

Charlie began to feel warm again, not just at the reassurance but at his determination not to hurry. "When was this?"

"Four days ago."

He'd met Lieutenant Colonel Rupert Jackson, the military attaché, in Berlin five days ago. It fit the urgency of the Ministry of Defense panic. "Did you make your brother's letter available to him?"

"Didn't come into the conversation. He asked specifically about the official War Office communications and that's all he saw. That's why I asked you when you got here if you were in charge of the investigation, although Sir Rupert had already told me you were when he telephoned."

"What did Burbage tell you?"

"That he was."

"I *am*," insisted Charlie. "It's been a problem from the beginning, too many departments, getting in each other's way."

Norrington nodded in further understanding. "Burbage asked me to tell him if anyone else approached me about Simon."

"Did you tell him I was coming?"

Norrington shook his head. "I didn't know you were, then. Decided to wait. See you first. Hear what you had to say."

"I certainly don't know of him. But it makes sense to stop this duplication. Which I will. Can I have Burbage's number?"

Norrington carried the card back with the whiskey decanter, adding unasked to Charlie's glass. All that was listed was the name and a telephone number. No ministry was identified. Neither was any department. Norrington said, "You haven't told me what you've got to say, Mr. Muffin. Not properly. Not why, for instance, Sir Rupert asked me when we originally spoke to keep secret the discovery of my brother's body in some place I'd never heard of, nor make any public announcement about finally burying him as he should be buried, after all these years. I think I've been remarkably patient, but now that patience has gone."

Shit, thought Charlie. Shit! Shit! Shit! Family pride, he told himself desperately: family pride and honor. "Your brother was officially in Berlin; his death there was accepted. His being in Yakutsk is considered, even now, something that shouldn't be made public. Until we find out why and how he came to be there—to be one of at least four victims in a planned killing—it's still considered a potential national problem."

"That's very difficult for me to accept. Or understand."

"It's even more difficult for me to ask you to accept or understand," pleaded Charlie. "Which is why I'm asking you for all the help I can get."

"My brother would not, under any circumstances, have done anything wrong: illegal or unofficial! He was proud to be an officer. To serve his country."

An opening, Charlie recognized. "He couldn't have been where he was *unofficially*. He was obeying an order. Which was what I told you when we first began talking: what I'm trying to do is find out who gave that order. Which it would seem the Ministry of Defense is also trying to find out." If Burbage was from the Ministry of Defense, which Charlie now doubted.

"According to the newspapers, the Americans consider their officer to have been a hero. There's a hero's burial planned. Why hasn't the same been said—planned—about Simon? And why was I asked to say nothing, do nothing, about burying him?"

"The American is being buried as an unknown victim," seized Charlie. "Your brother won't be, after I've found out the truth. Then, maybe, he'll be accorded the honor he's due."

"No," agreed Norrington, quietly. "Simon won't be buried as an unknown. And I don't want any maybes about his being accorded every honor to which he's entitled. I'm not given to threats, Mr. Muffin—the need to prove myself. So what I am going to say isn't a threat. It's a statement of fact. I am not without official influence—access to private as well as public platforms. I am prepared totally and fully to cooperate with you in every way I am asked. But with a time limit. Unless I am convinced otherwise—and you must understand I will take a very great deal of convincing—I will announce two weeks from today that it was Simon's body in the Yakutsk grave. I will disclose that somebody else was killed to fill a grave in his name in Berlin. And I shall demand a public inquiry into the circumstances of both deaths, and although it will offend me deeply I shall turn my brother's burial here into a media event. I don't, of course, expect you to be the messenger. I'll telephone Sir Rupert to tell him myself. Do you think what I've said is unreasonable?"

Charlie said, "I think you've already shown a great deal of patience and I'm grateful for another two weeks. In your position I'd have probably kept it to one."

Norrington's smile was abrupt and open. "Interesting reply. When I said roughly the same to Burbage, he said he'd stop me doing anything under the Official Secrets Act, and when I told him I wasn't a signatory to it, he told me I didn't know what I was talking about and that it didn't matter whether I'd signed it or not. That's the real reason I didn't call him when I agreed to your coming. Didn't like the fellow. Very rude."

But far more important, very stupidly indiscreet, bullying like that. Suddenly reminded of Richard Cartright, Charlie decided the standard was definitely going down.

Charlie refused the offer of lunch from Norrington's willowy blond fourth wife, who said to call her Davinia and whom he guessed to be half the baronet's age. Instead he accepted rare beef sandwiches he didn't get around to eating at the borrowed library desk, working steadily through the two wooden boxes of personal effects under the frozen, smiling gaze from three pictures of the man whose mysteries he was trying to solve.

He did so careful to retain the exact order in which each item had been kept, not removing one until that which preceded it had been replaced. The crocodile wallet was an early disappointment. It contained Simon Norrington's English driving license and visiting cards in his own name—both necessary and easy identification, Charlie acknowledged—but no one else's cards, letters, photographs or anything connecting him to Berlin or his unit. His army pay book was endorsed for his pay to be credited automatically to a Coutts Bank account on the Strand and although he didn't expect it to lead to the long-lost army records Charlie made a note of the pay book number. Charlie looked over it all, laid out on the desk in front of him, every item perfectly preserved, intact and undamaged, despite its age. How, he asked himself, could it have been accepted, apparently without a single question? Carried as it would have been, in the breast or inside pockets of the uniform, it should—and would—have all been totally destroyed by the massive force of whatever had killed the substitute Berlin victim.

The official notification of Simon Norrington's death was as cold as the grave in which the man had lain for fifty years, a formal printed notice with the choice of striking out sir or madam, whichever was inappropriate, and gaps in the text for the details of names, relationship and date of death to be inserted by hand.

Charlie got the first of what he considered important information from the handwritten letter of condolence to the father from Norrington's commanding officer, a colonel who signed himself John Parnell, and which was dated July 2. After the predictable eulogy of Norrington's bravery and dedication to duty, it read:

> *I cannot, of course, disclose the nature of Simon's very special work in these most recent months but I can say he was the only person in the unit with the very necessary qualifications to carry it out. Neither can I give any precise details of how or when he died, although of course we have made strenuous efforts to discover both. His body was returned to us from a Russian-occupied part of the city. The Russian documentation merely indicates that he was found dead, by Russian troops, on or around May 10. You will be aware that at that time there was still sporadic fighting in Berlin, an indication of the bravery of your noncombatant son to which I have already referred.*

So much and yet so little, agonized Charlie, easing briefly back into the bucket chair, which creaked like all the other leather furniture. What was the work so very special that only the noncombatant Lieutenant Simon Norrington was able to undertake it in the Russian sector of Berlin in which there was still fighting? But who hadn't been there at all but thousands of miles away?

There were thirty-two letters, all still in their envelopes and all in dated sequence, which was how Charlie read them, searching for people with whom Norrington had worked, particularly for references to the names he'd gotten from the Berlin photograph. A Jessica appeared in the third letter, addressed from London when Norrington was clearly still attached to the War Office, and by the fourth it was obvious she was employed there with him. From the way the next was written, she'd spent a weekend at Kingsclere. Norrington had been glad his father liked her as much as he did, but she disappeared from the correspondence just before Norrington's transfer to the art-loss unit. Norrington was relieved at the transfer: *Bloody French go on all the time as if I was personally responsible for Dunkirk and seem to forget we got almost as many of their soldiers out as we did our own.*

There wasn't another name until Charlie was halfway through, and then it was clearly a nickname, Scotty. Norrington described him as *a good man, salt of the earth. But hard.* There were frequent references after that, but none of them hinted at particular friendship, more admiration. Then there was someone identified only as J, and as more single initials followed, Charlie guessed, disappointed, at Norrington's own effort to obey wartime censorship rules. J was *a tyrant, but fair, who knows his art.* HH was a bully who'd clearly made an early choice about being a criminal himself and decided *to step the other way over the line.* And then there was the appearance of G, at which Charlie felt the tingle of recognition as he read. The letter was dated February 9, 1945. G was brilliant: *I sit at his feet.* G saw telltale brush detail—*despite his problem*—which Norrington missed: *three fakes, in one day. It's good to know the Nazis were cheated but it would have been even better if we thought they'd paid good money instead of stealing them.*

By March they were a two-man team *with the highest identification rate in the combined group.* It was *exhilarating* to be *so immediately close to it all.* But *the scale of the pillaging is indescribable: so much lost that will never be recovered.*

Practically every letter written after Norrington had been posted to Europe exhorted his father to keep Matthew from enlisting, *whatever you have to do.* War was filthy. Men were animals. It was inconceivable what one could do to another. *I don't want Matthew seeing what I've seen, hearing what I've heard, doing what I've done to conform and despised myself for not being brave enough not to do it.* The last letter was dated April 2. The concluding sentence read: *It truly will be over soon. I shall be coming home.*

Finally, after fifty-four years, thought Charlie: hardly soon enough.

"Well?" demanded Sir Matthew Norrington from the doorway.

"Your brother probably does deserve a hero's recognition," said Charlie.

"Give it to him, then."

"I need to talk more," said Charlie. Always more, he thought.

"Tell me about your brother?" asked Charlie, simply.

"Simon was the golden boy," declared Norrington, at once and admiringly. "There was nothing he couldn't do or achieve, usually twice as quickly and twice as well as anybody else. Everything came naturally, easily, to him. Our mother was French, so we grew up bilingual. I stopped there, but Simon didn't. He was practically as fluent in German and went on from Greek—which he took as part of art history—to more than passable Russian."

"He spoke German *and* Russian!" seized Charlie. There was a reassuring foot twinge.

"Both, very well," confirmed Norrington.

Abruptly recalling what now seemed a long-ago half thought, Charlie said, "What about *reading* it?"

"Of course," said Norrington, appearing surprised at the qualification. "He read both as well as he spoke both."

"He left the War Office at the end of 1943, to join the specialized art unit?"

"Yes."

"But obviously didn't go to Europe until after June 1944—after the invasion?"

"Almost immediately after: before the end of June. That was his job, trying to identify the national heritages that had been plundered and trace where they'd gone. He needed quick access to captured Germans, before they were dispersed."

As fifteen Germans were dispersed to Yakutsk, recalled Charlie. "Did he ever get leave, come home after being posted abroad?"

"Once," said Norrington. "December 1944. Father had his first heart attack. Simon was in Belgium then, I think. Wherever, he wangled a compassionate trip. Just forty-eight hours."

"Did you talk about what he was doing?"

"Of course. It upset him, the degree of Nazi looting. It was so complete: whole museums, galleries, stripped."

Charlie paused, unsure how to phrase his question, hoping for the answer he wanted but not wanting to lead. "What about anything else?"

Norrington, who had resumed his former seat, stared steadily across at Charlie. "You need to explain that."

"Did you ever get the impression, from anything that Simon said, that his function had been in any way expanded—that he'd been given a role beyond the location and recovery of looted art?"

Norrington took a long time to answer. "Nothing specific," the man said, finally.

"What wasn't specific?" persisted Charlie, refusing to give up.

"There was something about the languages he could speak—that he was often called upon by other people, in other units, to help them."

"Did he say which other units?"

The older man shook his head. "Not that I can remember."

He couldn't avoid leading, Charlie accepted. "Nothing about military intelligence? Intelligence of any sort?"

"No," said Norrington, positively.

"Who was Jessica?" demanded Charlie, abandoning one direction for another.

"One of the personal things I mentioned."

Charlie waited.

"Someone he met in London. There was talk of an engagement. They had a flat, in Pimlico. He had to interpret one night at a reception. Churchill, de Gaulle, a lot of Roosevelt's staff; America was in the war by late 1943, remember. There was an air raid. When he got back to Pimlico, their block had been destroyed by a land mine. Jessica was one of the ten who died."

"What about people Simon worked with?" Charlie hurried on. "Did he talk about any in particular? Refer to anyone as a friend?"

Again Norrington took his time. "There were things in the letters, but not until after he went back for the last time that December. I never knew who they were."

"I want to put some names to you," said Charlie, taking from his pocket the list from the Berlin group photograph. "I know it was a long time ago, but one might trigger something."

"I doubt it. But let's try."

"Wilson?"

"No."

"Allison?"

"No."

"Larisa Krotkov?"

"Russian?"

"Yes."

"I don't ever remember him talking of working with Russians."

"What about using the language?"

"No."

"Smith?"

"No."

"Raisa Belous?"

"She's the woman found in the grave! The Russian woman?"

"Yes."

"I suppose he must have known her, mustn't he?"

"You don't remember his ever mentioning her?"

"No."

"Bellamy?"

"No."

"Timpson?"

"No."

"Dunne?"

"No."

"Jacobson?"

"No."

Silence fell between them.

Norrington said, "Who are they?"

"People I believe Simon worked with."

"Where'd you get the names?"

"America," said Charlie, which was close enough to the truth. "Some of them *were* American."

"He worked with the Russian women, as well?"

"There was a connection. I don't know what, not yet." Would he ever? Charlie asked himself.

"I'm sorry," apologized Norrington. He gestured over his shoulder, toward the two repacked boxes. "I know everything there by heart. If there'd been a hint, I would have recognized it. I was waiting for an obvious Scots name, for 'Scotty.' " The man paused. "I've already spoken to Sir Rupert: told him what I told you, about my time limit."

"What did he say?"

"That he hoped you'd meet the deadline."

"So do I," said Charlie.

"The media release brought the American woman back but not the Englishman?" demanded Nikulin.

"Yes," said Natalia. There were just the two of them in the chief of staff's office. He'd served tea and sweetmeats.

"And he hasn't been in contact?"

"Not since the day he left." It had been a bad mistake for Charlie not to have telephoned Lestov.

"There's no doubt that the button found in the grave was British?"

"None," said Natalia, uncomfortably.

"They must know who the second man was: have an identity they want to hide."

"Possibly."

"Everyone knows Stalin was a monster, that the regime then is not the government of today. Why don't we turn the announcement of this new discovery into the finding of the evidence of a second mystery Briton? Put pressure upon them? We could even keep our understanding of cooperation: tell London what we're going to do, before we do it. And we'd have to tell them direct if their man isn't here, wouldn't we?"

Exposing Charlie to every sort of criticism, Natalia thought. How could she manipulate a delay? "I don't understand how the woman, Larisa Krotkov, can have disappeared so completely."

"You think you're being blocked?"

"Yes," exaggerated Natalia, eagerly.

"Then let's see if the obstruction extends to the president's office," accepted Nikulin.

"Perhaps we should wait until we establish that—and a reason, if it is the case—before moving on the British idea?"

"Not for much longer," determined the man. "So far we've been ahead in virtually everything. That's how I want us to stay."

On the other side of Moscow, Fyodor Ivanovich Belous nervously opened the door of his apartment only sufficiently to see it was Vadim Lestov, backed by a three-man squad.

"Don't be shy, Fyodor Ivanovich," said the militia colonel. "We've come back for a second look."

29

The telephone was lifted at the first ring. A man's voice, toneless and nameless, said, "Yes?"

Charlie said, "I understand you're interested in a Lieutenant Simon Norrington, who died a long time ago a very long way from home."

"Who is this?"

It would be a dedicated line and number, equipped for instant trace. But there would be no one in place and Charlie had chosen a telephone on the platform of the Euston underground station and estimated it would take them as much as thirty minutes, maybe more, to get anywhere near him. And by then he would have gone, as far as they were concerned, in any of a dozen different directions. "Someone else who's interested."

"Are you sure you've got the right number?"

Trying to prolong the conversation, to get the trace. All the buttons would have been pressed, everyone mobilized, waiting for the location. Charlie felt a flicker of nostalgia. "You tell me." Charlie was timing the call: forty-five seconds so far.

"Where did you get this number?"

"It's been left with quite a few people, hasn't it?"

"Who gave it to you?"

"Someone who was as interested in Lieutenant Norrington as we are." The Burbage identity would have only been on the card given to Sir Matthew and then logged personally against the baronet, the contact pseudonym providing an instant trace to the source.

"I meant the name of the person."

"I know you did."

"You seem well informed about certain things."

A full minute, Charlie noted. It would be a mistake to disclose too much tradecraft. He didn't try to speak over the loudspeaker announcement of a southbound train terminating at the Oval, which would be automatically recorded by the specially equipped telephone and mislead them to the Northern Line. "And about Lieutenant Norrington in particular."

"I think we need to meet."

"So did I." They might just alert a local police station—the transport police, even—for him to be held without explanation until they arrived. He'd allow himself another thirty seconds.

"Shall I come to you?"

"No. I'll come to you." They'd imagine he'd made a mistake.

"Where?"

"Somewhere open, obviously."

"How about Waterloo station?"

"That's convenient," said Charlie, for them to imagine another slip.

"How shall I recognize you?"

"Tell me how to recognize you."

There was a pause. "I'll wear a light fawn raincoat, unbelted. And I carry a closed umbrella as well as a copy of the *Evening Standard* in the same hand, the left."

The old ways were still the best, reflected Charlie, nostalgic again. "Whereabouts on the station?"

"Directly opposite platform fifteen."

"Time?"

"One o'clock."

"I won't be late," lied Charlie.

"Neither will I."

Charlie cleaned the receiver, which was sure to be checked for fingerprints, with the handkerchief with which he'd been careful to insert the coins before briefly returning to ground level to cross to Euston Square for the Circle Line. He made it before his feet began to protest. One o'clock gave them two and a half hours to get into position, which was a lot. A big team, then. A high-alert designation. They'd already be swamping the Nothern Line, imagining from his convenience remark that he would use it to reach Waterloo from Euston.

It was immaterial in which direction he went; the only need now to get away from Euston as quickly as possible. The first train to arrive was heading east and he got on, settling himself for the long, circuitous loop to the south. It was only the beginning, but Charlie was pleased with the way it had gone. He would, obviously, go through it entirely, although he was already sure he'd been speaking to an MI6 section controller. He hoped things were going as well at his own headquarters building on the other side of the Thames. Sir Rupert Dean had promised a team and there were only five obvious Britons from their uniforms in the Berlin photograph. Hopefully it would not be difficult to trace any who might still be alive. Charlie would still have preferred to do it himself—trusting no one but himself to do anything properly—but had deferred to the director-general's argument that the search and the sources were routine and that this had priority. He checked his watch as the train turned south at Liverpool Street: a third of the way in twelve minutes, faster than he'd estimated. Some would already be at Waterloo by now, getting into position, gaining vantage points, borrowing uniforms, parking off-duty taxis that would never ply for hire. How many more, Charlie wondered, were doomed to a day's travel up and down the Northern Line? And how many more than that would spend an even more frustrating day sitting on each of the intermediary stations between Edgeware and Morden, mentally promising themselves, if they ever discovered his name, the pleasure of slowly castrating with a blunt and rusty penknife the bastard who'd caused them such misery?

Even with the necessary change at the Embankment, Charlie still reached Waterloo with an hour and three-quarters to spare before the appointment he had no intention of keeping. He ambled easily along the concourse, establishing from the indicator board that trains from platform 15 served local suburban stations. Equally casually he bought himself a ticket to Windsor and on his way to the first-floor station bar purchased a selection of that day's newspapers. He had to drink standing at the bar for fifteen minutes before a table became vacant at the panoramic window overlooking the concourse itself, immediately checking adjoining tables with the same view for anyone as prepared as himself for a long wait. There wasn't anyone.

Charlie worked his way through three disappointingly blended scotches, four newspapers—all of which kept the mystery Russian announcement on their front pages—and was sure he'd definitely identified a yellow-jacketed cleaner sweeping the same stretch of the concourse, a station attendant who didn't seem to know the answer to anyone's question and a shuffling, bottle-clutching wino as the immediate watchers by twelve forty-five, when the fawn-raincoated man with the *Evening Standard* and a tightly furled umbrella in his left hand actually emerged from platform 15 on an arriving train and began studiously studying the display board. Almost at once the uniformed station attendant passed close and the sweeper chose a patch by the adjoining platform 14 and Charlie thought again that standards were definitely dropping.

The waiting man's impatience showed almost at once in constant attention to his watch and head-twisted checks to the station clock. Charlie remained where he was until one-fifteen, abandoning his newspapers when he moved. As he went across to the designated platform, he wondered if the easily spotted group had ever learned the old adage that the most successful way to follow was to be in front. He went on to platform 15 without pausing, settling himself in the rear car to see each person coming onto the platform to board the train after him. Neither the man in the fawn raincoat nor the others he'd isolated did, which he hadn't really expected so soon. At Vauxhall he explained to the ticket collector he'd changed his mind about going to Windsor and made his way unhurriedly toward the antennae-haired edifice by the river at Vauxhall Cross to get into position himself. He had to wait two hours on an embankment bench, sympathizing afresh with those who would still be buried underground, before he saw the raincoated man coming from the direction of the station. The Waterloo sweeper was with him, but they weren't talking. Neither looked happy. The two others he'd identified were in the first of two returning taxis.

"So our colleagues across the river are running a rival operation," accepted Sir Rupert Dean, an hour later. "And you were right. Well done."

"There's certainly an operation," agreed Charlie. "I'd like to know what its purpose is."

"It's another blank wall with your names," said the director-general. "Norrington's unit was nominally military police: all of your five were, in fact, seconded from civilian forces. Every one of them is dead. . . ." He paused. "And as far as we know are in their proper graves. I guess that only leaves you with your Americans: and we know that one of them is dead, too, don't we?"

Charlie felt a sink of disappointment, which almost at once became embarrassment, at his having to concede an oversight so quickly after being congratulated. "Maybe not," he said. "I left one out. John Parnell wasn't on my list. He was Norrington's commanding officer who wrote the letter of condolence. A colonel."

It took two hours to locate a Colonel John Wesley Parnell on the retired officers' list, with an address in Rye, in Sussex. The quivering-voiced man answered the phone himself and said if it was important of course he'd see Charlie that night. He'd enjoy the company but apologized for not being able to offer dinner. Charlie said he wouldn't think of imposing.

As Charlie headed south across the river yet again, this time in the rented car and slowed by evening rush-hour traffic, he thought happily that when you're on a roll you're on a roll and it was one of the better feelings. He probably wouldn't have time to call Natalia, but she'd know there was a working reason, would be pleased to hear tomorrow that at long last there seemed to be some movement. As he had going to and from Sir Matthew Norrington's Hampshire estate, Charlie drove constantly checking his rearview mirror for any obviously following cars. There weren't any. Would Henry Packer have been replaced in Moscow? Charlie's being in London meant Natalia and Sasha were safe, he realized, relieved.

It was a small house, its only attribute, in daylight, a partial view of the distant sea from what had to be the last road from which it would have been possible, the final stop of a lonely widower to genteel poverty. Charlie guessed the grandfather clock with the sticky, heartbeat tick in the hall and a few pieces of silver and engraved glass in the open-fronted cabinet were all there was left to sell and thought of Fyodor Belous in Moscow. Charlie guessed, too, that the rugs that covered most of the furniture were to hide the splits and escape of their stuffing. It wouldn't have been difficult to make a prosecution for gross indecency against the anally intrusive chair upon which he was sitting, with some twisted difficulty. Charlie was taking only token sips of the supermarket sherry retired Colonel John Parnell had insisted on serving from a decanter, not because it wasn't any good but because he didn't like sherry. He didn't imagine the old man was eating any dinner that night, either.

Charlie remained silent and uncomfortable while the old soldier pored over the photographs Charlie produced of the Yakutsk grave, the bodies inside it, the mortuary shots of the corpses and the group copy of the art-recovery squad he'd obtained in Berlin. There were what appeared to be a lot of wartime photographs in the stark room in which they were sitting, but Charlie hadn't been able to locate any of the people in whom he was interested from where he was sitting.

It was a long time before Parnell finally looked up. "Incredible. Absolutely incredible." The voice was frail, like the man himself. He was thin and bald, shrunk with age inside an enveloping cardigan heavily and badly darned at both elbows. "Such a good, fine man. Unbelievable."

Incredible and unbelievable had been the constant interjection during Charlie's recitation of yet another edited account of the discovery of Lieutenant Simon Norrington's body.

"You commanded the unit?" began Charlie, gently. "Know everyone in the Berlin photographs?"

"Only commanded the Britons, although I knew George Timpson and Harry Dunne, who everyone called Hank. But I didn't know either of the women. You say the dark-haired one at the end was found in the grave with Simon? Incredible!"

"I didn't know the fraternization was quite that close."

"Neither did I, to tell you the truth. Us and the Americans, certainly. Good working relationship, for our particular job, but then most of them were only token soldiers: really professional policemen and art experts like Norrington and Timpson and Dunne. Surprised I didn't hear about the women."

"So you've never seen them before? No idea of their names?"

"Afraid not."

"When do you think that photograph might have been taken?"

"Right at the very end, obviously. We were always at the sharp end: needed to be there before people and what they stole got dispersed. Difficult enough to track stuff down as it was."

"Can you recognize the building in the background?"

Parnell pursed his lips, squinting down at the picture. "Could be the Pergamon Museum, which contains the fantastic Greek altar: it's the most impressive building in the entire Museumsinsel complex."

"But isn't that in what was East Berlin?" pressed Charlie, the mistake intentional. This really was like trying to sieve mud in search of a gold nugget.

"The actual partition hadn't happened then, but it would certainly have been in that part of the city the Russians controlled and later occupied. Explains the two Russian women, I suppose."

"Simon and the others would have had to be there by invitation? Have permission, certainly?"

"Without a doubt," agreed Parnell, at once. "So it must have been *very* early. Almost from the first days they occupied the east of the city the Russians established patrols, checking everyone, turning people back even though officially they had no right. Always amazed me how the rest of the Allies seemed surprised by everything the Russians did afterwards. I thought from the beginning their intention was to take Berlin entirely, which they would have done if it hadn't been for the airlift."

"Sir Matthew let me read your letter of condolence about Simon, to his father?"

"Never enough right words to say what you properly mean," complained the old man.

"In your letter you said Simon's body was returned by the Russians? I don't understand what he was doing there, if the Russians were turning non-Russians back."

"You've got to understand the chaos that was there, even after the supposed surrender. It was total. Not *everyone* got turned back—just those that couldn't satisfy the intercepting patrols. And Simon was unique in our section, had Russian as well as German. And enough charm to use either language to talk himself into and out of anything.

I *gave* him the assignment to go into the eastern part, as well as all the accreditation I could think of.”

It was coming! Slowly, awkwardly, but it was coming. “When was that?”

The old man shrugged. “Difficult to be precise, to a date. First day or two of May, something like that.”

“Was there still fighting in Berlin then?”

“Not in the way I think you mean, but a lot of shooting, certainly. Mostly in the Russian sector. Hate to sound like the Nazi propaganda machine, but the Russians really were subhuman the way they took their revenge.”

“Wasn’t it dangerous for Norrington to go in?”

“He was an Allied officer with all the necessary accreditation and authorization. Officially he had the right. He was a very confident young man. And I sent all these in the picture in with him, although as I said I didn’t know anything about the Americans or the Russian women being there, too. Can’t understand that.”

“What *was* the assignment?”

“Because of the way the Russians were behaving, there was a huge exodus of people from what became East Berlin, everyone trying to justify their right to stay in the west. You’ve heard what an art rapist Goering was, literally looting museums by the trainload?”

Charlie nodded.

“There was intelligence, from three separate sources, that Goering had an enormous amount of art he hadn’t been able to ship to Carinhall, his hunting estate north of Berlin, stored in the basement of the Air Ministry. I sent Simon and his group to see if it was true.”

“On May first or second?” pressed Charlie.

“As far as I can recall. It was certainly very early in the month.”

“How soon after May first or second did you hear from Simon Norrington?”

The myopic man shook his head. “I’m not sure I did, personally. There *was* some communication, as far as I remember, although it’s difficult to be precise after all this time. Something about his following up some information, as far as I recall. I had other search groups, in Munich and Hamburg. But all the message exchanges will be in ministry records. Ours was regarded as an important unit, which is why I'll never understand why they kept us so short of staff. Records were important, though. Everything was kept, filed. I insisted on that, even though we had to keep a pretty loose command, by the very nature of the job, here, there and everywhere. I was actually off base, in Munich, for most of May. That's when the message came from headquarters that Simon's body had been found, terribly injured."

"Do you remember the date?" asked Charlie.

Parnell shook his head. "It'll all be in War Office records. You need to look them up."

"Yes," said Charlie, not bothering to explain the disappearance to the older man. "Do you remember how his body was returned?"

Parnell frowned at the question, offering more sherry, to which Charlie shook his head. "Of course I do. Star of my unit; only lost two during the entire war, and him when the bloody thing was officially over. The body was in a coffin. Damned awful thing, too. Changed it, of course. At once. The injuries were terrible . . ." The old man shuddered. "Wouldn't have known a thing, thank God."

"What about belongings?"

"Not as much as I would have expected. Decided at the time the bastard Russians had stolen a lot of stuff. Money, certainly. I clearly remember there wasn't any money. Suppose we were lucky to get back what we did."

"Uniform?"

Parnell shook his head. "There wouldn't have been anything left, after the injuries he suffered. It was a shroud. . . ." The old man stopped in abrupt realization. "But it wasn't Simon, was it?"

"No." Charlie had decided it was easier for the man to speak as he had been doing.

"So the body I saw . . . with Simon's things. . . . was someone else!"

"Yes."

"Do you know who?"

"No. I don't expect we ever will."

"Bodies were easy to come by," remembered the former soldier, with an unexpected hardness that surprised Charlie. "Was it simply a body? Or someone killed specially?"

The question surprised Charlie even more. "Killed specially, I would think."

"Like Simon, in . . . ?"

"Yakutsk," supplied Charlie. "Yes, killed specially." He straight-ened, refusing the maudlin drift. "There are some things that trouble me. Simon Norrington went into East Berlin on the first or second day of May? There's a message you didn't personally receive about his following up something there, and the next, at the end of the month, is that he's been killed?"

"That's as I remember it."

"What about the squad that went into the east with him at the beginning of May?"

Parnell frowned. "I can't properly remember, as I say. I wasn't there. There was something about their coming back, but I can't recall whether Simon was with them or not. Obviously he wasn't."

"Wasn't there a need to keep in closer touch than that?"

"Apart from myself and one or two other officers, we were one of those gypsy units, chosen for a particular expertise—in this case a knowledge of art—and an investigatory ability. That's why, officially, we came under the aegis of the Military Police and why there were so many civilian police officers seconded to us. It took me and other professional officers a long time to get used to it. In the end—certainly by the time we got to Berlin—there was an odd pride at being regarded as cowboys: it all went with the camaraderie of win-ning the war and of being part of a special unit." He got to his feet, with difficulty, and went to a carefully arranged photographic display on a wall too far away for Charlie to have focused from where he sat. There was a startlingly clean square against the age-darkened wallpaper when Parnell took the photograph down to carry back to Charlie. "There we all are," he said, proudly. "All thought we were pretty special then. Recovered a hell of a lot of stuff. Not enough, of course, but far more than we expected."

The old man gazed nostalgically down at the photograph before handing it to Charlie. "There was a halfhearted attempt to keep in touch afterwards, but as I said, most of them were enlisted policemen, from all over the country, so it could never have really worked. It got down to exchanging Christmas cards and then gradually that stopped. . . ." There was another nostalgic pause. "As far as I know, Peter and I are the only two of the original team still alive."

Parnell finally offered the print to Charlie. It was one of those vaguely self-conscious group photographs, the officers in the fore-ground, the unit behind them. Parnell himself and Norrington were in the front, with two other officers flanking them. The five men whom Charlie recognized from the Berlin picture were lined behind. There were a further five whom he didn't. Charlie said, "Which one's Peter?"

The old man pointed to a saturnine, unsmiling man seated next to him in the picture. "*Sir* Peter Mason. Seconded to us from the Foreign Office because what we were doing had all sorts of political dimensions, trying to decide who owned what art, that sort of thing. Ended up a permanent secretary. We kept in touch for a while, but it drifted off, like these things do."

"But he's still alive?"

"He was three months ago. Saw him on television, *Newsnight*: something about loss of sovereignty in the European Union, like it always is."

"What was he, in your unit?"

"Second-in-command, I suppose. Kind of self-appointed, actually, but he was a very able administrator. Incredibly hardworking."

"Would he have been the person Norrington would have dealt with in May, when you were in Munich?"

"Possibly. Difficult to remember after all this time. I really think you'd stand more chance going back through the War Office records."

"Of course," avoided Charlie, again.

"What happened?" demanded the old man, abruptly. "To Simon, I mean. And the poor bugger who ended up in his grave. What was it all about?"

"That's what we're trying to find out."

Parnell shook his head. "Murdered. Unbelievable."

"You told me you knew Timpson?"

"Wonderful man. Not as personable as Simon, but they got on very well together. Timpson had the most terrible eyesight, but it didn't seem to get in his way doing what he did. He and Simon were great friends. Always thought Simon had a great admiration for George: thought George was better at what he did than he was him-self."

"What about Dunne? Was he an art expert, too?"

Parnell shook his head. "Political adviser, like Peter. God knows why everyone thought it was so important to be politically correct: that was a phrase even then. He and Peter palled up, like Simon and George, as far as I remember. Can't actually recall the going of them."

Charlie said, "You've been very helpful."

"Like to think it would help find whoever killed Simon," said the former soldier. "How on earth could he and Timpson have been where they really were, in the middle of Russia?" Before Charlie could respond, Parnell said, in sudden awareness, "Whatever Simon said while I was in Munich would probably give you a clue, would it?"

"Yes," agreed Charlie. "It probably would."

Vadim Leonidovich Lestov was a clever man becoming cleverer with each passing day and had known from the moment of the first discovery how most quickly to break Fyodor Belous, a fervent Party zealot well aware—until now perhaps even an admirer—of how information could be extracted from an unwilling informer.

Lestov simply left the man in total, soundless isolation to feed off his own fear throughout the first night of his detention and most of the following day. Belous was also denied food or water or lavatory facilities, which made the interview distasteful because Belous had shit himself at least twice by the time he was led into the interview cell. Already laid out on the table between them were some prints, a small, single-framed icon, the oil portrait of a woman, what appeared to be a gold-framed religious triptych missing its third panel, a single gold-framed pastoral scene picked out in precious stones, two rings, both set with heavy red stones, and a ribbon-suspended medal. There were also four photographs. The first showed Raisa Belous at what was obviously an official ceremony, the medal on her chest. The second was of the woman alone, in front of the Catherine Palace. The third was of her with a blond woman featured in the first picture. And the last showed Raisa yet again with the woman and the American who had been found in the grave in Yakutsk. The American and the blond woman had their arms around each other, laughing, and Raisa appeared to be looking on approvingly.

The display was set out to face Belous when he sat down, which he did uncomfortably. Further to demean the man, Lestov exaggerated his disgust at the smell.

Belous said, "You can't do this to me!" His voice was hoarse from dehydration.

"I am doing it," Lestov pointed out, logically. "And I will go on, as long as it suits me." He splayed his hand over what was set out on the table. "You're obviously a thief. A burglar."

"You know they're my mother's things."

"Not if I want to jail you for ten, fifteen years I don't. A thief, from a church or a museum."

"They're my mother's!" repeated the man, whimpering.

"You recognize anyone in that first photograph, apart from her? I think I do. I think the man with the heavy mustache was most often known as Joseph Stalin. And the balding man next to him wearing glasses is Lavrenty Beria, who headed Stalin's secret police, the NKVD. You recognize them, Fyodor Ivanovich?"

"It was when she was acknowledged as a hero of the Soviet Union." He briefly touched the medal. "My grandparents told me."

Lestov picked up the jeweled pictures. "Do you know where this was from?"

"The Catherine Palace. Part of the Amber Room."

"Was there more?" persisted Lestov.

"I think there was. My grandparents sold things, to survive."

"What have you sold?"

"Nothing!"

"Liar!"

The stinking man touched the two rings. "Just some jewelry, like this."

"Do you know who the man is, in the picture with your mother and the other woman?"

"The American from the grave?"

Lestov nodded. "Why did you keep these things?"

"I thought I could sell them—the pictures, I mean. I wanted the American to be identified before I approached the American reporters who came to me after the *Moscow News* story. I was going to say I'd discovered all this: sell them the photographs and see if there was a reward for the Amber Room stuff that everyone wrote about after my mother was identified."

Lestov decided it was too pitiful to challenge. "There would have been some papers, documents, belonging to your mother?"

"Beria tried to gain power after Stalin died. Was purged. My grandparents were frightened: destroyed everything they thought might dangerously connect them to the man."

"So your mother was NKVD?"

"I think so. That's what it was known as then, wasn't it?"

"Do you know who the woman is, with the American and your mother? Did your grandparents ever tell you a name?"

"No."

"You're in serious trouble, Fyodor Ivanovich. If I discover you're still lying, I shall be very angry."

"I don't *know* anything more! Please give me something to drink. Let me clean myself. This isn't right!"

Lestov shook his head. "I'm going to let you live in your own shit so that you can think extremely hard to make sure you haven't forgotten to tell me all that you know."

"Please!" wailed the man.

"This is how people were treated all the time in the old days— that time you admire so much. Enjoy it while you can."

Marina Novikov stood with the official notification in her hand, her eyes too blurred to read it again. She said, "I never imagined this day would come."

"Neither did I," said the doctor.

"I'm frightened."

"So am I," admitted Novikov.

Marina looked around the room. "My father built this house. It's still the best in Yakutsk."

"Then it'll be easy to sell."

"What will Moscow be like? Big, I expect. Difficult to understand at first."

"But we will," promised Novikov.

"I'm frightened," she repeated.

"We've got the boys out," said Novikov. "They won't have to live the lives that we've had to."

"No," she accepted. "That's what's important. Do you think your side of the bargain with the Englishman will be enough?"

"We've got the official notice!" insisted the man, actually taking it from her.

"What if what you have isn't enough and it's canceled?" she asked.

Novikov shook his head in refusal against her doubt, but he didn't reply.

30

The instruction had been for Charlie not to be late and he'd set out from London before the early morning rush hour, although not to comply with Sir Peter Mason's autocratic demand. After his even earlier telephone conversation with Natalia, in a three-hour-time-difference Moscow, Charlie's impression was of events closing in upon him in ever-constricting circles without his being able to orchestrate the process, and it was always necessary for Charlie to be the one with the baton in his hand. Which was why, driving unhurriedly and still constantly checking his mirror through the low Norfolk countryside, he wasn't happy. And why he needed the time properly to analyze what he and Natalia had discussed to rearrange the score to his own tune, not that of the other players.

Unquestionably to Charlie's benefit was the virtually speed-of-light granting of Moscow residency for Vitali Novikov and his family, which would bring them into the city and the already-provided apartment in the next two or three days. Even more unquestionable was that he had to be ready and waiting when the Yakutsk doctor arrived, finally to learn what the man knew about the murders.

If anything.

That nagging, persistent uncertainty was Charlie's primary concern, as it had been from the first, initially unexplained approach from the thin, intense man. Charlie accepted with Novikov that he was in an all-or-nothing situation: all if the doctor had enough to unravel the riddles, nothing if he'd fallen for the desperate bluff of an innocent exile who'd greatly exaggerated his knowledge of a long-ago-eradicated camp and its special prisoners. The only thing he could do—had ever been able to do—was call that bluff, if that's what it was.

Which meant delaying his going on to Washington to try to find out if an American named Harry Dunne was still alive and had a nugget or two to contribute. In addition to trying equally hard to discover, either there or in London, the obvious although unknown importance of fifteen Germans imprisoned in the very last month of the war in a barely living hell on earth.

Was a shortcut possible with the Germans? Charlie knew—although she wasn't aware of his knowing—that Miriam Bell had the fifteen names when she'd gone back to Washington; was prepared, even, to believe her return might well have been connected with that identification. She could, after all, easily have gotten the FBI in Washington to make the inquiry on her behalf. But Charlie, who'd objectively seen similarities between himself and the American, gauged Miriam Bell's ambition to be such that, like him, it was always necessary for her to do things herself rather than rely upon others.

Could he trick her into disclosing whatever she'd found out, if indeed she'd discovered anything? He could certainly try. She'd even been anxious for him to get back to Moscow. And given a warning he hadn't really needed, about watching his back. He had Timpson's name as well as that of Hank Dunne: more than sufficient to bargain with. It was certainly something to consider, at least until all the greater uncertainties about Vitali Novikov were resolved.

Letting the reflection run, Charlie acknowledged the very practical argument, beyond anything the Yakutsk doctor might or might not have, for his going back to Moscow immediately. According to Natalia that morning, Nikulin's threat to go public about a second British officer had been prompted by Charlie's unspecified London recall and continued absence. Which made it possible to delay any public announcement *by* going back. Charlie reckoned he certainly knew enough from Natalia to invent a plausibly fictitious reason for the London return; he could even infuse something in the negotiations with Miriam for her to pillow talk about to Vadim Lestov to keep all the balls juggling in the air. Perhaps not as difficult to orchestrate to his own personally composed tune as he'd initially thought.

What about, even, an entirely different concert? Convinced as he

was that he and his fighting-to-survive department were being bug-
gered about by their own gods on high, Charlie abruptly wondered
what or who might fall out of the woodwork if Russia *did* disclose
the presence of a second British officer. His not being in Moscow at
the time of any announcement would avoid any personal or departmental blame. All he had to do was not warn the director-general of
his prior knowledge. At once the counterargument presented itself.
If he didn't give the easily explained warning, he could stand accused—almost inevitably by Gerald Williams, another unresolved
problem—of not being properly on top of the Moscow end of the
investigation, whether he was physically there or not. Not an alternative, then.

He definitely had to go back, Charlie accepted, as he began picking
up the signs to East Dereham. But without the intended American
detour on the way, quickly to get upon the rostrum, baton in hand.
And now with the score set out more clearly in front of him than it
had been at this journey's beginning.

The estate of Sir Peter Mason, a former government mandarin of
Her Britannic Majesty, was minuscule by comparison to that of Sir
Matthew Norrington but still impressive to someone born in a ter-
raced council house, which Charlie had been. The period of its construction, which favored a confusing mix of towers and castellated
battlements, was indeterminate, but Charlie had the impression that
it was far more recent than the Hampshire mansion, and the grounds
didn't have their grazing herds, but even to Charlie's Philistine eye
the paintings and artwork appeared comparable.

Sir Peter Mason was an intimidatingly large man, immaculate in
the sort of waistcoated dark pinstripe, complete with fresh rose buttonhole, that Charlie imagined the man would have worn every day
of his working life in Whitehall and couldn't bear to abandon in
retirement. The virgin white shirt was hard-collared, the tie Charlie
guessed to be the Carlton Club, although he wasn't sure. There was
scarcely any gray in the long, polished black hair, the advantage of
either remarkable genes or an equally remarkable, dye-adept barber.
The face was so pink and smooth it could have been genes. The man
only just managed to stop himself from checking Charlie's arrival
timekeeping. He remained seated behind the sort of desk Charlie

could believe permanent secretaries had made from the plans of air-craft carrier flight decks. There was no offer of a handshake. As well as several oils, the study was festooned with photographs of Sir Peter Mason with every world political leader Charlie could remember and some he couldn't. There didn't appear to be any of Mason in military uniform, though. The man said, "I talked to Sir Matthew, after your call. This is a dreadful business."

"You'll understand, then, why I need your help," said Charlie.

"Of course, although I'm not sure I did at first last night. Or what I'll be able to give you today." Mason was leaning intently forward on his desk, one hand cupped protectively over the other. "Looked out what might help, but I'd like to hear as much as there is from you first."

A man accustomed always to power and obedience, Charlie recognized: velvet-covered condescension. Charlie said, "You remember Simon Norrington?"

"Of course. Wonderful man as well as being superb at his job. First-rate mind." The voice was measured, carefully modulated. There was a nod in the direction of the oil paintings. "Would have appreciated his opinion of some of these."

"And George Timpson?"

The former civil service supremo frowned, creasing an uncreased forehead. "Not so well. American, wasn't he?"

"An art expert, like Norrington. Colonel Parnell described them as friends?"

"They were," said the large man. He lounged back at his desk, hands deep in his pockets. "Timpson had very bad eyesight, as I remember, although it didn't seem to affect his work. Had no idea they were the two referred to in the newspapers. With the Russian woman all the fuss has been about, weren't they?"

Instead of answering, Charlie offered Novikov's grainy, insect-blurred photographs of the bodies in the grave and then the better, more professionally taken ones after the recovery from Yakutsk. Mason physically shuddered and said, "Horrible! How much else have you been able to discover so far?"

Mason listened to Charlie's now almost automatic recitation, gazing down at the photographs, occasionally shaking his head in apparent disbelief. He looked up inquiringly at the end of Charlie's account, ensuring it was over before saying, "Now tell me how I can help. Which I will, of course, in any way I can."

"The month of May 1945," identified Charlie. "Norrington went into the eastern sector of Berlin, with a squad, to check intelligence that Goering had an art cache somewhere in the Air Ministry?"

Mason frowned. "It was a very long time ago for a recollection as definite as that. I certainly remember the Goering information: it was thought to be very reliable. And exciting."

"But not Simon being sent to check it?"

"He would have been the most obvious choice, with the expertise and the languages, but I don't specifically recollect it, no. There was so much happening. Or not happening. You've no idea what Berlin—Germany—was like: no administration, no utilities. Total devastation."

"So I keep being told," said Charlie, covering the sigh. "Colonel Parnell was in Munich virtually all of May. And Norrington doesn't seem to have come back from the Russian sector. He can't remember about the squad, either. But he is sure there was a message: maybe a reason why Norrington stayed there. Perhaps, even, *why* he went on to Yakutsk."

Mason slowly shook his head. "That doesn't mean anything to me—nothing that I can recall. Except that it wouldn't have been anything to do with Yakutsk. We were assigned to Germany. It would have needed Supreme Allied Command authorization to have gone into Russia. . . ." The man hesitated, shaking his head. "Not even sure that would have been sufficient."

"Don't tell me it was impossible for Norrington and Timpson to be where they were found!" pleaded Charlie.

"None of this makes sense!"

"I keep being told that, too. You said you'd looked something out, to help."

Mason groped into an unseen drawer at his side of the desk, taking out a faded brown leather-covered pocketbook. "Kept my wartime diaries: a log, really. This is '45." He finished the sentence looking down as he fingered left-handedly through the pages, exclaimed, "Ah!" and went back to turn the pages more slowly. "May, you say?"

"Yes," confirmed Charlie, hopefully.

"Went to Hamburg on May sixth. Got back into Berlin on the twenty-eighth." He looked up, smiling with what looked to be natural teeth. "And here it is!" He looked down again, to quote verbatim " 'May 2. Simon. Goering. Strong Louvre possibility.' "

"That's all?" pressed Charlie, disappointed.

"No!" said the man, triumphantly, " 'May 5. Goering unsubstantiated. Squad back.' "

"Squad back?" echoed Charlie. "What about Simon Norrington?"

Mason offered the sepia-brown pages. "I didn't make a note. Doesn't look to have been my decision. I usually put in a lot more detail, for my fuller reports later."

"Colonel Parnell issued the order. Just before he went to Munich," confirmed Charlie. "So both of you were away?"

"There was still a support staff running the office," stressed Mason. "Organized it myself. Anything that came in while we were away would have been automatically and immediately passed on to headquarters. Parnell was a stickler for records; insisted that we were trying to restore the art heritage of Europe. Which we were, of course. Had every damned telephone call logged." He waved the leather-covered diary again. "That's why I kept this. Parnell had to know where everyone was, what they were doing, every minute of the day." He smiled again, confidently. "So you don't have a problem! You go to War Office records and you'll get every scrap of paperwork that ever passed through our unit. Including any message from Norrington, even if it was telephoned. You'll know *exactly* what happened—or was supposed to be happening—to the man."

"We've already done that, sir," disclosed Charlie. "There are no records covering Norrington during May. Not until his body was returned."

For a very long time Sir Peter Mason regarded Charlie over the huge desk. Then he said, "Do you know what I did, after the war?"

"I understand you were a permanent secretary at the Foreign Office," ventured Charlie.

"*The* permanent secretary, to the foreign secretary, for fifteen years. I know about government files."

"Then you'll know that these have been destroyed," said Charlie, bluntly.

"That is impossible. It cannot be done."

"It has been done. So it is possible."

"What are you suggesting?"

"I don't know enough to suggest anything," admitted Charlie, honestly. "All I can tell you is that files that should still be in existence—as you believe they should still exist—have disappeared."

"Government files go automatically into the Public Records Office at Kew after a prescribed period of time," insisted the expert. "Even if the release time is extended beyond the normal fifty-year period, it is noted at Kew. Has there been the proper check?"

"I understand so," said Charlie, who truly didn't.

"An illegal act has been committed, if they've been tampered with. Or unless a special exclusion or extension-of-release order has been imposed."

"They no longer exist," insisted Charlie. He really was wasting his time. There wasn't any reason to delay his Moscow return.

Sir Peter Mason lapsed into renewed silence. "Do you imagine you'll ever fully get to the bottom of it all?"

"At this precise moment I doubt it," admitted Charlie, honest again and hating the admission. "Everything has been dispersed between too many separate departments here in England and is compounded by supposedly shared but in fact quite separate and conflicting investigations by America and Russia."

"In May 1945, we received a body with Simon Norrington's identification from the Russian authorities in Berlin," stated Mason, more to himself than to Charlie. "The three in Yakutsk—and whoever it was in Berlin—were killed by Russians. Who else could it have been?"

"The Russians have evidence of another British officer having been present," declared Charlie, flatly.

"The present British government knows this?"

"Yes."

"What evidence?"

"A bullet from a British gun. A button forensically proven to be from a British battle-dress uniform."

"That, potentially, is appalling! Unthinkable! You should have told me about this last night. . . . I still have friends in government: people I could have spoken to . . . got a better understanding . . ."

Careless of his desperation showing, Charlie said, "Don't you remember anything about Norrington around that month?"

"His death, that's all. Suddenly being told by the Russians that they had his body and were returning it."

"Wasn't any inquiry made about the circumstances? Colonel Parnell says your unit only ever lost two people during its entire existence."

"Of course," said the older man. "I *do* recall discussing that very fully with Parnell, obviously. It went higher, to headquarters, for them to use their authority to demand an explanation. All we got back was that his body had been found, by a Russian patrol, with no evidence of how he'd been killed."

What, Charlie wondered, had been the explanation given to the Americans for the death of the man they'd believed to be George Timpson? "Is it conceivable Norrington would have gone to Russia *without* telling anyone?"

"Totally *in*conceivable!" insisted the other man. "Okay, we were an irregular unit and maybe did things in an irregular way. But as I said, Parnell was a stickler and everyone followed his rules if they didn't necessarily strictly follow army regulations to the letter. For Norrington to have decided, off his own bat, to go to Yakutsk would have amounted to desertion! And *how* could he have gone, of his own accord? There were only military flights, in and out of both Berlin airports. And those flights were checked, by nationals of whichever country the plane belonged to. The one fact I am positive about is that the only way Norrington and Timpson would have got to Yakutsk would have been as prisoners of the Russians. Who were then prepared to murder to cover up what they had done. . . ." The man paused at a new awareness. "Is there a phony grave in Berlin for Timpson?"

"An American war cemetery in the Netherlands."

"Why on earth isn't the government—America, too—demanding an explanation?"

"The possible embarrassment of a second involved Briton."

"Rubbish. Preposterous rubbish," rejected the man. "By 1945 there were millions of British handguns all over the place. And tens of millions of uniform bits and pieces. And it doesn't matter whether there were one or two British officers. The unalterable, unchallengeable fact has to be they were prisoners of the Russians, without whom they wouldn't have been there in the first place. . . ." He paused, close to being breathless. "Instead of inventing conspiracies and spying missions and possible international embarrassments, has anyone thought that even if there was a second British officer his body might be somewhere else in another unmarked, unknown grave?"

"I don't believe they have," conceded Charlie. He certainly hadn't, until now. Which he should have. A second body in a second grave would make nonsense of a lot of his theories and arguments so far. It could even, he further conceded, refute a Russian accusation.

"Suggest it!" insisted Mason. "At the same time as suggesting an explanation is demanded from the Russians for what's clearly cold-blooded murder!"

Charlie said, "I appreciate the time you've given me. It's been very useful: put forward different perspectives."

"I don't at all like the sound of how this is being handled," said the other man. "You've got my number. Anything else comes up you think I might be able to help you with, you let me know. You've no idea what the Russians were like in Berlin."

"Colonel Parnell tried to give me some idea."

Mason shook his head dismissively. "You had to be there, truly to believe it." There was a further, more vehement head shake. "And I can't believe how this is being treated now."

When Charlie phoned from a public kiosk in the center of East Dereham, Sir Rupert Dean insisted it should be a full meeting, not confined just to the two of them.

In Moscow Dmitri Nikulin announced the same decision and Natalia traveled to the White House in the same car as Colonel Vadim Lestov. She was curious at the strange harshness there had been in the presidential chief of staff's voice when he'd summoned them, apprehensive of what it might mean.

"You're sure you seized *everything* Belous had hidden?" demanded the tall, austere man.

"After finding what we did, we virtually stripped the apartment," assured the militia colonel. "There's absolutely nothing more."

"Where is it now?" Nikulin appeared distracted, looking around his huge office as if he expected to see it laid out for inspection.

"All in my personal office safe."

"Fyodor Belous?"

"In custody, in Lefortovo. Held on suspicion of theft," said Natalia.

Nikulin said, "The NKVD accreditation is the most important."

"It's with everything else," guaranteed Lestov.

"I want you, personally, to bring it to me today," ordered Nikulin. He hesitated, looking away from them, his mouth moving in apparent rehearsal for what he was about to say. Then, coming back to them, he said, "As of today, this moment, the investigation into the Yakutsk murders and the apparent disappearance of Larisa Krotkov is ended. Neither of you will take any further active part and certainly make no contribution." He looked directly at Lestov. "You will *appear* to continue working with the American and the Englishman, to monitor everything they do or might discover, until such time as they announce the case unsolvable. At that time we'll devise a public announcement, which at this stage isn't something that has to be considered."

Natalia broke the stunned silence that followed, stumbling to arrange her own words. "But we surely need—"

"There will be no professional reflection upon either of you," interrupted the presidential aide, misunderstanding. "In fact, both your records will be personally endorsed, by me, that your investigation has been exemplary and the confirmation of your promotion, Vadim Leonidovich, will also be endorsed with presidential approval."

"We have already issued a statement of a potential breakthrough, hinting at Tsarskoe Selo," reminded Lestov, uncomfortable that it had been his idea.

"Which we can easily make it to be," said Nikulin, another decision already made. "We can produce everything else you found in Belous's apartment and disclose it as art she saved from being plundered by the Nazis: continue building Raisa Belous into a heroine, which she was. And we'll keep the man silent by using his fear of security organizations. Tell him if he as much as speaks to the press again he'll spend the rest of his life in a Yakutskaya labor camp."

"Are we to be told why and how Raisa Belous became a heroine? Larisa Krotkov, too, presumably?" demanded Natalia, her thoughts in order now.

Once more Nikulin hesitated. "They were both instrumental in one of the greatest-ever services to the Motherland, which continued to benefit for decades. But which will never, ever be revealed."

"When?" demanded Aleksandr Andreevich Kurshin.

"Immediately," said Vitali Novikov. "Everything's fixed."

"Full citizenship . . . residency permission . . . ?" groped Kurshin.

"Everything."

"But you never said . . . talked about it," complained the local homicide detective. "I would have expected . . . ?"

"You know how many times I applied before. I thought I'd be refused again," said the doctor, close to the truth.

It was midafternoon in the mortuary laboratory and Kurshin had already consumed one flask of vodka, squinting to focus and to understand. Befuddled, he said, "You'll be gone! Forever!"

"I shall miss you, too, old friend."

Kurshin came awkwardly forward, arms outstretched, and the two men bear-hugged. Novikov felt his boyhood friend shaking.

Kurshin said, "A farewell drink?"

"Of course," accepted Novikov. "Several." He had a lot to celebrate. Everything, in fact.

31

"A total waste of time, in fact?" judged Gerald Williams, wearily predictable, the moment Charlie stopped talking.

"No," denied Charlie. "There was no way of our knowing, until I'd spoken to all three, *what* there might have been. Which made it essential that I come back to do it." Charlie, who'd never had to hold up a wetted finger to gauge which way the wind was blowing, discerned a changed attitude in everyone in the conference room. During the last confrontation, only days ago, Sir Rupert Dean himself had intervened to remind the constant attacker that he'd ordered the withdrawal.

"And having spoken to them, you learned nothing!"

"No." Charlie was forced to admit.

"So there hasn't been the slightest step forward?" persisted the committed finance director.

Because Williams's attitude *was* so predictable, Charlie had withheld Sir Peter Mason's alternative theory about a second officer, to which the fat man's reaction was for the first time slower.

It was the director-general who said, "That would certainly be a total rejection of any Russian claim. Put us in the driving seat, perhaps?"

"More than that," encouraged Charlie, who'd prepared his second presentation during the drive back to London more interested in the maximum benefit than in its absolute accuracy. "As I've already told you, I believe the accusation of a second British officer is what's being threatened by the Russians. If we, in advance—today, even—made the demand for a Russian explanation, we'd completely preempt them." He'd only spent a few minutes—five at the most—with Sir Rupert Dean before coming into the conference room, but it had been enough to detect the man's misgivings at previously allowing so much to be withheld from the people now ranged around the table against him. It was therefore the director-general—upon whom above all others his future in Moscow depended—that Charlie was the most anxious to convince or reassure. Or both.

"Unless they know more about another officer than we do," countered Patrick Pacey. "In which case we'd be admitting a spying mission in advance of being accused of it." The political officer shook his head. "It's too risky a strategy and there's a lot of other people who'd agree with me, I'm sure."

"Which brings us back, as we are always brought back, to how little has been achieved during this entire mishandled investigation," Williams said.

"The opinion is not mine," conceded Charlie, unhappy at what sounded like an excuse. "It was suggested, most strongly, by Sir Peter Mason. Who *was* the permanent secretary to the Foreign Office."

"A long time ago," deflated Pacey. "The Cold War eyeball-to-eyeball confrontations are things of the past."

"Perhaps unfortunately, as far as our future is concerned," remarked Jeremy Simpson. "I accept all the political arguments, but speaking as a lawyer there's a lot in the cliché of attack being the best form of defense."

Charlie at once saw the opportunity further to allay the director-general's discomfort. "Sir Peter also insisted that it is impossible—his word—for Simon Norrington's records to have disappeared. According to him it's an inviolable Whitehall regulation that everything is transferred to Kew. Even if something is withheld for reasons of sensitivity, the fact that it *is* being withheld is publicly noted."

"Are you suggesting there's been positive obstruction?" demanded Dean, sharply.

What everyone else would believe to be outrage Charlie recognized as the man's relief at his committee having belatedly put in front of them a lot of what he and Charlie had earlier kept to themselves. "I'm telling you the opinion of someone who knows the system," Charlie said, following the older man's lead. So unproductive had the interviews with the three men been that the latitude Dean had allowed *did* seem pointless now. It irked Charlie to have to agree, even only to himself, with Gerald Williams's assessment.

"It's most definitely something to be raised at the next meeting of the Intelligence Committee," acknowledged the political officer.

"If it is positively being withheld or has been destroyed against the government's procedural rules, then there is something extremely serious to hide," the deputy director-general, Jocelyn Hamilton, began to warn.

Before he could continue, the finance director quickly intruded, "Which means there *is* a very severe embarrassment. And that we can't risk demanding explanations from Russia. So here we are again, in a full circle and back to where we began. Precisely nowhere, with nothing."

Charlie realized he very definitely wasn't getting the support he'd become used to, especially from Jeremy Simpson. He wondered if Dean was going to pick up on the suggestion of internal obstruction by pointing out how disastrously failure could affect the future of the entire department, but when no guidance came, Charlie decided against putting it forward himself. Instead, deciding it might be an occasion to keep his head as low as possible behind the parapet, Charlie said, "Wouldn't we still be able to get an indication of that by posing the question at the next combined meeting of the involved agencies?"

"Presenting yourself as our representative at Downing Street now?" goaded Williams, overeager.

"No," rejected Charlie, at once. "Presenting myself as the field officer most directly involved and therefore most in need of positive guidance."

"You've already been given all the positive guidance that should be necessary," came in Hamilton, aggressively. "You're surely not suggesting obstruction from us!"

Oh, to have had sufficient proof to reply as he'd like to have, thought Charlie, looking directly at Gerald Williams. He said, "Of course not. I'm simply reflecting the views of a highly experienced civil servant who found what I told him inexplicable." Enough, Charlie determined: if the director-general wasn't going to present the doubt outright, then Charlie certainly shouldn't. The conclusion had to be that Dean had changed his mind.

Hamilton said, "Don't we have another problem to consider? What are we to do about Sir Matthew Norrington's ultimatum?"

"With just ten days of it to go, the first thing to accept, here and now, is that there's no chance whatsoever of our being able to meet it," suggested Williams.

"Shouldn't we wait for the ten days to elapse before conceding it?" questioned Simpson.

"I don't think there's any point in wasting any more time," said Williams. "I propose we start making contingency plans at once."

"An excellent idea," enthused Simpson, happy for his antipathy to show at last toward the financial director. "Let's hear what yours are, Gerald, so that we can talk them through to get ideas of our own."

"I'm suggesting the need for serious discussion, not offering formulated proposals." Williams flushed. "It's only been an hour since we've been told of the ultimatum." A staged pause. "And that our part of the investigation is totally stalemated."

"So you don't yet have any positive ideas?" persisted the lawyer.

Williams's redness remained at his awareness of being mocked. "Let's hope you can find things so amusing in a few days' time," he said, stiffly.

"In a few days' time we could know all about everything, wondering even why it was such a mystery at all," said Simpson.

"At the same time as standing over there at the window, watching pigs fly over the river," Williams came back.

"Ten days really is a very short period of time, so let's *not* waste it," said the director-general, stopping the exchange and the meeting.

In his office, immediately afterward, the director-general said, "That wasn't very good."

"*Give* me the ten days!" urged Charlie. "Make that your deadline, too, for letting me work as we've agreed."

"I don't want it to go on that long," insisted the older man. "Before the ten days are up I want some idea, at the very least, what the hell's going on." Dean paused. Then he said, "You did very well last time. This time it doesn't seem to be working out as it should. In fact, it doesn't seem to be working out at all."

Charlie was tempted to buy a dewy-eyed giraffe bigger than Sasha herself but remembered Natalia's injunction not to try too hard, as well as realizing he'd have to take an additional passenger seat to get it back to Moscow. He settled for its more easily transported baby, which was still awkward hand-lugged. He bought Natalia a white and yellow gold love bracelet with a key to lock it permanently on her wrist.

Miriam Bell insisted they had a lot to talk about when he called from the hotel and Lestov said he was interested in hearing what progress Charlie's London visit had achieved and agreed to a meeting for the following day without offering anything about the enigmatic press release that Charlie finally went through the pretense of asking about. Charlie thought he detected an uncertainty in the man's voice, so much so he called Miriam back. She said the son-of-a-bitch had been avoiding her for the past three days, a problem the Russian had probably contracted from him. Charlie thought her suggested get-together the following day, ahead of that already agreed with the Russian, was a good idea.

Charlie didn't call Natalia because the Interior Ministry number would be logged on his hotel bill, which had to be submitted with his expenses to Gerald Williams, determining on his way to the airport that the situation with the finance director was something that had to be resolved although still not knowing how. After today Charlie wasn't even sure of the confidence of the rest of the group, particularly Jocelyn Hamilton.

All or nothing, he thought again, his mind fixing on the meeting with Vitali Maksimovich Novikov.

"We still need to know what the Russians have got," reminded Kenton Peters.

"They're hardly going to do anything about whatever it is they think they've got when they dig deeper, are they?" questioned Boyce, in return.

"Don't like frayed ends," said the American. "But you're quite confident now, as far as Britain is concerned?"

"Totally."

"So we just let it all seep away into the sand?"

"Wasn't that the intention from the beginning?"

"Not often it works out *exactly* right, though."

"Kenton!" said Boyce, in London. "How many times in your very distinguished career has anything not gone *exactly* as you intended, from the very start?"

In Washington the American chuckled into the telephone, enjoying the flattery. "There's always a first time. I didn't want this—of all things!—to be it. Things got too close at times, because of that damned man Muffin."

"But not close enough. But you're right about Muffin. No need to dispose of him as we intended, but I think he should be put out to grass. I'll see to it."

"You were the one under the real pressure, James," commiserated the other man, returning the mutual appreciation.

"But you who personally intervened when it was necessary," said Boyce.

"Only too pleased to help," assured Peters. "It's been a useful exercise."

"But not one I'm anxious to repeat too soon."

The American laughed more positively. "I suppose we can look back on this as our own very special meltdown, like the Russians had Chernobyl?"

Boyce laughed with him. "Without any contaminating fallout. As you came to me last time, I thought I'd come to you to wrap it all up?"

"Make a weekend of it: we can go down to Virginia," suggested the American.

"Wonderful. I'd like that."

"You get a call from Charlie that he's on his way back?"

"No!"

Miriam felt Cartright turn toward her in the darkness and was glad she hadn't told him earlier. It might have distracted him from the main reason he was in bed with her. On balance he was better than Lestov—enjoyed longer foreplay, as she did—but she still intended to end it soon. It was one of several decisions she'd made. The most important was to manipulate the now-established one-to-one association with Nathaniel Brindsley to get a transfer somewhere more civilized than Moscow. This episode had soured Russia for her. It was still instinctive, though, for her to go on picking and probing, right now to decide if Cartright was lying about not having heard from Charlie, to prepare herself for the following day's lunch. "I asked him what sort of trip he'd had and he said pretty good—that there were a lot of things to talk about."

"But not, apparently, to me—a colleague!"

Miriam thought the indignation sounded genuine enough; and although it had lessened, there had been those odd questions about Charlie when she'd first gotten back from Yakutsk. "You two guys have a problem?"

"He's the one heading for a problem," said Cartright, unthinking in his bitterness. With convoluted reasoning that defied logic or sense, Cartright was now blaming Charlie for his own mistake of getting involved with Gerald Williams. If he hadn't avoided Williams's call late that afternoon, he'd have probably known about the damned man's return, but he didn't care. He was sick and tired of the whole damned mess, Charlie most of all.

"What do you mean by that?" questioned Miriam.

"Nothing," said Cartright, belatedly realizing his indiscretion.

He moved toward her and Miriam responded at once, but her mind wasn't immediately on what he was doing, pleasant though the hardness of his tongue was. Maybe it was time to make another decision. Several, in fact. She still hadn't devised a way for Kenton Peters to kiss her ass—which Cartright was close to doing at that moment—without the bastard knowing it was she making him do it.

32

By chance Charlie had been given the same table in the Minsk Restaurant as before and, as before, Miriam's arrival in a severely tailored trousers suit caused the same head-swiveling contortions. The suit material was close to matching that of Sir Peter Mason's, but there wasn't a fresh rose buttonhole. Charlie stood to greet her, aware of the palpable envy throughout the room but not enjoying it as much as at their last lunch, now with too much else to think about, mostly the homecoming announcement he hadn't expected. As Miriam sat, he poured the vodka, unasked.

They touched glasses and Miriam said, "I missed you. Which isn't a pass; I'm better at making them than that. I mean workwise."

Surprise upon surprise, thought Charlie, not as much surprise, though, as there had been at Natalia's news. Bewilderment, tinged with suspicion, fit that better. He tried to reassure himself that if Natalia was reverting to the earlier nonsense, she wouldn't in the first place have created the atmosphere between them by telling him the Russian investigation had been officially ended but insisting she didn't know the reason.

Upon reflection it even seemed to mesh—although he didn't know how—with the official runaround he was convinced to be going on in London, again without his knowing how or why. Which elevated this lunch to more than hopefully learning what Miriam might have found out about the German POWs in Yakutsk. Now to complete the circle he had to gauge, if he could, whether America, too, had from the beginning only ever been interested in suppressing instead of solving murders they already knew about. But if it did mesh, it created an even bigger mystery: what was the secret so overwhelming, after more than fifty years, that all three involved countries were determined it remain forever concealed? With the delicacy of a man tightrope-walking across a snake pit, Charlie said, "I should have kept in closer touch, but there really was a lot to do. Didn't you find that in Washington?"

"No," said Miriam, shortly. Charlie was playing the same old game, she recognized. Did it matter a fuck anymore? Why didn't she come straight out and tell him she'd been closed down, that she was thoroughly pissed off about it and that from now on she was just going along for the ride without knowing who was driving where? Because she *had* to know, she answered herself at once. Washington—the cocksucker Kenton Peters in particular, the lapdog bureau director and Nathaniel Brindsley in general—was treating her like a dummy. It didn't matter a damn what was written on her record, to which she anyway didn't have access to confirm, she'd still be remembered by those who knew for obediently rolling over and dying. Far better, for her pride and reputation and career, to prove to Brindsley—and anyone else— she could close a case and make them the roll-over dummies doing nothing about it.

Shit, thought Charlie, disappointed. "How long were you there?"

"Coupla days."

"Useful?"

"Bits and pieces. How about you?"

"Bits and pieces."

"Who's going to blink first?" she smiled, letting him know she understood.

Charlie held up the empty vodka carafe toward their passing waiter. Every reason for her to think it would be him, if that's what she wanted. He could imply a lot of what he'd learned from Natalia to have come from London that she'd know to be true from the coitus conversations with Lestov. "My people have come up with the names of some Germans imprisoned in a camp that existed close to where the bodies were found."

Necessary for him not to think that was a trade. "So have mine."

"That why you were recalled to Washington?"

"Yes," she said, straight-faced.

When the waiter returned with the vodka, they ordered quickly, to get rid of the interruption. To hint his awareness of the real source, Charlie said, "Lestov give you any lead on what the development is?"

"Maybe they've identified the Germans, too?"

The first blink, isolated Charlie: identifying went beyond *knowing* the names. "So we're all three making progress?"

"Are we?" This was becoming a struggle.

"I think so," said Charlie. What could he afford to volunteer, to edge her further forward?

"I'm not so sure."

The moment to convince you, then, thought Charlie. "You think it's time for us to stop playing silly buggers?"

"It might help. Seems to me we're almost starting from scratch again. And I thought we'd come to an understanding."

Blitzkrieg, decided Charlie, the pun intentional. "I thought so, too. We've got the Germans. We know who your guy was. Both of them, in fact. And we can make a lot of *very* informed guesses—not actual proof, I know, but enough to take us a long way forward—so why are we fucking about like this?" He was pleased of the feigned irritation he managed at the end.

Miriam was glad the blintzes arrived, although she'd forgotten she'd ordered them, needing the recovery and the time to assess. She'd heard enough to know he hadn't been positively closed down, as she had. Point one. He knew about the POWs, which she knew Vadim Lestov hadn't told him, so London must have another, maybe better, source. Point two. Proof of that better source was his saying he knew who *both* Americans were, when she'd only been trying to find the name of the one in the grave, which she still didn't have. Point three and the biggest of all. And if London had that much, they had to be nearer to knowing a damned sight more, which put Charlie—England—way over the horizon. Thank Christ she'd played it this way so far. How to raise the bidding? Appeal to his macho, the male need to boast what was between his legs. She offered her glass, clinking it once more against Charlie's. "Like I said on the telephone, we've got a lot to talk about."

Somewhere he'd hit a target. But which one? Not the time to stop the bombardment. And the next shot was easy. "You first."

Fuck, she thought. He was too good—too clever—to try any sort of bluff. She could only play the cards she held. "I think the coincidence is incredible, your being *so* right at that goddamned press conference."

Not as good as he'd hoped, but he still believed himself ahead. "I'd liked to have found out earlier. Or rather that London had been quicker. Whom do your people regard the most important?"

Miriam frowned. "Don't you think it's Frederich Dollmann? He was the chief secretary in the bunker."

Charlie felt the slow, warming burn move through him. It still wasn't an answer, but the middle of the jigsaw was beginning to fill at last. "I'm not making the analysis. London is, as Washington obviously is with you. All I got was the names and a thumbnail sketch of what they'd so far come up with." Plucking a name at random from the list, Charlie went on, "Our guys seemed to think Werner von Bittrick was important."

"An aide-de-camp, admittedly," said Miriam. "But it was Dollmann and Buhle who saw him every day: took the dictation."

Franz Buhle, completed Charlie, as he filled in a lot more. At least three of the fifteen Germans had spent the last months of the war in daily contact—two of them taking the dictation—with the demented Adolf Hitler, fighting battles already lost with armies that no longer existed: the bunker that the Russians were the first to seize as they were the first to seize Berlin. Forcing the casualness as well as the conversation—but letting his mind run ahead—Charlie said, "Let's face it, the combined knowledge of everyone who was there would have been astonishing. But to historians—"

"I know the problem," broke in Miriam, which Charlie had hoped she would. "Why art experts? I could understand practically anyone else except them." When—or how—was she going to get the American names?

Charlie believed he could understand. Partially, at least. If he was right, it was the conspiracy to beat all conspiracies ever conceived, reducing those of the courts of Rome, Tudor England, the Borgias and Machiavelli to children painting by numbers.

Caught by his silence and her belief in his greater knowledge, Miriam said, "But you can?"

Distantly, virtually thinking aloud, Charlie said, "They wouldn't have known, would they?"

What were the right words? Miriam thought desperately. Maybe to follow with another question. "Known what?"

"What they were going to find in Yakutsk. Why they were being allowed there," suggested Charlie, still thinking aloud. "We can't look at it from today's perspective. We've got to look at it as they would have in Berlin in March or April or May 1945. Total chaos, total confusion. Suddenly to have made available the last support staff around Hitler: people who knew intimately every moment of every day in the last months of one of history's greatest monsters! People who knew where all the treasures were. That would have been too much to have considered rationally. There was no rationale."

"But there weren't any art treasures in the bunker!" protested Miriam.

"You sure of that?" demanded Charlie. "They wouldn't have been, not then. I'm still not sure now, after half a century."

Now it was Miriam who remained silent, pushing the blintzes away. Charlie didn't speak, either, needing to think as much as the woman. Eventually Miriam said, "You're saying they didn't go to Yakutsk because of Hitler's staff?"

"No," denied Charlie. "They went *because* of Hitler's staff. But that's not what they were taken there for. There was another reason."

"There couldn't have been another reason!" protested Miriam, belatedly accepting Charlie's earlier argument. "To get to the Germans would have been incredible!"

"That was only part of it," said Charlie. "There has to be more, otherwise none of it makes sense."

They ate—both duck—but were unaware of what they were eating and neither properly tasted the wine, either, each engrossed in private thoughts, hands and mouths working automatically.

Charlie felt instinctively that he was close, maybe close enough to reach out and touch, but there were still too many bits missing. His mind—his hope—was on Vitali Novikov, who according to Natalia was arriving the following day. *All or nothing* throbbed through Charlie's head, like a drumbeat. It wouldn't—couldn't—be absolutely nothing, he reassured himself. No matter how desperate, the man wouldn't have risked a total and outright lie—not someone as aware, as Novikov was, of the return expected for his freedom from the inherited exile of an innocent father. A bargain, in fact, that the doctor himself had volunteered.

Miriam was more confused now than when she'd arrived. Nothing that seemed to make sense to Charlie was even vaguely comprehensible—guessable, even—to her. So he was still out of sight and she couldn't see a way to catch up. Richard Cartright suddenly came into her mind: Richard Cartright, with the too-ready questions inexplicable then and even more inexplicable now, if London was operating with the sort of harmony Charlie was inferring. Tentatively she said, "How'd you find the attitude in London?"

"Attitude?" queried Charlie.

When the fuck was she going to get a half-useful answer instead of another wrong-position question? "Thought maybe you might have heard something about Peters's visit, on his way back from here?"

No, she didn't, Charlie recognized at once, concentrating fully. "It was a pretty big meeting, I gather. There's a lot of different interests, in London—too many, in my opinion. I didn't hear in any specific detail how it went with your guy. What playback did you get?"

A way at last to avoid the question! "I didn't, as such. But I kinda got the impression there was . . ."—the apparent search for the word wasn't necessary—"some rivalry in England?"

"How?" Charlie's demand was as unhelpful as she'd tried to make hers in the beginning.

"I *will* keep to our agreement," said Miriam. "And for me I guess it's easier. It's been left entirely to me—okay, so my head's on the block—but at least I don't have the irritation of someone riding shotgun on me. That's how mistakes happen." Cartright had tried to use her as she'd been happy to use him, before realizing that he knew nothing. This was just getting a repayment for what he'd gotten in another way.

Could he risk the guess? No. A guess, even though he was sure of the answer, would change the balance, weighing the scales to her advantage. Not another blitzkrieg. A softening-up salvo, to continue her belief in his superior firepower. There was only one thing she could be missing, apart from the full answer which she clearly hadn't gotten. He said, "I've got both American names and I know where the grave is of the one who was really buried in Yakutsk." And waited.

Miriam said, "Cartright."

"Personal?"

"Very much so. Carried out badly, too."

"Your lieutenant was George Timpson. Buried in the American cemetery at Margraten, in Holland. The second American was a Harry Dunne. He survived the war, as far as I know. I've no idea if he's still alive." Charlie was glad the encounter with Miriam was the first of a busy day and that he'd fought off the embassy ambush earlier that day.

"This come to your people from Washington?"

She shouldn't need to ask that! "No."

"Have they been told?"

If they had, she, in turn, would—or should—have been told. So her question manifestly showed that she hadn't been. No need even to guess now. "Have you been cut out entirely? Or sidelined?"

Abruptly—frighteningly—Miriam felt the emotion flood through her, her eyes briefly blurring. Her recovery was as quick as the near-collapse. He knew too much—was too intuitive—to go on with the charade anymore and in any case she was too tired and dispirited and pissed off and pissed over to try anymore. "Entirely." Bitterly she added, "You know what that motherfucker Peters told me? He said I was the fall guy. That you were, too. Both of us at the bottom of the heap, to take the shit if it came down. Denies it, of course. But I taped the son-of-a-bitch!" Miriam's emotions switchbacked again. This time she was suffused by an enormous feeling of relief. "That's it, Charlie! All of it. I don't have anything more to tell you. Nothing held back."

"He use my name? Or was it by inference?"

Miriam considered the question. "By inference, I guess. But you were the only person he could have been referring to."

"That what you meant about watching my back?"

Miriam looked steadily at Charlie for several moments. "I think Packer was a hit man."

"I'm *sure* Packer was a hit man."

"Who?"

"It wouldn't have been you," Charlie said.

"Which only leaves you."

Charlie decided he didn't want to go any further. "I still think it was a separate Agency thing. It's past."

"I hope. What do you think I should do now?"

"You sleeping with Cartright *and* Lestov?"

"Yes," said Miriam at once, totally without embarrassment.

"Tell Lestov you've been cut out. And that you don't know why." And if Natalia relayed that to him, from Lestov, he might be better able to decide if Natalia was being truthful or troubled by integrity again, decided Charlie.

"What'll that achieve?"

"There'll have to be some reaction. Let's see what it is."

"What about Cartright?"

Charlie thought about it. "Maybe we should satisfy his curiosity. A name, even. You mind being the messenger in your own special way?"

She sniggered. "It was my decision to begin with, wasn't it? I guess now it makes you my unpaid pimp."

Charlie smiled back. "I've always accepted that was what people like you and I are, whores and pimps. The professional ones just get treated better."

Charlie went through all the required motions with Vadim Leonidovich Lestov, talking of assessments and reevaluations and complaining there appeared to be very little progress and even conveyed some irritation at Lestov's refusal ("There are still facts to be checked before any disclosures can be made") to hint at the intended Russian announcement. Charlie actually went as far as asking if there was any official Russian impatience, which Lestov countered by asking about London's attitude after insisting that as far as he was aware Moscow was prepared for the investigation to continue indefinitely. Charlie said he hadn't detected any London restlessness.

He was back at the embassy an hour before the scheduled meeting with McDowell, Cartright, and Gallaway. He considered passing on to London what he'd learned about the German POWs but decided against it until after the encounter with Vitali Novikov the following day. He limited himself to cabling that the Russians were still refusing to disclose their intended media release and occupied the remainder of the time deep in paper-plane-building reflection. He ended it even more instinctively sure that only one or two doors remained closed against his understanding virtually everything.

Charlie put on a very positive performance in the head of chancellery's office, guessing at progress in Washington as well as that the impending Russian announcement would be startling but admitting that London had been an entirely unproductive, embarrassing expedition. He was, further conceded Charlie, anxious for whatever input any of them might have.

"Jackson called, from Berlin: some crossed wires with London about your going there," said the military attaché. "He thought you learned a lot?"

"That someone else had been murdered to fill Norrington's grave," said Charlie. "We'll never know who it was."

"But the Russians did it?" said Cartright.

"They returned a body," lured Charlie. "I'm not sure they can be blamed for the murder."

"Who else could have done it?" demanded McDowell.

"There wasn't any law, order or anything else in Berlin at the time," said Charlie. "It was a perfect place for a perfect murder. Don't forget the second officer at Yakutsk. I'm keeping an open mind."

"Did you tell London that?" asked Cartright.

Charlie shrugged. "No reason to fill their heads with theories I couldn't substantiate."

The three other men looked uncomfortably between themselves.

Cartright said, "You're telling us. Why didn't you tell them?"

"Because they've got to act upon what I tell them, so they need facts, not impressions. There's no reason why I shouldn't tell working colleagues something about which they're not going to act, is there? I've got quite a few others I'm keeping to myself, too."

"Like what?" pressed Cartright.

"It doesn't matter," refused Charlie. He only wanted to see how far one red herring would swim.

"What's the general feeling in London?" asked McDowell.

"I don't know about a general feeling. I don't think my own department imagine I've got a clue which is why I'm going to surprise them." No reason why one red herring shouldn't be channeled in the right direction.

Vitali Maksimovich Novikov stood slightly apart from his family, as if wishing to disassociate himself from them, his eyes moving toward anyone in uniform. His wife fidgeted tightly with their two sons, string-tied packs of belongings between them. The larger cases had already been loaded. No one talked. The elder boy, Georgi, looked constantly and unblinkingly at the arthritic indicator board. Everyone jumped at the sharp, metallic departure announcement.

Novikov joined his family at last. "Ready?"

Marina nodded, saying nothing. The boys began collecting the packages. Novikov had not put down a bulging briefcase since their arrival at the airport.

As they walked toward the departure ramp, Marina said, "We're never coming back, are we?"

"Never," promised Novikov.

"You haven't forgotten anything?" the woman said, looking at the briefcase.

"Nothing."

Natalia stared at Charlie, letting the shock show. "Why?" she demanded.

"All I want is a name. They'll all be on file, won't they?

"Why?" repeated Natalia, insistently.

"I am not going to trade currency," said Charlie, equally insistent. "I just want the name of one of the biggest dealers, that's all. Might be necessary to mislead someone who's taking an irritating interest in me."

33

Vitali Maksimovich Novikov kept the door on its security chain, easing it open just sufficiently to see it was Charlie. The man hesitated before opening it. As Charlie entered, the doctor said, "You are very quick."

"So was your residency permission."

"I meant we're glad to see you," said Novikov, instantly apologetic. "We never—"

"I know," stopped Charlie. "But it *has* happened. You're here."

It was a wide but short entrance hall, leading directly into the one living room. Cases and tied bundles were piled in its center. Marina and the boys were grouped around their belongings, as if awaiting permission to unpack, still wearing the quilted outer coats that were normal for Yakutsk. It was another Napoleon day outside.

Charlie said, "Welcome to Moscow."

"We didn't expect it to be so big," said Marina. Hurriedly, correcting an oversight, she said, "Thank you. We all want to thank you." The boys on either side of her nodded.

A tiny kitchen was to the left, already furnished with a cooker and cupboards and a table, although only with two chairs. There was also a glass-fronted cabinet and a fabric-faded, wooden-armed settee in the living room. There was a door to the right that Charlie assumed to be to the one bedroom and wondered where the boys would sleep. The entrance hall was big enough, he supposed.

Aware of Charlie's examination, Novikov said, "It's a wonderful apartment. I've already met the concierge. He wants to sell me some allotment space in the garden at the back."

The apartment was on the eighth floor of one of the Brezhnev-era blocks that ring Moscow—this one in the Lyublino suburb—like decaying teeth in need of treatment. Vegetable-growing allotment spaces came automatically with each flat, but Charlie decided against telling the doctor. There was nothing to be gained by alienating the concierge by challenging his private enterprise. Novikov and his family had to learn for themselves how to live in the big city. He handed the Macallan whiskey to Novikov and offered the chocolates to the woman. "Housewarming presents," he said.

The man said, "Thank you." His wife accepted the box and said, "It's all we ever seem to do, to thank you. There's so much." Her voice faltered. She swallowed heavily and said, "I'll make some tea."

"I feel numb," said Novikov. "We all do."

The man was blinking more rapidly than Charlie remembered. He said, "I kept my promise."

"We both have," said Charlie.

"Let's talk in the kitchen," invited the doctor, leading the way. It was cramped with the three of them in it until the two men sat facing each other across the table. Marina put their tea in front of them and left. At once, defensively, Novikov said, "I only ever told you I might be able to help."

"I remember everything you told me," said Charlie. "What is it you have?" At last, he thought. What would it be, all or nothing?

"My father was originally sentenced to Gulag 98."

"You told me that, too."

"Even after he was allowed to transfer to the town, he remained the camp doctor—"

"In 1945?" interrupted Charlie, impatiently.

"Yes."

Charlie felt the stir of anticipation. "What did he tell you?"

"He didn't *tell* me anything. He was a doctor. He kept medical notes. There are conditions particularly prevalent to the region, frostbite the most obvious. A lot of crush injuries, from the mines. In my father's day he often had to improvise treatment. He kept records to help me."

Charlie sipped his milkless tea, letting the man talk. How many missing pieces would Novikov have? Charlie said, "You read them all?"

"I've got them all," declared Novikov, simply. "I'd not read every single entry. Never intended to, until the bodies were found. Then I did, for any reference to a camp near Yakutsk in 1944 and 1945. I knew Camp 98 existed, knew my father had been sentenced to serve there, but I never knew its exact location."

"Got them?" echoed Charlie. "You mean you brought them with you, here to Moscow?"

Instead of answering, Novikov leaned beneath the kitchen table to a briefcase Charlie hadn't been aware of until then. There was a marker in the scuffed hardback ledger the man lifted on to the table, rotating it for Charlie's convenience. Novikov said, "The first date you need is May fourth, 1945. Read on from there."

The brittle, easily split paper would have been the cheapest and the ink would probably have been watered to make it go further. It was already beginning to fade, in places quite badly, but the handwriting was legible, missing letters and words easily filled in where they had become unreadable.

May 4. Camp 98. 8 p.m. Infirmary emptied. Ordered by Moscow officials. Unidentified woman. Early 30s. Blond, well nourished. Severe abdominal trauma. Extensive venous hemorrhage, blood in wound and mouth. Very pale. Obvious hypotensive. No exit wound. No AB transfusion available. Plasma. Pulse erratic. Pressure ninety over fifty. Sedation. Exploration impossible until stabilized.

10 p.m. Male Caucasian. America. Officer. No physical trauma. Deep shock. Unresponsive visual or pain stimulation. Involuntary temporary spasms. Hallucinations. Mutterings of an execution. Sedation.

11:30. Search for second Caucasian. Fierce arguments about his disappearance. Warn of frostbite. Ignored. Request for heating for transferred patients to administrative building refused. Gangrene concern for crush victim Osadochy. Communication with Moscow opened by officials. Clearly security. Drugs and plasma requests refused.

Charlie felt out unseeing for the now-cold tea, needing the respite. Not the victims in the grave. Raisa had been brunette: shot in the head. Timpson, too. Larisa Krotkov? Hank Dunne? Who was the missing Caucasian? The Englishman? Why had they been allowed to live, the others killed?

May 5. 1:30 a.m. Woman deteriorating. Persistent severe hemor-rhage. Continuing hemorrhage. Violent hallucination. Name repe-

*tition—Georgi. Assassination. More Moscow officials. Deep
concern.*

*2:15 a.m. Oppose adrenaline resuscitation of American. Risk of
psychological damage counteracting chlordiazepoxide. Accepted after Moscow contact. Permanent line established. No-one allowed in
the infirmary except myself. Patient spasmic. Killing fixation.*

Charlie lifted and replaced the cup, without drinking, conscious
of Novikov still sitting before him, motionless. There wasn't any
sound from the other room, either. It *had* to be Larisa Krotkov and
Hank Dunne. Some intentionally put to death, some intentionally
allowed to live. Nothing about Hitler's bunker staff in the same camp.
Wouldn't be, Charlie acknowledged, irritated at the intrusion. This
was a doctor's log, nothing more. He had to work out the rest. Closer
but still not close enough.

*3:30 a.m. Woman died, without regaining consciousness. Calls for
Georgi. And a priest. Progressive exsanguination and hypotension.
Body claimed by Moscow officials. No reference in camp infirmary
log. Commandant instructed.*

*6:45 a.m. Arrival of British officer. Severely traumatized. Hy-
pothermic. Frostbite to extremities. Hot baths. Massage. Repeated
assassination fixation. Hand washing obsessively. Speech refusal.*

*10 a.m. Able to save most extremities, although possible damage
ulnal two digits. No obvious functional impairment. Left ear lobe
gangrenous and amputated.*

*3:30 p.m. Refusal to allow evacuation to Moscow overruled.
Deep sedation necessary, to subdue psychologically driven violent
spasm. Evacuation by stretcher to military aircraft. American com-
prehending but still in shock. Sedated. After departure amputated
left arm of crush victim. Gangrene.*

Beneath that final entry for May 5 was a list of drugs and the
amounts that had been administered, each listed against a time. Also
noted were temperatures and blood pressure counts, ironically
marked under the believed nationalities as the man's son had itemized
his findings against the bodies of the Yakutsk grave more than fifty
years later.

"It was the same incident, wasn't it?" demanded Novikov, anxiously.

"Yes."

"So there were witnesses? Others involved?"

Which he'd already known, thought Charlie. There was nothing new; nothing that took him one step—one millimeter—further forward. And yet . . . ? His mind remained blank. Trying too hard; hoping too hard. Nowhere else to go. Nowhere else to look. "There's nothing more?"

Novikov's face was ashen. "This is not enough?"

"I'd hoped for more." Charlie heard the faintest of noises from the entrance hall behind him and guessed Marina had eased herself to within hearing. "It won't affect your being here."

The man opposite him visibly sagged with relief. "I'm sorry. I thought it was valuable, would help."

Instead of immediately replying, Charlie went back to the notes, reading everything for a fortnight prior to May 4 and for a full month after May 5. Camp 98 was not mentioned again. It became a repetitive catalogue of mine injuries often resulting in amputation and of illness and disabilities caused by the climate. There were a lot of deaths recorded and frequent complaints of Moscow's refusal or inability to provide drugs. At last Charlie said, "I'd like to take this ledger, for the May entries."

Novikov's concern was immediate. "It would have been an offense for my father to make notes like that. Still would be, for me to have kept them. The references to Moscow officials? They had to be security, didn't they? The Narodny Komitet Vnutrennikh Del, then?"

"No one else will ever see it but me. And I already know you have it."

"You are asking me to trust you: putting ourselves in your hands."

"You did that in Yakutsk."

Abruptly, a man making an impulsive gesture he might quickly regret, Novikov thrust the log farther across the table toward Charlie. "Promise me that no one else will ever see it. And that when you no longer need it you will destroy it."

"I promise," said Charlie, putting the log into his own briefcase before the doctor could change his mind.

"Will I see you again?"

"I don't know. Perhaps not."

"Thank you, then, for the last time. I think of you as a good man."

That wasn't Charlie's impression of himself, riding the metro back into the center of Moscow with his briefcase clutched to his chest. At that precise moment he thought of himself as a failed man, not knowing where else to look, what else to do. And yet . . . ? He physically shrugged aside the unanswerable self-question, irritated by it and the foot twinge that came with it and which he never usually ignored. This time, for once, it had to be wrong. Charlie didn't like not knowing what to do.

"It was obviously something you had to know immediately," said Lestov.

"Of course," accepted Natalia. She'd accepted Nikulin's refusal to disclose any reason for the Russian decision because she'd had no alternative; had secretly been relieved at the thought of the whole thing drifting to an inconclusive end just as long as it ended without any danger to her and Charlie—and Sasha—personally. Now, in minutes, everything was thrown into total confusion again. "She wouldn't say why?"

Lestov shook his head. "Just that it was an official instruction from Washington."

"It could be a trick," suggested Natalia.

"Where's the trick?"

"Lulling you into believing you could safely share with her something you might be withholding," guessed Natalia.

Lestov shifted uncomfortably. "I don't think so."

Natalia got up from her desk, walking head bent toward the huge ministry window. She arrived in time to see a GIA traffic policeman, on foot, extract payment from a flagged-down motorist preferring to pay an instant bribe rather than waste a day in court protesting an invented speeding offense. Charlie hadn't told her anything about the American withdrawal. He'd insisted nothing had emerged from the lunch with Miriam Bell: claimed to be worried about the lack of progress. The American girl was sleeping with Lestov, according to Charlie. Maybe she'd told her lover but not Charlie. Or Charlie was keeping things back from her in the belief that she'd lied about not knowing why the Russian decision had been made. Which took them back to their distrustful beginning. Her fault, then—her decision, she acknowledged. Surely it wasn't necessary for Charlie to balance everything, like for like? Over her shoulder Natalia said, "What about the Englishman?"

"He claims the London visit was for reevaluation," said Lestov. "He didn't offer anything new yesterday."

"You believe him?"

"No."

"So he's still actively investigating?"

"He gave every impression of doing so. Kept pressing about what our announcement was going to be. Are you going to tell Dmitri Borisovich?"

Natalia turned back into the room. "That's why I asked to see you. Dmitri Borisovich intends to issue the press release today. Wants to know about Belous."

"He's still in custody."

"Have you told him what will happen to him if he says anything about his mother being NKVD?"

Lestov nodded. "And he believes me."

"Keep him in custody for the next few days, just the same."

"Are you going to tell Dmitri Borisovich about America?" pressed Lestov. He was where he was now—liked being where he was now—because of some earlier internal intrigue he still didn't properly understand. As the bearer of the message, he didn't himself want to become a victim by its not being passed on to everyone who should know. Searching for the persuasion, he said, "It might affect his making the release."

"I know," said Natalia, coming back to her desk to pick up the telephone.

Openly boasting to colleagues in the embassy of deceiving his own department, thought Gerald Williams, triumphantly. Colleagues who could be called as witnesses, if an internal tribunal could be convened. There'd be no way Rupert Dean or Jeremy Simpson could go on protecting their precious pet monkey once that was brought out. It all came very nicely on the back of Muffin's appearance before them earlier in the week. Even Dean and the legal adviser had been hard-pressed to support the man then and the deputy director-general had certainly been receptive to the suggestion afterward that the investigation was going to fizzle out inconclusively, exposing the department to criticism if not open ridicule.

In fact, *everything* was coming together very nicely indeed.

34

Kenton Peters's weekend house was original old colonial, white, columned and with an encircling veranda overlooking the immediate, oak-treed grounds and the paddocks and stables beyond, where the Arabians were bred. There was a stallion and three mares in the nearest one. Peters and Boyce sat savoring the tranquillity and privilege in shared contentment and in matching, high-backed wicker chairs that crackled slightly when they moved, their highballs on the separating table between them. It was their second. They were still dressed for golf, which had ended an hour earlier. Boyce had intentionally taken five on a par four on the back nine, to let Peters win their $25 wager. Boyce knew the American would have done the same for him, if they'd been in England. Everything in their ordered lives had understood rules.

Peters said, "Had some trouble with the damned woman in Moscow, towards the end. Impudent. Had her fired."

Boyce said, "Really! I had the impression from some of the message traffic I've seen that she was still on station."

"She hadn't better be," said the American, indignantly. He made a mental note to check.

"Was there any resentment, from the Bureau or the CIA or your military people?"

"I simply told the Agency and the military to keep out of it. The military are getting their Arlington glory with the president, so they're happy. Bureau director was a bit stiff at first. But he's a political appointee and they do as they're told in the end, particularly if they get to like the job, which most of them do. As I said when all this began, it was your difficulty I sympathized with."

"Used the principle of divide and rule," reminded Boyce, toying idly with the tee he found in his pocket. "Knew all the archives were clean, so I just told each of them a little about the need to avoid difficulties if they had any skeletons in their department cupboards and left them to stumble around and get in each other's way to cause as much confusion as possible with Dean's people, whom I had the Intelligence Committee supposedly give the full investigation. It was all a bit of a farce, really. None of them knew they were performing in one, of course."

The butler came inquiringly on to the veranda and Peters nodded to more drinks. To Boyce he said, "Eight suit you for dinner?"

"Perfect," accepted the Englishman.

Peters said, "I've officially told the Bureau the investigation is over."

"Was it wise, to do so officially?" queried Boyce. "Being professionally curious is the job of most of these people."

Peters coaxed a slim but long cheroot into life, expelling a perfect smoke ring toward the distant horses. "I told the director it was national security, that most convenient of panaceas, and for everyone below it was on a need-to-know basis and they had no need to know."

"The number of people that I had to deal with has given me a problem there," admitted Boyce. "I'm just going to let them thrash around until they themselves have to admit defeat. Might be necessary to initiate an internal inquiry, to apportion responsibility for failure. It's the sort of thing that would be expected."

They stopped talking while the drinks were served.

As the butler left, Peters said, "That mean you're not entirely sure your archives *are* clean?"

Boyce smiled. "It means I don't like losing control. And that everything is going to appear to have been done properly and fully."

Now the American laughed. "Losing control is a sin we neither of us will ever be accused of." He sipped the new drink and said, "You spoken to your man?"

"Day before I flew here."

"And?"

"He's fine. Quite remarkable, for his age."

"No risk of his giving way?"

"Why should he? That's the last thing he'd allow."

"Of course," accepted the American. "Media have been more of a nuisance than I expected. Still are, in fact. You thought what to do about that?"

"Not really," conceded the other man. "Future role of Dean's department is a bit uncertain, so they're convenient if public scapegoats are necessary. Muffin's the obvious choice. He was on television from Yakutsk, remember: he's identifible. Useful, really, that we didn't go ahead with the other idea."

"Always good to get the maximum benefit," agreed the American. "When's your Arlington ceremony?"

"Next Friday. It'll stoke the media pressure, I guess, but it can't be helped."

"You won't be there, of course?"

"Of course not!" said Peters, actually surprised at being asked if he'd ever appear at any public, media-recorded event.

"You know," said Boyce. "While all this has been going on, I've thought several times how much I'd like to have met Clarence Mitchell, the man who set the whole thing up on our side."

"Peabody did it from here," supplied Peters. "Samuel H. Peabody. Hell of a brain, both of them, for devising it."

"And keeping it going for so long," said Boyce. "That was the true brilliance."

"Genius," agreed Peters.

"And it can't be said we've failed them," said Boyce, self-congratulatory. "It could have gone very badly wrong if we hadn't acted as quickly and so effectively as we did."

"True," agreed Peters. "Very true indeed. I wouldn't want it any other way, but sometimes I wish people knew what we did to keep them safe in their beds."

Boyce gestured expansively, encompassing the house and grounds. "It has its rewards."

"My own money, not a penny from the taxpayer," reminded Peters. "We're eating pheasant tonight. Shot them myself. Been hanging just long enough."

"Wonderful," said Boyce.

"Why?" demanded the presidential aide, as he already had several times. "There's no logic; no rationale."

He was pacing the room, sometimes driving his fist into the palm of his other hand. It was the first time Natalia had witnessed Nikulin display any sort of emotion and she wondered if she'd get any clue why the man had ended the inquiry. "It was obviously something she knew Vadim Leonidovich would report back. To which we would have to react."

"Too clumsy," argued Nikulin.

"I believe there's a personal relationship."

Nikulin stopped pacing. "Why did he—" he began, outraged.

"For benefits beyond sex, I'd guess," said Natalia. It was something that had to be taken into their consideration, which was why she'd met Nikulin alone.

"Might not she be doing it for the same reason?"

"That's why I mentioned it." It wasn't the primary reason. She wanted time, the opportunity to talk it through with Charlie before the release of the art recovery, staged though it was intended to be.

"I'm glad you did. It's very confusing, though."

"As it is my not knowing the reason for our decision," said Natalia, openly.

"It was one of the greatest—and most secret—of coups," confided Nikulin. "And it must always remain secret, even from someone like you."

Natalia nodded, resigned. It wasn't something she'd tell Charlie, she decided. "The American would have known he'd have to act upon it," Natalia repeated.

"So it's intentional, *to* confuse us?"

"Shouldn't we consider delaying the announcement about what was recovered from Belous?"

"It has no significance," dismissed the presidential aide.

"Can we be sure of that, not knowing what this is about?"

"Where is Belous?"

"In custody. I've ordered he stay there, until we decide otherwise."

Nikulin finally sat down. "Whatever the Americans are up to has no affect whatsoever upon our decision. Which stands. We go ahead with the release."

Gerald Williams realized how totally he was committing himself and he was nervous about doing so. He wished he belonged to the sort of club to which Jocelyn Hamilton had taken him, which seemed the proper venue for such discussions, instead of a public restaurant, even one close enough to Westminster to be the favorite of MPs and cabinet minsters. Williams had spotted three and a minister within minutes of his arrival. He filled the time waiting for the deputy director-general's arrival studying the menu, horrified at the prices. Hamilton was greeted as a regular by the restaurant manager who had initially regarded Williams as an unwelcomed intruder, and on his way to the table Hamilton stopped to talk to the cabinet minister and after that to an MP frequently quoted in newspapers as an espionage expert.

Hamilton finally arrived with flurried apologies for being late and as he was seated told the manager to ensure there'd be that day's special available. From his study of the menu Williams knew that was lamb chops and ordered the same. He chose Margaux, too, remembering it was what Hamilton had selected entertaining him at the Reform Club.

"What's all the mystery about?" demanded the department deputy, the moment they were alone.

"Not mystery," said Williams. "Concern."

Although Williams had spent a long time sanitizing his account, Hamilton said the moment he'd finished, "You've been talking like this to the people across the river!"

"I spoke to my counterpart, Horlick, once: to assure him the expenditure was coming off our budget, not his. Which I consider it should because we're heading the investigation. With his agreement I talked direct to Cartright in Moscow: didn't want anyone imagining unlimited expenses. And have done a few times since, to make sure costs remain under control. What I've told you has come up in general conversation."

"It doesn't sound like general conversation to me," refused Hamilton. "To me it sounds pretty specific—improper, in fact."

"I'm prepared to make allowance for that," said Williams. "I'm far more worried at the greater danger which we've talked about too many times to need repeating. This man is openly talking in Moscow of treating us like fools. You saw for yourself what it was like, just days ago. Something's got to be done!"

"Why are you telling me, like this? Why not officially, to Sir Rupert?"

"Because it *is* only gossip. And, all right, improper gossip at that. Any case against Muffin has got to be backed by a proper inquiry, supported by fact. Witnesses."

"So?" persisted the other man.

"I've become involved in this by accident. I'm the financial director. I've done my bit auditing accounts that virtually prove the money dealing, which amounts to a criminal act. You're operational. I'm suggesting for the sake of the department—for us all—you ask Cartright's people to authorize his providing an official account. Factually checking what the hell Muffin's up to."

Hamilton sat with the lamb halfway to his mouth, regarding Williams across the table in disbelief. "Are you serious?"

"Deadly serious."

"I don't like it."

"I like less the thought of what will happen if we don't move."

"I need to think about it very seriously indeed," said Hamilton.

"The time for thinking is over," insisted Williams. "Now we've got to do something positive."

Charlie was kept at the embassy cabling the full text of the Russian release to London and afterward answering the queries that came back, which distilled down into contributing nothing new, and Natalia was at Lesnaya when he got home, Sasha already asleep.

There was still the reservation of the previous night—the uncertainty there'd been at the beginning—although not quite so awkward. Charlie told her about the encounter with Vitali Novikov and then showed her the log. While she read it, he made drinks.

When he returned to the main room she said, "This isn't anything. Just confirmation of what we already believed."

"I know. I've read it a hundred times, trying to find something." He decided against telling her the nagging feeling that kept pricking at him. There were enough mysteries without the need to invent more.

Natalia said, "What did you tell Novikov?"

"That it won't affect their residency."

Natalia looked at her watch. "Let's see the result of the Russian contribution."

The Russian announcement was the lead item on all the English-language satellite news programs through which Charlie flicked. Photographs of the recovered art had been issued with the release claiming them as further proof of Raisa Belous's heroic wartime work keeping Russia's heritage—particularly actual treasure from the Amber Room—out of Nazi hands. Fyodor Belous was included in the eulogy for returning the safeguarded articles the moment he'd discovered the truth about his mother. CNN and the BBC also carried footage outside Belous's empty apartment, with reporters quoting official sources suggesting the man was helping the authorities search further for things still hidden. Inevitably every program carried library pictures of the treasures of the Catherine Palace and the other royal residences at Tsarskoe Selo, as well as film of the devastation after the Nazi occupation of the park. Just as inevitably there was speculation that the further lost art that Belous was helping locate was the missing Amber Room itself.

"I tried to get it delayed," disclosed Natalia.

"Why?" Charlie frowned.

The expression remained as she talked, although more in guilt at his disbelieving her—and at setting the test she was at that moment passing—than at anything else. Charlie was glad Natalia would never know he'd doubted her. He said, "Nikulin was right. Whatever brought about the American decision won't be influenced by the art announcement: that was only bait in the first place. All that's going to happen is America refusing to bite and a lot of renewed publicity."

Natalia offered the log back to Charlie. "You were relying on that, weren't you?"

"Yes," he admitted.

"What now?"

"I don't know," Charlie forced himself to admit. And then, in a rush and without warning, he thought he did. He had sufficient about the mystery English officer, at least, and most of it allowed the pieces to fit.

"What?" demanded Natalia, seeing the expression on Charlie's face.

Instead of immediately answering, Charlie flicked the television back to the permanently running CNN, leaning forward intently to study the pictures of what had been recovered from Belous. And then he told Natalia.

"Are you sure?"

"Positive." He looked down at the log of Novikov's father and said, "And it *was* here, all the time!"

35

Charlie's satisfaction ebbed by the following day. Sitting in his shoe-box office, surrounded by a squadron of reflectively folded paper airplanes, Charlie acknowledged reluctantly that Natalia was right. His conclusion—even more positively confirmed by examining in detail the Tsarskoe Selo treasure catalogue of Catherine the Great's palace—didn't explain America *and* Russia quite independently closing the investigation down.

And there was only one way to try to prove what he now did know. With no guarantee that he'd succeed and, after Henry Packer, possibly physically dangerous. If he made the attempt and it went wrong by just one millimeter—even excluding the Packer-type risk—he'd be dismissed and withdrawn from Moscow. On top of which he couldn't discuss it with the director-general, who couldn't possibly condone it, even if the man's personal support hadn't been wavering as much as Charlie knew it was. So he'd be totally disregarding—defying!—the department and going off station without authority, which was very definitely a firing offense.

But what choice did he have? It was the only way forward, it did fit sufficiently for him to be sure of at least part and there was Kenton Peters on tape describing him as a fall guy, if one was necessary. So he was damned if he went solo and damned if he didn't. He refused to think about being dead.

Charlie forced his mind from the negative to the positive. It was physically possible to fly to England and back in one day, leaving on the first morning plane and returning on the last at night. So he'd only be away for twelve hours at the most and it wouldn't be difficult to give London an excuse in advance for his absence from the embassy. The newspaper coverage of the art recovery—particularly the speculation that Fyodor Belous was guiding the authorities to more treasure, possibly even the Amber Room—had been enormous, but Charlie already knew from Natalia there wasn't going to be anything more London might panic about, so that wasn't a bar to his going. What else? An ally, he decided, now that he and Miriam had resolved their personal war. She'd been described as a fall guy, too. It would require slight adjustment to his dislike of being dependent on someone else, but Charlie Muffin's rules of engagement were always adjustable to suit his needs and at that moment he judged his need to be quite extreme.

The positive fell far short of outweighing the negative, but there was a balance of sorts. And he took as an omen the fact that when he inquired there was availability on both the outgoing and incoming British Airways flights the following day. He made reservations and then set about establishing the cover for his absence. Which would be easy. He could use the art recovery. Charlie was later to remember the startled look with which Richard Cartright greeted him when he entered the MI6 man's office.

"I don't like this," objected the military attaché at once, looking to Raymond McDowell for support.

"Neither do I," agreed the head of chancellery.

"Do you think I do?" demanded Richard Cartright. "They're my instructions, from London!"

"Why?" asked Gallaway. They were in the military attaché's office and theatrically the man got up and locked the door.

Cartright's relief, at being told officially by his own department to assess Charlie Muffin's investigation, was limited: it had briefly been shattered by the scruffy man's arrival in his office an hour earlier, which Cartright had at first thought, frightened, to be a confrontation. Since then he'd tried to rationalize what there was to work from and realized how limited that was, too. Apart from the contempt with which Charlie Muffin had dismissed his superiors on his return from London, everything else remained totally unsupported, mostly bedroom tittle-tattle. But what increased Cartright's unease was being asked, in the authorizing message from his operational officer that morning, if the man had boasted of making misleading telephone calls during his London recall or had ever referred to someone named Lionel Burbage. A confused Cartright was still awaiting clarification on that.

His explanation prepared for the inevitable question from one or the other of them, Cartright said, "I didn't like his attitude, when he came back: behaving as if what we're all supposed to be doing wasn't important. I asked London if anything had happened there to sort the whole business out. When they asked me why, I told them." Seeing the look on the faces of the other two men, Cartright added, "I don't consider that disloyal. I see it as self-protection, for us all." He looked pointedly at McDowell. "You forgotten what happened to your predecessor?"

"Muffin certainly hasn't tried very hard to be a team player," conceded the diplomat.

"And from what I gather, he caused Jackson some embarrassment in Berlin. Me, too, for that matter," joined in Gallaway. "I had the ministry on, demanding to know why I wasn't aware of his going there. Looked a bit of a bloody fool having to admit he hadn't told me, after I'd already assured them we were working well together."

"Which is another joke, this time on us," insisted Cartright. "He came to see me this morning. Said he thought there might be something in this Russian statement and, when I asked him what, said he couldn't tell me until he'd looked into it properly."

"You think we should tell London?" asked Gallaway, at once.

"I'm certainly going to cover myself," said Cartright. "Nothing specific because I can't be. Just an advisory, that there might be something. That's what he said he was doing."

"Probably a good idea for us all to do the same," said McDowell. He paused. "I suppose it's true to say he's treated us all a bit shabbily. But I'm still not sure it justifies an official inquiry."

"Not by itself, perhaps," Cartright admitted. "But I think there are things going on in London we don't know about, which, let's face it, has been our problem all along, not properly knowing what's going on. I think what I've been asked is part of a far deeper inquiry into how the investigation has been conducted from the start. As far as we know it's got nowhere. I, for one, don't intend having any responsibility for failure off-loaded on me."

The other two men shifted uncomfortably. Gallaway said, "I understand your point of view."

McDowell said, "Yes, quite."

Pleased with the way it was going, Cartright said, "All I'm asking is to be able to say you were with me when he said what he did. And to know you'll support me if you get asked about it from London direct."

"It would be the truth, would it?" accepted McDowell. "He *did* say what he did, in front of all three of us. Virtually made a joke of it, in fact. Think maybe I should tell the ambassador, though. Not exactly conducive to the smooth running of the embassy."

"Probably wise to make our position clear," said Gallaway.

"Thank you. I'm glad we're agreed," said Cartright. He hoped it would go on being this easy. He hoped Irena wasn't on a long-haul flight. It would be better—more convincing—if he had a Russian with him. He shouldn't forget Miriam, either.

"I thought we'd stopped all this shit!" protested the American. The reaction from the high-class hookers—imagining unequal competition—to her entry at the Savoy hotel bar was only just subsiding. They had, Charlie remembered, agreed on his role as Miriam's pimp. It would be a job with career prospects.

"If it goes wrong, you don't *want* to know about it," said Charlie. "My plane arrives back at ten, local time. I'll call you by eleven. If there's time, I might check in during the day."

"If it goes right, you'll know it all by tomorrow night?"

"Enough," assured Charlie. Once he'd always needed to know it all, he remembered. Another adjustable rule.

"If anyone asks, you're following up something about this art recovery but haven't told me what it is?" Miriam clarified.

"That's all."

"It's an odd coincidence."

"What is?" asked Charlie.

"Richard Cartright's called. Invited me to dinner."

"You going?"

"I stalled. Waited to see what you wanted first."

"What are you going to do?"

Miriam shrugged. "A gal's got to eat. You never did give me a name, incidently."

"Orgnev," supplied Charlie, glad of the reminder. "Arkadi Orgnev. Operates from a pitch near the Buratino Café, in the Arbat."

Charlie spent longer than necessary assuring Sasha that the giraffe's neck hadn't been stretched by someone pulling its head, hoping Natalia's concern-driven anger would have lessened by the time he went back into the living room. It hadn't.

"You're trying to convince yourself as much as me," she accused.

"Don't you think I have to go?"

"I think it's madness. You don't know anyone's going to try to make you a scapegoat and even if they do you stand more chance of surviving than risking everything, which is what you're doing. Risking *us*!"

"I don't think so."

"I love you, Charlie. I love you and Sasha loves you and I really do want us to spend the rest of our lives together. But I don't know how much longer I can go on like this."

"That's why I have to go. To get the whole damned thing over. Make us safe."

"I don't think we're ever going to be safe. That's why it might be better to make a decision about us now. Stop putting it off."

"No!" refused Charlie. "I'll get it right and we'll survive!"

That night they lay stiffly side by side, untouching, and Charlie knew every time he woke up, which he did often, that Natalia was awake, too. She remained stiff even when he tried to kiss her good-bye, only just responding. It meant he spent more time thinking about himself and Natalia on the flight to London than about what he had to do when he got there, but there was time during the drive.

Sir Peter Mason personally opened the door. The man said, "You didn't ring for an appointment."

Charlie said, "You might have refused to see me."

"I still could."

"But you won't, will you?"

36

Despite the totally unexpected intrusion, Sir Peter Mason was as immaculate as he had been at Charlie's first visit, even to the fresh rose buttonhole, although today's pinstripe was blue, not gray. The hair was as neatly barbered and in place, too, which made the last detail for which Charlie was looking easy to find, although he would have missed it, as he'd missed it before, if he hadn't specifically looked. And today's walk to the library had provided all the confirmation he'd really needed. The man sat easily on the far side of the desk big enough, Charlie reckoned, for a real delta wing, not a paper reproduction, and in the chair in which he'd been placed opposite Charlie tried to appear as relaxed. The man said, "Well, now, how is it you think I can help you further?" There was just the faintest unctuousness.

Charlie curbed the tingling euphoria, knowing the confirmation was only significant to him and that to get the admission he wanted, the conversation to follow—with a man whose entire life had been listening and talking in nuances and doublespeak—had to be the cleverest he himself had ever conducted in a lifetime of nuance and double-speak. "You could give me your own version of what happened at Yakutsk, to compare with the one I have."

The laugh was of disbelief, the one word stretched in astonishment. "*What?*"

"I know," declared Charlie, hopefully.

The other man's face was stiff now. "I haven't the slightest idea what you're talking about. You're clearly suffering some mental aberration and I think it best that you leave, before I call the police." The tone was controlled, unemotional, just mildly irritated.

Could he risk it? wondered Charlie. "That might be an idea. They could take your statement officially." He decided against completing the threat.

"I've asked you to leave."

The moment to hit hard, judged Charlie. "It was your battle-dress button, wasn't it? And the casing from your service revolver?"

"This is madness."

He hadn't reached for the telephone. Or threatened to call Sir Rupert Dean, to whom he'd referred intimidatingly several times at the previous meeting. "No, Sir Peter. It's fact. Forensically proven, evidential fact."

"Which you've communicated—discussed—to others?"

The first crack? "Of course," said Charlie. It wasn't an actual lie: only the inference that Sir Peter Mason had been connected with it wasn't true.

"In writing?"

"Yes."

"Then you're guilty of libel."

Not the first crack at all! "Which you'd need to take me into a court of law to prosecute," said Charlie. "You sure you can afford to appear in court, Sir Peter?"

"More, I'm sure, than you, in every meaning of the word 'afford.' "

Bullying—pompous—but that was all, assessed Charlie. Still far short. "You haven't called the police."

"I'm more interested now in the total extent of your aberration. And your libel."

That was a crack, although again not sufficient. Cleverly outtalking him, in fact, Charlie conceded: the bastard was trying to learn how much he knew. "Was Larisa already dead when they found you and brought you back to the camp infirmary?"

"Larisa who?"

"Larisa Krotkov."

"I've never heard of anyone named Larisa Krotkov. Nor do I know what camp you're referring to."

There was no euphoria or satisfaction left. Charlie was hot, perspiring, aware he was losing. "Gulag 98."

"That means nothing to me."

"What about Raisa?"

"I did not know Raisa Belous."

The hardest hit he could think of, Charlie decided. "She's the woman you killed: shot in the back of the head to go first into the grave, before Simon Norrington and George Timpson were thrown on top."

Mason actually jerked back in his chair, his face bloodred, eyes bulged, hands no longer cupped but splayed against the desktop to support himself. His mouth moved several times, but there were no immediate words, and when they finally came they were strained, wheezing from the man. "I will see to it that you are prosecuted! Put away! Your life . . . everything . . . is over. Finished."

He'd been within a hairbreadth, Charlie recognized. He'd rocked the man, had him teetering on the edge, but at the last minute Mason had pulled back, turning the near-collapse into apparent outrage. He had to push again, Charlie acknowledged—push with everything else he had to topple the man on the second attempt. The uncertainty was not being sure just how much there really was left.

Charlie said, "I can't imagine what it must have been like. No one can. Not surprising that you ran like you did: no one could blame you for wanting to get away. Remarkable that you managed to get so far, although not that they didn't shoot. They had other, more long-term needs for you, of course. As they had for Harry Dunne. Didn't stop them from shooting Larisa, though, but then she'd served her purpose, hadn't she . . . ?" Georgi, he suddenly remembered: how Larisa, in her dying delerium, would have referred by the Russian name to George Timpson, who'd carried the cut-off photograph of them both together. "And Larisa did try to stop George Timpson from getting shot, didn't she?" he guessed. "Got hit herself doing it . . . couldn't be saved . . ." He nodded to Mason's hands and the deformed fingers, still splayed on the desk. "Not like your fingers were saved, despite the frostbite. He was a good doctor, wasn't he? If I hadn't known he'd had to amputate your earlobe— particularly looked when you opened the door to me today—I wouldn't have known you'd lost it. I'm sure not many people have, all these years. . . ."

It didn't work.

Sir Peter Mason retained his rigidly affronted stance, although his color went and his voice returned to near-normal. "I've heard enough—too much—of this absurdity! You'll leave my house. Immediately. I intend contacting Sir Rupert, at once. To carry out the threats I've made, about every report you've filed. . . ." The control went, at the end. Color abruptly suffused the man's face again and he roared, crack-voiced, "GET OUT!" and rose, actually pointing toward the door.

And Charlie did.

Charlie drove obliviously, thoughts in free fall, for several miles before the most essential awareness forced its way to the forefront of his mind. How much—how badly—had he lost?

It didn't matter that Sir Peter Mason, without any doubt in Charlie's mind, was the murdering second officer or what the obvious implications were of his having been all his life at the heart of British government. He'd failed to get an admission, and the log of a long-dead doctor was insufficient evidence. What about the rest? He needed a jury, Charlie decided: a tribunal, at least. And there was no way he'd get that now. Mason would have an explanation, no matter how thin.

The man *would* complain to the director-general. Probably to a lot of other people, as well. There wasn't a defense against confronting Mason, but Charlie needed to get his explanation—and what little was left—to Sir Rupert Dean first. What was initially indefensible was his being unofficially in England at all, which he knew and the consequences of which he had to accept. By the end of the day he'd doubtless have had confirmed what he already knew them to be, so he could wait until then to call Natalia. Would she give up everything and bring Sasha to live in London? Or would she look upon it as the obvious breaking point that she'd virtually declared during last night's row?

As always, too many questions with too few answers. The first step—which professionally would be his last—was to get through the encounter with Sir Rupert. So totally upon that was Charlie's concentration that he wasn't aware of the siren or of the flashing lights of the police car until it actually came up alongside, with the observer waving him into the roadside. Charlie's first thought was of Henry Packer.

He kept the window closed and the locks down, pointless though that would have been, until he was satisfied the two uniformed men walking back toward him really were policemen. And not armed. When Charlie finally wound down the window, the observer said, "Every unit in Norfolk is looking for this car and this number. I don't know what you've done, my son, but it's upset a lot of important people."

"I know," said Charlie. He gave the same reply to the Special Branch officers who greeted him at Norwich police headquarters with the practically identical remark.

"I thought we were going to do some ourselves!" protested Irena.

"Of course not!" said Cartright, irritably. There was a virtual sea of tourists washing around the Arbat and it really was like forcing their way against a fast-running current. He felt more disoriented than discomfited.

"What are you going to do, then?"

"Find a particular man. Ask him to identify the photograph." He patted the pocket containing the picture of Charlie Muffin, to reassure himself it was still there. There'd be a lot of pickpockets in a crowd like this.

"Why did you want me to come?" demanded Irena, still protesting.

"The man I'm looking for will feel more comfortable with a Russian than with a foreigner."

"They have some nice jewelry in the foreign outlet store on Serebryany."

"We'll look afterwards," sighed Cartright.

"What's the name?"

"Arkadi Orgnev. He works around the Buratino."

"There it is," she said, pointing to the café with the illustrations of Pinocchio after which it was named.

Cartright prompted Irena to ask and they were misdirected to two people before a short, rotund man in a baseball cap, T-shirt and Levi's jeans was pointed out to them.

"Arkadi Orgnev?" asked Cartright, taking over.

"Maybe," said the man.

"I think you might be able to help me."

"How much?"

Cartright pulled the money from his pocket sufficiently for the man to see it was dollars. "Of course, I'm prepared to pay for what I want."

The man put a whistle in his mouth and blew it and five men

materialized from the crowd, surrounding them. One was the second
person Irena had asked to point out the money-changer.

"How did the cocksucker find out I hadn't been fired?" demanded
Miriam.

"I don't know," said Nathaniel Brindsley, in Washington. "Asked
the director outright, apparently. The director didn't have any alternative."

"The son-of-a-bitch!"

"I'm sorry, honey. Really sorry. When Kenton Peters comes on
the line, God takes the call."

"What am I to do?" Miriam suddenly felt lost.

"Pack up. Close your apartment. We'll do our best about sever-
ance. Personal word of the director himself."

"Fuck you. Fuck all of you!" Miriam shouted down the telephone.

"Know how you feel," sympathized the Bureau's overseas director.

"You know fuck-all, like the rest of them," said Miriam.

37

There was instant professional-to-professional recognition and they
didn't ask Charlie why they'd had to arrest him and Charlie didn't
offer any explanation, which would have been difficult anyway, his
not being precisely sure. There was bound to be a wide choice under
the Official Secrets Act. The policemen tried with soccer, to which
Charlie couldn't contribute because he didn't follow it on his satellite
sports channels, and eventually they found common ground with
movies, agreeing there was too much sex and violence. The driver
mourned the passing of those wonderful musicals and admitted an
unrequited passion for Doris Day.

Charlie's curiosity was answered when they passed between the
headquarters of both intelligence agencies on opposing sides of the
Thames to sweep into the entrance tunnel of the Foreign Office. As
Charlie was signed into the custody of a Foreign Office uniformed

custodian, like the special delivery he supposed he was, one of the Special Branch officers wished him luck and Charlie thanked him. As the custodian escorted Charlie along darkened corridors and into noiseless elevators, the man said Charlie would probably need it because James Boyce was a bastard. Charlie didn't bother to reply, passingly surprised at the indiscretion, more immediately aware that his not being escorted into the building by the Special Branch—being brought in fact to the Foreign Office instead of a police station—meant he wasn't under arrest. It was essential for whatever was awaiting him to seize every pointer like that.

The corner office, on the fourth floor overlooking the statued square, the Houses of Parliament and across Westminster Bridge, immediately designated the sleek, diminutive man behind the regulation landing-strip desk as a permanent secretary. Charlie assumed him to be James Boyce, although once more there were no introductions. There were six other men already waiting. Sir Rupert and Patrick Pacey, the department's political officer, both sat stone-faced, unsympathetic mourners at a funeral.

Charlie guessed the only way Sir Peter Mason could have arrived ahead of him after giving Special Branch the rented car number was by helicopter, which was significant.

It put the final piece in the puzzle to make everything crystal clear. Charlie had only once before, a long time ago, been involved with a traitor who had been given amnesty in exchange for all that he'd known and done for the other side. It had been one of the few occasions—apart from now with Natalia, which was totally different—that he'd been unable to separate business from personal animosity. He could recite backward all the professional justification for turning a traitor back upon his masters, but it was one of the few established practices of a totally amoral professional that was anathema to Charlie. He assumed from the proprietorial way Mason sat easily in one of the encompassing leather armchairs by the Parliament Square windows that the room had once been the man's own.

It was not the tribunal Charlie had expected, and with this new and complete realization he wondered how much advantage he could maneuver out of it. Follow their lead, he told himself. But not necessarily subserviently, which was always inherently difficult anyway and would be especially so now that he understood all he needed about Mason. What else could he read from the situation, before it began? They clearly believed he *did* know it all to have picked him up and to have arraigned him at this level of authority. And were shit-scared. There was obviously no question of his relaxing, but Charlie began to feel vaguely comfortable.

Boyce said, "You appear to have made very serious allegations."

"I am carrying out an assignment," said Charlie. The bastards were going to make him stand, which was stupid. To their disadvantage, not his. It put him on the orchestra podium, baton ready.

"It was not part of your assignment to leave Moscow without authorization."

Like a lot of small men, Boyce was a bully, Charlie guessed. He was also a lousy interrogator, if indeed that's what the man saw his function to be. There was no hurry: let them set out their battle formations. "I was authorized ten days ago to come here from Moscow to carry out inquiries as part of that assignment. I considered my going back to Moscow for the Russian announcement merely an interruption of that original authorization. I had not finished the inquiries I came here to complete. Now I have." Charlie hoped the director-general appreciated not having any responsibility off-loaded.

"That's a fatuous explanation!" rejected the permanent secretary.

Blustering, deciding Charlie. He wondered how many times pompous men at this echelon were openly opposed. Not often, he wouldn't have thought. "Then that must be your judgment. Mine is that by coming back today I have totally obeyed my director-general's instructions to find out how—and why—a British lieutenant, with others, was murdered fifty-four years ago in a remote part of what was then the Soviet Union. . . ." He turned slightly, to look directly at Mason. "Wouldn't you agree that to be a reasonable assessment, Sir Peter?"

It became so quiet, Charlie could hear the sound of the long-cased clock; even its tick was respectful. He thought the chill that permeated the room would be akin to that at the depth of winter in Yakutsk itself, when the climate was at its subzero worst. They really did have to be shit-scared to be staging this performance.

Boyce said, "I'd like your response to what I said about your making serious allegations against Sir Peter."

Thin-ice time. Charlie said, "I put a number of points to Sir Peter as part of my investigation."

"Points you claim to have communicated to others," said Boyce, briefly looking directly at the director-general. "Yet Sir Rupert does not appear to be aware of them."

The bloody fools were seeking damage limitation, Charlie accepted. "I was responding to a question from Sir Peter about a battle-dress button and a shell casing from a revolver," said Charlie. "Both of which formed part of a very early report to London."

"That is so," cut in Sir Rupert Dean, from the side.

"From *my* battle dress and revolver!" interjected Mason.

Why, apart from overwhelming pomposity, was the man this confident? Looking around the room, Charlie estimated that the man, whom he knew from the Who's Who entry to be close to eighty-five, had to be at least twenty years older than anyone else. "I'll take that as the confirmation you didn't provide earlier."

"I meant that's what you claimed them to be," flustered the man.

One of the unidentified men leaned briefly to his companion, whispered, and then said more loudly, "This isn't getting us very far, is it? Let's discuss it more directly, shall we?"

"I think you should tell us everything you know," ordered Boyce.

If he hadn't been one hundred and one percent right about Sir Peter Mason, he wouldn't be standing on increasingly painful feet in front of this Star Chamber, Charlie knew. So he could be far more accusative than he had been trying to trap the man into an admission earlier. How much further could he go? He could bring in the Hitler bunker staff, although cautiously. And the fact that Larisa Krotkov and Raisa Belous had switched from art conservators to Trophy Brigade looters to NKVD intelligence officers, using their art expertise as a cover for their association with Norrington and Timpson. And what about Mason, too? Charlie reminded himself. He still wasn't sure how to bring that accusation in.

Charlie talked not to the assembled men but to the former permanent secretary, intentionally in the manner of a prosecutor, careless of the personal contempt being obvious. He embellished the scene he'd read about in the log of Novikov's father, confident from the references to the mental collapse of both Mason and Harry Dunne that Mason wouldn't clearly remember. Very quickly Charlie became alert to Mason's reaction. It wasn't the bombastic refusal of earlier in the day, although his face grew red again and his body stiffened. Mason was hardly looking at him. Instead his eye-flickering concentration was upon everyone else in the room: men who, with the possible exception of James Boyce, were for the first time hearing a full and detailed account of the Yakutsk incident. With those aware-nesses came a further understanding. Mason, so sure and cocooned for so many years, felt himself humiliated, particularly by the con-tempt with which the accusations were being leveled. Briefly Charlie turned back into the room and caught expressions of disdain on the faces of two of the unidentified men. Boyce was gazing pointedly down at his desk. Standing as he was at that moment, Charlie missed the moment when Mason broke, brought back to the man by the near-shout. "It wasn't like that at all!"

The bastard thought he could justify it, Charlie recognized, amazed. "Maybe you should tell it, instead of me?"

"I'm going to," insisted the man, still looking beyond Charlie to the others in the room. "You've got to know the real truth, not this. Understand how it happened. . . ."

Behind him Charlie heard the stir move through the room but didn't look back again, his total attention upon the man straightening, commandingly, before him. He couldn't be wrong! Charlie told him-self. It was impossible. Yet . . . ?

"It was the political opportunity of the entire war . . . of the cen-tury," began Mason, forcefully. "Something that couldn't have been ignored. Hitler's staff, the men and women who knew everything! Where all the documentation was, all that Hitler had done and said in the last months of the war. His actual will, which the Russians seized: still have. Gold, literally, for Dunne and myself. And the hiding places of the Nazi loot, for Norrington and Timpson. . . ."

Mason paused, swallowing. The color was lessening. The man would have made hundreds of presentations in this room but none so impassioned as this, Charlie was sure: not since, maybe, the first time he'd been called upon to explain.

"We knew it was genuine," Mason picked up. "The Russians got to the bunker first: had all the staff names, which checked out against those we had. Tricked Norrington and Timpson, to begin with. Linked them up with the women when they went into the Russian sector to check out the Goering rumor, which wasn't true, of course. Promised them everything that was stolen from Tsarskoe Selo: even the Amber Room. Then they talked about all the political material. I didn't know then . . . didn't know for a long time . . . that they'd identified Dunne and myself as political officers . . . commissars, they called us . . . I took the call from Norrington: Dunne spoke to Timpson. Special clearance, they said. No problem with documentation for Russia. Norrington was perfect: had both languages. According to the Russians, the bunker staff had agreed to cooperate—tell them where everything was from Tsarskoe Selo and make Hitler's will available to us—in return for being transferred away from Yakutsk. But they wanted the guaranteed safety of British and American officers, to ensure they wouldn't be cheated. All be over in two or three days, they said. There was certainly no problem for any of us to take off for two or three days. Made our own rules. Everyone did."

Mason stopped again, as if to judge the reception. Charlie's feet began to throb.

"There were a lot of Russians, but only Norrington could properly talk to them," resumed the old man. "They were very friendly. A lot of drinking. Toasts to friendship. Lent us protective clothes for the flight and for when we got there. They said it was summer, but I've never known anywhere so cold. . . ."

He parted his cupped hands briefly to cover the ear that had been frostbitten, as if he could still feel pain. "Separated us, when we got there. Dunne and I were by ourselves: that's the way it had to be, they said. Politics for us, art for them. Hitler's bunker staff were all assembled. Dollmann. Buhle. Staubwasswe. Stoelin. The Russians said Norrington and Timpson were elsewhere, with the rest. We talked through Russian interpreters. The Germans were willing to tell us all they could to get away from the place: that was the first we—anyone—knew that Hitler's last will and testament had survived. The proper discussion was planned to begin the following day. Dunne and I slept in a barrack in the prison camp. When we asked about the others, we were told they were in another part, with the Hitler staff who knew all about the Einsatzstab Reichsleiter Rosenberg für die Besetzten Gebiete. . . . There was a van waiting to take us to what they said would be a conference room. It had been dark when we arrived—it was dark practically all the time—but there was enough light in the morning for us to see prisoners in another section. The interpreters said they'd committed very serious offenses, mostly war crimes. It was light enough, too, to realize that we were being taken out of the camp. . . . Then we heard some explosions and saw smoke up ahead. . . ."

Mason trailed off, bringing a handkerchief up to his mouth, head bowed. His voice was cracked when he started to speak again. "I'll never forget that scene. Can't. There was still a lot of smoke around the crater. Debris still falling. And Russians. I don't know how many, but at first too many to see that Norrington and Timpson were shackled and kneeling by the hole, with the woman. Larisa wasn't shackled, but she was crying. Everyone around them had guns and the men in the van pulled guns on us, too. They made us get out and I thought we were going to be shot, as well. Norrington was talking in Russian, loudly, arguing. Raisa was crying. Timpson didn't see us until we got very close, because of his eyes, but when he did, he shouted out: said he didn't know why, but they were going to be killed . . . told us to make them stop."

Mason abruptly sobbed, then coughed, and Boyce said, "Peter, you don't have to . . ." but the old man waved the deformed hand and said, "I *do*. I won't be wrongly accused . . . !" He looked up, swallowing, for the first time looking steadily at Charlie. "They took my revolver, put one of theirs literally to my head, the barrel touching me. Made me stand directly behind Raisa and said I had to kill her. Put my gun back in my hand and told me to press the trigger. I refused. Told them to kill me. There was a terrible explosion and then another and I thought they had, but someone had shot Timpson. I saw him thrown forward into the crater, and there was another flash but no sound and I saw there were photographers on the other side of the hole, taking pictures. Larisa was on the ground, screaming. They told me again to kill Raisa, but I wouldn't. Norrington was yelling in Russian. The next shot killed him, knocking him into the grave on top of Timpson. I think they were still shouting for me to fire, but I couldn't hear properly because the shots had been very close. Someone grabbed me from behind—put their hand over mine and pressed the trigger, and Raisa's head seemed to split in half and there were more photographs and then I was let go. . . ."

There was a further, gulping break. "I stood there, waiting to be shot, but nothing happened. There was a lot of confusion. Dunne just stood there; I don't know if he'd been made to fire or not. Everyone was concentrating upon burying the bodies. I got back to the truck. I remember being sick. Then running. I just ran, anywhere. I don't know where. It had got very dark again. And cold. Dear God, it was so very cold. I couldn't find any road. Kept falling over, and in the end I couldn't get up anymore, so I lay there, knowing I was going to die. I didn't hear men, only dogs that were brought from the camp. That's what I remember next, being in the camp. Being wrapped in blankets and looked at, by a doctor. . . ." The hand went up to his ear again. "Being operated upon. We were flown out that night, back to Berlin."

The gaze, totally upon Charlie, was defiant. "They had the photographs of us by the graveside but not of Russians. They'd been painted out. . . . They planned to blackmail us, as killers of our fellow officers."

"Enough!" stopped Boyce, at last. "There'll be no more! Sir Peter is not on trial, has nothing whatsoever to answer for. All that's necessary for each of you to know further is that Sir Peter has performed for this country—*his* country—one of the bravest and most successful services in its postwar history. At any time in history. For a full twenty years, until his retirement, Sir Peter—with Harry Dunne, who provided what appeared to be confirmation from the State Department in Washington—fed Moscow with whatever we wanted them to believe. While all the time they understood they were receiving information from a priceless source, for fifteen of those years from the permanent secretary to the Foreign Office himself! In effect, for twenty years, we and the Americans ran Russia's foreign policy, as and how we wished. Not just in espionage terms but politically as well, we conducted the coup of this or any other century. Because the discovery of the bodies was made publicly known, an investigation had to be publicly staged. As of this moment it is officially closed, as I can tell you it has been by America. . . ."

He looked at Charlie. "Except for you. You learned far too much. I want your sources."

"And I want a total and complete apology," demanded Sir Peter Mason. He looked pointedly across the room to Sir Rupert Dean. "And other assurances to go with it."

"One at a time," said Charlie, to the director-general's undisguised wince. "The source first. There is nothing that cannot be bought or bribed in Moscow, for the right price. Apart from what I deduced for myself, in Yakutsk and what little—far too little to matter—was shared by the FBI, everything came from Russian intelligence archives. Sir Peter was not named, but there were details of his frostbite injuries to his ears and hand, which I recognized when we met."

"Did you understand from the archives you read that the Russians still believe everything they were told was genuine?" demanded the permanent secretary.

"Yes," said Charlie.

"How much of it do the Americans know?"

"The cooperation wasn't good. I'm not sure."

"It doesn't matter. Everything has concluded very satisfactorily," declared Boyce.

"Except for an apology," reminded Mason.

"There's just one or two things that aren't clear," said Charlie, ignoring the demand. "There are photographs, of the bodies as they were found in the grave. Which show that Raisa Belous was shot *first*. Was at the very bottom, not the top. In fact, when the grave was first uncovered the local investigators only thought there were two bodies, not three. That confuse you like it confuses me, Sir Peter?"

"It happened as I've said it did," insisted the man.

"Something else," pressed Charlie. "You sure there wasn't a *third* British officer at Yakutsk? As far as I can see there would have had to be, from what you've told us. According to you they immediately started filling in the grave after shooting Raisa. Who do you think told them where to find the duplicate tailor's label in the trouser waistband that enabled me to trace Simon Norrington? And stripped the body to provide the identification in Berlin . . . ?"

"You will stop this!" said Boyce.

"I'm confused about the start," Charlie bulldozed on. "You—and Harry Dunne—reported what had happened to military intelligence the moment you got back to the western sector of Berlin in late May?"

"Of course!" said Mason, flushed again. "It was before I left Berlin that the planning began to deceive the Russians, which we did for so long."

Easily recalling the dates from his Who's Who reading, Charlie said, "Planning that wasn't put into operation until five—or was it ten?—years later, not until you became part of the Foreign Office secretariat?"

"I won't be subjected to interrogation!" said Mason.

"And I've told you to stop!" shouted Boyce.

"This is important, now that we know everything has to remain the secret it's always been," ignored Charlie, again. "We know, because he's just told us, that Sir Peter didn't know Raisa Belous before meeting her in May in the Russian-controlled eastern section of Berlin. But you've seen the Russian photographs released a couple of days ago, of some art objects that Raisa Belous saved from Catherine the Great's palace. One of the prints was a Dürer which is the next in sequence to the one I saw this morning—and on my first visit, although I didn't connect it then—in Sir Peter's house in East Dereham. And there's a small pastoral scene—I think it's a Watteau—just at the beginning of the hallway corridor which makes a pair with the one also in the photograph. . . ." Charlie felt the chill begin to settle in the room again. "And it might not be a good idea to offer for sale on the open market the small canvas of Sophia of Anhalt-Zerbst hanging just inside your study door, Sir Peter. That was Catherine the Great's maiden title before her marriage and is listed in the palace catalogue as one of the masterpieces still missing."

"This meeting is ended," announced Boyce.

Not until you supercilious bastards know just how firmly I've got you by the balls, Charlie decided. To Boyce he said, "I take it you'll explain everything to Sir Matthew Norrington? I wouldn't want to tell him anything he shouldn't know."

"You've gained us a lot of enemies, yourself more than anyone," said Sir Rupert Dean.

Before Charlie could respond, Patrick Pacey said, "But guaranteed the continuance of the department, in my opinion."

"Don't you ever again as much as think of going AWOL as you did," threatened the director-general. "I'll accept no excuse, no apology. It wouldn't be politically acceptable for me to fire you after today. If I could, I would. And still might find a reason for doing so. Don't think of your survival as anything other than a temporary postponement."

He never had, thought Charlie. They'd walked back from the Foreign Office and his feet were on fire. "I understand. At no time did I intend any disrespect to you personally. Or to the department."

"I said I didn't want to hear any of that. You're not going back to Moscow. There's another problem to deal with first."

First, seized Charlie. So his return was only a postponement, too. "Can I ask what?"

"Richard Cartright was arrested by the Russians: some nonsense about currency-dealing. Diplomatic immunity was invoked to get the bloody fool out, but he's implicating one of us."

"Who?" asked Charlie, just for the pleasure of hearing the name.

"Gerald Williams," said the political officer.

"Incidently," said Dean, "how much did you pay to get to the intelligence archives?"

"It wasn't a lump-sum payment," said Charlie, anticipating what was to come. "I'm keeping the man on a permanent retainer. It's expensive but proved invaluable in this instance alone."

On the telephone Natalia sounded as subdued, as desultory, even, as she had that morning. She accepted his remaining in London without asking why and told him not to bother when he asked what she thought he should bring back for Sasha. Natalia added that she didn't want anything for herself, either. When he said everything had turned out perfectly and that he loved her, she said good but didn't say she loved him in return.

It took several moments for Charlie to pick through the obscenities when he spoke to Miriam Bell, not immediately understanding what she was telling him.

"Stop off in London," Charlie said. "And tell your people you'd like to meet Peters in person, to talk about Harry Dunne and Sir Peter Mason."

"They going to save my life?"

"They just saved mine. What's the story with Cartright?"

"He kept on that night we met about how I imagined you really got the money to afford the apartment, so I suggested the name of the man at the Arbat. And then anonymously telephoned the local militia post."

"I'll buy dinner when you get here," promised Charlie.

38

It was scheduled as a tribunal hearing into the civilian arrest of Richard Cartright, but within the first hour of the first day Gerald Williams virtually became a coaccused, with Jocelyn Hamilton and SIS case officer Malcolm Covington only just avoiding an indictment.

Desperately Cartright insisted his Arbat approach—which had not been to a money dealer named Arkadi Orgnev but a posing militia currency investigator—had been part of an investigation into the activities of Charlie Muffin officially authorized by SIS case officer Malcolm Covington, and that he had the Moscow cable to prove it. The dollars he had shown the Russian had not been to trade but to pay for the identification, from a photograph he'd been carrying, of Muffin as a client. He had not known his woman companion, an Aeroflot stewardess, was carrying $430 she'd admitted to the militia she'd intended to sell. Cartright produced a diary of every conversation—and what was discussed—with Gerald Williams and called as a witness his department's financial director to confirm his having checked Williams's London conversation with the man about expenses claims, from which he'd assumed he was at liberty to talk to Williams on a combined agency investigation.

Miriam Bell arrived in London that afternoon, took a room on the floor below Charlie's at the Dorchester and was waiting in the foyer when Charlie got back.

She said, "I'm pissed off. Been here half an hour and haven't got propositioned once." And smiled.

"This is London, not Moscow."

"It shouldn't make any difference!"

Charlie took her to the Rib Room because he thought she'd like the steaks, which she did. She agreed that Cartright sounded like a prick but didn't deserve to be dismissed but Williams did. Charlie said that if he'd had any pity, which he didn't, it would have been pitiful to listen to. Her steak covered half her plate, as his did, and she'd eaten it by the time he finished filling in all the details of the Yakutsk murders.

She said, "Jesus H. Christ! That was an operation and a half! Who d'you think got caught and turned first, Peter Mason or Harry Dunne?"

"I don't know. Whoever it was immediately shopped the other."

"Great idea, turning them and maintaining them for so long," she said, admiringly.

"I wonder if it balanced out the damage they did before they got caught."

"How am I supposed to know about this?"

"I told them we didn't cooperate—that I didn't know what you had. No reason why you shouldn't have found out about Timpson like I did. Or that there's a grave in Holland. No reason, either, why you can't have established a paid source at Lubyanka Square."

"I'd have had to share a source like that with Saul: he's the Bureau chief. You've got a hell of an inside track there."

"One I'm going to guard with my life."

"I'd do the same, if I was that lucky."

"What feedback did you get from Washington?"

"Panic. Demands for a full explanation."

"What did you say?"

"That I'd give it in person, when I saw Peters. I'm not sure this'll save me, but it's going to be better than any lay I've ever had to make Kenton Peters kiss my ass. Never thought I'd be able to keep the promise to myself. So thanks a whole lot."

"You think you'll come back to Moscow if you survive?"

Miriam shook her head. "I don't want to. If it goes good, I'm going to ask for a reassignment. Somewhere warm and nice: Australia or Spain, maybe."

Because it was Miriam's first time in London and she wanted to, Charlie actually compromised to window-shop past Harvey Nichols and Harrods—deciding to look in both before going back to Moscow, despite Natalia telling him not to buy presents—but they hailed a taxi after about half an hour. They had a nightcap—two, in fact—at the Dorchester Bar, and during the second Miriam said, "You know something?"

"What?"

"I've just decided it would spoil things if you and I went to bed together."

"Yes," agreed Charlie. "It would."

"You want to know something else?"

"What?"

"I've never felt like that about a guy before. Not sure if it makes you special or what. Special, I think."

The tribunal lasted a further two days, extended by the determination of everyone involved completely to exonerate themselves. The Foreign Office cited the expense for refusing to recall Raymond McDowell and Colonel John Gallaway from Moscow to recount Charlie's disparaging conversation, insisting instead upon signed affadavits, and Williams produced his carefully amassed examples of unsupported expense claims, which Charlie said he'd already talked about with the director-general, who at once insisted the explanation was totally satisfactory upon his personal authority and forbade any further discussion. Calling Charlie was nothing more than a token gesture to procedure. He said he couldn't remember the actual disparagement—which the diligent Cartright had produced verbatim, alongside McDowell's written recollection—but didn't deny saying any of it. There had been intentionally introduced operational difficulties—to which the investigation of one department upon another had contributed—and he felt his remarks were as justified now as they had been at the time. He was apprehensive that Malcolm Covington might produce a voiceprint of his Waterloo runaround telephone call—sure it was Covington he'd spoken to—but it didn't happen.

The hearing was impatiently concluded by the middle of the second day. Richard Cartright was assigned to the travel and communications desk at the Vauxball Cross headquarters. Gerald Williams accepted the invitation for early retirement, with his index-linked pension adjusted to what it would have been had he not left until he was sixty-five. Jocelyn Hamilton and Malcolm Covington had severe reprimands attached to their personnel files.

"All that was ridiculous," dismissed Sir Rupert. He'd insisted Charlie accompany him from the hearing to his office.

"Totally," agreed Charlie.

"One has nothing to do—has no effect whatsoever—with the other," warned the director-general. "I will not, ever again, tolerate your affectation to be the lone vigilante. And don't patronize me by meekly agreeing. Understand that I mean it."

"I do," said Charlie.

"It's right that I thank you, for what Pacey tells me you've achieved for the department. I do so, but reluctantly."

"Thank you, anyway."

"Now bugger off back to Moscow."

It was the first time Miriam Bell had been in the presence of the FBI director, Judge Colin (pronounced *Cohlin*) Hibbert, who was avuncularly fat and prematurely bald and disappointed at being both. He was also disappointed at the confrontation that had just ended— he hoped—between someone as awesomely influential as Kenton Peters and a woman young enough to be not just his daughter but possibly his granddaughter. He knew from Nathaniel Brindsley that Miriam Bell had told Peters to kiss her ass and from ten years' previous experience on the bench his verdict was that she'd effectively if not physically made him do just that.

"You were told your participation was over," Peters continued to argue.

"I had initiated inquiries before I was recalled to be told that," said Miriam. "They obviously had to be concluded. Not to have done so would have aroused suspicion with the Russians and the British."

"Concluded very successfully," contributed Brindsley, who'd enjoyed the spectacle.

"Have you anything else to say?" demanded Peters.

"I consider I have been wrongfully dismissed."

"I wasn't aware that you had," said the State Department man to whom no responsibility ever attached.

"That's my understanding."

"A mistake, a misunderstanding, I'm sure," said Peters, talking to the director.

"I'll look into it," promised Hibbert.

"Good!" said Peters. "And I'd like personally to congratulate you, for a brilliant investigation. I think that's it, isn't it?"

My bended knees, kiss-ass time, not yours, determined Miriam. "And I'd like to be reassigned."

"Where?" asked Hibbert.

"Spain, perhaps?" She'd decided that Europe was better than Australia.

"You have it," promised the director.

"Thank you." Miriam smiled. "That's definitely it." She'd send Charlie a card: make him feel jealous.

39

Kenton Peters stood with his back to the room, legs apart, hands linked behind his back, gazing out toward the British Parliament. He'd come straight from the airport, deputing Boyce's chauffeur to register him into the Connaught. He was vociferously proud not to suffer jet lag. "You know the difference between England and America?"

"What?" asked Boyce, dutifully.

"Permanence. That's my impression. Everything here's permanent: been here for a thousand years, will still be here in another thousand years. Too much in America seems to me to be *im*permanent: a gust of wind and it'll all blow away."

"I thought Washington was supposed to be the re-creation of a Greek city," said Boyce. The antiquity reverie was a familiar one. Peters claimed to have Founding Fathers ancestry.

"That's what it is," said the patrician-featured man. "A copy. Not original. And Greece stopped being great about two thousand years ago." He sat down in one of the armchairs, the leather of which subsided with a sigh under his weight.

Boyce thought the Greek era had ended long before that but didn't bother to query it. Instead he said openly, "Not quite as clear-cut as we thought it would be."

"A readjustment," suggested the American. "The need was for containment. And we achieved that, didn't we?"

"I think so."

"How was Sir Matthew?"

"Persuadable, to the argument of the national better good. It was a family interment: advantage of owning half a county is that he has walls and barred gates to keep out unwelcomed intrusion."

"Permanence. Tradition," mused Peters. "I suppose I was lucky all Dunne's family are dead, like him."

"So your ceremony can go ahead?" Boyce knew it was to be re-assured about the Arlington ceremony that the man had flown in from Washington overnight. Personal attention to the smallest detail was the hallmark of their unique profession.

"You know how it is with these sort of things, no unexpected loose ends?"

"Quite."

"Mason surprised me."

"Bloody man. I actually think he believes he was a hero who didn't do any harm and worked out the deception all by himself. I obviously needed to find out precisely what Muffin knew before having the damned man fired or disposed of, but Mason insisted, without any warning, on talking like he did to impress people who didn't know the full story and didn't need to. If he'd left it to me, everything would have been all right. He's only himself to blame for the humiliation in front of the cabinet secretary and the head of SIS."

"I reread Dunne's interrogation transcript. He was full of self-justification, too. Managed to make his identification of Mason a patriotic act. You didn't know about the heritage art Mason had?"

Boyce shook his head. "I should have reread Mason's debriefing, as well, instead of relying on the précis from my predecessor. It's there. The Russians targeted Mason and Dunne months before Berlin. Put Raisa Belous beside Mason in Belgium. He was using Norrington's expertise to treasure-spot for himself even then, although Norrington didn't know it, of course. Mason was a veritable magpie and Raisa was busy recording everything he stole. He was a golden goose waiting to be plucked and the Russians recognized it. That would have been the original blackmail, of course: why they couldn't go to the military authorities after Yakutsk. Never really understood why the Russians went to all that trouble: truss them both up completely, I suppose."

"We subjected Dunne to a polygraph," disclosed Peters. "He said the Russians didn't think their art-thieving was a strong enough pressure—that murder was better and knowing the choice he and Mason would make with a gun to their heads. The art-thieving was enough to keep them from going to their own authorities when they got back to Berlin."

"Makes some sort of sense, I suppose," said Boyce.

"Larisa got to Dunne's looting investigation squad in Poland," continued Peters. "Ironic that's where Raisa's husband died. Wouldn't be surprised if he wasn't involved in some way, although the question wasn't put to Dunne. Belous and Larisa would have known each other from Tsarskoe Selo, after all. Larisa really did put herself in the way of Dunne's first bullet, incidentally: they'd had an affair going since Poland. In his statement Dunne seemed more upset by that than being forced to shoot Timpson."

Boyce shrugged. "Dunne and Mason were real bastards, weren't they? But useful, in the long run."

"Wonder where Larisa's buried," said Peters.

"God knows; we never will," said Boyce. "Damned clever of the Russians to have used their Trophy Squads like they did. Already to be looking that far ahead, well beyond the ending of the war. And putting Larisa in Gulag 98, trying to trick Hitler's bunker squad into disclosing all they knew. It was probably down to Larisa that the Russians still have Hitler's will today."

"To get our hands on that really would be a treasure," said Peters. "But I'm not surprised how far ahead Stalin and Beria were thinking. That's what Stalin was doing at Yalta and Potsdam, carving up Europe for himself."

"All very clever," mused Boyce.

"Muffin really did turn out to be a nuisance," said Peters. "It was a bad mistake not eliminating him."

"Not only chopped Mason up into little pieces but coated himself and his department in Teflon. Can't do anything to any of them now.

Too many people know after that damned confrontation."

"Who's going to be your scapegoat?"

"Not sure we need one at the moment. The MI6 man in Moscow made a fool of himself, so he's available. I'll wait to see which way the media hysteria goes."

"Muffin back in Moscow?"

Boyce nodded. "Your woman?"

"Spain. It's only a temporary respite. We'll transfer her from the foreign division after the normal two-year tour there. Bury her in a home station somewhere like Montana or North Dakota."

"Bit of a waste, for someone so clever."

"That's not the point," reminded the American. "She was impertinent."

"Of course not," apologized Boyce.

"There we are, then!" said Peters, in finality. "All's well that ends well, as long as the bumps in between don't derail anything."

"The club special today is steak and kidney pudding."

"Tradition!" said Peters. "Excellent."

Charlie and Natalia sat side by side, watching George Timpson being buried as an unknown hero in Arlington. There was a rifle volley over the grave and the poignant Last Post and the president talked of America's great and good, and of the hostilities of the past becoming the hope for the future. At one stage he choked to a halt and wiped what appeared to be a tear from his left eye. His rating was to climb five points by the end of the week.

Charlie sighed and said, "That's it. All over."

"Until the next time."

"There'll never be another one like this."

"I couldn't stand it if there were."

He reached out for her hand and Natalia let him take it. "My internal problems are over, your internal problems are over. Like Sasha's storybook says, we can live together happily ever after."

"There were some changes in the Duma while you were in England," announced Natalia.

He looked at her, unspeaking.

"Viktor Romanovich Viskov got elected deputy of the Communist faction. I think I should still keep the Leninskaya apartment."